STREET LEGAL: THE BETRAYAL

BOOKS BY WILLIAM DEVERELL

Fiction

Needles
High Crimes
Mecca
The Dance of Shiva
Platinum Blues
Mindfield
Kill All the Lawyers
Street Legal: The Betrayal

Non-Fiction

Fatal Cruise

STREET LEGAL: THE BETRAYAL

WILLIAM DEVERELL

M&S

Canadian Cataloguing in Publication Data

Deverell, William, 1937 –
Street legal – the betrayal

ISBN 0-7710-2669-2

I. Title.

PS8557.E84S87   1995   C813'.54   C95-932015-6
PR9199.3.D48S87   1995

Street Legal and the Street Legal Design Mark are trademarks and official
marks of the Canadian Broadcasting Corporation.

The publishers acknowledge the support of the Canada Council and the
Ontario Arts Council for their publishing program.

Typesetting by M&S, Toronto

Printed and bound in Canada on acid-free paper

McClelland & Stewart Inc.
The Canadian Publishers
481 University Avenue
Toronto, Ontario
M5G 2E9

1 2 3 4 5   99 98 97 96 95

AUTHOR'S NOTE

I am proud to dedicate this novel to the fine actors, writers, artists, producers, directors, and crew who made "Street Legal" one of the longest-running series in the history of Canadian television. I mention particularly those who worked with me so assiduously to bring a dream to fruition: Maryke McEwen, Peter Lowther, and Don Truckey. They brought passion, compassion, and justice to the small screen and were proud to showcase the vibrant city of Toronto in a series that has been sold throughout the world, and can be seen from Russia to Abu Dhabi.

My thanks also to Marian Hebb, an entertainment lawyer who worked so unswervingly to resolve a dispute with the Mother Corporation over use of the title.

The characters in this novel are as I originally conceived them many years ago and, with minor exceptions, were rendered on the screen in a manner faithful to my original concept. The story is set during the early days of a small, struggling law firm . . .

W. D.

January 14, 1980. Temperature outside minus thirty Celsius. From a window in the Chelsea Hotel, Tommy Chu looked down at columns of smoke from the chimneys, vertical plumes on a windless day. Tommy Chu thought of Hong Kong, where he was born, where the air was damp and hot. He thought of Vancouver, where he now lived, where the grass was green all winter. Here nothing was green; the trees were skeletons, branches like bones and claws. Toronto the Good, they called this city. Toronto the Dead.

From the direction of the bed came a pop like a cap pistol firing, and Tommy Chu felt, again, a tremor within.

Chu turned, and gazed solemnly at Speeder Cacciati, who was sitting on the bed chewing bubble gum, blowing little pink balloons until they popped. Was he doped up on something? Some drug that made all his parts move incessantly? Cacciati's hands fussed with his hair; now he was cracking his knuckles, now picking sores. Of which there were many. A scrawny body, a face that looked to have been stepped on at some unlucky moment with a heavy boot: almost concave.

Tommy Chu and Speeder Cacciati each had an armed guard in the hotel room. Chu's man, Sherman Lott, had a .38 revolver strapped to his checkered sports shirt. He was being watched by

1

Jerszy Schlizik, who was called the Undertaker, and whose gun was hidden behind the drapes of his long black suit jacket.

Cacciati cracked a big onc, and grinned, and peeled the gum from his lips. "Let's do business," he said.

Tommy Chu picked up his briefcase, and placed it carefully on the bed. Cacciati leaned over and snapped it open. He pulled out a kilo of white powder, triple-wrapped in thick plastic.

"Ever do this stuff yourself?" Cacciati asked.

Tommy Chu shook his head.

"You're a smart Chinaman. You use the expression over in Hong Kong there, get the Chinaman off your back? That's when you're hooked. You gotta get the Chinaman off your back. It's like the monkey."

"No, we don't have that expression."

Speeder nodded, blew a bubble, held out one of the bags to the light from the window. "This as pure as the sampler?"

"Do you want to test it?"

"Naw, Billy says to trust you."

"I can offer this much again in two weeks. Also more in a month."

"Billy's interested, he says to talk about it. How do you bring it in?"

"That's not for the world to know. I might tell Mr. Sweet." The notoriously shy Billy Sweet, their boss.

"As I already once explained, Billy don't talk to strangers."

"It is necessary to make arrangements at the top."

"Not with some flunky, eh?" Speeder gestured to Jerszy Schlizik. "Pay these boys off."

As Schlizik bent to an attaché case, Tommy Chu felt an odd sensation of distress – he didn't know where it came from; it was just a momentary flutter. *Pay these boys off.*

Schlizik, the man who looked like a mortician, retrieved from the case a stack of bills banded with elastic. He tossed the money to Sherman Lott, who licked his fingers and began his count, fingers flipping through the bills soft and easy and quick.

Tommy Chu then saw Schlizik, still bending, pull a silencer-equipped revolver from the attaché case.

2

Schlizik shot Sherman Lott twice in the chest and stopped Tommy Chu with a third bullet as he was running for the door.

As Cacciati snapped bubbles, and picked up the money and the heroin, Schlizik made absolutely sure. He fired bullets into the back of their skulls.

"Two stiff dicks," said Speeder Cacciati.

1

July 25, 1980. Temperature outside plus thirty Celsius. Carrie wasn't sure how hot that was. Multiply something by five and divide it by nine? She had not mastered metric conversion; she wasn't good at numbers. Which is one of the reasons Carrington Barr became a barrister instead of an economist or an engineer. Not that she'd ever dreamed of being anything *but* a lawyer.

Even in the courtroom it was stifling: the air-conditioning didn't seem to have much poop. Thirty above, add to that the hot human sweat from the packed gallery, from the jury box, the press table, the counsel bench. In a heavy black gown, Carrie felt sticky, damp at the armpits, and her own smell offended her.

The courtroom was silent, breathless. The witness, Julia Yates, a brave and spunky woman of nineteen, had been invited to leave the witness box, and now was strolling beside the gallery railing, studying all these good burghers of Toronto, who were sitting still and calm upon their benches, like observant church-goers in their pews.

Julia Yates was looking for the Midnight Strangler.

She had picked out Edwin Moodie five months ago, in a police lineup. She had written on a slip of paper Moodie's number: six. But she had put a tiny question mark after that number. And that lineup, Carrie felt, had been so unfair: Moodie standing there with five men all slightly smaller than him. Though it would be hard to find someone larger – Carrie's client weighed in at something like two hundred and sixty pounds.

"He was big," said Julia Yates, still patrolling the fence line. "Real big. And sort of bald."

The Midnight Strangler had left this young woman for dead after choking and raping her, but she had been conscious all the time, feigning death. The jury loved her, they would do anything. They would convict for her, Carrie feared, on the slightest evidence.

The judge, too, seemed eager to put away poor Edwin Moodie. Someone had to pay for these terrible crimes; someone had to be sacrificed upon the altar of justice. But at least His Lordship had allowed Carrie to place Moodie in this packed gallery.

Julia Yates stood for a moment before a beef-chested, balding, fiftyish man in the third row. A yellow bow tie hid one of his chins. His face was deadpan and his eyes stared blankly past her, at the wall.

Now, silent and intent, Julia Yates focused on the man beside him, also balding and about the same age, but he was even bigger, thick neck and massive chest, his face a full moon decorated with a tiny, groomed moustache in the French style, two smiling curls. This man was not staring off into space like his seat-mate, but looking directly at her, bemused, contemplative.

Carrie watched as Julia cocked her head at him, bird-like, then moved on, walking along the railing, stopping in front of yet another large man near the end of the row. He was younger, in his forties. He wore a poorly fitted hairpiece – like a golf-course divot. Carrie had fitted him out in the toupee, *hoping* it would be obvious. She had also placed several other big men in the audience, as many as she dared: ex-footballers, weightlifters, a couple of reluctant conscripts from the police force.

One of these was Sergeant Horse Kronos, in charge of the lockup at the Queen Street Provincial Court. He was shorter than Carrie's client, but otherwise fit the bill. He had been in the original lineup, too, at police headquarters, and Carrie had prevailed upon him to come to court today. For a moment, Carrie thought Julia Yates was going to finger Horse, but she gave up on him.

"I'm sorry, I . . . It was so dark."

"Take your time," said Mr. Justice Trueletter.

"She must be absolutely sure," said Carrie.

"She simply has to do her best," said Oliver McAnthony, the prosecutor.

"That's right," said the judge. "This is just a form of lineup."

"My client is accused of six murders," Carrie said. "If she isn't sure, how can the jury be sure?"

"Mrs. Barr, you are out of order. I've given you a lot of leeway so far."

Oh, sure, Carrie thought. A lot of rope, he might have said. But Carrie had got her two cents in, that's what mattered. Her father would have approved, Charlie Connors, the Terror of Temigouche, New Brunswick.

Julia Yates shook her head, and finally returned her concentration to the man in the third row, the man with the yellow bow tie who was so carefully studying the wall behind her.

"I think . . ."

Carrie held her breath.

"I think that's him. The man in the bow tie."

The man's mouth went slack, and one of his chins bobbled, the bow tie moving in lock-step with it.

"Are you *sure*?" Carrie said.

Her voice carried a scold, and Julia Yates's back seemed to stiffen.

"Yes, I *am* sure."

"The witness," Carrie said, "has just identified Detective-Sergeant Jock Strachan of homicide."

Oliver McAnthony sat for a while and seemed to be studying his hands. Then he stood. "That, I regret to say, is the prosecution's case."

"I move for a dismissal," said Carrington Barr.

Outside the courtroom, Carrie tried to beat her way through the blockade of reporters. "I have nothing to say right now."

They then descended on Oliver McAnthony, the Crown's senior prosecutor for Toronto, as he emerged set-faced from the courtroom. "No comment, ladies and gentlemen, thank you." He stopped in front of Carrie, and brushed aside some microphones.

"You have arrived, Carrington. Your first murder trial – a serial killer, and you got him off."

"Don't be a poor loser, Oliver."

"I may be appealing."

"You'd be more appealing if you smiled."

"What happened in there, Mr. McAnthony?" a reporter asked.

"What happened?" He turned on his jury voice, mellifluous and forceful. "Let us just say that six of the Midnight Strangler's victims could not enjoy the pleasure of giving their evidence. That was unavoidable because they are all dead. The only woman who lived to tell her tale could not identify him. And the Strangler is now a free man."

Carrie was shocked by the innuendo. "The Strangler always *has* been a free man," she said angrily. "Go out and find him, Oliver." She turned to the press, furious. "They think they can go out onto the street and pick up any poor old oddball . . ."

She hesitated, seeing her client Edwin Moodie at the open courtroom door, still handcuffed to Detective Jock Strachan. Moodie blinked and looked around, as if not comprehending. The media parted, like the Red Sea, as the two men walked out.

"They think they can pick up any poor old fellow," Carrie continued, her voice rising again, "and charge him with a series of murders they've been incompetent to solve."

Which is exactly what they'd done, of course, grabbed a street person, a man slow of thought, bereft of alibis, and shoved him in a lineup. He just happened to be living in a building behind the lot where Julia Yates had been attacked – some inconclusive hair and fibre matches, that was all.

"I want you to know that Mr. Moodie has been the subject of the proverbial railroad."

Carrie heard her own shrill voice. She never does that, never shouts. Cool, collected Carrington Barr. She turned and walked briskly toward her client, while the reporters pursued McAnthony as he marched down the hall.

Moodie was still blinking, his wispy moustache twitching. He was a mountain of a man – there was rock in him as well as fatty fill – but his features were gentle, his blue eyes small and sad and liquid.

As Detective Strachan unlocked the cuffs, he said to Moodie, *sotto voce*, in his Scots burr: "If ye kill one more poor girl, I'll blow your diseased brain away."

"Jock!" She was furious. "You apologize!"

"I'll apologize, lassie, when you prove he didn't do it." He pocketed his handcuffs, adjusted his bow tie, and stalked away.

Watching him go, Moodie looked puzzled. The world had always been a strange place, Carrie believed, for this lonely fellow. He'd been one of her first clients – a vagrancy charge three years ago, then a street begging offence. She'd won those. When arrested for six recent murders, he'd come back to her.

His eyes turned to her, a pulling, needy look.

"Now, Mr. Moodie, I want you to see Major Andrews at the Salvation Army."

She always called him Mr. Moodie. The first time they'd met, Carrie had asked him, "What do they call you? Ed? Edwin?" "They call me Mr. Moodie," he had answered in his absurdly thin voice. It seemed comical, a kind of tough-guy response, but she was sure he hadn't meant it that way.

"Major Andrews will fix you up with a place to stay."

Moodie blinked and nodded. "Okay."

"And if he can't find you a place, I will."

He nodded again, seemed to struggle to find words. "I'm not the Midnight Strangler."

"I know that. You couldn't hurt a bug."

She wondered if he would shake her hand with the strange, soft grip he had, as if holding a wounded bird. But he was rubbing his wrist, where the cuffs had chafed, and then his eyes left hers and he looked down at the floor, shy. She patted his arm, his hammy biceps, and he started like a nervous horse.

Now he was looking at her hand, the gold wedding band, her only decoration. She'd often found him staring at it, as if checking to see if she was still in a state of wedlock. You'd like Ted, Mr. Moodie, she thought. He's sort of like you, uncommunicative.

8

Becoming more so every day, secretive, like a man who – don't even think about it.

Moodie glanced up at her again, and looked quickly away, as if embarrassed. She wondered if he saw the sadness in her eyes. Sadness – what sadness? She had just won the trial of the decade. She was the queen of all she surveyed. She was happy, damn it.

Moodie mumbled something she couldn't make out.

"When you're settled, we'll look for a job for you. I have some contacts. Well . . ." She shrugged. "Good luck."

Moodie seemed unable to say anything more and just stared after her with his small, liquid eyes. Finally, as she turned to go, he spoke in a soft voice.

"Thank you."

In the female barristers' robing room, Carrie hung her gown in a locker and shed her white blouse and black skirt. She thought of showering before changing back into her beige cotton suit, but she settled for an underarm wash and some Mitchum roll-on.

She studied herself in the mirror. Her wine-red tresses sat like a damp mop on her head. Tall and angular, long of neck and flat of chest. The bra held up nothing, but she always wore one, a properly raised young lady. She had Golly Miss Molly eyes that seemed constantly wide and alarmed. She was striking, people said. As opposed to, for instance, incredibly attractive. Always so *tastefully* attired.

Would the *Star* use that terrible shot they'd taken earlier? Looking like she'd just been goosed. Or today's confident smiling one?

How vain, the victor.

How she wished her dad had been here to see her. It's the big time here, Charlie, in the media capital of Canada. Here's where you should have tried your talent, here, under the big top, not some pokey country carnival – although your renditions of "The Ballad of Reading Gaol" might not milk as many tears in the cynical city as it used to among the jurors of the gentle hills of New Brunswick.

She should have kept her own name, Connors. But she'd been brought up in the old-fashioned way, a late-blooming feminist.

Was Ted seeing someone? Such a furtive phrase, *seeing* someone. Seeing someone, involved with, sleeping with, she couldn't utter even to herself the impossible four-letter word. His secretary, Heather? Impossible. Though she was smitten by him, available, and cute.

Get with it, Carrie. So he's been strange. Men have moods. Men are human.

Carrie thought a walk would freshen her, and she departed the Armoury Street entrance of the courthouse and headed up to Bloor, toward her offices. But the afternoon heat of the midsummer Toronto swelter quickly caused her energy, her clothing, her entire body to wilt. She took a route past the Parliament Buildings, through Queen's Park, seeking shade under trees.

Ted would kiss her, praise her, be all sincere. *Marvellous* work, Carrie. She would be sincere back to him. Thank you, Ted, it feels great. And Leon and Chuck would emerge from their offices, wanting to hear all about it, how the witness fingered Jock Strachan (whom she must have seen numerous times – how could she *make* such a mistake?). And poor Edwin Moodie, she would say, he *still* doesn't know what happened. And Oliver McAnthony – well, the old smoothie almost had a cat fit.

She stepped with relief into the air-conditioned lobby of the General and Commercial Trust Building, a three-year-old tower on Bloor. A formidable rent had to be paid each month for their tenth-storey suite, and her firm had outrageously overspent on furnishings and equipment and decor. They had been too optimistic when they signed that lease three years ago – they hadn't counted on recession and reflation. She and her partners had borrowed for these expenses, and a cruelly high rate on the floating loan – 16 per cent, 19 per cent, and rising into the stratosphere – now nearly had them on the rims. Well, maybe all this publicity over her win would send the clients flocking.

ROBINOVITCH, BARR, BARR, TCHOBANIAN, said the raised heavy brass lettering on the wall outside their suite of offices.

Ted was the first Barr. He was thirty-two and had been called eight years ago. Carrie was twenty-eight, had been practising for five years, as had Chuck Tchobanian, a pal from law-school days.

Leon Robinovitch, who at thirty-three was already into his second midlife crisis, was a nine-year man. He had founded the firm with Ted, a former fellow university activist. They first had been called Robinovitch, Barr, Connors, and Tchobanian. Three years ago it became Robinovitch, Barr, Barr, and Tchobanian. No more Carrie Connors.

The receptionist, Pauline Chong, gave her a brisk military salute, and Leon Robinovitch came out and made one of those Eastern mystical bows, the hands rolling lower and lower as he bent reverently toward her. Something from his Buddhist retreats, she assumed.

Some clients were in the waiting room. A prim, worried-looking woman being comforted by a cleric, Roman or Anglican with his reversed collar. And an older couple: the Jepsons or Jessons, a house conveyance.

"We are ennobled by your presence, O great lady." Leon mimed rolling out a red carpet for her, bending, stepping back until he bumped his ass into Chuck Tchobanian's groin.

"Not in public, *please*, darling," Chuck said.

The minister frowned. Carrie's two clients looked uncomfortable. "I'll be with you in a few minutes, Mr. and Mrs. Jepson," Carrie said.

"Jessup," said the husband.

Where was Ted? In his office no doubt, with one of his divorce clients, being all sympathetic and charming.

"Trixi Trimble called," said Pauline Chong. "Wants to know when her trial is."

"Oh, for God's sake. Phone her and tell her it's Tuesday. And not to embarrass me by nodding out on heroin while the judge reads the verdict." Carrie spoke too loudly; the Jessups were pretending to be absorbed in magazines, but their eyes widened with alarm.

She urged her partners toward the staff lounge, through the secretarial pool, weaving through the planters, glossy, bushy vegetation – they almost needed a full-time gardener. Everything was grossly tasteful: oak panelling, recessed lights, a heavy wool pile on the floor. Ted had insisted: clients aren't impressed by plain

11

vanilla, he wanted an office that said, *Open the wallet, folks.* It worked for his clients maybe, Carrie thought. Didn't impress the crooks and the seekers of civil rights, their major clientele.

"It was on the news, Carrie," Leon said. "Dramatic win. So why aren't you smiling?"

Carrie looked at them with her wide startled eyes. She tried on one smile, then another; they didn't feel real. Why was she tense?

"She's in a state of emotional paralysis," Leon said, always diagnosing everybody. "It's common after a dramatic event."

"Yeah," said Chuck, "she's spacing out. Quick, get some caffeine into her or she'll float out into the ozone thinking she's God."

Carrie suddenly relaxed and did a real smile.

"What may end up being truly significant about this case," said Leon, who looked as if he was about to pontificate, "is that the trial was run – with no help – by a woman. At last, they are forgetting their place in society, one reserved to women for centuries. Second place."

"Leon, you're so cloying when you condescend," said Carrie.

But she realized he had made an attempt at irony and she immediately felt bad: Leon looked like a hurt puppy. Still a hippie in 1980, bearded, hair curling below his shoulders, a long, aquiline beak, dark inquiring eyes. Always searching. Mostly for himself.

"I have to be honest, Carrie," said Chuck. "I'm insanely jealous."

Chuck was the firm's other criminal lawyer. He hustled more than Carrie; he was brash, pushy in court. Armenian roots, tough: an amateur boxer in his late teens, a decade ago. Slicked-back black hair, dark darting eyes. Reckless, irreverent. He and Carrie went back a long time; she had introduced him to one of her best friends, Lisa, an artist. Now they were married.

"So how're you going to feel when he kills again?" Chuck said.

"That's disgusting, Chuck. I've known Edwin Moodie for years. He has about as much killer instinct as a bunny rabbit."

"Oh, he'll fight it for a while. What is it, six months since his arrest? Every six to eight months he gets this urge, right? Puts on his black mask and goes out to seek a victim to satisfy his cravings."

"You're despicable." But there had been that report by one of the psychiatrists, who said Moodie hated women . . . A fraud, that shrink, Dr. Humbug. Thank God she never showed the court *his* report.

"I hear she picked out poor Jock Strachan," Leon said.

"Well, maybe because he *is* the Midnight Strangler," Carrie said.

"Get real. How did she make a mistake like *that*?"

"A couple of women officers did all her interviews. She probably half-noticed Jock a couple of times at the police station. He rang the wrong bell for her in court. Anyway, that's my guess. I'm going to find Mr. Moodie a job."

"That cartage company I'm doing an impaired for," said Chuck, "maybe they need a specialist in carrying fridges and pianos. Or hauling barges. Maybe I can get him a spot on Thursday-night wrestling. The Midnight Strangler takes on all comers." He turned serious. "Carrie, in this business, you do the gig, you go on to the next one. You let your old clients go. You don't bottle-feed them and tuck them in every night. He's a cookie cutter, Carrie. He belongs in a padded room."

He passed her a cup of coffee. Carrie sipped at it. She was hungry and wondered if there was a stale doughnut in the fridge. She wanted a cigarette badly. Three months now, the addiction still burning within her.

"I know you believe he's innocent, Carrie," said Leon, "and he may well be, but do you think it's wise to, ah, get involved with him?"

Involved. It seemed a strange term for kindness, for helping out some poor sod without family or friends or means. "Involved with a client" was an expression lawyers often used when referring to a more illicit, intimate activity. Where had Ted been those afternoons he was neither in court nor in the office? She wanted to talk to Chuck about it – Chuck shared Ted's secrets, they were fellow jocks, squash buddies, dirty talk in the locker room. Chuck used to be so close to her, but had become Ted's best friend; Ted had stolen him from her.

"I'm not *involved* with Edwin Moodie."

"I'd be careful," said Leon.

Carrie then heard her husband's hearty, backslapping voice, and she could see him through the doorway, ushering from his office Melissa Cartwright, the socialite: designer body, day-glo pant suit. A minor film star once, before she married a rich surgeon. Dr. Cartwright, the heart specialist, who couldn't repair his own broken one.

She saw Ted and Melissa exchange a look that seemed too confiding, too promising.

No. *Very* unlikely. A client. What is going *on* with you, Carrie? Whence this sudden neurosis, this doubt? What proof is offered?

Ted was by the coffee-lounge door now, and he peeked in. "Way to go, Carrie, I'm proud of you. Damned good work."

She looked at him with her startled eyes. "Thank you."

"Carrie, darling," Melissa said, coming in. She gave her a buss on the cheek – she stank of expensive perfume. "Congratulations, I heard about it."

Carrie flicked a cool smile at her. Melissa and Ted disappeared, and were replaced in the doorway by Chuck's secretary. "Don't forget your appointment. Mrs. Klein and that minister."

"Send them in." Chuck gulped back the last of his coffee. "Mrs. Klein is the doting mother of a son gone bad. She wants me to bail him out. Chance of a snowball. Walked into a mom-and-pop with a sawed-off shotgun."

They left the lounge, Carrie returning to the waiting room to fetch the Jessups. They'd been referred up from the ground floor: General and Commercial Trust, their landlords. The referrals paid the rent.

She sifted through the mail in her slot. Diner's Club bill. She daren't look at that. Offer of settlement on Mrs. Myers's whiplash, way too low. Newsletter from the criminal justice subsection.

Ted and Melissa were by the front door, talking in low tones.

Carrie could hear: not to worry, he was saying, he'll handle that husband of hers, wait until he gets him on the stand. Melissa was touching him, her hand resting on Ted's sinewy wrist, his racket hand. Graceful and handsome and athletic was Theodore Barr: Varsity tennis champ, chairman of his college debating society, a former long-haired campus radical. Short-haired divorce specialist now. Moving into commercial and corporate law. Favoured three-piece suits.

"Ta-ra, Carrington, dear." Melissa waved a goodbye to her. Carrie pretended she didn't see it. Out of the corner of her eye she saw Ted glaring at her.

More bills. The usual stuff: Law Society bulletins, charity mailouts. Copy of Trixi Trimble's police record, worse than she thought. The twenty tickets she promised to sell for the chamber-music series this fall.

A scribbled screed on lined paper from a man who had seen her "pickture on the TV" – an item on the news about the Moodie trial, she assumed. Unsigned. He wanted to meet her alone. "They" were watching him. Carrie was a celebrity now. This was the price. She shuddered.

Ted joined Carrie, talking low, pretending he was also reading his mail.

"You could try to be more pleasant to Melissa. She's paying us a whack of money."

"She's a cheap hustler, Ted, and you know it. A gold-digger. A bloody rich tramp!"

Good Lord, she was almost shouting – what was wrong with her? She looked at the Jessups. The wife stole a glance at the husband; they weren't concentrating on their *National Geographic*s.

She hated herself for this . . . shrewishness. But they had been like this for almost two months: caustic, sniping, acting like children. Love him but don't marry him, Leon had said. Live together, sure. But don't marry another lawyer. Especially Ted, a great guy but spoiled, still growing up. But she wasn't interested in such logic three years ago. Blinkered by love.

15

Ted spoke brusquely now, and loud. "All I ask is you treat her with at least the same civility you bestow upon your friend the serial killer."

She suddenly felt nauseated – she could still smell the perfume, it was on Ted now.

"Damn it, Ted, let's not do this now. I have clients."

She turned to where the Jessups had been sitting. But they were gone.

2

Beneath the feet of Perez and Hiltz, the floor vibrated: muffled explosions, bowling balls, pins scattering. From the portable radio, Anne Murray kept asking if she could have this dance.

Normie the Nose Shandler watched them working, felt their nervous energy, smelled their jittery odour. The night was hot and humid, their skin was wet and shining and their shirts stained. Normie the Nose waited, mellowed out, as he watched them pour heroin into a punch bowl, sweet delicious smack, dream porridge, the joy ride. Escape and forgetting.

"That first hit was kinda chippy," he said, and he was lying, because it actually had a pretty good lift. "Too much buff."

They ignored him, mixed up another sample, one part smack, six parts lactose. The Nose continued to stare at that punch bowl with his tiny pinned pupils. He was short and bony, with a sharp nose like a terrier's, a good nose – he could tell what kind of kick a mix had just by smelling it. Though it wasn't much of a way to get off.

The loft was above the Roll-a-Bowl-a-Ball Alleys on St. Clair West, and there wasn't a lot of working space in it. Surrounding the table was a clutter of movie props, costumes, furniture, backdrops with minarets. The Nose figured the movie had been set in a casbah maybe, with belly dancers. A sex comedy or something. Then he decided it was more of a shoot-'em-up because he read the words on Perez's T-shirt: LAST FLIGHT FROM ISTANBUL. SOON FROM HELIOTROPE STUDIOS. A thriller, maybe he'd catch it: he liked chase scenes.

Perez, yeah, he was in the movie business – what did they call him? – a gaffer. What he couldn't figure out, these guys worked for Billy Sweet, so what were they doing playing around with his junk? Packaging it for quick sale, it kind of looked like.

On the table were a kitchen blender, a bag of lactose, a set of fine scales, a bunch of six-packs of Ramses safes, and a stack of film cans, sealed with tape on which was printed in big black letters: EXPOSED FILM! DO NOT OPEN! Hiltz and Perez were opening them, removing full freezer bags, dumping the powder into the punch bowl that the Nose couldn't keep his eyes off.

"Listen, you wanna unload fast, cut down on the cut. Go easy on the additives, man."

Hiltz gave him a mean look. He was family, a kind of brother, he and Normie the Nose had both been raised in the same foster home. Hiltz was heeled, carrying heavy weight, a .45 in a harness.

"Who said anything about unloading fast, Normie? We're just doin' the back end."

"For Billy."

"Yeah."

"Sure. Sure you are." The Nose smiled. He could be trusted.

Perez looked at Hiltz. The Nose figured a signal was passing, a question.

"He's okay," Hiltz said, and he turned on the blender. When it stopped they could hear Anne Murray again, still wanting that dance. The Nose thought he'd like to dance off into the night with that punch bowl.

Hiltz handed the Nose a spoon with a taste of the new mix in it. He sniffed, nodded, then made soup of it. He sucked it into his outfit, and searched for a place where the scar tissue wasn't too stiff, and shot the spike home.

Perez and Hiltz watched him, waited.

"*Isn't she beautiful?*" the radio said. "*Old gold from Queen Anne. This is Night Country, 1350, all night long, cool country on a hot night in Hogtown. Comin' up, the Pickens Brothers, but first a timely reminder . . ."*

A roll and a boom. The Nose felt the room jiggle. Everything felt okay.

"Yeah, this has a better blast." Smooth runway, he was soaring, fuck the world. "Yeah, yeah, I feel like I'm coming from every pore, man." He felt the throttle ease, and he was in the gentle bobbing ocean, the waves lapping at him. "Levels off real good."

Dreamily, he looked at the reel cans. Ten, twelve pounds of pure. They wouldn't dare steal it all. He guessed Perez would tell Billy Sweet some of it went missing on the way, and he never figured out how.

"Yeah, that's fine, that's sweet. Dazzling."

"He got off awful fast," Perez said.

"Maybe it's too rich now," Hiltz said. "You think we oughta step on it a little more?"

"Hey, man," said the Nose, "take my advice, step it *up*. Moves faster. It'll all go in two, three days."

Hiltz poured some of the new mix into one of the condoms, tied it with an elastic, and threw it hard at the Nose. "Take your ounce and go, Normie."

"I got a couple of good connections."

"We ain't cuttin' you in," Hiltz said.

"Reason you guys might wanna unload quick is 'cause Billy Sweet might think you're cuttin' him *out*."

"You say that on the street," Perez said softly, "I'll cut somethin' outa you."

The Nose pocketed his ounce, but he didn't leave right away. He picked up one of the empty rubbers, rolled it out, played with it, felt its texture, smooth and creamy like sex, or what he remembered of sex. He rocked gently on his heels. An ounce. He wanted more.

Perez and Hiltz bent to their work. A rumble of a rolling ball. A strike. Distant shouts of triumph. The radio talked about the bargains in Car City.

Hollis Lamont and the boss were listening to a remote receiver unit in the back of a darkened van parked across the street from the Roll-a-Bowl-a-Ball.

"Sounds like they ripped Billy real good," Lamont said.

"We should have put extra mikes in there. That radio makes it hard."

They heard Perez: *"Didn't we say to split, Nose?"*

They heard a sharp explosion.

In the loft, Normie, who had blown the empty condom to the size of a watermelon, had just pricked it with his syringe. Perez nearly fell off his chair. Hiltz went for his gun, then stopped, seeing the rubber dangling flaccid from the Nose's hand, seeing his big grin, his black, decaying teeth.

"You boys wanna shoot up, maybe ease the tension?"

"Get the fuck outa here, you ugly dumb shit!" Perez yelled.

The Nose drifted toward the door, still smiling, he couldn't help smiling. It felt like he was floating, he wondered where his legs were. He washed out his 'fit in the sink, went behind a plywood partition where there was a toilet, and took a leak, mellow yellow, comforting.

He thought, maybe insist on one more bag, the price of silence. Ugly dumb shit, eh? Fuck 'em, maybe he should drop a dime on them, a friendly word to Billy Sweet. Billy would set him up for life.

The Nose zipped up, left the toilet, took one last fond look at the punch bowl full of magic powder, and slid back the latch on the door. He paused again. Maybe he should do a little jab more, enough to get him on the street, enough to get home on. He watched them work. Maybe he could wheedle a half out of them, just a half more.

"Hey, it's Happy Hank Jones here for the next four hours, and here's number eight, movin' up with a bullet, Jimmy and Joey Pickens, 'I'm Just Sick to Death of Lovin' You, Betty-Sue . . .'"

A great force from the other side of the door pushed it inward, propelling the Nose face-first over a crate and into a stand-up wardrobe full of veils.

En route, he heard sounds like *whump, whump, whump,* and through the gauze of a pink veil he saw Perez, an astonished look on what was left of his face, and he saw the lights go out on that bloodied face. And he saw Hiltz fumbling for his .45, ducking, not ducking fast enough. *Whump, whump.*

Hiltz staggered, clawed at the table, and brought the punch bowl down on him, where the heroin formed a glutinous mix with the blood that pumped from his heart.

"Billy Sweet don't like gettin' whizzed, fellas," said the gunman.

Schlizik. Jerszy Schlizik. The Nose couldn't see him but he knew the voice. Billy's main button man. Schlizik who took out those two undercover bulls last winter in the Chelsea Hotel. He felt the panic rising, billowing clouds of fear pushing out through his skin, a helpless loaded total junkie kind of fear.

"I'm just the tester!" he screamed. "I'm just the tester!"

The door was still ajar, and the bowling sounds were louder. The Pickens Brothers sang of their pain, "*I ain't gonna be used by you, Betty-Sue, I ain't gonna be used no more.*"

"Where are you, Nose?"

The Nose could see Schlizik now, he could see him through the film of silk, dressed in his long black suit jacket, the Undertaker. He was coming around the wardrobe, looking for the shape of him in the veils, in the tangle of imitation-gold chains, hidden and still like a trapped rodent.

Then the Nose saw someone else, just entering through the doorway, lounging there now, a tall man, six and something, also dressed in black, black hair, black gloves, dressed for Normie's funeral. His gun was held down, loose.

Schlizik, too, caught sight of him, wheeled, swiftly levelled his gun at him. Then he relaxed.

"You almost bought it, André. You're supposed to stay at the goddamn wheel."

André shrugged, looked at the dead bodies.

"*Vouz avez du visou.*" A Québécois accent.

"What's that mean?"

"You have a dead eye."

21

"Yeah, well, talk my language," Schlizik said.

André raised the barrel of his gun without moving his arm, and fired once from the hip, and his bullet went dead centre between Schlizik's eyes. The explosion rebounded from the walls just as, from below, there came another explosion, and people cheering, a strike.

The Nose saw Schlizik's body fold up and drop from view. Normie didn't move, didn't take a breath, he begged God that the man wouldn't spot him, wouldn't see the figure hidden in the silk.

André stooped to Schlizik's body, checked his eyes, then looked around the room as a director might, studying the stage. He picked up Schlizik's legs by the ankles and moved the body around a little bit. He stood back, frowning, then nodded, and went over to Perez and pressed his gun, a .357 Magnum, into the palm of Perez's hand, tightening the fingers around the butt and the trigger.

Preoccupied, he didn't see Normie the Nose slither from the wardrobe, shoeless now, bent double, making himself small, and now stepping carefully behind some packing crates, along the wall, toward a fire-escape door at the back. He unlatched it, and slipped out.

André moved back to get a better perspective, then returned to Schlizik, adjusted his position once more. Then he calmly strolled to the sink, wet his face, and walked out.

Carrie hardly slept a wink the night that Ted stayed out until three o'clock in the morning. The evening was sultry and she was hot and anxious, haunted by the sounds of their house. It was a comfortable dwelling, a brick semidetached on the west side, in Parkdale, an old Victorian house with gingerbread and plaster mouldings and the original stained glass. A well-built house, yet it creaked as if heavy ghosts were roaming upon the burnished oak floors.

She played her cello for a while in her studio, solo passages from a Beethoven quartet she was practising for her chamber group. Usually she could lose herself in her music, but not tonight.

Too many ghosts, too many memories, too much Ted in her head . . .

Tonight he was out with her, with Melissa. *Seeing* her. Business, of course. *Her trial's next week, Carrie, she's under strain, so I have to babysit.*

Chuck was the only person in whom she'd confided her worries about Ted – Chuck, who was like a brother, a confidant since law-school days. He'd airily dismissed her fears. But why hadn't he been able to look her in the eye?

If only her mother were still alive to give the comfort mothers give. How cruel God was to have taken her so suddenly and mercilessly after Charlie's disgrace. Cancer. Maybe she hadn't wanted to live.

She poked through the kitchen, the drawers, not sure what she was looking for, then realizing. A cigarette, a pack forgotten beneath the linen or behind the cutlery. She felt the hunger in her throat, her lungs – it was oppressive.

She tried to read in bed for a while, then sought oblivion in sleep. With the lights off, the house noises seemed louder, almost like feet shuffling about. She thought of that strange letter, the man who'd seen her "pickture" on the TV. She thought of the Midnight Strangler – he'd broken into houses in safe residential areas . . .

A scuttling noise, a mouse, or maybe the raccoons were back.

A creak. A moan, wind in the branches outside, but somehow human.

She crept from the bed, and padded barefoot to the open window overlooking the elm-lined street, the flat black lawns, the slumbering houses. A distant streetlamp, moths attacking it, the boom of a nighthawk somewhere above, circling, hunting, the anonymous buzz of the city, a siren from afar, the sound rising and falling, another siren, more distant. There, in the shadows, something . . . A man?

The figure moved again, and stopped, a dark blur beneath a tree. She strained, tried to make it out. Nothing. She was seeing things.

She went downstairs, checked the doors.

Nervous Nellie. She hated it when Ted stayed out late. She hated it when he didn't come home.

At two o'clock she subsided into sleep. Some time later – she wasn't sure what time – Ted climbed into bed with her reeking of wine and something else. Carrie squeezed her eyes shut and gripped her pillow.

Over coffee in the morning – just a few hours later – Carrie erupted.

"Where the hell were you?"

"Looking after business. Melissa's a goddamn *client*, Carrie."

"You were taking a brief of evidence from her all night?"

"She insisted on after-drinks. She got maudlin. Christ, Carrie, I'm suing her husband for a vast gob of money, and I'm not going to walk out on her in the middle of Barberian's Restaurant when she's crying and has had too much to drink. I took her back in a taxi and came straight home."

"By way of Winnipeg?"

"I swear to you, damn it, nothing's going on!"

Then he called her paranoid.

She threw her wedding band out the window of their kitchen nook. It fell among the wilting rosebushes outside.

Ted seemed shocked. She was suddenly uncertain, wanted to believe in that hurt expression.

She hated being in love with him.

3

Outside Toronto's Old City Hall, now the Provincial Court Building, a dozen people had gathered, and more were arriving. Two women unfurled a banner: PORNOGRAPHY IS DANGEROUS TO YOUR HEALTH. Another woman passed out signs: PORNOGRAPHY IS A DIRTY WORD, END PORNO'S YELLOW REIGN.

Harry Squire could see them from the back of the unmarked cruiser where he sat handcuffed and in a state of dismay. The police car wheeled by the demonstrators to the back of the building, to the prisoners' gate.

Squire, a man of forty with quick, restless eyes beneath beetle brows, swivelled his head and saw – with not much relief – that his lawyer seemed to be on the job, B.J. Festerton, Q.C., was pulling up behind the police car in his Cadillac.

The raid had occurred last evening, just after the last customer of the day left Squire Books International, Yonge Street branch. Squire estimated that something like fourteen thousand books, half the stock of his main Toronto store, had been carted away. Those women out front, those picketers against free speech, had laid the charges.

While the police were packing out the books, Harry Squire had made a hurried call to Festerton. The lawyer had finally arrived, imperious and insulting, demanding to see warrants, threatening to call the chief, the mayor, the premier. Fur was going to fly.

It had been the wrong tack, Squire now realized, for the morality squad, who had merely intended to serve a summons upon him, arrested him instead, and coolly advised him he would have to apply for bail after spending the night in jail. It was a night of sleepless horror. He'd also been subjected to the ignominy of prints and mug shots at the police station, and now was on his way to court.

Festerton had said the arrest was a technicality; he had promised Squire he would be back with his family in an hour. Festerton was connected. He golfed with the mayor.

A barred gate opened and the cruiser entered a narrow passage leading to the building's lockup, and Squire was helped from the car. As B.J. Festerton, with his articled student in tow, strode to the gate, Squire complained loudly to him: "This town is overpopulated with drug dealers, pimps, and armed assassins, and the police have little better to do but harass an honest businessman."

A woman poked her head around the side of the courthouse. She was waving a sign: JAIL HARRY SQUIRE.

"It's him!" she shouted.

She ran forward. Others joined her.

"It's Harry Squire!"

"Dirty Harry!"

He heard boos, catcalls. Press photographers rushed forward, bent, kneeled, stood on tiptoe, getting all the angles.

"Send him to jail!"

"With the other perverts," said the woman with the JAIL HARRY SQUIRE sign. She was pert and plump, pleasant-looking enough, but obviously – beneath the skin – just another mindless censor.

"How am I going to get a fair trial?" A rhetorical question, unheard above the shouted insults.

Festerton tried to walk in past the gate, but an officer blocked his way.

"Sorry, sir, you'll have to go in by the front. We have to process him before court."

"You will *not* continue to treat my client like a common criminal."

"Looks like another hot one today," one of the officers said to the other. "Be great to be at the lake."

They led Squire past the prisoners' door. Inside, he could hear the clanking of metal doors, raspy barks, commands, the obscene shouts of imprisoned thugs.

The courthouse, facing south on Queen Street and looking down the narrow tunnel of Bay Street, had served as Toronto's City Hall back in the days when Toronto was Anglo-Saxon and staid and upright and closed on Sundays. The courthouse was dwarfed now by the financial towers which had sprung up around it, high spires of tinted glass, and by the two tall, arc-shaped structures across the street that comprised the new City Hall.

The nineteenth-century building in which the city's main criminal courts were housed lacked the proper ponderous look of a courthouse – too ornate, the sandstone exterior grey and pink and pigeon-shit white, the interior metallic and lacy with its bronze facings and wrought-iron railings, its mosaic tiles, its stained glass and oak panelling. But the lawyers who worked it endured it; some even loved it: the familiar creaks, the dark corners where they gathered to hatch their plots, the awkwardly shaped courtrooms with the lions and the unicorns of the Canadian crest.

Outside One-Eleven, the first-appearance court, waiting for it to open, pacing up and down the lobby, Chuck Tchobanian felt strangely oppressed by all the hum and bustle: clerks scuttling back and forth, yelling greetings; coffee-gulping cops memorizing their notes; other witnesses, civilians, wandering lost or gathering in small knots to debate their causes. And the lawyers: tense men and women, racehorses before the bell, making hasty notes, brushing up their witnesses, doing deals on sentence, gossiping, telling jokes.

But most of the talk today was about the triple murder last night above the Roll-a-Bowl-a-Ball. A French Canadian was in custody, Chuck had heard, one André Cristal, presumably a button

27

man for Billy Sweet; a cop had mentioned something to Chuck about stolen dope.

He knew there wasn't a lawyer here who wouldn't give his or her bicuspids to be retained for Cristal's defence. Big fee if Billy Sweet were indeed the paymaster. Lots of ink and the chance to notch a major win.

Chuck Tchobanian was ready for his first murder after four years of defending bums and drunk drivers. When was something big going to come his way? He needed a nice, fat, rich crook with lots of troubles, a milch cow. Not much milk in criminal work, though: look at Carrie, a measly fifteen grand in legal aid for six months doing a serial killer. Maybe Ted's got the right idea: divorces, corporations.

All Chuck had today was young Timmy Klein, an armed robber of convenience stores, a picayune five hundred clams for a bail application, although there'd be more if he could get the kid out. Also, he was supposed to babysit a hooker, Carrington's client, Trixi Trimble, who probably wouldn't show up – she had a heavy habit.

"Hold Trixi down," Carrie had said on the phone. "I'm just getting dressed, I may be late."

"What do you mean, hold her down? I'm a married man."

But Carrie hadn't found this funny. She was grumpy, only a couple hours' sleep.

"Why no sleep?"

She hadn't wanted to discuss it.

Then she had added, before hanging up: "That son of a *bitch*."

Carrie didn't often swear: a genteel woman, civil, a cultivator of the arts. So Chuck feared Carrie had caught Ted – figuratively – with his pants down. What had Ted been up to last night? But of course Chuck knew, Ted had mentioned something about "eating out" with a client. He hadn't been so crass as to wink, but he had smiled too confidingly.

Chuck had seen this coming. He had warned Ted. Melissa was not worth a tenth of Carrie. Melissa was a rich, beautiful mistake. Lust was blind. You're letting your dick do your thinking.

Chuck was conscience-smitten about his role as Ted's cover

man, his personal Alibi Ike: the fishing weekend that Ted had not really shown up for, the afternoons they'd supposedly taken off to play squash and tennis.

He prayed Carrie hadn't figured out he'd lied and weaseled for Ted and betrayed his old pal Carrie Connors with whom he used to study torts in law school, used to play Scrabble and chess, who used to drag him out to ballets and concerts – never anything physical between them; they were like brother and sister, the sister who used to tell Chuck *her* secrets, who'd once confided she was falling head over heels in love with a certain senior partner of the firm they'd both joined.

Was it as bad as it sounded? Should he try to phone Ted, to get the whole gruesome? Or should he just back away, stay the hell out of it? No, talk to Leon, that's what he must do, the wiser, older head, together he and Leon would work Ted over, get him to see reason . . .

Al Costello, a grifter who had somehow managed to scam a law degree, pulled up in front of him, a clean suit today, sharp.

"How's it hanging, Chuck?"

"Loose and easy."

"I see this Cristal guy's got two counts of murder so far, maybe there'll be three. The bulls haven't figured out *what* was going on up there, a fucking Chinese fire drill. He got a lawyer, you heard?"

Chuck shrugged. "He's just a small-time hit man. Billy's got plenty of 'em."

"Billy, that's who they really want. The Bullet creams his shorts thinking about it. But they'll never nail him. Too careful."

Not once in his mottled career had Billy Sweet been tagged for anything, not even speeding. It seemed they'd *always* been after him, looking for him to stumble, to make a mistake, even before he became Toronto's kingpin, before he cornered the city's drug market.

"I'll bet this Cristal was in on the job Billy did on those two narcs, too," Costello said.

The Bullet – Inspector Harold Mitchell, head honcho of the RCMP's narcotics division – had developed an almost neurotic

29

obsession about Sweet, it was said, especially after his two under-cover officers were murdered in January, men borrowed from E Division headquarters in Vancouver. They'd been running a reverse sting that backfired.

"Billy will go deep-pockets on this one."

"He usually hires the best and the swiftest for court, Al. Don't get your hopes up."

Costello looked at him sourly, adjusted his tie, a conservative stripe; he looked like a corporation guy from Bay Street.

"Who's prosecuting?" Chuck asked.

"The man himself." McAnthony, the A.G.'s top gun. "I just saw him talking to some feet from homicide."

Costello was looking around now, on the hunt for game, defendants without lawyers whom he could hustle and make a buck off. "This joint is a zoo today. You see all those pickets out front? Burn the books, and throw the bras into the fire, too, while you're at it."

Chuck watched him amble off. Books and bras, he had no idea what the guy was talking about. Chuck had come in a side door, hadn't seen any pickets.

Oh-oh. Here was Carrie striding toward him, purposeful yet looking – to someone who didn't know her – wide-eyed and inno-cent: those big green startled eyes. But the mouth was firm and set.

"Has she shown up yet? Trixi?"

"No."

"Damn her. She's using again."

Carrie looked pretty bagged, white.

"Okay, what's up?"

"Chuck, I want you to be frank."

"Okay, and you can be Geraldine."

"Please, Chuck. Is he involved with someone?"

Chuck looked for means of escape. The doors of the remand court were opening, people starting to flow in.

"In particular, is he seeing Melissa Cartwright?"

Chuck gritted his teeth, and lied for all he was worth. "Come on, Carrie, she's a client. Ted would never do that. Get him disbarred."

30

"He was out 'til almost three o'clock with her."

"Well, that's . . . you know, that's business. Man, Carrie, he's got a big contingency on this, 15 per cent, and Dr. Cartwright is worth about five million bucks."

"Look me in the eyes."

Chuck did so. "I'm telling you the truth, Carrie." He despised himself then.

The doting mother of Timmy Klein, boy armed robber, was standing at the courtroom door, looking anxious.

"I got a worried mom over there, Carrie."

Carrie went off to search the premises for Trixi Trimble, and Chuck – suppressing all guilt feelings for the moment – tended to Mrs. Klein. The minister was with her – Chuck had told him to make sure he wore his collar today.

He walked them into the courtroom. "We'll be half an hour anyway. Grab a couple of these empty seats up front."

The prosecutor seemed harried already, though court hadn't yet been called into session. It was going to be a long morning, a hundred cases on the list. And Chuck knew Judge Revere to be a stern and righteous soul who kept saying things like "Come to the point, counsel," and "I'll brook no nonsense."

"Give me a break on this one, Andy," Chuck said to the prosecutor.

"He's got two previous."

"In *juvenile* court. You can't even mention that. He's eighteen, for God's sake."

"He scared the wits out of that poor couple."

"Hey, they're real tough birds: the old man pranged him with a bottle of Pepsi. No harm done except to my client. Andy, I've got a bail application that will take an hour, I've got *viva voce* evidence. You want to get out of here by midnight? I'm only asking for bail, not the moon."

"He's an armed robber, Chuck." Then Andy leaned to his ear. "Talk to the arresting officers. One of them's grumbling; it's his day off."

"Hold the case down."

Outside the door to One-Eleven Court, Chuck was accosted

by a scraggly-haired young man who seemed stoned on something. Not booze but pot, Chuck caught it on his breath.

"Where's the place for bail? I gotta bail my buddy out."

"Next floor down."

Chuck found the two case officers having a smoke in the rotunda, a corporal and a constable from the holdup squad. He tried to soften them up with a couple of jokes, then made his pitch. "Look, guys, what about bail on this thing? Andy says he'll go along if you agree. The guy comes from a good family, I'm going to try to get him some help."

"Get him a brain," said the constable.

"You want to take the kids to the pool today, you guys. Summer comes but once a year."

The corporal, the guy who supposedly wanted to get out of here, said, "No way, Tchobanian. I'm going to stick around."

"I'm going to spring him anyway."

"That's better than your last joke. You got Judge Revere sitting in remand."

"He loves me."

Carrington could see Chuck working the policemen, pushy, glib – he was tireless. She was feeling much better. Chuck had seemed so forthright, firm, his eyes hadn't wavered from hers. Ted is *not* having an affair; Chuck wouldn't lie. She'd been acting childishly, filling her mind with extramarital ghosts.

She turned to the Queen Street entrance as Trixi Trimble waltzed in, painted, in brunette wig and high heels and miniskirt, carrying a little black evening purse, as if on her way to a good time. The part of the picture that didn't come together was the cowboy hat.

She waved and smiled at Carrie, and explained, as she reached her: "I got tied up at a cattle-breeders' convention, honey. If you can dig it, two hundred *breeders*."

Trixi was cheery, seemed clean, no new marks on her arm.

"Get rid of that ridiculous hat."

Carrie grabbed it from Trixi's head, and as they walked

toward the stairs to their second-floor courtroom, she plunked it on the head of a court officer passing by. "Join a rodeo, Freddie."

"Oh, hey, Carrie, there's someone in the lockup wants to talk to you."

"I'll be down in half a sec, thanks." A repeater, she guessed, someone she'd won a case for once.

A long-haired young man, looking bewildered, stopped her at the top of the stairs.

"Hey, lady, you work here? I gotta bail someone out, nobody'll take my money."

"Main floor," Carrie said.

"I been there. I think." The man stumbled off.

"I hope this dotty judge hasn't forgotten the evidence again. Trixi, you still owe me a thousand dollars."

Trixi went into her purse and pulled out a wad of hundreds.

"Well, holy cow, don't flash it," said Carrie. She tried to be surreptitious, quickly stuffing the bills into her briefcase. But after five years in this business she no longer suffered guilt about where her money came from. It was a kind of tax the naughty had to pay.

She led Trixi into 126 Court, where Judge Klotzman was sitting in judgment upon one of the regulars, a drunk. Carrie heard the clerk read the charge, a 175, causing a disturbance by fighting on Parliament Street, in the Cabbagetown area.

"Guilty wit' an explanation, sorr," said the prisoner, a grinning leprechaun with Newfoundland accent.

"Yes, Molloy?" said Klotzman.

"Well, Jasus, I need toime to t'ink of one. I rest on y'r marcy, that's for damn sure, y'r warship."

"A hundred dollars or three days."

"That's koind of you indeed, y'r warship. When can I collect the hundred dollars?"

Molloy got his laughs, a rich rumble from the bulb-nosed judge, a man of drink himself. This was good, thought Carrie, she had caught the Klotz in a merry mood.

"Can you fit me in, Joan?" she asked the prosecutor. "I have to see a client in the lockup. I have Trixi Trimble, number eighteen."

"Gosh, I wasn't on the trial," Joan said. "It's Joe Wiebe's case. I don't know anything about it." She looked through her files and found the one marked "Trimble," and puzzled over it.

"Next case, please, Madam Prosecutor."

"Oh, just call it," Carrie said. "It's for decision, all the evidence is in."

"Number eighteen," Joan announced, though a little uncertainly. "Trimble."

Carrie brought her client forward, and Judge Klotzman studied Trixi pensively for a long time, probably wondering what it would be like, thought Carrie. He was a softie when it came to the young women of the street.

"I remember Miss Trimble," Klotzman said. "But I can't remember the case."

"It's a 195, prostitution," Carrie said. "It's for decision, your honour. You said you wanted to mull it over."

"I had some notes somewhere . . ." The judge picked through some papers that were in disarray in front of him.

"I can't help, your honour," said the prosecutor. "I wasn't there."

Carrie decided to risk it. "You thought the arresting officer's story was full of holes."

Judge Klotzman scratched his head, gave up looking for his notes. "Okay, well, I think . . ." Then he began talking quickly, getting it behind him. "On reviewing the evidence, I find the Crown has not made a sufficient case. I have a reasonable doubt and I find the accused not guilty." He peeked over his glasses at Trixi. "Though it was obvious what she was up to."

"I'll tell her to be careful the next time," Carrie said.

The judge chuckled.

Outside the courtroom, Trixi said, "You're the best, honey."

It felt good. A slightly brighter edge to the day. The sweet tranquillizer of victory.

"You're going to stay off the stuff, Trixi?"

"Oh, you bet, I cross my heart."

"Otherwise you're heading up a dead-end street, Trix. I want you to think about that office retraining –"

Trixi stopped her. "Don't worry, I'm gonna find myself a nice rich sweetie one of these days. The way I look at it, I'm retraining for him."

"Stop by the office, we can talk, I'll get some forms. You'll learn about computers."

Trixi looked doubtful. "Sounds kinda boring."

"Jail is boring. So is dying young."

4

Chuck waited glumly outside the remand court. He'd argued with those cops until he was blue in the face on behalf of the spoiled brat who was his client, but ultimately to no avail. He'd almost had them, though; it was close.

There goes Carrie, seeing Trixi to the door – from the look on their faces Goddess Victory had once again smiled on Carrie, that's five in a row including a monster murder, she's good. Better than him in the library, he had to admit, better prepared.

Damn Ted. He'd better not bring everything down around their ears. A serious talk was needed, Leon and Chuck and him.

Nearby, two men were studying a list posted to the wall, the court docket. Strangers to Chuck. One of them was older, well-dressed, but looked like a shark, a corporate crook of some kind. Chuck took him to be the client of the other fellow, a young man with a briefcase.

"Ask somebody," said the older man.

The young lawyer approached Chuck. "Are you familiar with the routines?"

"What's the problem?"

"Can't find a client's name on the list."

Chuck studied the other man. He looked monied, maybe a businessman charged with impaired driving. This punk was just out of law school, already getting the wealthy clients, it didn't seem fair.

"What's your guy charged with?"

The older man caught this, and moved to join them, affronted, haughty.

"I am B.J. Festerton, Q.C., of Lichtburn, McDonald. This is my student. I don't usually appear in these courts." He looked around, somebody trapped in the cellar with the rats.

Chuck stuck out his hand. "I do. Chuck Tchobanian. The reason your client's name isn't there is probably that he's just come in and they haven't reissued the docket. You are at the right court, B.J."

"Do you know who the judge is?" Festerton asked.

"Revere. We call him the Reverend – he's a deacon of the Anglican Church. Your guy should be all right as long as it's not a morals beef."

Festerton blanched. "Actually, it's a charge of selling obscene literature. Harry Squire. Squire Books International Ltd. I normally, ah, represent his corporate interests."

Ah, thought Chuck, that's explains the pickets, the book-and-bra burners Costello had carried on about. Harry Squire, stroke books and tit art, he had a big chain of stores. As in whips and chains.

"Revere couldn't find a reasonable doubt if it sat on his face. I'd find a way to wiggle out of his court, if I were you."

Festerton adjusted his tie, it seemed to have become a little tight. "And how would that be done?"

"You learn to pull a few levers around here." He wasn't about to let this prig know how to work them. One *earns* one's spurs, it takes experience to survive in the jungle.

A voice sounded through the loudspeaker system. "B.J. Festerton, One-Eleven Court, B.J. Festerton."

"Better get in there," Chuck said. "Revere is a time freak, he's obsessed with punctuality. His favourite line is 'I don't like late.'"

He followed them in. This is something he might enjoy watching.

Judge Revere, a major imbiber of stomach medicine, was a small man with an unsettling tic in one eye. He was scowling now, tapping his finger, his worst habit, a device also used to warn windy counsel to cut it short. But Chuck got along with him, he'd learned you pare to the bone, you zero in, you don't waste time.

"I don't like late, Mr. Festerton."

Chuck saw Harry Squire in the prisoners' box, wearing a creased suit. An odd-looking man with eyebrows knit together, he had one of those upside-down faces you used to see in cartoon magazines. He was glancing about the courtroom.

Festerton made it to the front of the court. "It couldn't be helped, your honour, there was some confusion –"

"You'll wait. Call the next case."

Squire looked at Festerton, as if assuming some tart rejoinder would issue from the lips of the mayor's golfing companion, but the lawyer meekly sat down.

"Ah, I see Mr. Tchobanian is here," Revere said. "Let's do him."

Favouring him, Chuck realized, was the judge's way of punishing Festerton, the guy should have apologized.

Squire was openly glaring at Festerton now from beneath his beetle brows. Timmy Klein came up the stairs from the lockup and joined Squire in the box, but didn't turn around, couldn't look at his mother to receive the loving messages she was sending. The prosecutor explained at length why this armed robber shouldn't get bail, then sat down when the judge started tapping his finger.

Chuck cut his own pitch to the quick, then said, "I have Reverend Whitson here to say a few words. He's young Klein's godfather."

Revere looked down at the minister. Chuck caught the slightest nod of recognition. Pay dirt; the judge had probably been at church teas with him.

"Has the boy been attending services?" Revere said.

"He tries, your honour," said Reverend Whitson.

The judge nodded. "I won't need to hear from the good reverend."

The prosecutor glanced at the arresting officers, who were sitting on the front bench. The corporal gave Chuck a rueful grin and raised both his hands slightly, palms forward, in surrender.

"I don't have any reply," said the prosecutor.

Revere released Timmy Klein on a bond with a strict curfew and told him to report three times a week to his neighbourhood police station until his trial.

"It might be a good idea to order him to continue his counselling with Reverend Whitson," Chuck said, setting things up for a suspended sentence.

"So ordered. All right, let's hear about Mr. Squire."

Chuck walked over to Mrs. Klein, his ego plastered all over his face, he couldn't hide his smile. As he ushered her and the excellent Reverend Whitson from court, he could hear the court clerk sombrely intoning the words of the information against Squire:

". . . did have in his possession for the purpose of sale the following publications, to wit: *Sin Slaves*, *The True Story of Mitzi O*, *I Was a Harem Girl*, *Stud for Hire* . . ."

As Mrs. Klein stood in the corridor numb with joy, Chuck quoted a handsome fee for the trial, enough to pay his mortgage for another month anyway.

He didn't want to miss the action in One-Eleven Court, and when he strolled back inside the clerk was still reading the information.

". . . *The Gang Bang Girls*, *Case Histories of Foot Fetishists*, *I Had the Biggest Dick in the World*, *Handbook of Pain and Bondage*, *Adventures of a Toe-Jam Queen* . . ."

"Is there no end to this?" said Judge Revere, whose face was unreadable.

Chuck watched as the clerk flipped through several pages. Must be several hundred titles, the prosecutors had worked overtime last night. Somehow Chuck couldn't imagine Revere ever reading all these books – a trial would take a year.

"That's enough, I get the picture," the judge said. "Well, Mr. Festerton?"

"I have an application for bail, sir."

"Bail? *Bail?*"

The prisoners' holding area was bustling, a flow of people in and out, crooks, drunks, cops, court officers, probation officers, legal-aid lawyers, the wagons outside filling with today's losers on their way to the Don Jail, other luckier prisoners heading out to the bail counter, on their way to the street.

On hot days the place usually smelled like a sewer, with an overlay of chlorine disinfectant. Carrie could barely stand it. She weaved through the crowd toward the desk of Staff-Sergeant Horse Kronos. They called him "Horse" because he was built like one – he'd been used in the Moodie lineup. Horse had been boss of the bullpen for as long as Carrie could remember.

She saw Chuck's client, Timmy Klein, being taken from the bullpen. It looked as if he was on his way out, good for Chuck. Molloy, the Newfie leprechaun, was in the tank with about twenty others. "Horse," he yelled, "are me t'ree days up yet, b'y?"

Horse ignored him. He was attending to a man with a red rooster haircut, punk or new wave or whatever they called it. "He was supposed to show up with the bread three *days* ago. Aw, man, what's going *on* here? It's like Dante's *Inferno* or something around here, I'm in a cell with a psycho."

"I think I bumped into your friend – someone trying to post bail, anyway," Carrie said. "He's probably paying it now. Sergeant, someone in here wants to see me?"

Horse smiled at her in the way of one bearing good news. He said, "Cristal."

His look suggested he expected a more interesting response from her, but Carrie was lost.

"As in chandelier?"

"Cristal. The Frenchman. André Cristal."

Finally this rang a bell for her – she had seen the story in the morning *Star*, "THREE SLAIN IN DRUG WAR." Three bodies and three guns found in a loft along with five million dollars' worth of heroin. One man arrested. André Cristal.

"You have competition, though," said Horse.

She walked down a passageway lined with cubicles. The competition, Al Costello, was sitting on a stool, talking to someone on the other side of the metal grate. Carrie saw him pull a card from his wallet and poke it through the mesh.

"First thing is get you out on bail."

Costello didn't see her stroll up behind him. The man he was engaged with, obviously André Cristal, was tall, dark, and handsome, though not conventionally so – his features worn and tough. Longish dark hair, a dimpled square chin, and piercing eyes, pupils like nuggets of coal. He was wearing a denim shirt and pants, prison issue.

He seemed quite at ease, puffing contentedly on a hand-rolled cigarette, showing none of the tension one might expect from a man accused of a bloodbath. He was not looking at Carrie, although he must have observed her there, but at Costello, examining him as one might an interesting bug.

Cristal hadn't taken the lawyer's card.

"Who sent you?" A Québécois accent – the newspaper said he was from Montreal.

Costello winked. The boys, he was intimating.

"I am suddenly very popular," said Cristal, deadpan. "You are the t'ird one."

"Why don't you go chase an ambulance, Al," Carrie said.

Costello turned quickly, and flushed. "Listen, a friend of his sent me." He opened his briefcase, dropped his card back into it. "Hey, you're in good hands, Mr. Cristal." As he retreated he pretended to be absorbed in some papers.

"Thank you for coming, Miss Barr." Cristal's eyes seemed to drive right into her. Suddenly, his face was creased by a smile that was oddly boyish, lopsided. Cute.

The interview area was too open, too many ears. "I'll arrange for some privacy, Mr. Cristal."

She found a small, empty room and sent for him. She tried to

41

remember what she had read in the morning paper. Cristal had been arrested leaving a stairwell from a second-floor loft, a back-end operation, a mixing room. Blood and bodies galore, men with criminal records: gangland slayings, that was the speculation. Billy Sweet was probably mixed up in it.

The officer who escorted Cristal to the interview room said, "I'll stand outside."

"You'll do nothing of the sort."

"He's charged with three murders, ma'am."

"I'm not worried."

Cristal came in and took a chair. She closed the door and held out her hand. "Carrington Barr."

A curious thing then happened, a spark as their palms met, a click of static. But after that, his hand felt firm and dry, comfortable.

The smile again. "We 'ave different polarity."

She smiled, too. "I'm positive."

"I am very 'appy to hear, Miss Barr. Maybe you will turn me positive."

Oddly nervous, Carrie busied herself with pen and notepad, then glanced up at him. The white line of an old scar ran over the bridge of his nose, otherwise his features were unsullied. A bit of wrinkling near the eyes, either from laughing or squinting. About mid-thirties, she guessed.

"You're not to talk to anyone, you understand that."

Cristal nodded. "They say in here you are a very good lawyer, Miss Barr. Someone here call you one of the best t'roats in Toronto."

"T'roats?"

Cristal worked on his phonemes. "Throats. They mean lawyers." He brought out a packet of Drum tobacco and some papers, and began rolling. "I t'ink you 'ave done a very big murder trial a few days ago, for the Midnight Strangler, yes? He was accuse of killing six nice women and I only t'ree bad men. So with you I 'ave hope."

"He was innocent, Monsieur Cristal."

"And so am I."

She wasn't quite ready to accept that. The roll-your-own told her this gentleman had done time. She was fascinated by his fingers, nimble, practised, one, two, zip, a perfect cigarette.

He offered it to her. *"Une rouleuse?"*

"Thanks, but no. I've managed without for three months now."

He started to place it in his shirt pocket.

"No," she said quickly, her hand reaching out, touching his wrist – why did she do that? She jerked her hand back, afraid of another shock. "People smoke around me all the time. I want you to be relaxed."

He shrugged, and put the cigarette in his pocket anyway.

"You are from Montreal?"

"I should 'ave stayed."

"What do you do there?"

"Manage a dry-cleaning business."

It was an answer she didn't expect. Usually, one got evasion, professional bad guys claiming they were between jobs.

"Do you have a record?"

"None. Okay, one, assault, a guy was bod'ering a woman in a bar." He shrugged. "Well, who cares? Of these murders I am innocent."

The last was said with emphasis. She wanted to believe him. "Let's not talk about the evidence right now." One never, ever does that right off the bat. One first collects the facts from the prosecutor, and builds defences into them.

"I want you to believe in me, Miss Barr, I am innocent. If you are my lawyer, I want you to know that."

"Mr. Cristal, it may be that you were just visiting Toronto, and you like to bowl, and you went up those stairs looking for a wash-room, and you just happened to be the wrong man in the wrong place, but if that is the case, I'd like to hear it later."

Kind of shady this, but all lawyers do it, lay out a possible line of defence. But it would be highly improper to hear one version of a client's story, then urge him to give a different one in court.

"Good. First I will listen to what they claim I 'ave done." He seemed to understand the ethical nuances. "But I promise you, I am clean."

43

"If you manage a laundry, I'm sure you are clean."

Cristal flashed that big smile. "Can you get me bail?"

"If the case is very weak, maybe. I doubt it."

"It is very important that I get bail."

"Why?"

He shrugged, gestured at the four cold walls. "*C'est pas le paradis*. So. How much will be your fees?"

"Fifty thousand dollars assuming a preliminary hearing and a two-week trial. In advance."

Cristal slowly went for the cigarette.

"No beating t'rough the bush. I am the same." He lit it with a wooden match, blew the smoke away from her. "Will you write this down, please? There is a man I work for in Montreal. His name is Leonard Woznick, Lavanderie Woznick, on Boulevard Saint-Laurent. He is a friend, like a father. He will 'ave the money."

When she glanced up from her notepad, Cristal was looking at her with those coal-fire eyes, but with a slightly amused expression.

"So . . . will you be my lawyer, Miss Barr?"

"I . . . accept. Mrs. Barr, actually."

His eyes went to her hand, a ring of untanned skin where the wedding band had been. She got up quickly. She was embarrassed, she wasn't being cool Carrie.

"Yes, I'll represent you."

Their hands didn't spark this time, but she felt something feral in his touch.

5

Carrie walked quickly through the thinning throng in the central
lobby, and headed down to the Crown Counsel offices to see if
Oliver McAnthony was about. He'd been against her at the
Moodie trial, and it very much looked as if they'd be facing off
again. M. Cristal seemed to have utter confidence in her. M.
Sang-Froid.

What *had* he been doing here in Toronto? A man from that
strange other nation of Canada, insecure Quebec. Carrie felt bad
about knowing so little French – it was rather disloyal. There'd
been bigots in the town where she grew up, franco-bashers,
though New Brunswick was supposedly bilingual.

By now, with her doubts about Ted somewhat quelled, she
was feeling strong, good about herself. Another major client, a
paying one this time, an important career break. Win it, and
Toronto is at her feet.

Was her interesting new client as innocent as he claimed? He
seemed like a man with a dark past, but he professed to have had
only one previous, a minor assault. That could be checked:
McAnthony would have his record. No weapon found on him –
it sounded like a pretty threadbare case. Were there witnesses?
Merely a businessman from Montreal, m'lord, off to do a spot of
bowling during a visit to our lovely city.

Well, maybe she *was* defending another innocent man. It feels

45

good to defend the innocent. It happens so rarely. She knew that only a tenth of the acquitted are actually innocent. But any other system is wrong, her father had sermonized, in his booming – through often slurred – baritone. Better a hundred guilty souls go free than one who is innocent be jailed. In Canada, the state *proves* guilt, my pet. Until not a tittle of doubt remains. You can't tell Charlie Connors the Napoleonic Code is better. France, Germany, Spain: they were uncivilized countries that lacked that greatest of British institutions, the common law.

Charlie Connors had turned down offers to practise in Toronto, in other cities. He preferred his country juries, he always knew half a dozen folks on each of them. He was happy being the big bullfrog in the little swamp, the Terror of Temigouche, the Great Orator. When she was a girl she'd suffered – and now missed – his long, soaring, whisky-voiced soliloquies from *Hamlet*, from *King Lear*, the sonnets, the verse of Keats and Yeats and Blake.

He'd pretended disappointment when she said she'd chosen law. Always claimed he wanted her to be a poet. Or a concert cellist – music was his third love: law first, then Shakespeare, then the great Ludwig.

But deep inside he'd been so proud when she entered law school at Dalhousie. And if events had not conspired against him he could have been prouder. You should see me now, Charlie – she had always called him that: it was Mom and Charlie – you should see your sole-begotten taking on the big ones in Toronto, the multi-murder cases, up against the top prosecutors, blunder-busses like McAnthony.

Carrie saw the door to the inner offices was open and she just barged past the secretaries, and found Oliver McAnthony, Q.C., in deep conspiracy with two senior cops: Jock Strachan from homicide and Harold Mitchell from RCMP narcotics.

"If either of you can make head or tail of this ring-dang-do . . . ," McAnthony was saying, and he stopped in mid-sentence as she entered. "Ah, Carrington, how delightful, what business honours us with your lustrous presence?"

"What can't you make head or tail of, Oliver?"

"The meaning of life, my dear. The nature of the universe."

"I've just been retained by André Cristal."

"Ah, yes," said McAnthony. "Interesting chap. Good luck."

"Thought I'd drop by to seek some quick disclosure of your
. . . ring-dang-do."

McAnthony looked at the two policemen. "She demands what
is her right according to our fastidious traditions of justice.
Disclosure of the evidence."

McAnthony seemed relaxed, well recovered from the petulant
episode he'd suffered outside Moodie's courtroom. He was
nearing seventy, handsome, white-maned, in shirt sleeves and a
vest, a fob and chain strung across it. He liked to fiddle with his
gold watch when opposing counsel was addressing the jury.

"He is a hit man, Carrie. I don't know yet if we can prove it, but
we will give it the old college try. We don't know how many he
killed, so to be on the safe side we're charging him with all three."

"He had no gun."

"Too true, we cannot put a weapon in his hand just yet. But we
do have him running out the stairwell into the arms of an off-duty
constable."

"Running?" Carrie said.

"We dinna have him running, Oliver," Strachan said. His bow
tie bobbled as he talked. Carrie liked him, he was abrupt, but
honest.

"We have the individual *proceeding*, to use the argot of our
minions of the law, from a stairwell which *accesses* – another fine
technocratic word – only one area, a loft in which motion-picture
props were being stored, and which was being used for mixing up
– what do you call the process, Harold?"

"Cutting smack, Oliver, bundling," Mitchell said. "A back-
end operation."

"Cutting smack. Marvellous are the uses of the English language. We have a stolen vehicle outside, and its motor, unlike Mr.
Cristal, *was* running."

"That's *all*?"

"An expert in the developing science of blood spatter examined the scene. His opinion is Schlizik's body may have been

47

moved after he was shot. A possible theory: Cristal rearranged some human furniture and placed his weapon in one of the dead men's hands to make it appear as if a gunfight had ensued."

"He's a soldier for Billy Sweet," Mitchell said, as if that were the end of the matter.

"We're working on it, Carrie," said Strachan. "The labs haven't all reported in."

"Well, while you work on it, give him bail. Or maybe you should just drop all charges, and I'll accept a letter of apology in lieu of damages."

"The background is this," said Mitchell. "Perez and Hiltz were stealing a shipment of smack, the property of Mr. William Sweet." The name was spoken with utter loathing. "Dope brought to Canada in film cans, grade-A Turkish heroin."

That's why the RCMP was involved, Carrie surmised. They usually handled the trade in foreign commodities. Mitchell reputedly ran a secretive, mean crew in his narcotics section, hard-nosed men and women. They called him the Bullet not because he was gun-happy but because his head resembled one, coppery and bald on a thick neck. She remembered that before being posted to Toronto he'd been involved in some scandal, an entrapment sting in Newfoundland that went wrong.

"Did you have them under surveillance? How do you know they were stealing it?"

"Obvious," said Mitchell. "You don't have to be Sherlock Holmes. The third body, Jerszy Schlizik, was Sweet's number-one gunner. He did one thing for a living and he did it very well. He was a stone-cold psycho killer, a vicious fucking son of a . . ." His voice had suddenly raised alarmingly. "Sorry. We're pretty sure he's the guy who took out our two undercover men last winter. I don't know how Billy narked them, but he did. Anyway, he and this Cristal went into that loft to ice Perez and Hiltz. There was a gun battle. Only Cristal survived."

Carrie had a feeling Mitchell knew a lot more than he wanted to share. He had been targeting Billy Sweet for many years, obsessed with the man.

"Do you gentlemen have a single witness?"

48

"We wish," said Mitchell.

"No one saw Cristal with Schlizik."

Silence.

"Or in the stolen vehicle. Can you put him in that loft? Did his clothes analyze for gunpowder? Were there prints? Do you have *anything*?"

"We have some rather interesting antecedents," McAnthony said. "Your gentleman apparently works in Montreal for an industrial dry-cleaning firm. I do not mind telling you – because it will be a part of our case – that this dry-cleaning business washes more money than clothes."

Here it comes finally, thought Carrie, the criminal connection. So much for the innocent client. She was disappointed – not all that much. She never totally believed in him. And these fellows still had to prove their case – they hadn't much of one.

"Take over," said McAnthony to Mitchell.

"The business is a front. It's supposedly run by a guy named Big Leonard Woznick, a well-known rounder in west-end Montreal, but I think Sweet really owns it. The money washed there comes from narcotics." He added: "So will your fee."

"Take him to the cleaners, Carrie," McAnthony said. "Don't undervalue yourself, charge a fair fee. You're a fine counsel. But I'm afraid that's all we have for you so far, my dear. Motive, association, opportunity. We have no secrets, do we, gentlemen?"

"Aye, none," said Strachan.

Mitchell just smiled. A cagey guy, thought Carrie.

"You don't have a *case*."

"It is all rather weak, isn't it?" McAnthony said.

"You won't get this past a preliminary hearing, Oliver. Please, end this silly charade, it's almost embarrassing."

"Her Majesty has been embarrassed before."

"What's on Cristal's sheet?"

"One common assault," said McAnthony.

"Reasonable bail at least, okay?"

McAnthony looked at Mitchell, who shook his head. Carrie got the impression he was running things here. Odd, it wasn't really his department, this was murder.

49

"I'll agree to bail," Mitchell said. "How does a million dollars sound? Be interesting to see just how it gets paid – and who pays it."

She turned to McAnthony. "Are you taking orders from him, Oliver?"

"Harold is my trusted adviser."

"You opposed bail for Edwin Moodie."

"Ah, yes, the gentle giant, the alleged – I emphasize that word, of course – Midnight Strangler."

"And he spent a wasted six months in jail because of that." She turned to Strachan. "I hope you've stopped harassing him, Jock – the day he got out he was followed all over town."

Strachan folded his arms, as if in a gesture of defiance. "The chief spoke to me about it."

"And?"

"He is to be treated as innocent. I protested, but we are a wee short of manpower. If he kills again, let it be on *your* head, Carrie."

"I hope you're still looking for the real murderer."

Strachan said simply, "The file isn't closed."

Carried sighed and went to the door. "I'll see you in High Court, Oliver." That is where bail was heard in murder cases, before a superior-court justice.

"It will be a pleasure being up against you again." McAnthony gave her a mock salacious leer, then a wink to let her know he was really over the hill. "As it were."

Horse was busy with the man in the rooster haircut again, so Carrie had to wait for permission to meet with Cristal. She wondered if she should call the office, cancel the day's appointments.

"I'm in here three days, and you tell me there's a mix-up on my charges? Oh, *man*."

"We have you down here, section 220: did commit rape of a female person."

"Rape? *Rape?* Hey, man, where do they get *rape*? It's a *weed* charge." He seemed very rattled suddenly. "Jeez, what's this, some kinda horror movie? I'm just charged for a little bit of

50

smoke. They popped me with a couple of joints in my ass pocket. Look, the judge set bail at two hundred bucks, I got a buddy who's gonna post it, I don't know what happened to him, lost in the freakin' bureaucratic maze in this freakin' joint."

Horse scratched his head. "I'll try to find out what's going on. Your name is Blaine Johnson?"

"*Blair* Johnstone. Johnstone with a *t* and an *e*. Man, someone get me a freakin' *lawyer*." He turned toward Carrie. "Hey, lady, help, this is right outa Kafka."

"I'll arrange to see you."

It looked like a real snafu, a time-consumer, something you'd hate to get on legal aid. But it would seem a big mistake had been made, and she'd try to help him out.

As Horse escorted Blair Johnstone back to the cage, a man holding his beltless pants with one hand stormed from the interview area, followed by a lawyer Carrie vaguely knew, B.J. Festerton.

"I'm going right to the top on this one," Festerton said, hurrying after his client, almost running. "Heads will roll. I'll argue the appeal tomorrow, we're taking it to High Court."

"You couldn't argue your way out of a crowded bus."

Harry Squire, Carrie realized – she'd seen some demonstrators outside.

Squire went through his pockets, then said to Festerton: "Do you have a quarter?"

Festerton handed him one.

"Thanks. Your services are no longer needed. Now, where's the nearest pay phone?"

"No phones here," said Horse. "You can call from the Don Jail. The wagon's waiting."

Squire looked dispirited.

"Who do you want to call?" Carrie said.

"A lawyer called Tchobanian," he said.

"I'll ask him to see you."

"I watched him in court," Squire said. "Seems to know his stuff."

"He's good," Carrie said.

She realized she was getting a cold stare from Festerton. She returned her best wide-eyed, innocent look, and went into the locked area.

Cristal gave her the Pepsodent smile again as he joined her in one of the cubicles. He took a wooden chair in one hand, turned it and sat on it backwards, straddling it, all this done in one fluid motion. Athletic. He probably worked out, lifted weights or something.

Cristal was silent throughout as Carrie recited the Crown's particulars. She found herself speaking somewhat sternly, disappointed in him: she assumed now he wasn't any innocent bystander, though God knows what his role was. Big Leonard Woznick – Cristal said he was like a father to him. More like a Godfather maybe.

He fiddled with another of his *rouleuses*, but didn't light it for a long time.

"It's okay," she said. She wondered where he'd picked up the habit of smoking rollies. Not jail, but it somehow suggested a man who had been alone a lot.

He tried to blow the smoke away from her, but it filled the little room. She could take it, she was strong. Just a little second-hand smoke passing from his lungs into hers.

"They'll be trying to connect you with organized crime. They think you're not as innocent as you appear to be."

"I am guilty of many t'ing, Mrs. Barr, but not murder."

She thought about this. It's true, he'd said nothing about *not* being a criminal. "Okay, do you want to tell me now what were you doing up there? You don't have to, you can think about it."

A slight grin this time, no blinding flash of teeth. "Do you want me to lie? Would it make it easier?"

"No. Frankly, I don't want to be caught by any surprises at the trial."

"I work for Leonard Woznick. It's true, he does some t'ings for Billy Sweet."

"What things?"

"He is in the business."

"Please be plain."

"Drugs. Washing money. Big Leonard sent me to that place to pick up some product."

"Product."

"Heroin. Does it matter? I am a bad guy. I am a dealer." His eyes hard into her. "But I am not a killer."

Carrie nodded, sad that the veil of innocence had dropped – she had really hoped he was that rarity, an innocent like Mr. Moodie caught in a web of suspicion. But she was content at least that he was being straightforward, not holding back.

"They were all dead when I walked into the room. I 'ave never seen any of them before. I ran downstair, and suddenly I am grab."

"None of the guns can be traced to you?"

Cristal shook his head, then leaned close to her. "I t'ink someone tried to set me up."

"Why do you say that?"

"The police, they knew exactly when I will be walking down those stair."

"Well, there was an off-duty cop, he just happened to be . . ."

"How did he happen to be?" Cristal's eyebrows went high, emphasizing the question.

"He heard a shot."

"Below? In the bowling alley. You must go there and see if you can hear."

It *was* an odd thing, Carrie thought, the officer being right on the spot. No, don't go looking for stray dogs, it'll muck up a perfectly good defence.

"The matter of bail, that has been discuss?"

"You should be entitled to a cash or property bond, with sureties. Unless they can allege harder facts. You could never be convicted on what they have so far."

"But they will 'ave more? Bail would be good, Mrs. Barr."

She wondered if he was planning to skip.

"Okay, M. Cristal, tell me all about yourself."

6

"If you don't mind me being blunt, Mr. Tchobanian, how much is this going to set me back?"

"Chuck, they call me Chuck." His mind raced. Harry Squire, he had to be worth a couple of million. Fifteen hundred dollars a day? The trial could take years. Don't get greedy, you'll lose the fish off the hook. "I normally bill a little higher, Harry, but let's say . . . a thousand a day. As I see it, there's a principle at stake here."

"It's more than a principle. Democracy is at issue. When are you going to get me out of here?"

"Not to worry, Harry, we'll get that bail review heard tomorrow morning."

Chuck put down the phone, got up with a happy grunt, and ambled into the coffee room. Leon and Ted were there, munching on deli food, salads and sandwiches.

"I brought you some dead animal on pumpernickel," said Leon.

Chuck peeked through the Saran. Pastrami. He put it in his briefcase. "I'll have to eat on the go. I've just been talking to Harry Squire."

"Oh, God, the biggest porno pusher in Canada," Ted said. "There go the tattered remains of our image." He looked wan, hungover, cranky. Must have been a hell of a night. Chuck hadn't managed to get him alone yet.

"Image?" said Chuck. "What's this image? An image is what my wife's ad agency uses to sell aftershave lotion."

"I think an effective argument can be made that pornography involves a profound form of misanthropy –" Leon began.

Chuck waved him off. "Don't get all preachy, Leon. I'm billing a K a day. Bucks. Dollars. Negotiable notes with the queen's loving countenance on their faces to back them up. That's the kind of image I'm into."

Leon said after a pause, "Of course, there's also a valid question of prior censorship involved here." He was piling into a plate of sprouts, a vegan, he ate like a rabbit.

"And what's Lisa going to say about you championing the cause of schmuff?" Leon said, his mouth full of greens.

"Schmuff?"

Leon swallowed. "Smut."

"Aw, she's just going through a militant phase." He thought about Lisa for a moment, suddenly aware of some unhappy implications. "Anyway, she doesn't have to know about it."

"Hold on," said Leon. "She doesn't have to *what*?"

"Hey, even Harry Squire is innocent 'til proven guilty. It's a free society, people can do any damn thing in the privacy of their . . . You're right, she won't understand. Listen, you guys, we go back a long time, longer than Lisa – whom I love, don't get me wrong – we're like the three musketeers."

"You want us not to tell her," said Leon, "is that the point you're desperately trying to make? Be a man, Chuck. You'll be in the news in any event."

"Jesus, I'll have to talk to her. Okay, I'll break it somehow." He gathered himself together. "I'd better go over and sew him up."

As he was about to leave for the lockup, he said, "Hey, Ted, you got a second?"

No point in involving Leon in this just yet. He waited until Ted joined him in the corridor outside the waiting room, then said, "You're up to your ass in alligators, buddy."

"Yeah, I nearly blew it. Just got drunk, loose, and late, that's all."

"Eating out all the time gets costly." Was that it, he wondered, the sex? Could it be *that* good? Carrie was probably a little prudish in bed, but Chuck didn't think she was frigid. And she loved Ted. Maybe, he thought, it was also the money, Melissa's claim to half of Dr. Cartwright's five million bucks. But he refused to accept that. Not Ted.

"When's it going to end, Ted?"

"I don't know. It's confusing."

Chuck spoke softly but fiercely. "You better get your head on straight, man. You're treading on a minefield. Get *rid* of that dame."

"I . . . I'll have to talk to her."

Chuck wanted to hit him right in the chops. "Don't hurt Carrie. I'll kill you."

Ted seemed stunned. "Hey, Chuck, don't get . . ." Then he spoke abruptly. "You're right. You're absolutely right, I'll end it."

"You mean that."

"Yeah. I don't know what's been getting into me."

"Or vice versa. I lied for you, pal: Carrie came onto me like a freight train. Don't make me hate you for doing this."

"Thanks, Chuck."

Ted grabbed his arm as Chuck turned to go.

"I'll end it. I mean it."

"Okay."

Just then three officers of the Cool Aid Society came noisily in, shouting greetings to Ted and Chuck. They were the favourite official office characters and looked wild: two men with unkempt beards and a woman with an Afro as big and busy as a jungle canopy. Parjanya was her name – she had about ten rings stuck in one ear. Roy, who was nearly seven feet tall, was their intellectual leader. His T-shirt read: I GOT OFF BY GETTING OFF. Elmo, who was shirtless, exhibited an ample, hairy kitchen, which flowed over his belt.

Grinning, he bumped Ted with his stomach. "I'm bellying up to the Barr."

Ted gave him a playful combination, a light one-two to the mid-section.

"What's up, you guys?" said Chuck.

"Is the lion in?" said Roy. That's what they called Leon, he was their hero. Cool Aid was one of Leon's pet projects, peer help for kids on drugs. "We got a problem, a hassle down at Ex Park, a strip search, they went right up his winkie with a flashlight. But he was clean. We wanna sue those ass-poking porkers."

It was only then that Chuck noticed the landlord standing in the doorway, Robert Barnsworth, manager of G & C Trust, and he was looking upon the three freaks in the waiting room with a mixture of disgust and trepidation.

Ted led the Cool Aiders inside. Chuck turned to Barnsworth, guessing he'd come about the overdue loan payment.

"Do you have a moment?" Barnsworth said. A small man in rimless spectacles, he had a fussy air.

"Well, I'm on my way to court."

"I shall briefly make my point. We sent a mortgage up the other day, a Mr. and Mrs. Jessup. They were rather disturbed by the, ah, atmosphere here, and we recommended they go elsewhere. Your office does seem a little, shall we say, informal in its approach to matters. It doesn't quite *do*, Mr. Tchobanian. And I must say, some of your clients look like rough trade indeed."

Chuck took his elbow and patiently shepherded him out. "Sorry, Mr. Barnsworth, things have been hectic around here."

He led him into the elevator, and made soothing noises all the way to the ground floor. As they exited, Barnsworth finally mentioned the overdue loan payment.

"Yes, we're late," Chuck said. "We'll rectify it."

How? he wondered. Their general account was alarmingly low. They'd better get some big fees in fast. Harry Squire to the rescue.

As Chuck headed out the front door of the G & C Trust building, he almost bumped into his wife, who was coming in.

"Lisa." Chuck, caught off guard, stood there for a moment, staring at her.

He saw she was holding a sign, stiff cardboard stapled to a lath. He couldn't make the words out, it was upside-down, facing away.

"You're not at the office today?" he asked. Lisa worked in an ad agency, indispensable there, one of their best artists.

"I took the morning off. I had more important things. You having lunch? Want to take me?" A short, feisty woman, plump and bubbly, she seemed in a good mood.

"Gee, Lisa, I was just running out to court, a little emergency . . . What's this?"

He turned the sign around. Upside-down letters spelled JAIL HARRY SQUIRE.

"W.A.P. – Women Against Pornography – called me this morning. They finally got Harry Squire busted."

"Uh, yeah. Honey, I can't join you for lunch. I've got this client . . ." He couldn't tell her, not yet. "A rich . . . ah, broker, it's complicated, wash trading, a curb market in worthless shares."

"Sounds boring. Okay, darling, I'll see you at home for dinner."

Chuck scurried away. He would work it out with her over dinner. Ethically, he'd explain, one just can't turn a client away. The presumption of innocence, darling, it's basic. Every person, however scummy, has the right to a fair trial, a right to counsel of his choice . . . No, that wouldn't work, an appeal to principle and reason, not with Lisa. She had been so apolitical when he married her, so innocent, so . . . non-troubling.

Life shouldn't be this complicated.

Edwin Moodie was in the waiting room when Carrie returned from court, his bulk spread across an upholstered chair which seemed to be a little insecure, and wobbled as he shifted. He looked up at her, then averted his eyes bashfully, kneading his thick fingers.

"Those two computer salesmen are here again," said Pauline Chong.

Carrie saw them sitting there, clones in business suits and briefcases. Ted was all for getting computerized; Chuck was against it, a waste of money.

Carrie scribbled a note for Moodie and handed it to him. "This is the address of a cartage company I spoke to."

"Thank you." His eyes went to the paper – he seemed to be studying it intently. He probably couldn't read very well.

"Everything all right? You have a place?"

"Yes, on Jarvis Street. The Eagle Hotel."

She thought she'd seen it. One of those dingy joints with a big beer parlour and little sordid rooms.

"Police have stopped bothering you?"

"Yes, thank you." So polite, he must have been raised well.

He seemed rooted to his chair. "Well, on your way, Mr. Moodie. Kelver Moving and Storage. Just a couple of days a week, but it'll put food on the table. They're good people, and they know all about you."

The chair groaned with relief as he stood. "There's stuff nobody knows about me."

What did he mean by that? "I hope it's good stuff." She saw him to the door. "*Ciao.*"

He turned. "I ate already."

"So long, Mr. Moodie, that's what I meant. Good luck."

As he turned to go, Trixi Trimble came in wearing a too-revealing halter top and hot pants. Moodie's little blue eyes bugged at the sight of her, and his pencil moustache twitched.

"Hi, there, cutie," she said. "What's your name?"

"Um, Edwin. I'm . . . I'm . . ."

"Shy, right?" She winked at him. "Mr. Edwin Shy."

Moodie couldn't find words. He became beet red. He fumbled his way out the door.

"He's quite a gentleman once you get to know him," Carrie said.

She was about to lead Trixi to her office when one of the computer people said, "Mrs. Barr, we thought we'd drop by and try a little demonstration on you." They had brought in one of their machines, which sat between them, bulky, expensive-looking.

"I'll see what the others think."

In her office, Carrie handed Trixi some forms for the secretarial course she had been urging her to take. Trixi looked good, healthy and perky, no needle marks.

59

"Honey, thanks, but I don't know if I can afford the tuition, you know?"

Carrie wrote her a cheque for three hundred dollars.

"This will get you going."

"You are an absolute doll, hon. I won't forget it."

"Stay straight."

"I promise on my deathbed."

Trixi gave her a kiss and a hug, and Carrie escorted her to the waiting room. Chuck, who'd just come in, was dismissing the computer-sales team.

"Gentlemen, I don't think we have time to look at that thing right now," he said, herding them out.

He grumbled to Carrie: "Computers – always something new to waste money on. You pay fifty grand for a bunch of machines, and in two years they're obsolete and they're pushing some other kind of junk at you. I'm in a rush: I've got to prepare a bail review for Squire tomorrow. He didn't even blink at the fee. A thousand a day."

"Let's see the retainer," said Carrie.

"I'm not going to insult Harry Squire by insisting on cash on the barrel like a criminal. Have to soften him up. Did you make a hit with the hit man?"

"Get your money in, Chuck, rule number one." That had been one of her father's problems, he actually *lent* money to clients. Then she remembered: hadn't she just done the same? Three hundred dollars to Trixi; she'd never see it again. "Cristal is paying *fifty* thousand, in advance, though I have to go to Montreal to pick it up."

"God in Heaven, Thou hast been bountiful today to the firm of R., B., B., and T. I was worried we were going to have to stall the bank next week. I just saw our general account, not enough to keep us in dog food. Maybe we'll get the mob business now, *organized* crime, people who pay their bills."

She could hear Ted approaching, with Royce Boggs in tow.

"She's a voracious cunt," Boggs was saying. Carrie flinched.

Ted's voice: "Royce, I'm sure she'll see reason after the discovery."

60

She could see Boggs now, florid and large. A corporate pirate with some major electronics holdings.

Ted looked ravaged all right, but he was keeping himself together, being all Rotarian, clubbish, his hand on his client's elbow.

She saw that Boggs was giving her a once-over. "Mrs. Barr, you are looking radiant."

She barely acknowledged him, and began checking her mail.

"Oh, I forgot, Mr. McAnthony's office called," said Pauline Chong. "He has a judge for your bail hearing tomorrow."

"Oh, good. I have to make a trip to Montreal. Book me for, let's see, day after tomorrow, afternoon flight." She didn't expect that Mr. Big Leonard Woznick got up very early in the morning.

Boggs seemed unaware that Carrie was ignoring him. "Still hotter than a bitch out there?"

"Very hot, Royce." Hotter than a bitch in heat, old sport.

Oxfam, John Howard Society, Ban the Bomb, the firm was on everyone's mailing list. Alumni newsletter, a reminder from her optometrist. Invitation to formal reception for Justice Clearihue, he's just been raised to appeals. No scary letters today. Another legal aid referral, a pot pusher . . .

Oh, God, she suddenly realized she had promised that rooster-tail, Blaine or Blair, that she was going to get a pass to see him. Tomorrow, she must do that, before he disappears into the bureaucratic void.

Boggs was speaking to Ted in some kind of arcane language. "Big recapture value." "Achievement-oriented players." Then: "We want you on board, Ted, on the ground floor."

"Let's just concentrate on that divorce, Royce." Ted gave him a squeeze on the elbow, flashed his famous crooked grin.

Boggs disappeared, and Carrie returned to the main office, where Leon was standing beside the copier, studying it with an expression of dismay. He called to his secretary: "Shirley, the machine just ate Mrs. Urquhart's will."

Carrie could sense Ted behind her, reproachful. She turned to face him.

"Carrie, I know you're still angry at me." Ted spoke softly, but

61

she could hear the stiffness in his voice. "I don't know what I can say to convince you that I'm guilty of only the minor misdemeanour of not phoning you last night. For that, you have a right to be totally pissed off at me. But please don't take it out on the clients. You did it again, honey, you gave a terrific cold shoulder to Royce Boggs."

Honey. It sounded odd. Too intimate right now, too casual. Hello, honey, I'm home. Sorry about the spat this morning. What's for dinner? Carrie was confused, unsure whether to feel guilty and forgiving after hearing Chuck's assurances, or still furious, or just stupid.

"Boggs is a venal corporate manipulator, and a very boring one at that. *And* brutal. He beat his wife to a pulp. I hope she beats him to a pulp in court."

Ted bristled. "Behind the egalitarian facade, I sometimes think there's something of the snob in you, Carrington."

Leon was taking this in now – their voices had raised. Shirley found the will, lying on the floor, and handed it to him. "You know, Leon, you're really helpless."

"I side with Carrie," said Leon, suddenly a part of their conversation. "I'm starting to wonder, Ted, what *are* you doing joining cause with corporate warlords like Boggs? What is this sudden obsession with money I am noticing?"

"I'm tired of living in constant fear of the bank, Leon. I'm tired of this office being up to its eyeballs in debt. Listen, Boggs has leveraged Sky Electronics to the hilt. He wants me in for a piece of the action, I'd work with a crack team of lawyers. We're talking some humungous money here."

"My God," said Leon, "this is what we've descended to. That poor but proud civil-rights firm we founded in 1971. My partner, a mere decade later, grovelling for mammon. The other two leading lights of the firm acting for purveyors of heroin and pornography."

"We pay ten grand a month in rent, and more than that on interest payments," Ted said. "Civil rights doesn't buy paper clips. Nor does criminal law, Carrie."

"We have some big fees coming in," Carrie said.

"Carrie," said Leon, "it may be hard to visualize this, but try. Picture your husband as he was a dozen years ago, hair down to his fourth vertebra, in sandals and leather fringes, expanding his consciousness on mescaline, and shouting 'Off the fascist pigs' while police arrest him and me and our brother and sister sit-ins at Lochdale College."

"Leon, times change, so do people." Ted studied Leon for a moment, the beard, the baggy old corduroy jacket. "Some people," he said.

"Taste in clothes and hair lotion changes," Leon said. "Sometimes we change a politician or two. But some things never change." With that announcement, Leon returned to his office.

Watching Leon leave, Ted seemed lost in some private world. Carrie felt shut out.

"Ted, we have to talk."

Ted sighed. "Carrie, I'm truly sorry for last night. I should have just abandoned her, but she was drunk, she was making a scene. I should have called, I know. It's just . . . things got out of hand, and then it got too late."

His eyes looked raw, sunken; suddenly she felt a compassion, a sadness.

"Yes, let's talk," he said. "Tonight."

At home that evening, they ordered in. They talked over curried fried rice and sweet-and-sour shrimp. Ted had a couple of drinks, became charming, got the smile working. He went out into the roses to look for her ring. Carrie thought of going out there with him, but the act would have been too forgiving, almost obsequious.

Ted came back scratched from the thorns after a fruitless search in the dark.

Carrie laughed a little. She couldn't help but observe he still wore his matching ring, prominently, flashing it: the vows still bound, he was announcing. Again, he reassured her: he was not interested in anyone else; he was committed to Carrie.

Committed. It sounded like someone being sent to an institution. Love. Just say you love me.

"She came on, didn't she?"

63

Ted was silent for a moment. "Yes. She had her hands all over me in the car. And I *was* a little drunk, and I . . ." He seemed lost now, Carrie thought he was going to blurt something out, something awful. *Okay, I admit it, I did it, you got me.* And Carrie would have forgiven him then, she knew that, a drunken act of lust, regretted, forgotten, thrown out with the rest of life's casual garbage.

Get it out of the way. Now. "Did you . . . do anything, Ted? With her? Just tell me. Honestly."

"No," he said firmly, looking at her square and hard. "I absolutely did not." Then he smiled. "I suppose now she's very embarrassed. Poor Melissa. You're right, she's really quite ridiculous."

For some reason, finally, Carrie found herself wanting to cry, maybe a surge of relief. But she collected herself, changed the subject, told him all about the Cristal case.

"It sounds a little fishy to me," Ted said at the end of this. "You're sure they're not holding something back?"

"Not Oliver McAnthony. He's fair, a professional."

"Carrie, it's great, it's a big case. The only thing . . . I worry, you know, all these murder trials, aren't they putting you under a little strain?"

"It's not the work that's doing it, Ted."

"Yeah, well, *touché.*" He paused, then continued in the same vein: Was this really what she wanted to do for the rest of her working life, defend social misfits? Criminal law – it was ill-paying, and rather . . . dirty. It had left a trail of victims.

Ted didn't mention her father, of course.

She didn't argue with him. Sure, the criminal courtroom was stressful – she silently admitted that to herself. Sure, you see the seamy side of things. It *wasn't* easy. But she owed.

7

That evening, Chuck somehow just couldn't get around to talking to Lisa about Harry Squire. He had planned to have his heart-to-heart after dinner, but the Sisterhood came over, the coalescing women, a strategy session. Chuck should have interrupted there, just when they were starting merrily to put Harry Squire to the sword.

Chuck listened to them, spying from the kitchen, sipping a beer. He would find out what the enemy was up to, and when the troops left he would confront Lisa with the unhappy fact of her conflict of interest, tell her about the thousand a day, what it could buy.

Women Against Pornography, that was what they called themselves. W.A.P. These Wappers seemed malevolent women. There was much evil laughter, they were stoned on the drug of their mission. How had Lisa begun to run with this pack? She'd been such a homebody. Why do people change? It was those socialist artsy friends of hers, man-haters.

He heard Lisa say she couldn't possibly make it to the bail review tomorrow.

"We want that courtroom packed," said one of the Wappers.

"Maybe I can try to pop in. But I just *have* to show up at work. I'll do some of the phoning."

"Give us all your clothespegs." A peal of laughter.

After the conspirators left, Lisa spent two hours on the phone. Chuck knew he should interrupt, things were going too far, but he drank another couple of beers instead.

By the time he'd summoned courage, Lisa was in the bathroom. He had another beer.

When he went up to the bedroom she was fast asleep. The sleep of the innocent, the righteous.

Chuck showed up in County Court the next morning with a bit of a head. He was late, and had flown right out of bed to the courthouse. No picketers outside – maybe they'd gone to the wrong building. No, they'd all be in court, waiting, with clothespegs over their noses. Lonely, empty, cynical women, what right had they to tell citizens what they could read? Chuck was finding comfort in his cause, identifying with it.

Tyrone Slocum, a prosecutor, was in the barristers' lounge when Chuck went up to change into his robes.

"I just popped into Judge Blake's courtroom," Slocum said. "The libbers are there in force."

"I'm telling you, Ty, it's not going to end here. The intended final result is emasculation of the whole male sex." He could talk like that to Slocum, a man, like Chuck, confused by women, not sure why a whole generation of them seemed so mad at everyone. "I'm acting for the poor bugger."

"I'm prosecuting him," said Slocum. "The boys at the top want your guy's balls served up on a platter before the next election."

A warm glow began to suffuse Chuck. Ty Slocum – this was great – a comrade in the camp of the enemy.

"You well retained?" Slocum asked.

"A fair per diem."

"Well, I'm happy to spin this thing out."

Chuck liked this idea. "It's going to be hard to do that if he's not on bail."

"I'll agree to twenty-five thousand, his own recognizance."

"Hey, ah, do you think we can slip this thing into O'Leary's courtroom?"

"It's posted for Court 2-4. They got a murder thing in there first in front of Justice Blake."

"I want to do an end run around those ladies."

"Right. Good idea."

When Carrie walked into Court 2-4 she saw all the women there, clothespegs at the ready – a few already had them on their noses. One of them was pretending to spray the room with a deodorizer, guerrilla theatre.

Fortunately, the judge wasn't there yet: Blake didn't like shenanigans. Poor Chuck, she thought, Lisa probably had kittens when he told her about the new client. Lots of reporters in court, too – she and Chuck would make the papers again.

Oliver McAnthony was at the counsel table with one of his juniors. On the front bench sat Inspector Mitchell and Jock Strachan from homicide. There was a third man, obviously a cop, thin as a pole, with animated clever eyes.

Carrie guessed he was the off-duty officer who made the collar on Cristal. Lamont, that was the name. He was looking mighty proud, surrounded here by brass, a hero. Heard a shot, they said, ran outside the Roll-a-Bowl, saw the car with its engine running, grabbed Cristal as he was heading out. Cristal hadn't resisted, which was good.

They had a feeble case, even tough old Blake would see he had to give him bail, though this wily judge was Crown-minded and ungenerous.

She had a lot else going for her. Cristal, she had been sur-prised to learn, had gone through college, had been an industrial architect, then worked five steady years with a construction company in Montreal. When it went bankrupt six months ago, he became manager at Lavanderie Woznick, industrial dry-cleaners. Not a portrait of a criminal. A bachelor all his life, but a long-time address, a normal, hardworking, taxpaying citizen. On the sur-face, anyway.

"Oliver, I know you pride yourself on being fair. What are you asking for?"

"Carrington, do you really think I can be swayed by an appeal for fairness? I am not paid to be fair. Judges are paid to be fair."

"How did we end up in front of Blake?"

"I asked for the meanest son of a gun they had available."

"We can post a property bond of thirty thousand. He owns a cottage in the Eastern Townships."

"My dear, he will be on the first plane to Amsterdam, where one can purchase a new identity."

"How much bail do you want, Oliver?"

"Three hundred thousand dollars."

"That's . . . that's crazy." Carrie looked over at the Bullet, who was absorbed in his notes. What was his game? Why was McAnthony playing the servile court jester to him?

"Order in court!"

Justice Blake came in scowling at everyone, especially the women in the gallery.

"I don't want any scenes in this courtroom. Take those ridiculous things off your noses."

There were murmurs of protest, but the women complied.

André Cristal was led into the prisoners' box, a police guard close behind him. They'd returned his clothes: Carrie didn't like his outfit, all black, the uniform of a man who does bad things in the dark. He *looked* like a hit man. She was irritated at herself – she should have found him something else to wear.

Cristal looked around the courtroom, detached at first, then sort of bemused, she thought, as he saw all the women there.

Carrie went up to him, waiting for the judge, who seemed to be looking for something in the *Criminal Code*.

"Those women aren't here for you, M. Cristal."

"T'ank God for that."

"How do you feel?"

His dark eyes shot through her. "I am never better."

"Okay, Mr. McAnthony," said Justice Blake, "this is a bail application on a first degree?"

"Murder one, m'lord. Planned and deliberate."

"I see." Blake took the measure of the alleged hit man, and frowned.

Already, Carrie wasn't liking the way this was going.

McAnthony delivered a précis of the evidence, pitching it in a relaxed and offhand way: the Crown had a reasonable circumstantial case, important facts were soon to come to light, police were still investigating, there were "ties" with organized crime.

In her turn, Carrie said all the good things she could think of about Cristal, then suggested that the case for the Crown was so bad maybe the clothespegs were appropriate.

Blake smiled at that, but began to give her a rough time.

"Mr. McAnthony says the accused has ties with organized crime, as I think he put it."

"Works for a man with a long criminal record, m'lord," McAnthony said. "A Mr. Leonard Woznick."

· "My learned friend believes in guilt by association."

"He was on that stairway, Mrs. Barr," the judge said. "It leads to only one place."

"I'm not about to reveal our defence." She was being too abrupt. "There could be many explanations."

"What about the gloves?" The judge was looking at Cristal again, appraising this man in black.

"Well, he had gloves in his pocket. The important thing is he had no gun."

"You make a big thing about his fingerprints not showing up. What's he doing with gloves on a hot summer night?"

Afterwards, Carrie went quickly down to the lockup to see Cristal before he was moved back to the Don Jail. She was trying to still her fury.

"Three hundred thousand dollars! That miserable son of a . . . the old Scrooge."

Cristal seemed unperturbed. "Will they take a post-dated cheque?"

"I can try to get it reduced on appeal."

"I do not have the time."

"I'm afraid you may have plenty of time."

"What if suddenly they find a witness?"

"What witness?"

"When I went up there, I saw there were washings in the sink."

Washings? Heroin residue. What was all this?

"A cotton swab, a little blood on it. I t'ink somebody just do up, and maybe he will say he see me in there."

Carrie was unhappy with this conversation. It was starting to sound as if Cristal had been in that loft longer than a second or two.

"I'm not following."

"Mrs. Barr, how can I explain . . . I 'ave a strange feeling, somet'ing is not right. Maybe the police, they 'old t'ings back from you. Maybe . . . Sometime, you know, I feel . . . how do you say? Psychic?"

She looked into his guru eyes, felt oddly uncomfortable, somehow compelled by those eyes. "Psychic, yes."

"So in my 'ead I see anod'er man in there."

"But how could someone slip out unseen?"

"There is a back door, a fire escape. But maybe I am making ghosts."

"Let's assume a witness. What could he say? More than you have told me?"

"No more. I walk in, I look around, I am in shock, I walk out. I walk out past that sink. I 'ave a feeling I am being watched. And also, I 'ave a feeling I am being set up. But maybe I am not psychic. Maybe I am crazy."

Carrie fiddled with her pen. How much of what he was telling her was false? Possibly he had actually *seen* some other person in that loft. Probably he was being more than a little evasive. Probably he was – no, not guilty, don't make that jump.

"Why were you carrying gloves?"

"To 'ave no prints on the bundles I pick up."

Carrie nodded. Logical. "Can Big Leonard raise the three hundred thousand?"

"Big Leonard, I don' t'ink he has so much money, but od'ers have."

"Who?"

"Billy Sweet. Maybe he owes me some worker compensation."

"Do you know him?"

"I 'ave never met the man. He is not so public. But I 'ave met Speeder."

"Speeder . . . ?"

"Speeder Cacciati. Second in command."

The name seemed familiar. Then she remembered a trial a few years ago – she'd been in court. Cacciati had beaten a murder charge, got it down to manslaughter and a sentence of a few years.

"Maybe they will worry I might name names to the police . . ." Cristal was musing. "Maybe they will be generous." He nodded to himself, as if he'd confirmed something in his mind. "Yes, you will see my friend, Mr. Woznick? I'm sure he will talk to Speeder Cacciati and Billy Sweet."

"I am certainly not going to threaten anyone with blackmail to get bail for you."

Cristal's smile enveloped her. "They will see the possibilities. Just tell them how un'appy I am to be 'ere."

Carrie didn't like the idea of being bearer of his subtle threats. She liked even less some of the dangers that seemed inherent in such an approach.

"I'll talk to Mr. Woznick. I'm not going to suggest where the money might come from. I don't want to be responsible for any *further* deaths, including yours."

Cristal poked into his packet of Drum, then quickly looked up at her. "T'ree 'undred t'ousand dollar, that would be a good fee for you, yes?"

"What do you mean?"

"Billy, he will want to give me cash for bail. I will assign the bail to you."

It was often done; criminal lawyers got many of their retainers that way. She could hardly think he meant it: three hundred thousand.

"If I . . . disappear, then you keep it all."

71

"If you skip we get nothing. They seize the bail."

"If I disappear in a different way." No smile now, just the eyes, like drills. "If I die." He rolled one up. "Then it will be a good year for your office."

He smiled. She didn't.

"Good luck, Mrs. Barr. I t'ink I am in good 'ands."

He reached out for one of those hands, studying it, as if reading a future. Another little spark as their fingers touched. She jumped.

He laughed, a gentle, easy sound. "We 'ave 'igh voltage, eh?"

Everything went smooth as silk in O'Leary's courtroom, and Chuck walked out of there with his bail order before the feminist vigilantes in the other court realized they'd been had. He thanked Ty Slocum, and sped off to the court clerk's office to get Harry Squire admitted to bail.

The clerk seemed to take an interminable time getting the order signed. Chuck wanted to slip out of this building quickly and quietly with his client. Then he would call Lisa at her office, suggest lunch, tell her about the hilarious coincidence of his being retained just this morning by Harry Squire. They could agree to be on opposite sides of this issue. It would be fun, lots of laughs.

Squire was finally brought out to sign his recognizance.

"I'll never forget this, Chuck."

"Hey, no problem." Come on, sign it, sign it.

Here, unhappily, came that newspaper guy who covered the court beat.

"Thought there was something strange up," the reporter said. "Court was adjourned, no Harry Squire."

"Okay, we have to go." Chuck took Squire's elbow, propelled him forward.

"I'm from the *Star*, Mr. Squire. What do you want to say to the public?"

"He wants to say nothing."

But Squire wasn't so reticent. "No, I want to say something. I simply don't understand how the police can come in and seize half my stock and yet I'm presumed innocent until proven guilty. If you're Hugh Hefner, you can get away with anything; if you're a little fellow like me, the forces of reaction jump all over you. This prosecution is anti-democratic and intolerant. It strikes at the very heart of our so-called free society."

"Okay, Harry, that's enough." They were almost to the University Avenue entrance of the building, but the reporter was following. Chuck hoped there were taxis on the street.

"How are you going to elect to be tried, Mr. Squire?"

"I'm electing jury, I'd like our citizens to know how their tax dollars are spent. And for the record I want to say one more thing . . ."

"Harry . . . ," Chuck warned.

"This gentleman here . . ." He put an arm over Chuck's shoulder. "He's a true fighter for freedom of expression."

They had paused at the door. Chuck had a sinking feeling: he could hear a rumble of feet, a herd of buffalo, and now they came swarming around a corner, the W.A.P. posse, with more reporters.

Squire grabbed Chuck by the wrist, raised their hands in a gesture of defiance. "Together Mr. Tchobanian and I are going to make a stand for freedom," he called out.

Chuck found himself staring into the amazed eyes of Lisa Tchobanian. She was holding her cardboard sign: JAIL HARRY SQUIRE.

"I can explain," Chuck said. "No, I can't."

She swung the sign like a baseball bat, and the cardboard ripped as Chuck raised his arms to defend himself from it.

"You rotten two-faced sexist pig!" she screamed at him.

Chuck tried to push Squire out the door, but he was resisting, determined to brave the enemy. "That was a clear case of criminal assault, are you going to let that woman get away with it?"

✢ ✢ ✢

As Carrie walked back to the office, she was lost in thoughts about Cristal. *If I die.* What had he meant by that? Had his so-called psychic self foretold his own demise?

Odd, odd man. Powerful emanations. You needed a voltage regulator to be around him. Electronic imbalance or something. Dope dealing, running other criminal chores for Big Leonard Woznick – a picture of Cristal as somebody's busy, crooked gopher didn't come together. He seemed very unlike a man who simply accepted orders, more like one used to giving them.

But a picture of him with a smoking gun in his hand was not that hard to make out. He looked too much the part in court today – Justice Blake had seen it. A button man, an expert? Someone called in for the big, special jobs? Hired to kill the killer – had Billy Sweet for some reason wanted him to remove Jerszy Schlizik? Cristal had said he didn't know Sweet, but he'd said a lot of things Carrie was beginning to suspect were not true.

But here she was, doubting her own client's innocence. You're a hell of a better lawyer if you believe in your client, her father had told her. Makes you work harder. You don't believe in him, the jury won't.

Well, perhaps more would come to light about the man when she visited his friend tomorrow, Mr. Woznick. Cristal had been working for him only six months – why was there already this bond between them?

She reminded herself she had to do some checking on that rooster-head, Blair Johnstone. Or was it Blaine?

Another searing day – when was this stretch of weather going to end? But in the cruelty of winter one hungers for days like this. The climate back home had been softer, less extreme.

There was her building, a busy branch of General and Commercial Trust occupying most of the ground floor. G & C Trust was their bank, their creditor to the tune of a few hundred thousand dollars, money spent on their fancy furnished offices. They were also major providers of clients, though, and were sending up another mortgage today.

A man was lounging near the front door of the G & C Trust

74

Building, a grungy little person who looked as if he was on something – he was swaying, his pupils hugely dilated.

As she tried to go past him, he said, "You Mrs. Barr?"

She stopped. "Yes."

"I know you're the Frenchman's lawyer." His voice was slurred. He seemed to have trouble focusing on her. "I seen your picture."

"What can I do for you?" A handout? Was he offering some kind of threat? This was a busy street, but she was a little frightened.

"Maybe I got inf'mation."

Carrie looked at his left arm: the scars of a user, a fresh mark there, a spot of blood.

"Maybe I was in that loft where Perez and Hiltz got greased. Maybe I can be of assiss . . . assiss . . . help."

My God, thought Carrie, the other man in the scenery loft, Cristal's psychic creation, that swab of bloodied cotton in the sink.

"Maybe I was the tester."

"Look, can you come upstairs to my office?"

"Don' have time."

"Of course you do."

"No, I gotta . . . I gotta . . . ."

"What? Shoot more heroin? You are on one hell of a habit. What's your name?"

"Normie, but I ain't sayin' nothin' yet. Yeah, I'm beltin' ever' half-hour, and when I run out I'm gonna need some . . . some more."

"Come on up for a second."

"No, I jus' want you to think about it. I figure I oughta have a consider . . . sider . . . reward for what I seen or what I ain't seen."

"What sort of reward?"

"Big, flashy reward." He grinned, his teeth were black. "What I call sweet money."

Billy Sweet, she inferred. Normie the tester . . . he'd been paid off with product, was going through it fast, worrying already about where his next hit was coming from. How was she going to

75

handle him? Lasso him, drag him by the ankles to the elevator – this man represented the whole case for or against Cristal, murder one or nothing.

She was desperate, there was only one way with a junkie. "I'll give you a key to the office washroom." He could do up there, it was a sick, last, reckless offer.

He took a step away from her. "I ain't talked to the bulls. I won't go to them. 'Cept as a last resort."

He began staggering across the pavement, toward the street. Carrie pursued him.

"I'll call," he said.

"Where can I reach you?"

"You can't." He hailed a taxi, got in.

She ran, her business card extended, and he grabbed it and slammed the cab door shut despite her efforts to keep it open, to keep him talking.

After the taxi left, she waited for a few seconds in the hope another cab might show up, so she could follow him. Then she gave up and went inside.

This was a potentially dangerous situation, she thought as she rode up on the elevator. Inspector Mitchell might offer a great deal for this man's evidence, especially if it could be shaped to fit the Crown's theory.

The waiting room was empty. Carrie asked Pauline Chong: "Where are those new clients the trust company was supposed to send up?"

Leon overheard her and came out. "Barnsworth cancelled them. He was up here the other day complaining about our image. Doesn't think we run a sufficiently dignified shop."

"That little *prig*."

"He's starting to send people down the street to Jensen and Company. I don't know, we may lose G & C Trust altogether."

How depressing. General and Commercial's referrals had paid the overhead, kept them afloat. "Some big fees had better come in soon," Carrie said.

"Well, Ted can keep us going through the rough patch. He has some major billings. Boggs, for instance. Melissa Cartwright."

She didn't tell Leon about the three hundred thousand dollars they might earn from Cristal. It was looking as though they might need it.

Carrie went through her mail and messages, freshened up in the washroom, and headed out to the Provincial Courts.

"Blair Johnstone," Carrie said.

"No one by that name."

"Or Blaine. Johnstone with a *t* and an *e*."

"No current file by that name."

The clerk went through her list a second time, accused persons who were before the Provincial Courts. Carrie was feeling more than a little frustrated.

"A pot charge, simple possession. He was here *yesterday*."

"Maybe he pleaded. Maybe he's out."

Carrie went to the lockup. It was four o'clock now, things weren't busy. Horse was reading a copy of *Hustler*, his lips oddly puckered. He tried to slip the magazine out of sight when Carrie came up to him, but she spotted it. She was disappointed in him, a family man.

"That guy, Johnstone, with the *t* and the *e*. With the awful dyed red hair. Is he still here?"

"Shipped out, I don't know, last night, this morning. I wasn't on duty."

"To where? The Don?" The main Toronto jail, where prisoners awaiting trial were kept.

"Yeah, I guess so."

At the office, she phoned the records clerk at the Don. To her relief she discovered they did have a *Blaine* Johnson. The court lists must be gummixed up. She would go out to see him. Tomorrow. Heavy date with Ted tonight. No, tomorrow she was in Montreal. Friday then.

They dined across town on the Danforth, in one of their favourite Greek restaurants. Ted was attentive, didn't stare at the waitress's legs as he often did. Their talk was mostly about work, her frustrating day, his new divorce case, another wife-beater.

"Like Boggs," she said.

"All right, look, I can hardly stand the guy myself. Honey, you don't pick and choose your clients in this business."

"You don't get in bed with them either." That wasn't exactly what she had intended to say.

Ted looked shocked. "I thought we had that straightened out."

"I'm speaking figuratively. You don't want to get too close to Boggs, some of the grease might rub off."

"He's a door. It opens to other clients." He leaned toward her. "Listen, there's a big directors' meeting tomorrow in Montreal, Sky Electronics, he's going after them, and they're trying to stop him. Buy Sky, he said. Buy quick and sell in two weeks."

"Ted, that sounds like insider trading."

"I'm only telling my wife."

"But he told you."

"I'm his *lawyer*. For some things."

"Ted, you're going to get in trouble."

"Hey, Carrie, what do you think, I'm *that* dumb, I'm going to mortgage the house and buy stock? Forget it, I'm just interested in seeing how the whole thing works. Anyway, look, Boggs is laying on the dog in Montreal, the whole five-star-hotel treatment."

"So?"

"Do you want to join me for the evening? You said something about going to Montreal tomorrow. A suite in the Bonaventure. An elegant restaurant in the old quarter. A little champagne to restore order to our marriage."

"Will Royce Boggs be sharing this romantic evening?"

Ted paused as he thought about that. "Gee, I don't know, that may be unavoidable. He'll want to buy us dinner."

"Uh-uh. Three's a crowd. I think I'll come straight back, Ted."

Ted shrugged. "We'll be flying to Montreal together, anyway. I reserved the same flight. More retsina?"

"I have to have a clear head tomorrow."

"What's the deal then? Who are you going to be seeing?"

"A certain rounder named Big Leonard Woznick, who is connected to Billy Sweet, who in turn has three hundred thousand dollars."

"Aw, honey, I don't like the idea of you running around a strange city collecting bail from gangsters."

"It's what you have to do." She wasn't so sure, though, if she liked the idea herself. "Ted, he's willing to turn the bail money over, the whole thing."

"As a fee? Jesus, *that*'ll help out."

"But I think he plans to skip."

"What's he afraid of?"

"I don't know."

"Let's hope he sticks around – we keep the whole three hundred." Then he thought. "Unless Billy Sweet wants it back. Jesus, Carrie, there are some serious implications here. Don't you think – maybe Chuck or somebody should go along with you? I can't, I'll be tied up in meetings."

"It's my case. I'll do it on my own." She didn't need anyone to hold her hand crossing the street.

"She wants her star billing." He grinned. "What an egotist. Ah, hell, I'm jealous, I think you're a better counsel than me."

Compliments were flying fast and furious this evening. She thought it took a lot for Ted to say that. There's no more competitive creature than a trial lawyer.

"I'll bet in your heart you don't believe that."

"Okay, you're lousy. But I love you anyway."

He said it. He had to make a joke of it, but he said it. Carrie decided she wanted to make love to him tonight. Close the book, close the wounds.

✤ ✤ ✤

At the Tchobanian household, Chuck wasn't about to make love to anyone. He was making up the fold-out sofa in the living room into a bed for himself. A brief conversation with Lisa had convinced him it wasn't going to be so much fun being on opposite sides of the Squire case.

8

Herbert Orff's hero was Adolf Hitler. Sometimes he felt he *was* Adolf Hitler. Every once in a while, he heard himself speaking with a screechy German accent, like in old newsreels he'd seen. But he heard other voices coming from him, too, when you got down to it, although he never could quite make them out. They came when he was daydreaming and he would sort of lose touch with himself, and he would come back to earth realizing he was supposed to be filling out an inspection report on a landfill site, and Mr. Blumberg would be climbing all over his big round behind if he didn't finish it.

Herbert Orff was Sewer Inspection Clerk II for the Waste Management Office in Scarborough, ten years of unswerving duty with local government. Two years ago he had made Clerk II from Clerk III, his one promotion. That he had not risen farther in the hierarchy of the Waste Management branch was, he felt, a result of conspiracies hatched by the chief supervisor, Mr. Blumberg, whose constant mean kidding gave him migraine headaches.

Orff didn't look like Adolf Hitler. Though he was short – only five feet, four inches tall – he was shaped like a top, like those twins he saw once in a cartoon show, Tweedledum or something, his chin extending in an unbroken arc almost to his chest. At twenty-eight he was already starting to go bald, and his remaining hair was cut short in patchy bristles.

Mr. Blumberg kept referring to him as "you fat ugly flub," and "you dumb foul ball." Mr. Blumberg would say in front of the others in the office, "Herbert here can't pick his nose without putting his finger in his eye." "Nerd" was another word he often heard. Herbert the oversized nerd. Sometimes he even heard his disembodied voices calling him a nerd.

But some day people were going to stop saying that to him: some day he was going to change the world.

His own world changed last year. That's when Orff received in the mail a sample copy of a magazine called *The Simple Truth*, published somewhere in Alberta, which contained an article about Jews. He learned something about what they are like, how they victimize people. He subscribed to *The Simple Truth*, and discovered a lot of amazing things: for instance, contrary to what the media would have you believe, only a few Jews died in Nazi concentration camps, all from cancer and old age.

The Holocaust was just one of countless falsehoods propagated by owners of newspapers and TV networks, who were themselves Jews. That's where the power in today's society lay: in the media. Information was power; the masters of the media controlled information.

The publisher and editor of *The Simple Truth*, one Dr. Austin Yorvil, had written a book called *A Thousand Lies Exposed*, and Orff sent away for it with a cheque and a letter saying how his eyes had been opened. Not one but fifty copies arrived, with an extremely friendly letter from Dr. Yorvil telling him he could keep half of what he sold the copies for. "We must spread the word!" his letter exclaimed.

The book was thin at two hundred pages, but packed with fact, startling fact. How Stalin was actually a Jew. Why Jews go into law. How the media elite control you through the TV and the newspapers. The plot to fill Canada with non-Christian people of inferior blood. He read it over and over, relished it, felt stirrings, felt as if he'd been initiated into something big. But how to get the word out, how to sell these copies of *A Thousand Lies Exposed*?

They were not something Orff would want to show around the office, or to have Mr. Blumberg find during one of his snooping expeditions under the fill-site requisitions in his bottom drawer. At the very thought of that, he developed one of his headaches, and with them came the voices.

He took copies around to several bookstores, but quickly found they were controlled by the power elite, too, and a couple of the bookstore people were quite insulting. So after work on Monday, July 28, he set up a table at Queen and Parliament and began offering them directly to the public.

"Read about the mind enslavers before it's too late," he called out to passersby in his most forceful voice.

They ignored him. People don't tune in unless they're in front of a TV set, that's what Dr. Yorvil wrote. They're programmed every day by the TV. Much of it was subliminal, although Orff wasn't sure what that meant. He used to watch a lot of television before he learned what they were doing to him.

"Read how they use the state to censor truth and lawyers to twist it. Read the new evidence about races."

He heard a slurred voice, with what seemed like an Irish lilt. "I know all about races, b'y. They fix 'em." At first Orff thought this was one of those strange voices that tended to come out of the air. But he turned around and saw him: what the polite describe as a street person and what Orff would prefer to call a obnoxious drunken bum. About forty, shorter even than Orff – an elf with mischievous eyes.

"And wud ye happen to have a little spare change on ye, b'y? Oi has to make a phone call."

Orff tried to ignore him, and shouted out: "They own all the TV stations and all the newspapers and they're controlling your minds."

"Nobody controls *my* moind, b'y." He stuck out his hand. "Molloy. I'se a literary man, misself."

"Please move along." Orff didn't touch the little extended claw, and stepped back a foot – the man reeked of booze.

Molloy began pawing through the books on the table. "You got any Farley Mowat, b'y? Jasus, these are all the same."

"Get out of there unless you're willing to pay."

Molloy studied the cover. 1,000 LIES EXPOSED, it proclaimed. "What koind a shit is this?" he said, leafing through it.

Orff felt one of his headaches coming on. "You're living the big lie," he called out. "Read how the press covered up the truth about Hitler."

Molloy squinted his eyes at Orff, as if trying to make out the small features in the tub of flesh. "Me dad got kilt in that war."

"Go *away*."

"How much are these, b'y?"

"I am charging ten dollars. They normally go for twenty."

"Oi'll take 'em all." Molloy scooped as many as he could into his arms and proceeded down the street to a trash can on which was inscribed the words, KEEP YOUR CITY CLEAN. Orff ran after him, but by the time he tottered to the little man, Molloy had thrown the last of the books into the trash.

"Okay, you've had it, buster." Orff grabbed Molloy in a bear hug and they toppled to the sidewalk and struggled for a while there, Orff getting the worst of it, a couple of sharp knees under the stomach that had him gasping.

After a few minutes of this a patrol car stopped, and a man and a woman in uniform got out and separated them.

"Not *again*, Molloy," said the policeman, holding him outstretched by his lapels, his feet dangling in the air. He turned to the woman officer.

"This toime it's self-defence, b'y. Oi was strugglin' for me loif against a human blimp. He's a dorty racist."

"I wish to prefer a complaint of robbery," said Orff, brushing himself off, his good brown suit all grimy now. He began gathering his books from the trash can.

"Okay, Molloy," said the male officer, "causing a disturbance by fighting, you're coming with us."

"Oi'll take this to the hoighest court."

The policewoman was leafing through one of the books. She began wrinkling her nose.

"What are you doing with these?"

"I'm selling them."

The officer paused at a page.

"That chapter's about the immigrants," Orff said. "How they're taking over."

"Your name?" she said.

"Herbert Orff."

"These books are for sale?"

"For only ten dollars."

"They're normally twenty," said Molloy. "It's a hell of a deal, b'ys, for certain."

"I would like to buy one book," the woman officer said.

Orff tried not to show his surprise. This was an important customer: it was vital to educate the police. He took her ten dollars, his first sale.

She then wrote him out a ticket for operating a business without a licence on a public way, pursuant to the Street Licensing Bylaw.

Orff stared at the ticket with dismay, looked from her to her partner, then collapsed onto the pavement and calmly lay there on his back.

"What the hell are you doing?" the policeman asked.

"I have gone limp. I am not going to co-operate in this travesty."

"But you're not under arrest," said the policewoman.

"You'll be sorry," said Orff.

His migraine took full effect, and he lay there and heard the voices laughing at him.

Two days later a policeman came to Orff's house with a summons. He was now also charged with the additional offence, under the Criminal Code, of selling hate literature. The conspiracy had broadened in scope.

The charge read that he, Herbert Orff, did wilfully promote hatred by communicating statements in a book to wit "A Thousand Lies Exposed," contrary to Section 319 (2) of the *Criminal Code of Canada*. Orff went to the library and discovered that the offence carried a possible two years' imprisonment.

Orff thought a trial might be an excellent vehicle for exposing the truth: he would be in the public glare, the media couldn't ignore him. How could he be convicted when he had historical facts on his side? But at the same time he realized there was risk – and he was terrified of jail. Shortly after getting the summons he suffered a horrifying nightmare about being raped and sliced up like bacon by a gang of racially mixed persons in black-and-white striped prison clothes. So despite his absolute distrust of lawyers he decided to retain one.

He was turned down three times, by lawyers who claimed they were too busy or didn't do this kind of work. Someone suggested he make contact with the Civil Liberties Association. That body referred him to the offices of Robinovitch, Barr, Barr, Tchobanian.

So on this morning of Thursday, the last day of July, Orff found himself in those offices, waiting for Mr. Leon Robinovitch while munching on a bag of potato chips, his favourite food.

There were several others in the waiting room, one of them a man in pigtails, obviously of North American Indian blood, though he tried to disguise it by wearing a suit. Orff didn't believe Indians were necessarily inferior, but they *were* different. For instance, they were far better racially adapted than the white man to the hunting of caribou. Every race has its own specialties.

The postman who just dropped off the mail, a Hindu: very good at jobs requiring walking. The receptionist was an Oriental. They were good detail persons, and made excellent secretaries. But Orff really didn't like women – they always seemed to be laughing at him or something. They had their place, though.

Now a man came in with a stomach almost as big as his own. He was dressed in a kind of leather jacket except it was sleeveless to the armpits, and he wore a military cap and had big tattoos all over. His name was in big letters on his jacket: HARLEY DAVIDSON.

"I'm here to see Chuck Tchobanian," he told the Chinese girl.

Tchobanian – that sounded very foreign. Orff wondered if it was Jewish. Robinovitch, the man he was supposed to see, had a foreign name, too, Russian or something. A lot of Russians were atheists and communists.

After a while a man who looked like a lawyer came in from outside, well-dressed, shiny black hair, slender, a suspiciously dark complexion. He was carrying a big box of books. He spoke to Harley Davidson: "Be with you in a sec. I've got a bunch more of these to bring up."

As he was leaving, one of the books slid from the pile, and Orff observed it lying face-up on the floor, a naked lady shackled to a wall. This was confusing to him, unsettling.

The Chinese secretary picked up the dropped book, made a face, and said, "I think I'll wait for the movie."

"Hi, babe."

She turned around quickly and looked at Orff. "Was that you?"

Orff wasn't sure. He'd heard the voice, it seemed to have come from where he was sitting.

"No. Honest." The secretary frowned. Orff piled into his bag of chips, feeling uncomfortable. Everyone was giving him funny looks, including Harley Davidson and the Indian.

A handsome couple came hurrying out of the offices. "Pauline, we're off to Montreal. I'll be back tonight, and Ted is . . ."

"Staying overnight. I'll be in tomorrow in time for Mrs. Cartwright's discovery."

"*Mrs.* Cartwright, how formal," said the woman. She had big green eyes and red hair, Aryan for sure.

They left together, carrying their briefcases.

Orff became absorbed in the tattoos on the fat biceps of Harley Davidson, who was sitting beside him. He had an Iron Cross and . . . yes, that was definitely a swastika.

In a low, confiding voice, Orff said: "I think we may be . . . on the same side."

Harley Davidson turned to him, wrinkled his nose. "Get away from me, ya faggot creep."

"Yes, sir. Sorry." Orff had finished his chips. He was still hungry. He was always hungry.

Just then, one more man came out of the offices, with a long hawk's nose and hair to his shoulders.

"Orff, who's Orff?"

"That's me, sir."

He looked Orff over, a puzzled expression on his face. This was his new lawyer, Orff guessed, Mr. Leon Robinovitch.

The lawyer turned to the Indian. "Mr. Two Feathers, you're here on that Hudson Bay arbitration."

"I sure am."

"Let me . . . get rid of Mr. Orff here first."

Leon didn't offer to shake Orff's hand, and placed him on a chair that was reasonably distant from his desk. On that desk, a copy of *A Thousand Lies Exposed* lay open. Leon had read to chapter three.

All Leon knew about the man was from the newspapers, an item about him being charged.

"They're trying to suppress me," Orff said.

"Uh-huh," Leon said. A fat, short butterball, two hundred and some pounds, he guessed. The man might seem a little hard to suppress.

"I want to put *them* on trial, the people who run the system, the media barons, everyone dances off the end of their fingers. That's what I should have told those police: they're puppets."

"And what did you tell them?"

"I told them they'd be sorry. That wasn't strong enough. Toadies and bootlicks, that's what I should have said."

"They're part of the conspiracy," Leon said.

Orff paused. "Naturally I have to suspect that," he said carefully.

Leon tried to think of some way to kick this schmendrik out of his office fast.

"Yes, well, I have a very busy practice, Mr. Orff. I really don't think I can fit you into my calendar." Then he made the mistake of asking: "Why did you come to me, anyway?"

"The Civil Liberties Association said you'll defend anyone's right to express their thoughts. They said you're not afraid of unpopular causes. I know I'm unpopular. I can't even get a lawyer. I've been turned down by three of them."

Leon felt uncomfortable. Orff had rung the right bell.

"So you'll be like the rest of them," Orff said as he stood up to retrieve his book. "Afraid of the establishment. Or *working* for it."

Leon felt himself bristling. No one was more anti-establishment than Leon Robinovitch. He'd fought for the rights of the physically disabled, gays, unions, communists. He believed in free speech: it was a religion.

"I take it you're aware I'm Jewish."

"No. They should have told me that."

Leon felt relief, he would not have to turn the man away, his convictions need not be compromised. "On that basis do you still want me to defend you?"

"At least you're honest." Orff seemed to ponder his situation, then said: "Well, I guess it's okay you're a Jew. You see, I don't say Jews are inferior. They're just different. It's all in the genes. Just like the Negroid race makes good athletes, Jews make good lawyers. Every race has its specialty –"

Leon felt his spirits plummet. "I don't want to hear any more."

"Just like the others, afraid to rock the boat." Orff started to rise. "You'll be sorry."

"Sit down!"

"Yes, sir." He plumped back onto his chair.

There was a lull. Leon, depressed, wondered if there was still a chance to get out of this with honour. But he felt badly about turning away the undefended, even the indefensible. A warped kind of civil libertarian–Jewish guilt.

"Mr. Orff, I want to say something to you. I think you should be ashamed of yourself, you have some very twisted, wrong ideas. I would want that made clear at the beginning were I to defend you."

Orff merely nodded.

Leon sighed. "All right, when do you appear in court next?"

"Tomorrow. Friday."

"Understand this: I make the decisions. There will be no attempt to prove any of this garbage is true."

"Well, actually, I was thinking of a test case. I want to put *them* on trial, Mr. Robinovitch."

Leon found himself shouting: "Look, you can spew any kind of vomit you want to anywhere else, but I'm not going to help you do it in the courtroom." He tried to calm himself. "I shall only take the point that the hate-literature law is unconstitutional. Contrary to the Bill of Rights. This is a free country and you're the price we have to pay for that."

"How much is this going to cost me, Mr. Robinovitch?"

"A great deal."

"I don't want to go to jail. I know what they do to you there."

Leon took a few notes: the man's address, his place of work, some background on him. A bachelor – for obvious reasons – orphaned, a foster home, he'd managed to get as far as grade nine.

At the end of this, as Orff wobbled from the office, he seemed to be muttering to himself. Almost a kind of one-person argument. Having his name in the paper beside Orff's – what would Leon's mother and the members of her anti-defamation league think?

What the heck, he needed clients, anyone. One arbitration set for the next month, General and Commercial Trust sending its business down the street. A retinue of non-paying clients like Cool Aid. If Ted could act for Royce Boggs, Leon could act for a retarded Nazi.

He spent the rest of the afternoon with Victor Two Feathers, trying to sort out a complex aboriginal claim, then, weary, set off for home, pedalling his ten-speed to the ferry which took him to the string of islands that enclosed Toronto's inner harbour.

The air hadn't cooled, Toronto was still an oven, even on Ward's Island. After a few stretches and twenty minutes of tai chi, Leon set out his lounger on the porch of his small frame house, and he sat and stared over the choppy waters of the harbour at the city spires. It was lonely here, lonely since Margaret moved out. Two hurting years since his former female partner left him for another man. Two years of not figuring out how to make another relationship happen. Maybe he was boring, probably that's what Margaret had decided.

But maybe it was his mother, the non-stop leftist. She had scared Margaret off.

He waited for his mom's call. It came at six p.m. as he was putting his salad together.

"You got a minute, Leon?"

"Sure."

After a few preliminaries she spent half an hour on his case: Where was he getting his protein from, you've got to have it to live a normal life, only cows survive on grass, and they have two stomachs. Why does he never come over, what does he do at home all the time by himself? What are you, a hermit, Leon? There's a world out there, lights, action, camera: join it for a couple of seconds. Meet a nice woman, a companion, a partner, someone to share the tribulations of life. Who cares if she's Jewish? A Buddhist will do, an Arab, a Black Panther. As long as she's *progressive*.

His mother was Old Left, a marcher for peace, equality, workers' rights. Pete Seeger, Paul Robeson, Joe Hill were her heroes of song. She never wanted her son to be a lawyer. A union organizer, a social worker, okay, but not a leech on society.

"I want you to admit to me, Leon, if you think you have a problem. If you're gay it doesn't bother me, it's nothing to be ashamed of."

"Mom, for God's sake."

"Brenda Knopf's son is gay, he carries on a normal life otherwise. *Sees* people."

"Mother, I'm not gay."

"Well, you're acting very odd."

Maybe, he thought, his problem was that he couldn't get interested in just any member of the opposite sex. Thoughts of Carrington Barr always got in the way. Hopelessly impossible thoughts.

His life seemed stalled by this deep infatuation. She and Ted were obviously going through a rough time of it – maybe, he thought evilly, there was hope. But of course he felt terribly guilty for thinking that.

9

Carrie was in the depths of The Main, lower Boul Saint-Laurent. The area was seamy: cheap bars and hot-dog joints. Right next to a topless bar was Lavanderie Woznick. She saw the sign, hastily repainted. It had once read WOZNICK INDUSTRIAL LAUNDRY – you could still read the words in English, illegal now under Quebec's language-shelter laws.

The sky was overcast here in Montreal, a dark, threatening hue. Carrie thought: maybe the weather is breaking at last.

Through a large plate window Carrie could see men and women working, throwing uniforms into huge industrial washers. A quite elaborate front, if that's what it was.

Where was Mr. Woznick? In some back office likely. Big Leonard, yet another monster – sometimes Carrie felt she was surrounded by oversized men, big cops, big clients. She thought of the rape-murderer who was still on the loose somewhere, and shivered. But she was far from Toronto, and the time wasn't close to midnight.

She was beginning to regret her decision not to stay the night with Ted at the Bonaventure. It always felt creepy being at home alone. The price, though, would be Royce Boggs during dinner, and she had bluntly informed Ted she didn't want to pay it. She had three hours to do her thing here, then back on an early evening flight.

They had driven from the airport in a limousine and separated in downtown Montreal, Ted rushing off to meet Boggs to debate strategy for the takeover of Ace Electronics – an asset-stripping job most likely.

As she stood by the door of Woznick's, working out her opening lines for him, a man came from the topless bar next door. He wore a long raincoat, the kind that advertises something ugly about to be offered for display. He smiled at her. His eyes were animated, somehow familiar.

Carrie quickly escaped inside. A clerk was at a counter near the door, a skinny, pimpled man. He was on the phone.

"Yeah, I got twenty-five for you on seven in the eighth, and I can't take you on five, it's a scratch."

This didn't sound like industrial-laundry talk. He made a note and hung up.

"I'm looking for a man named Big Leonard Woznick."

"He's in the back but he don't want to be bothered right now."

The back presumably meant behind that door marked PRIVATE.

Carrie gave the young man her card. "Please tell him I'm here. I don't have an enormous amount of time."

"For Big Leonard, you're gonna wait. This is his do-not-disturb time."

"That's why you're taking his calls."

"As a matter a fact."

"Twenty-five hundred on the seventh horse in the eighth race."

"Twenty-five uniforms comin' in on August seventh, due out on the eighth."

"Give me a break."

"Have a seat. Big Leonard is a guy you do not interrupt in his favourite pastime."

Carrie walked toward the back door and the clerk moved quickly from his chair, ran and flattened his back against the door.

"Big Leonard *don't* want to be bothered."

"This is about André Cristal. I'm his lawyer."

She heard a lion's roar from the back room, raspy, angry.

The clerk opened the door a crack. Cigar smoke poured out. Carrie could hear the same booming voice, Big Leonard she assumed: "What's this? What's this? You moronic putz, with this you put me in six no trump? You got no spades!"

The door opened wider. Carrie could see three men, one was obviously Big Leonard's partner, cowed, a little guy with a big cigar. His cards were laid on the table – he was dummy.

"I t'ought you had the spades."

Telephones all over the place. A huge chalkboard, horses' names and various numbers written on it. A big block of cheese on the table, and a jar of pickles.

"That was a cue bid, jerk. I got a single *ace*." The voice descended to a grumble. "Now we're gonna be down eight grand for the afternoon. You couldn't get a pass mark in stupid school. Whadda ya want, Zoot? It better be important."

"André's tongue is here." Zoot opened the door wider, and Carrie finally saw Big Leonard. She smiled, a big, astonished smile that caught everyone off guard, including herself. Big Leonard was about five-five in his socks, shorter than his bridge partner but with a taller cigar. Wiry, in his fifties.

Big Leonard, in turn, surveyed her: prim, white blouse, a light cotton pant suit.

"Lady, you got twenty points and a fit in three suits but a void in spades. Would you leave me in six no trump?"

"I think I'd go in your first suit."

"The lady knows something about bridge. Take over from this schmoe, will ya? Diamonds! Six diamonds! It's a laydown!"

Carrie walked in. "You're Big Leonard?"

"I am."

"You guys ever heard of air-conditioning?" She waved at the heavy, smelly air.

Woznick put his cards face-down on the table. "So, how's André?"

"Can we find some place to talk?"

Woznick got up from his chair.

"Sorry to interrupt your bridge."

"What you are interrupting is not bridge." He turned to the others. "Take a beer break, we ain't through."

Woznick took her outside, to the back, and they sat in one of his vans, away from ears.

"I seen you on the TV news," Woznick said. "You got him bail."

"Three hundred thousand." She almost said G's.

"I don't know no one who can post that."

"I hope you do. You and whoever else got him into this business had better get him out."

The hint was not too veiled.

"Listen, he's my favourite guy, he's indispensable with me, I love him."

"Indispensable in what way?"

"Everything. Odd jobs."

"He helps run the book? And your heroin? That's an odd job."

"André tell you that? It's a . . . minor sideline, lady."

"Everyone knows, Mr. Woznick. The cops know you wash Billy Sweet's money."

Woznick's voice lowered, as if he feared being overheard. "I don't like to hear that name too loud. Billy is a very paranoid guy."

This gentleman was being a little too shy. Her plan wasn't to threaten him, but she couldn't help it, a little. "Trafficking in heroin, that's a grand slam. Twenty years. I'm just giving you fair warning, you could be at risk here."

"André will protect me." He sounded confident.

"Don't get the wrong idea. He likes you, Mr. Woznick. Very fond of you."

"He's my boy."

"Here's the problem: if he's forced to go to court he may have to say he was up there only to pick up some heroin."

"That's the defence? That's what he'll say?" He looked worried now.

"In cross-examination he could be asked who he was doing

94

this for. So we're in a kind of dilemma. I'm hoping we can avoid it. Maybe he won't have to take the stand."

"You mean maybe they got no case?"

"It's weak. So far. Could get stronger. A possible witness is wandering around offering his services. I think he was in that loft, an addict – Normie, he was the tester. His services may go to the highest bidder."

"You want I should ask Billy Sweet for the bail money? You think I'm crazy? He's a blowtop, Mrs. Barr. I made it to fifty-three good years, I wanna hold out for fifty-four."

Carrie decided to turn things up a notch. "After a man sits in a cell, six months, eight months, waiting for his trial, he starts to wonder where his friends are."

"André wouldn't rat." Woznick licked his lips, sat silent, and said, finally, "I'll pass word up the line."

"You have my number. We don't have any time to waste."

"Yeah." He shook his head, a wry smile. "Maybe you got *my* number."

They left the van, went back into the building. Woznick went to the phone.

"This ain't a neighbourhood for a lady. I'll call you a taxi."

"Thank you."

After he did so, he said, "I don't even allow my own daughter down here. Nights, it's dicey."

"I'll let you get back to your game."

But he wanted to talk. "She's gonna be a lawyer. Lemme show you."

He produced a snapshot. A high-school grad photograph of his smiling daughter. "Lenore. She's in first-year arts at Concordia." He paused, reflective. "André's goin' out with her."

Carrie looked more carefully at the photo. So this was Cristal's taste: sweet, petite, and very young.

Woznick showed her more photographs, unfolding a string of them in plastic. His daughter with her father. Lenore with Cristal – they were waving at the camera from the front seat of a sports car.

"Here, you keep that graduation picture, I got lots," Woznick said. "Maybe she'll ask you for a job some day."

"Yes, well, thank you."

"Like, I figure they're gonna get married soon. She's really in love with the cluck."

Something was distressing Carrie, she wasn't sure what. Cristal hadn't mentioned any Lenore.

As Carrie neared the airport in the taxi, she noticed the sky growing darker, and she could hear a low grumbling of thunder. The storm broke just as she got out at the departures level, a sudden flurry of rain.

Air Ontario advised her that her flight might be delayed an hour. That, she assumed, meant two. Ted's offer was looking better. Hell, she could skip the dinner with Boggs, and just stay in Ted's room and watch a pay movie over a bottle of wine.

She phoned his hotel and learned he was out. Five o'clock and a little – he was probably still at his meeting. The hotel receptionist asked if she cared to leave a message.

"Okay, tell him it's his wife –"

"Oh, Mrs. Barr, I have a message for you. When you come in, you're to meet him at half past eight in Le Castillon bar."

Carrie took a long while to respond. Ted's message wasn't computing. Had Ted checked with the airline, found out about the delays, assumed she'd changed her mind?

"When I come in from where?"

"From Toronto."

Another long silence.

"Okay, I won't bother leaving a message."

At six-thirty, Carrie's flight was announced. She didn't get up from her table at the noisy bar at Dorval. She ordered another glass of red wine.

At eight-thirty, when Mrs. Barr was supposed to be meeting Mr. Barr in Le Castillon Bar, Carrie was still sitting in the airport bar, unable to move. A man took the next table and tried to make conversation. Carrie couldn't hear anything he said, his words drowned by the screaming inside her head. He offered her a cigarette, coming on.

She took it. He extended his lighter. She closed her hand upon the cigarette, mashing it. Soon afterwards, the man finished his drink and left.

Three hours later, Carrie clambered awkwardly from a taxi and into the pelting rain. She dashed, a little unsteadily, to the hotel door. Six and a half glasses of wine – her head was spinning with it, and with the turmoil of her thoughts.

At the Bonaventure, the doorman greeted her with a worried expression.

"Bags?"

"No." Carrie walked stiffly in, affecting absolute sobriety, her bearing erect, a lock of russet hair wet-plastered to her face. She'd worn the same clothes all day, all night. She was rumpled; she felt unclean.

The young woman at the desk pretended not to notice her dishevelment, her signs of slight impairment.

"May I help you?"

"The spare key to our room, please."

A hesitation. "Of course, and . . . you are registered here?"

"Would I be asking for the spare key?" Too curt. "I'm sorry, I don't want to wake my husband." An explanation was in order. "He'll be exhausted."

"And your room number is . . . ?"

"I really don't remember. Barr. Mr. and Mrs. Theodore Barr. Toronto." She managed a smile. "Oh dear, I could be anyone, I suppose. Anyone off the street." She showed driver's licence, credit cards, and, prominently, a card showing she was a member of the Law Society of Upper Canada.

The clerk looked under "Barr," found a registration card, and consulted with the night manager. He gave her a spare key to room 1408 and wished her a pleasant night. She thanked him.

Waiting for the elevator, Carrie looked at her watch. Midnight, when the Strangler comes.

Hanging from the doorknob of 1408 were a plastic bag containing two brown oxfords and a do-not-disturb sign. There was no deadbolt inside the door and it slid open silently.

She heard a long, low, terrible groan, as if from a man in pain. The room was dark, the curtain drawn, but she could make out motion on the bed, the sheets moving. She heard him groan again and heard other human sounds from the area of his groin, unintelligible. Grunts, like something a sow would make rooting in her pen.

"Oh, God," Ted cried. "I'm coming!"

"No, Ted," Carrie said, "you're going."

She could hear Melissa choking on it.

✣ ✣ ✣

The storm front had avoided Toronto so far, but the night was close and sultry. Though it was midnight, light shone from a filling moon, which dappled the maple trees and silvered the little lawn in front of the residence of Carrie and Ted Barr.

Between it and the building to the left, a flagstone walk led to the back yard, to a tiled barbecue patio surrounded by thick clumps of rosebushes. In these rosebushes, Edwin Moodie stood, peering in through one of the windows.

He tried sliding some of the windows up, but they wouldn't move. Retreating from the wall, he accidentally broke a branch of one of the bushes and it snapped audibly. He froze. After a few moments he moved again, stepping back, looking up to the second floor, where the main bedroom was.

He was sweating, though he hadn't much exerted himself. A teardrop of perspiration rolled down his cheek, dripped off the end of his little moustache.

He looked down to where the droplet fell, onto a rose. He plucked it, smelled it, held the scent in. There, lodged between the petals, a glint of metal in the moonlight: a golden ring. Edwin Moodie removed it from the flower. He put it to his lips.

10

"Mom put me through law school washing floors for rich people. Be a lawyer, she said, it's all I ask."

Chuck was making a sympathy pitch to Lisa this morning, he figured nothing else was going to work. He'd spent another uncomfortable night on the sofa, endured another electric silence during the breakfast he'd prepared with his own hands. Now, over their second coffee, she listened like a stone-faced juror to his speech.

"A thousand bucks a day, Lisa, we're talking a million-dollar fee here. I could pay off Mom's mortgage just like that. You didn't come from an immigrant hard-times background. You can't understand how it feels when it's suddenly there, held in front of you like a lollipop. We could afford a bigger house, Lisa, maybe in Rosedale. Swimming pool. Cottage up in the lakes. Is there something wrong with these goals? Am I some kind of sicko for wanting us to have a few nice things out of life?"

He was talking to the wall.

Chuck wearily made his way to the office. There, he summoned his secretary, Gloria Walker, into the library. Paperback books were everywhere, on the floor, the table, on shelves, more than nine hundred of them.

"I'll never be able to read all this crap. Gloria, I want you to go through these and find literary merit."

She riffled through the pages of a few of the books. After a few minutes her eyes seemed to glaze over.

"This is out-and-out muck." She snapped a book closed, disgusted. *Hollywood Whores* was the title – the woman on the cover was stepping out of black lace panties.

"Do they do harm? Do they make you want to rape and kill or make love to goats? They're stroke books, Gloria, they actually provide a service."

"Well, maybe that should be your defence. No sane judge will acquit."

"Gloria, sweetheart, criminal law is not about the law. It is about business efficiency. It has to do with the time and cost of trials. We've got nine hundred and fourteen titles here, and let's say we elect a jury. About sixteen persons, including the judge and the prosecutor, have to read all this crap, almost a thousand books, on average a hundred and fifty pages . . . This is a trial that will never end, Gloria – they're going to buckle, eventually they'll find an excuse to enter a stay." He patted her on the head like his favourite poodle. "And I earn a bundle."

"How's everything at home these days, boss?"

"I'm enjoying the silence."

"I'll bet."

They saw Carrington Barr pass quickly by the open doorway. Carrie looked a mess, her hair unkempt, her eyes wild.

"Oh-oh," said Gloria.

A few seconds later Carrie returned the way she had come, this time carrying a weapon, a pair of sharp shears.

Chuck turned swiftly to his secretary. "Where's Ted?" His first thought: Carrie was going to kill him.

They heard a banging.

"Jesus." Chuck ran from the office.

Thankfully the waiting room was empty. Pauline Chong was standing, white, her hand covering her mouth. Another bang, coming from the corridor.

There, Carrie was working in a fury with the shears, chipping off some of the raised brass letters. Chuck didn't try to interfere, just watched until she finished. The sign now read

100

only ROBINOVITCH, BARR, TCHOBANIAN. The first BARR appeared as a shadow.

Carrie turned to Chuck, her eyes large and raw and wild. It looked as if she hadn't slept all night. He noticed that her fair complexion was spotted with pinpricks of red.

"You're a low, lying, slimy snake, Tchobanian." She pointed her dagger toward his heart.

There was no hole nearby Chuck could crawl into. "*Moi?*"

"Don't, Chuck, I *warn* you."

Carrie marched back into the office.

Chuck looked at the damage to the wall: Barnsworth would have a cow. He returned to the office, found Carrie, her back to him, standing by her desk, gripping it by the edge as if to keep herself upright.

He closed the door.

"Okay, Carrie, let's just simmer down a little. What happened?"

Carrie placed her palms flat on the desk, steadying herself. "He had the gall to register her as his wife. When I walked in, she was . . . I won't even describe it."

Head, Chuck assumed. The blow job that swallowed the firm.

She whirled about. "And you . . . *you*, Mr. Tchobanian, have played me almost as damn false."

"Now, Carrie . . ."

"Tennis, anyone? Little fishing weekend? You lying son of a bitch!" A shout, the whole office could hear. Chuck flinched. "What did you do, chauffeur him right to her bed? I feel like calling you as a witness at our divorce."

"Carrie, I . . . Let's calm down here."

"Oh, yes, be rational, be calm, Carrie, be nice. He . . . he . . . *paranoid*, he called me."

That bastard, thought Chuck. He had *promised*. He was going to lay off Melissa.

Carrie lowered her voice. "You can pick Ted or me, you can't have us both. I won't have him in the same house and I won't have him in the same office."

"Let's not do anything rash. We'll talk about it. We'll talk, you and me and Leon."

101

"How long have you known?"

"Come on, Carrie."

"About this one, Melissa Cartwright. I don't suppose I care about the others. But this is too blatant. A client! He should be disbarred! He's not only treacherous, he's stupid!" Someone turned on a radio loudly in the coffee room; Chuck figured some clients had arrived.

He suddenly felt his own anger release. "*Goddamn* Ted, I told him to lay off her, Carrie, I warned him, I begged. I'm with you, I agree, she's a mercenary, vamps a rich surgeon and dumps him after five years, but not before she gets her name on half of everything." He took a breath. "Ted's been making out with her for months, Carrie. I told him you're worth a million Melissa Cartwrights. But I guess she's worth a couple of million dollars."

Carrie studied him, a look of confusion. "He's . . . leaving me for her *money*?" She sounded weary now, the last of her energy expended.

"I don't know *what* the Christ is in his mind." Chuck came around behind the desk, and he put his arms around her, but she remained stiff in them, unyielding. "You go home, get some sleep. I'll track Leon down, we'll come over, we'll cancel everything today."

"Okay, we'll . . . yes. I have to sleep. If Ted calls, just tell him to keep out of my way. Please. Tell him I threw his best oxfords into the trash at the airport. Tell him that was the highlight of my night."

After Carrie left for home, Chuck stared at his wall for a long time, wondering if this was truly the end of the firm.

He tried to persuade himself Carrie would cool out; she was the queen of sober second thought.

No, he realized, there was not a chance. This wound was too deep: he had seen something in her face besides tiredness and despair. Something very determined. She would pull the walls down on Ted, herself, everyone, the whole firm. So this was it, the breakup of R., B., B., and T. Well, maybe there isn't enough criminal work in the firm for two lawyers, and if worse comes to worst it would only be logical: she goes with Leon; he goes with Ted.

The thought of the firm splitting up filled him with dismay.

Leon had to be tracked down immediately. Off somewhere in the Provincial Court with that nutty fat fascist.

He first tried to phone Ted in Montreal, but he'd checked out.

He found Gloria still in the library, struggling through the porn books.

"We're closing the office. Cancel all the clients. I don't care what you tell them, explain we're in mourning. If Ted comes in, tell him he better check in at the Y. I don't have to tell you what's going on."

Gloria nodded. She knew. Legal secretaries know everything.

Herbert Orff's case had been assigned to the court of Judge Avery Singh, an excellent draw, a scholar who enjoyed tangled arguments.

Leon led Orff into the court and placed him on a seat directly behind the counsel bench. Leon could hear the crinkling of cellophane behind him.

"How come there's no jury?" Orff mumbled from behind his ear. Leon turned slightly, saw Orff's mouth was full of Cheesies.

"We're not going to have a jury. Put those away, shut up, and sit still."

Orff sat back and obeyed orders like a good soldier.

"Mr. Robinovitch," said the judge, "what can we do for you?"

"Fix date, your honour." He led Orff forward. "Appearing for the accused Herbert Orff. It's a hate-law case. What I would like is a quick pre-trial hearing on the validity of the section."

"A free-speech argument," said the judge. His eyes lit up.

"Might make some history here." By way of a courageous decision to declare the hate-literature law unconstitutional.

"Will the accused please stand," said the clerk.

"I am standing," said Orff.

He was five foot four, and this was the old standard short-guy gag being played out. It was as if Orff had a sense of the burlesque, but Leon knew this humour was unconscious. There was

103

laughter in the courtroom, however, which Leon, who didn't believe in joking at others' expense, failed to join.

The judge explained to Orff he could elect to be tried by him, or by a judge of a higher court, or by a judge and jury. He asked how he elected.

"We elect this court," Leon said.

"I want a jury of my peers," said Orff.

Leon felt like throwing a net over him. "We elect summary trial in this court."

"Mr. Robinovitch," Orff whispered urgently, "the judge is . . . you know, *coloured*."

"You want to get together on this?" said Singh.

"Your honour, I'm thinking seriously about withdrawing from this case."

Orff agreed he wanted to be tried by Judge Singh.

The case was set over for one week to fix a date for the Bill of Rights hearing, and Leon left court quickly, with Orff scampering hard at his heels. As Leon reached the front door, he could have sworn he heard someone mutter behind him, in a kind of Teutonic accent, something about an "asshole lawyer."

When he turned around the only person there was Orff and his bag of Cheesies. "Did you say something?"

Orff looked at him and blinked. "I . . . don't think so." Then he frowned. "I have a headache."

Maybe Leon had been hearing things. "Okay, you go to work. I'll call you when I need you."

As Leon walked from the courthouse into the slap of another hot day, he saw Chuck Tchobanian running down the street toward him, waving his arms, calling.

✢ ✢ ✢

While her bath filled, Carrie wearily wandered through her silent, empty house. During the small hours of the previous night, waiting in the stillness of the Montreal airport, waiting for the first flight of the morning, her head clanging, she had ultimately

104

decided it was a matter of lust – Ted couldn't have liked that woman for her brain, her personality, her warmth.

Her money, though? This was a possibility she hadn't considered. It had never struck her that Ted would abandon her for *money*.

Carrie tried to work the concept through her mind: was Ted was just a sociopathic mercenary? She decided this was the theory she preferred. Ted abandoning her out of *love* for another would have been an act of greater enormity, harder to bear. But greed was a brand of bitter medicine that was easier on the stomach.

She tried to swallow her anger, to be totally-in-control Carrington, but it wasn't working today. She wept.

Outside, a rumble of thunder. The storm front from the east had arrived.

After her bath, she went not to the second-floor bedroom she shared with Ted, but the spare room downstairs, then realized she didn't have pyjamas, so she lay naked under a sheet. Outside, the skies darkened, more thunder, and the rain came, and lightning, and after a cruel time of continuing awareness she slept.

When she awoke it was dark, still raining, and she was disoriented. She was on a bed and a bearded man she thought she recognized was sitting on a chair nearby. She was in great pain – that's all she knew at first.

"Leon?"

"I didn't want to turn too many lights on."

She sat up, forgetting she was unclothed. Leon turned his eyes away as she pulled the sheet up around her.

"How long have you been here?"

"Since about three o'clock. We thought by then you'd be awake."

"We?"

"Chuck and I. He left a while ago."

"What time is it?"

"Half past nine."

"What have you been doing all this time?"

"Watching you."

Her face went slack. "What am I going to do, Leon?"

"You're going to eat. I bought some shrimp. I'm going to stir-fry them."

"You don't eat shrimp."

"I'll make an exception."

After a pause, she said, "I wonder if he ever loved me. I thought he did. Guess I'm not very good at reading people."

Leon looked away from her. He seemed awkward, embarrassed.

Speeder Cacciati always liked hanging around in Billy Sweet's games room, the decor was really tasteful. Billy was a collector: he'd got ahold of a lot of those old neon signs you used to see in stores, and old beer advertisements and displays.

Billy's big stone house, more of a fort, really, was near the Toronto Golf Course in Mississauga, on an acre lot with a wall around it and a guard at the gate. Billy did most of his business from his home because he didn't like to go out much, even to his downtown office. So most of his running was done by Speeder Cacciati, who was proud he was about the only guy Billy trusted.

Speeder couldn't figure out why Billy had changed so much, he used to let it hang out, used to be a free-wheeler. Maybe it was just age creeping in – Billy was forty-five now, about a decade older than Speeder, kind of thin and haughty with this perpetual frown and lines of worry that made him seem even older. He was a neat dresser, wearing a suit vest now: the air-conditioning was on full blast.

Speeder Cacciati wore a more casual shirt, tropical colours. At his belt was a pager. He was chewing gum, cracking his knuckles, fiddling with his hair, playing with his pool cue, sighting it, twirling it, moving ceaselessly.

"Stand still, for God's sake."

Sweet was aiming for the far corner pocket. He missed by a hair.

"I still don't get it," he said. "You send Schlizik and this Frenchman up there to whack those two rip-off artists, and only the Frenchman walks out – what's his name?"

"André Cristal."

"Cristal. So how does Schlizik get gunned down in the process?"

"A firefight, man. The fuckin' Frenchman saves the day, right? Billy, I figure we at least owe him something."

"So how come he gets charged with three murders?"

"He gets the book throwed, that's the way them bulls operate."

"I am not venturing three hundred thousand dollars upon a blackmailer."

"Who says he's a blackmailer?"

"That's what it sounds, according to what this lawyer said to Mr. Woznick. A possible singer."

Cacciati saw some openings and went into action, but after running two balls in he flubbed his next shot.

"Whom does this Mr. Cristal know?" said Sweet.

Whom. Cacciati always found his manner of speech grating, each word chewed off slowly, perfect diction, as if he was trying to be cultured.

"*Whom* does he know? He don't know you, Billy."

"That's good. That's the way I want it to stay."

Sweet watched Cacciati blow up a bubble, and waited until he popped it before going back to the table, cleaning off all his balls, mechanical, perfect.

"I was lucky. Another?"

"Naw." Cacciati didn't mind letting Sweet win, if it suited a purpose, but he couldn't beat him anyway. Nobody could. At anything.

Speeder popped a couple of truck drivers, little red capsules, hits of energy, as Sweet strolled to where he had furnished the room with those new video games that were the rage these days, and switched on Battleship.

107

"I am asking, whom can he finger?"

"He can sure finger Big Leonard."

"That is unfortunate for Big Leonard."

Cacciati put back his cue, pulled out his comb, began running it through his hair. "Yeah, but if he fingers Big Leonard, who does Big Leonard finger?"

"He fingers you. You finger me. Everyone protects theirselves in the end, isn't that it, Speed?" He sunk an enemy destroyer, it went flying in all directions. "Everyone protects their assets in the end."

"Come on, man, I once did a deuce in the joint for you."

"What have you done for me lately, Speeder? Find out who's stealing the stock-in-trade. There are rats in the grain bin, Speed. Catch them. Do what friends do to put theirselves above suspicion."

Cacciati watched him destroy the enemy ships. No one touched him.

"Ten pounds of lost product. This operation was supposed to be clean. Mr. Schlizik and this Frenchman were supposed to walk in there and take it. Sure, eliminate whom you have to. But you don't leave the goods behind."

"Things obviously got fucked up. Real cowboy job." The speed was hitting him now, he was feeling good.

"Where did this André Cristal come from originally, anyway?" Sweet said.

"He's out of the Dubois gang in Montreal. Big Leonard picked him up. I did the interview. You said you wanted another good iceman for Schlizik on this job, and that's what I got you."

"Yes, and he's hitting on us for a great deal of money. We are in a negative cash-flow situation, and I fear Mr. Cristal is not a very good investment. He is not worth the cost of his own release from prison. He will have to sweat it out."

"Big Leonard won't be pleased. André goes out with his daughter."

"Tell Mr. Woznick to hire smarter people henceforward."

"What about the junkie? Hiltz had this cousin or somethin', Normie the Nose, I think it's him."

"Well, check him out. A junkie named Normie the Nose – already I don't like him. Whom can you trust these days, Speed? I don't trust Mr. Cristal, and I don't trust Mr. Woznick neither. I don't even trust my accountants. Should I trust you, Speed? But this is what business does to you, you lose your love of people."

11

In his office, Inspector Mitchell and one of his undercover men, Hollis Lamont, were staring at a video terminal. On the screen: Carrington Barr walking along a sidewalk toward the camera, stopping, looking startled, maybe disgusted. In the background a sign: LAVANDERIE WOZNICK. Carrie turned her back to the camera, and entered the building.

"Nice buns, huh?" said Lamont. He was brazen, a cocky man who liked to perform. "Had the camera hidden under my raincoat, lens just poking out." The screen went dark, then showed Carrie leaving the premises, Big Leonard Woznick showing her to a taxi.

"Where does this get us?" Mitchell said grumpily.

"Cristal leads us to Big Leonard, Big Leonard leads us to Billy Sweet."

"Not enough. Where the hell is this Normie the Nose character?"

"We're still pulling blanks on that one, Inspector."

Mitchell didn't want to tell Oliver McAnthony about Normie, but things could get dicey if he didn't. Still, the prosecutor didn't have to know all the details of Operation Sweet Revenge.

At noon on Saturday when Carrie finally emerged from her house, the air was sharp after the night of rain. No clouds, a piercing sun. She was still feeling damaged, violated, still working through the pain, trying to pull the pieces together. Leon had been so good last night, generous in his understanding, letting her get it all out. But when she raised the matter of the firm's future, he seemed at a loss, evaded, kept saying things like, "We'll work it out."

From her house, Carrie walked the long stretch of Queen West, her favourite street, all the way to the other side of Spadina, wanting to walk, needing the exercise. She looked at the anonymous faces of passersby, stared bleakly into shop windows. Life was normal here, people busy, happy, in the Bohemia of Toronto.

Where was she going? The office, that's right, a crisis meeting with Leon and Chuck. She felt she could handle it, she could stifle her anger, her bile, and get through the afternoon. As long as Ted didn't show up.

She stopped for a bite at Le Select and stared for a long time at her quiche, unable to eat.

Why had she been in love with him? What was *there*, after all? Great mind, wicked sense of humour, an athlete's body, he was generous and open . . . but empty inside of all but a preening male vanity and self-centred ambition. Was it her competitiveness that made her want to beat out all those other women who panted after him?

He'd left her for Melissa's money – two and a half million bucks, that's what he was suing for and that's what he was selling himself for. He was a whore, not in the little leagues like Trixi Trimble – his immorality was far more exorbitant; Trixi sold her body *much* too cheaply. The Cattle Breeders' Association of Ontario, her husband should join it.

She could feel the doors of anger spilling open again, and when she took a sip from her grapefruit juice she felt nauseated. She rose as decorously as she could from her table, and walked to the washroom where she bent over the toilet and gagged several times, but nothing came out.

Repairing herself, she examined her raw eyes in the mirror,

red to match her hair. She took out her contacts and put on her reading glasses, hoping they would hide the hurt in those eyes.

You're tough, she told her reflection, you can get through this. You're not going to have a stupid breakdown. You're a trained courtroom lawyer, you take on murder trials. Be proud. Be happy. You've just got rid of some unnecessary baggage in your life: Royce Boggs's pal, the achievement-oriented player.

Why had Leon been so timid about reacting to her threats to bounce Ted from the firm? Maybe Leon and Ted had been together for too many years; there was a cement there that her marriage never knew. And with Chuck, Ted was far too close and confiding. She was the outsider . . .

She told herself she should do the noble thing: just quit the firm, let the guys carry on. She didn't need Ted, she didn't need Leon and Chuck, she was on her way. She could open her own office, here on Queen West, an area maybe a little too hip, but coming up, another gentrifying patch of this city of neighbour-hoods. Yes, she could make it on her own.

Alone. Single-O. The Carrie in the mirror stared at her with a bespectacled wide-eyed alarm.

Tucked in, hair combed and fluffed, lips re-reddened, she emerged with some dignity. She paid for her food without touch-ing it, and walked again into the heat of the day.

The G & C Trust building was abandoned on this August weekend – a three-day holiday, she remembered, Monday was Civic Day. On the tenth floor the letters she had chiselled from the wall had been glued on again by someone. The custodial staff, she assumed, on orders from Mr. Barnsworth, the landlord.

From the waiting room, she could hear a murmuring of voices, Leon and Chuck in debate somewhere in the inner offices.

She spotted the tops of their heads in a corner of the library – it was as if they were hiding there, behind a barricade of porno-graphic paperbacks. She walked in quietly, and sat and waited for them to notice her.

"Jesus, Leon, we have to stall this thing out, give her a chance to cool off. We're all four of us tied to a lease which is like a goddamn albatross, we co-signed a loan that could keep all of Biafra fed for a year . . . Look, man, we drown separately or we keep each other afloat."

"Ted owns all the life jackets," Leon said.

"That's what I mean – look at last month's statements, he did almost 50 per cent of our billings. Carrie – let's face it, hers is mostly legal aid, she did less than fifteen. The brutal fact is, Leon, without Ted we're tits-up. We go bankrupt and lose our licence to practise, we become shoe salesmen and hardware clerks."

Carrie could just see the top of Chuck's head, bobbing as he talked. It was amazing to think about it – this person had once been her closest male friend.

"Carrington wants him out," Leon said. "She is very resolved on that point."

"Look, a weekend in Bermuda, I'll make some reservations for her, she just needs time to settle down, reconsider . . ."

"Their marriage is kaput, Chuck. And maybe our office is, too."

"I'll tell Ted to grovel, I'll tell him to . . . Where the hell is he? I've been trying to reach – "

"I'll save you all this trouble," Carrie said, and they looked around the pile of books and saw her. "I'll make it short and painless. I intend to leave the firm."

A silence. The air-conditioning hummed softly in the background. Carrie glanced down at a book, a crudely illustrated woman's face on the cover, her painted mouth oval and open. *Fellatio Sue.* She picked it up and hurled it in Chuck's direction, missing him.

"Oh-oh," he said.

"Carrie," Leon began, "let's –"

Carrie shut him up. "I shall be giving notice of an extraordinary meeting under our articles of partnership. At that meeting I intend to give notice of dissolution. You may then reform the partnership among the three of you."

"Can we talk about this?" said Leon. "Can we *discuss*? Before you just go diving off the high platform?"

"Yeah, Carrie, without checking to see if there's water in the pool."

"Don't interrupt me, Chuck, please." Carrie spoke crisply, mechanically, as if she had thought the whole thing out. "I will easily survive on my less than 15 per cent of the billings. I plan a low-overhead practice. I don't want anything from the firm – you keep the assets and all the files, and *all* Ted's fantastic billings, I just want out of the lease and the loan."

"Carrie –" Leon began again.

"Please understand that the three of us will always remain friends. Close friends. I've forgiven you, Chuck, I believe Ted put you in a very awkward position, and you feel guilty about it."

"I haven't forgiven either of them," Leon said.

"Aw, come on, Leon," said Chuck. "Carrie, let's the three of us go out and have a cold beer. Man, you're in a pretty upset state."

"I'm *quite* in control."

"Carrie," said Leon, "I know right now you're summoning everything you've got within you –"

She lost it, began shouting: "Stop indulging me! I won't be made a fool of! Go with him! Both of you! I am *not* going to change my mind, I am leaving this firm!"

The sound of the front door being unlocked, then closed, was drowned by her outpouring, but now they could all hear the advancing footsteps, and in a few seconds Ted appeared at the library door.

He had recently showered, and wore clean slacks and T-shirt – he hadn't been home, so Carrie assumed he had just bought them. Brand new pair of shoes, too. His face looked ghostly, inanimate, and there were bags under his eyes.

Carrie found, to her surprise, that his arrival seemed to calm her, to clear her head.

"So what's this?" he said. "The trial or the hanging?"

"Oh, Ted, I'm glad you dropped by," she said. "I'd like to settle the terms without a lot of fuss and bother. All I want is the house and the furnishings. I don't want any of your money. Or hers." She watched him for reaction, sought blood. But he seemed oddly unmoved. It was as if he was ready for this.

"I don't have a problem with that, Carrie. The house is yours."

She realized he wasn't here to beg and promise amends – he had accepted their marital death, *finito*, the end, history. Already, they were divvying up the spoils of marriage.

"I'll have to decide if I need to subpoena her to the divorce hearing," she said.

"You will do what you must do, Carrie." His remorseless expression caused the knife to go in backwards – it was she who was bleeding, from the wound of his blunt consent to the inevitable.

She felt herself fighting for control, trying to be cool Carrie. She wasn't dealing with a husband here, she was dealing with a divorce lawyer. "I'm dissolving the office partnership, too, Ted."

He nodded and took a chair. She realized he wasn't going to argue about this, either – it was almost demeaning of him.

"Who wants to go with whom?" he said.

Chuck's mouth dropped. "Hey! Pause!"

"I am beyond redemption in Carrie's eyes. What is broken will not be fixed. I know Carrie. I'm truly sorry – that is all I can say. I don't want to quibble over paper clips, I have a lot of work coming in, and I intend to be generous whatever way we split up. Leon?"

Stunned, Leon said, "What?"

"Her or me."

"What is this," said Chuck, "some kind of comic opera? It's not funny."

Leon abruptly said, "I go with Carrie."

That silenced everyone like a rifle-shot. The deed had been done quickly, a bullet to the head, the firm had been executed.

Ted seemed taken aback by the suddenness of it, then recovered. "Okay, Leon, yeah, I kind of thought you might . . . Sure, it's better that way, it makes it easier, fifty-fifty."

Carrie saw that Leon was looking at her intensely, as if trying to send a message, something almost intimate. She felt a great affection for him just then.

Ted turned to Chuck. "Okay, Mr. T, is it you and me? I've got enough stuff coming in to keep half a dozen people busy. I'll be associate counsel on the Ace Electronics thing when it gets to court. Looks like I'm going to be swamped."

Carrie saw that Ted couldn't meet her eye. Nor could Chuck meet anyone's – his face was in his hands, hidden. "God," he groaned. "This is nuts."

Ted seemed in a stall, he was waiting. "You can do some of the divorces, Chuck, I can't handle them all."

"Shit."

"Choose," said Ted.

A long silence. Then Chuck spoke softly. "Carrie."

Ted turned ashen. He took a deep breath and slowly rose from his chair. Carrie closed her eyes – she couldn't bear to look at him. Despite all he had done to her, at this terrible moment she couldn't bear to see his pain.

"I'll . . . start making a checklist of the files I'm taking." Ted recovered slightly as he got to the door. "I guess you three, ah, can take over the lease. And the loan. Well, I'll get to work." He left.

Carrie opened her eyes and stared into the empty space where his body had been. She didn't cry. She felt the comfort of friends.

Oliver McAnthony's office, in the downtown courthouse, was all oak and mahogany, dark, muted, like his mood today. He had placed Mitchell square in front of him, on a heavy leather chair.

"It is unclear in my mind why you have withheld this from me," McAnthony said, trying to remain calm.

"There are complications," said Mitchell.

McAnthony found this evasiveness odd and distasteful. "And why have you just now come forward with this information about a certain possible witness? Norman . . ."

"Norman Shandler. Normie the Nose, they call him. We were hoping to pick him up before this, Oliver. I don't know why we haven't, he must stick out like a sore thumb. He's a mainline junkie, no fixed address, but we know him from around Queen and Bathurst. If he was the tester for Hiltz and Perez, they paid him with enough smack to blow a billion brain cells, maybe he did an OD . . ." Mitchell was rambling, squirming a little.

"Are we working on the same case, Harold?"

"I wanted to keep things quiet, Oliver, not that I don't trust
. . ." Mitchell may have realized he was heading in a dangerous
direction, and changed course. "I've got a general pickup on him.
They're supposed to do just a standard fan and tag – they'll find
he's dirty – and bring him straight to me. I have a deal ready for
him, witness protection."

"Very enterprising of you." The tone was ironic.

"Listen, I have the greatest respect for you, Oliver, but I've
been constrained . . . I have to clear everything with my boss on
this."

"I shall take this up with him. Perhaps with the solicitor
general himself, a charming man with whom I have dined on
many occasions. He will be vexed to learn that five days after the
murders the prosecuting counsel was finally informed that a
witness may have been in that loft. I have been acting in these
courts for king and queen for more than forty years, and this is the
first time I have ever been deceived by a senior advising officer."

"It's not *deception*, Oliver. I was always going to tell you – as
soon as I could. Look, we had to put a clamp on it – Billy Sweet
gets wind of this guy, he's toast, end of witness, end of case."

"And with your witness secured, you would never have had to
apprise me of the fact you knew of his existence all along."

"I'd like to say we just got word on him from the street, Oliver,
but it isn't the case." Mitchell looked hangdog.

McAnthony suddenly understood. He should have guessed –
it wasn't the first time for Mitchell. "You employed an illegal listening device."

Mitchell said nothing.

"That is how you know Normie the Nose was at the scene of
the crime. That is what you really didn't want me to know.
Wiretap obtained without a judicial order often causes cases to be
thrown out of court. The fear is I would have told Carrington
Barr. And let me tell you something, Inspector, I damn well will."

Mitchell went open-mouthed in alarm. "Jeez, Oliver, put a
hold on that. I mean, not yet – I understand the principles of disclosure – you've got to give her everything. But a man's life is at
stake here, just give me more time to locate him."

117

"Tell me about, as you put it, the complications."

"We had a bug in there. We were tipped there might be some action."

"This place above the bowling alley was under surveillance throughout?"

"Everything happened too fast, Oliver – gunshots, yells, you can't make much out, and then this André Cristal was walking out the door."

"And your man who was posted in the bowling alley made the arrest."

"Yeah, exactly. I was covering him."

"*You?*" McAnthony was truly astonished at the extent events had been misrepresented to him. "*You* were there?"

"I had Hollis Lamont in the van with me, and I sent him into the Roll-a-Bowl. Hollis is a top-notch undercover, does some amateur stage. I'm running a special unit, Oliver, it's not generally known. Operation Sweet. Anyway, Perez and Hiltz go up there together . . ." He checked his notepad. "At twenty hours, twenty-three minutes. Norman Shandler enters premises at twenty-one-thirteen. Stolen 1978 Bel Air pulls up at twenty-one-forty."

"What is that in my time, Harold?"

"Nine-forty p.m. Cristal stays behind the wheel and Schlizik gets out. Schlizik enters the premises. Cristal follows five seconds later. Three shots, the first two in quick succession. By the time we get our wits together, Normie the Nose has cut out the back way. We collar Cristal."

"This sounds like a true botch job."

"Yeah, well, we were undermanned, just the two of us . . ."

"Your underling has doubtless been sworn not to mention the illegal wiretapping. Did anyone else know?"

"Yes, one other . . . officer."

"I want all names."

"The other officer is my superintendent, Oliver. This was all done with his blessing."

"I am utterly at a loss for words."

Mitchell finally lost his temper. "Listen, for God's sake, this is

Billy Sweet we're talking about. If there's any hassle about cutting corners, I'll face it. We're talking Billy Sweet! Not some two-bit French-Canadian button man. The biggest horse connection north of the Great Lakes. He ordered the execution of those two undercover guys, two good men, family men – we owe! I'm going to nail that cocksucker if it kills me."

Mitchell was red-faced from his exertions, and now was standing.

"And how are you going to nail him?"

"Watch me. Give me time, Oliver, a couple of days. I mean it, lives are at risk. I haven't even told Jock Strachan about Normie Shandler. I'm begging you, Oliver."

McAnthony didn't want blood on his hands. A few days, he decided – what would be the harm? Surely Mitchell, left to his own ineffable resources, couldn't cause further damage to this already wobbly case.

"Two days," he said.

✢ ✢ ✢

Leon and Chuck had boosted Carrie's spirits, but she still felt a void that could be filled only by staying busy. She didn't want to spend Saturday evening alone, nor in the company of those dubious friends, Anger and Depression. Life had to be gotten on with. Work drowns sorrows.

Five days had gone by since Carrie had taken on the Cristal defence and she hadn't yet ventured down to the scene of the crime, so she made a date with Jock Strachan and drove to the Roll-a-Bowl-a-Ball on St. Clair.

The bowling alley was packed, loud with the buzz of physical exercise, a constant rolling thunder, sporadic clatterings of pins. Carrie wondered: could someone down here actually hear gunshots from above?

Detective Strachan was waiting for her in the coffee shop. He stood up, straightened his bow tie, and shook her hand. He was really one of the better boys in blue, she believed, unswerving and straight.

"Jock," Carrie said, "this is really good of you. Did you bring some blanks?"

"Aye, as you asked, Carrie."

"I'll wait down here. You go up to the loft. Fire three shots."

I t'ink someone tried to set me up. That is what Cristal had said. That off-duty officer, Constable Johnny-on-the-spot . . . Lamont, that was his name . . . claimed to have heard those shots. But did he?

Carrie could barely make out the sound of the first two muffled cracks of a pistol from above, but the bowling noises obscured the last one. No one seemed to prick up any ears.

She passed through a side door leading to the stairwell – where André Cristal had been arrested – and climbed to the loft, where Strachan was awaiting her verdict.

"He would have had to have very good hearing to be able to distinguish those noises as gunshots."

"It's a sound he's trained to hear, Carrie," said Strachan. But he seemed to be trying to convince himself.

He showed her around: the film props were all still here, wardrobes of clothes, crates with veils and fake jewellery, but the heroin paraphernalia was gone, of course. Fingerprint powder all over. There was the sink where Cristal told Carrie he'd seen some washings. Across the way, the rear fire escape, presumably Normie's route of escape.

"*Last Flight from Istanbul*," Carrie read, studying one of the packing crates. "Did they ever make this movie?"

"They're doing the editing now," said Strachan. "Reputable company, we've looked into them."

Carrie saw a long curved knife in a bloody scabbard. Some kind of schlock film, she supposed. Heliotrope Studios. Reputable company, its employees smuggling junk.

"Jock, that off-duty policeman downstairs, did he have a beat or something? What were his regular routines?"

"RCMP drug squad."

"RCMP . . . *Drugs?* He works under Harold Mitchell?" Suddenly, Carrie was overwhelmed by a flood of suspicions. "Jock, honestly, don't you think there was something awfully fishy about what happened here last Monday night? I mean, what's a *drug* cop doing there standing right under five million dollars' worth of heroin? Are you saying this was a coincidence?"

"He said he was bowling, he heard shots."

"Bowling with whom? Did he have friends or family with him? I'll bet you a hundred bucks he was alone."

Strachan shrugged, and his bow tie bobbled. "What are you saying, Carrie?"

"Jock, you know very well what I'm saying, and I wouldn't say it if I didn't trust you. You know Harold Mitchell. You know the kind of stings he runs. He may not be totally bent but he sure doesn't play straight."

Strachan said nothing but held her eye. "Would he lie to me, Carrie? Be sensible."

"I think Mitchell knew something illegal was going on here that night. I think he had eyes and ears on this place. I even suspect he knew some people were going to get killed – he didn't care, dope pushers, scum, especially Jerszy Schlizik, a cop-killer. And I think after it was all over, he needed a scapegoat. My client was handy." And she paused, struck by a thought. "Maybe Mitchell even engineered it."

"It's all a wee bit speculative, Carrie."

"Any harm in checking it out? Quietly?"

Strachan thought for a moment. "No harm."

"Thanks, Jock. You're a sweetie."

The Eagle Hotel was block-shaped, three storeys of peeling yellow plaster, a dozen rooms, a large, dank beer parlour on the ground floor decorated with pennants and posters for the Blue Jays, the Maple Leafs, the Argos. The pub was crowded on a late Saturday night, and customers – almost all male – were watching the Jays and the Angels on two raised television sets.

Their hubbub could be heard on the floor above, in room number seven, a spare, small space with just the essentials: a sink, a bed, a hot plate, a window with a view of an adjoining wall. And a warped wooden table, where Edwin Moodie laboured with a pencil and paper. The night was hot, and rivulets of sweat rolled down his face from his bald scalp.

The only decorations here were newspaper clippings, tacked to the stained, patterned wallpaper. The headlines, from various Toronto papers, read: "POLICE ARREST RECLUSE," and "IS IT THE MIDNIGHT STRANGLER?" and "LEGAL AID APPOINTS LAWYER IN STRANGLER CASE," and finally, "IDENTIFICATION FAILS IN STRANGLER TRIAL." That was accompanied by a photograph of Carrington Barr walking triumphantly out of the courthouse. The photo was smudged, as if fingered many times.

There was another photo, coloured, clipped from an arts magazine: one man and three women dressed in dark concert attire, a string quartet. Carrie Barr was playing a cello.

Edwin Moodie put down his pencil and closed his eyes tight. After a while he opened them again and stared down at the gold wedding band that sat beside the pad of lined paper on his table. He tried to put it on his little finger, but could work it only up to the first knuckle.

The clock beside his bed said eleven-thirty. He made a sound, a low, soft moan, and rose from his chair.

He left his room, and stepped down the creaky stairs to the dingy lobby. Moodie could hear shouts and cheering from behind the door leading to the licensed premises, an announcer saying, *"Ernie Whitt sends it downtown!"*

He walked out onto Jarvis Street, and then down to Dundas, and he kept going, sweaty and hot, clumping his way west, past Yonge, past University, through Chinatown, and further west into the quiet streets of Parkdale. Tonight . . . yes, tonight he would find the strength.

12

A ghastly nightmare awoke Carrie on a peaceful Sunday morning. It drove her upright in her bed on the second floor of her house. Through a window open to the street came distant bells, summoning worshippers to church, and sounds came, too, of children playing. "Ring around a rosy, pocket full a posy."

"Only a nightmare," she softly repeated to herself, wanting to hear her own voice. She was trembling and sweating, but alive, undefiled. As she tried to focus, she looked to the other side of the bed, as if for support, for comfort, and, on seeing it empty, for the fleetest foggy moment wondered if Ted had gotten up early to go jogging. Then she remembered.

She tried then to recall the dream – it seemed three-dimensional, physical, she could feel the hands upon her. The man who was about to rape her, the Midnight Strangler of this nightmare, was familiar – not Mr. Moodie, certainly, but . . . was it . . . Inspector Harold Mitchell? She decided that's who he looked like at the end, a face maskless suddenly, angry, red, a wet sheen of bald scalp. But no, earlier he had been someone else, a different monster . . .

Start the dream over. She'd been in court, and . . . Royce Boggs? Yes, the rich misogynist, *he* was on the stand, and she was cross-examining him – then it all changed, one of those ungainly dream-jumps, and Boggs was the pursuer. Then what? She had been hiding from him, then running down an endless corridor, and suddenly it was night and he was yelling something about a . . . "voracious bitch." Royce Boggs, yes, definitely. The Midnight Strangler.

How ridiculous.

She saw herself in the bureau mirror staring back with shocked eyes. The dream faded and, though she struggled with it, she lost the details.

The bedside clock read ten-thirty. It had read two-thirty when sleep had taken her. Again, her house had been haunted by sounds, clanks and groans, a distant, quiet knocking.

"Husha, husha, we all fall *down!*"

Suddenly tears came. From nowhere. No, from deep inside, where she had been storing them. A tidal wave that washed in all the ugly debris of marriage and separation and left her shaking.

Several minutes passed before strength and composure returned.

Get it together. Stay busy. Life and career carry on. It's Sunday. Try to track down the tester, the witness to murder. The Don Jail today. Talk to André Cristal. Maybe hire him to break someone's kneecap.

And she simply had to see Mr. Blaine Johnstone with a *t* and an *e*. And later this afternoon, a meeting with Leon and Chuck to talk about mundane things such as how they were going to survive.

As she was making coffee, Lisa Tchobanian phoned, worried, asking after her welfare.

"Chuck told me about the whole rotten thing, Carrie. I'm crying for you."

"Don't, Lisa. I'm okay. I bent, I didn't break. The guys stuck with me. Tell Chuck I love him for that. I really didn't tell him properly how I felt about it."

"He would *really* have been in trouble if he'd chosen Ted's side."

"You two have made up?"

"A truce. We're letting the Red Cross come in to care for the sick and injured. Hell, I didn't mind the idea so much of Chuck acting for Squire, especially if he bleeds the guy to death with fees – but he made me feel like a fool."

"It's not a marriage-breaker, Lisa."

"I have your point. Look, you need a friendly ear or shoulder or something, you know where I am. Like me to come over?"

"I'd love to see you. But I . . . I have some things to do, I'm just going to keep busy."

"You're sure?"

"Thanks, yes."

Later, Carrie sipped her coffee and stared at the empty chair at the other side of the kitchen table, where Ted was usually buried in the sports section. She fought tears, but they came.

✤ ✤ ✤

A short distance east of downtown and just west of the Don Valley, where Toronto's embarrassingly minor river, the Don, distorts into a canal before emptying into Lake Ontario, stands the Toronto Jail, known simply as the Don. An older prison had been built on the site in 1865, an ugly relic whose closing brought no tears to those who'd inhabited it. The Don was a short-term holding facility, and in 1980 boasted a population of four hundred and fifty mostly unhappy persons.

On the fourth floor of the Don were kept prisoners likely to come to harm from their mates, an area called p.c. – protective custody – and that was where Carrie was told she could find Blaine Johnstone. But the man brought out to talk with her was not her client – either that or he had cut off his rooster-tail and done some serious plastic surgery.

"Who are you?" he said.

"I'm a lawyer."

"I didn't ask for no lawyer."

"What are you charged with?"

"Rape. The crazy bitch is lyin'."

Carrie went back to the control booth and learned he was the only Johnstone they had, with or without *t* or *e*. This was becoming a little abnormal. Can people just disappear through a

125

hole in the earth while going through the court system? Right out of Kafka, the poor man had said: maybe he'd turned into a cockroach.

Where does one look for him? She wasn't sure.

"Where can I find André Cristal?"

This time she was sent into a visiting room on range 3A, a large stark room dominated by a long table.

Cristal marched in briskly, like an officer in the military, gave her a kind of inspection, and frowned. Carrie had done her face – maybe too much – but hadn't got rid of the shadows.

She didn't offer her hand. "How are you today?" she said with a wan smile.

"Not too bad. And you, Mrs. Barr?"

She was stuck for an answer. "A little . . . under the weather, I guess. Not in the best shape. Have too many things whirling around me." She was babbling. "I'm okay."

He waited, as if expecting her to carry on, to explain. She became busy with her bag, bringing out pen and pad and a sealed pack of Player's. "If you get tired of rolling them . . ."

"Thank you." He pulled out two, extended one. "But I should not offer, should I?"

Carrie felt a hand struggling to move up there, to grasp that little sweet tube of addicting drug. Miraculously, her hands remained near the table, fingers fiddling with her ballpoint pen, clicking the button in and out.

"No, you shouldn't."

"*Je m'excuse.* I 'ave deep admiration for you, *madame.* I 'ave tried to quit." He started to put both cigarettes back in the pack.

"No, you –"

"I can wait –"

"– can smoke if you –"

"– not important."

As their words collided, Carrie made a grab for the cigarettes, snatching one of them, lighting it, just one teensy draw on it, then handing it over to Cristal.

God, did that feel good. Why was she so nervous with this man?

Cristal was smiling broadly. Carrie felt foolish. She cleared her throat, and told him of her visit to the Roll-a-Bowl-a-Ball and the prop loft, and the blank-bullet test.

"This Inspector Mitchell," he said, "do you think he 'as tried to set me up?"

"He has a sort of Machiavellian mentality. I wouldn't put anything past him. If he has information he isn't disclosing, we can get the case thrown right out. Okay, I also saw your Mr. Big Leonard Woznick. I had to scare him a little bit. He says he will try to get some wheels turning."

"Don't be surprise if they will make contact. If Big Leonard is scared, Billy will be *very* scared."

"Sweet – he's a real worry wart?"

"Big Leonard says Billy has – I can't pronounce . . . anxiety neurosis. It is his weakness, but maybe for his business it is his strength also."

Carrie recited to him her conversation with Woznick. He listened quietly.

"I liked Big Leonard. Walked into the middle of his bridge game."

"I 'ave learn bridge from him. And you play, too?"

"A little."

"Maybe one day, you and I, we can play. We can be partners, eh?"

She met his eyes, saw something in them that made her feel strange and prickly.

Abruptly, she said, "His daughter wants to be a lawyer. Lenore."

Cristal drew deeply on the cigarette, blew out slowly. "Lenore. I am very fond of her."

"So it would seem. Frankly, M. Cristal, it would have helped my bail submission had I known you were seeing his daughter. Makes it a little easier to explain your association with a . . . well, a gangster."

"I do not want to involve Lenore."

"Okay, I guess I respect that." Why was this gentleman – for that's what he seemed to be – involved in something as sleazy as the heroin trade? It didn't quite come together for her. In truth, did he not follow a more noble criminal profession – was he not a runner but a gunner? Sadly, that seemed more likely. She *wanted* to believe he had nothing to do with those bodies in that loft – but the mental effort was taxing. He knew too much, for instance, about the witness in the loft. Psychic, he had said. Pretty unlikely.

"Well, your speculations – whatever they were – about a tester turned out to be correct. His name is Normie. He looks like a weasel."

She described her encounter on the street near her office.

"Normie – the name means not'ing to me," said Cristal. "And was he there when . . . does he say he see me in the loft?"

"He wants to be paid for his information."

"And do the police know about him?"

"No, they would have disclosed that. He hasn't talked to the law, not yet. He won't until he tries to work me for some money. I assume he'll phone me when he runs out of heroin."

Cristal studied his cigarette butt, slowly mashed it into the ashtray, damped the embers.

"He will be living dangerously, this Normie."

Carrie didn't like that, a heavy sound of threat. "I think I know how to handle him."

"I 'ave complete faith."

The smile made her relax, perhaps she had misread. "You're telling me the truth, M. Cristal, you didn't see him up there?"

"I tell the trut'. I am not a fool to lie to my lawyer. M. Cristal – it is too formal for me. André."

"André . . . well, okay. Carrie, for me. Carrington, actually. I was named after the town where I was born in New Brunswick. That's kind of silly, isn't it? My father's idea. I think he'd been drinking." My God, she was at it again, her tongue running the marathon. "Well, I guess . . . that's it."

She gathered her tools. She was suddenly conscious that he was beside her, holding her chair. Courtesy – they must breed it into Gallic men.

She stood with a little graceless wobble.

"I 'ope . . . I *hope* you will recover from, as you say, your being under the weather."

"I intend to." She smoothed down her skirt. She knew his eyes were X-raying her, seeking what was inside.

"And I hope everyt'ing goes well in your life, Carrie. Carrington. I prefer that." His tone was solicitous, gentle. His receivers had obviously picked up the intricate signals of her unhappiness: the strained face with all the cosmetics, the rigidity of limb, the body language. He didn't have to be psychic to read her.

Suddenly she wanted to tell him all about it, to pour forth Ted and Melissa and anger and sorrow.

She barely held it in. She wondered if this was like a nervous breakdown – she had never had one, she had no idea what they were like. Get it together.

His hand grasped hers. No sparking, thank God, but for a moment he wouldn't let her go, and she couldn't look at him . . .

"Okay, I'm off. I'll keep in touch."

"I'll be here."

Biting her lip, avoiding his smile, she left the visiting area.

Leon looked sadly around Ted's office, pillaged of its files now, sad and empty. Gone the exorbitant fees the firm had been expecting from Ted's wealthy adulterers, gone the munificence of Dr. Royce Boggs and Mrs. Melissa Cartwright. Gone forever were the offerings of G & C Trust, too, the conveyances and mortgages that had kept the wolf from the door. Robert Barnsworth, the manager at G & C Trust, the stern, forbidding moneylender their stricken firm was beholden to, had had a fit when he learned of the damage Carrie did to the wall outside their offices.

Ted had turned out to be an asshole. Why was he so successful? Did assholes make better lawyers? They care less, he supposed, they don't let obstacles like concern for the downtrodden or a yearning for justice get in the way of their greed. Leon was angry at Ted, and perplexed – he had known him for a century, it seemed, had known him better than anyone, better than Carrie. But he had never known him at all. Such a judge of character.

Despite his anger, in some small hiding place deep within him he felt a sense of relief, almost . . . triumph. The light was green, the road was clear. Carrie was a free woman now, and some day, some time, when the proper stars are in conjunction and Buddha is smiling from his throne in heaven, he would utter the unutterable, he would speak to her of matters of the heart.

A heart he feared would be broken if he offered it to her. She would be astonished, then perplexed. She would say, my goodness, I had no idea, and she would stifle a smile, and afterwards she would feel sorry for him and comfort him and tell him she has always loved him dearly. As a friend.

But she was in a fragile state now, vulnerable. It would be enough for now just to be there for her, to help her through it. And she'd survive – she had faced crises before: her mother's death, her father's conviction. His suicide. But he grieved for her, felt her pain as his own.

He paced, nervous, hot. It was nearly noon on this Sunday of the long weekend – tomorrow was Civic Day – and the offices were still and stifling. G & C Trust had turned off the air-conditioning.

Leon went into his own office. Books and papers covered his desk. He had been working on a brief for the Herbert Orff case, his thesis being that it should not be against the law to be a racist, just as it is not against the law to be retarded. Maybe a lack of mental competence *should* be his defence – his client was too simple to be guilty of anything. The little fascist beach ball who mumbles to himself.

Ted had been in most of yesterday cleaning his cupboards bare, and had left a memo listing files he hadn't taken "in case they are in dispute." Mostly clients he had brought to the firm and referred to the other lawyers. He'd left a phone number and an address, care of Boggs Industries Ltd. "Royce is lending me a little space," said his memo.

Chuck and Carrie arrived within a few minutes of each other, and both joined Leon in his office for the first meeting of their reformed partnership. They studied copies of Ted's memo.

"He has traded his soul for a little space from Mr. Boggs," said Carrie. "But let's not get sidetracked. What's on the agenda, as if I didn't know? We're broke, right?"

Leon thought she looked better; she had survived the first few days, now healing had begun.

"Yeah, we're in the hole," said Chuck. "Somebody's got to talk to Barnsworth. We've got to throw some numbers around, restructure the loan."

"Let me talk to him," Carrie said. "I'll explain the situation. Maybe I can break down in tears in front of him."

"I don't think it's fair to ask you, Carrie," Leon said.

"Look, I'll bloody do it."

Leon shut up. He was clucking, a mother hen, she didn't want that.

"I'll try to hit Harry Squire up for an advance on that thousand a day," Chuck said. "How about you, Leon, what do you have coming in?"

Leon was embarrassed. A Native land claim with a large fee, but the case would take years to settle. He had some labour arbitrations booked, but they were two, three months away. The rest was Herbert Orff and a little of this and that and a lot of free work. "I'll call the legal-aid people, get some referrals." But a few legal-aid billings wouldn't satisfy the needs of Mr. Barnsworth.

"If I can get bail for André Cristal," Carrie said, "and land that three hundred thousand dollars . . ."

"Then we're in hog heaven," said Chuck. "Have any of Billy Sweet's minions made contact?"

"No."

"Then we can't count on it. Listen, you guys, we've got to get out of these expensive digs, set up some place simple and cheap."

Leon stood staring out his window, fashionable Bloor Street below him, one of Toronto's high-rent areas – he had never been comfortable here. He turned to his partners. "We're stuck on a five-year lease."

"We have the right to sublet," said Carrie.

"We'll still take a bath," Chuck said. "Office rentals are way down."

"Maybe Barnsworth will take pity," Carrie said.

"The guy has a heart of stone, forget it," said Chuck.

They heard someone enter, and Chuck got up. "I asked Harry Squire to drop by. Here's where I go into action."

Chuck found Squire in the waiting room, dapper in a navy blazer, looking for all the world like the respectable businessman he felt he was.

"Glad you could make it on a weekend," Chuck said.

"These are nice offices," said Squire.

"Yeah, but we're thinking of moving. This is too uptown for us."

"That so? I have some space you might be interested in."

"Yeah? Let's go into the library." He would offer mute demonstration as to how hard he'd been working for him, analyzing all those books in terms of literary merit.

Squire looked around at the piles of paperbacks and sat with an unhappy grunt.

"Business is down. I had to replace most of my stock with, ah, softer material, it doesn't sell too well. I still have pickets outside all three of my Ontario stores."

"Where are the others?"

"Montreal, Halifax, couple cities out west, and I'm expanding into the States, Buffalo and Syracuse."

"So you can't be hurting too bad, Harry."

"Yes, but business is way down in T.O. I'm having to close one of the stores because I have these damned feminists out in front taking pictures of my clientele. The store's in an area where a lot of these damned bra-burners hang out, Queen West. Two dozen bookstores down that street, and I'm the one they select to harass. In each one of those stores you can find books with nude photos and sex manuals, far more graphic than anything I offer."

Chuck couldn't staunch the flow.

"I pay hundreds of thousands in taxes to this city. They treat me as if I'm in a communist state complete with self-appointed censors and busybodies. What happened to the Bill of Rights? Has it been repealed?"

"This store – is that the space you want to rent?"

"It's near Spadina, a walk to the Queen Street courts."

"How much?"

His big eyebrows curled into a frown for a moment. "Okay. The first six months free, and after that . . . let's say a couple of thousand a month. I feel I owe you."

This sounded like a hell of a deal, though Chuck thought the area a little unfashionable for a law firm.

"Harry, speaking of monetary matters, I wonder if I can get you to look at a little retainer agreement I drew up."

Squire glanced down at the paper that was laid in front of him, then crumpled it. "I don't think we want to leave evidence. No, that's not the best way to handle it. A thousand dollars every day you're in court for me, and I'm going to slip it to you each day, cash in hand. What the bureaucrats of Revenue Canada don't know isn't going to hurt them. It's none of their damn business anyway."

More than a little ignoble this. Could Chuck persuade Carrie and the overly noble Leon to think about it? It wouldn't be the first time, really: a client slips you a hundred-dollar tip, you don't bother to run it through the books.

"I'm not afraid of doling out for this case, Chuck. We're fighting for a principle here, and the principle isn't money. As far as I'm concerned I'm financing a blow for liberty. I'll cover your extras, too: for instance if you have to . . . you know, pass a few dollars around."

Chuck was beginning to realize this man was not exactly a paragon of business virtue.

He'd intended to ask him about an advance on that thousand a day – otherwise he would have some explaining to do to his partners – but he just couldn't bring himself to hit him up right away. He didn't want to appear greedy, it might diminish the man's infinite trust in him.

"Okay, we're in court Tuesday. We're going to elect for a jury, and the judge will set a date for the preliminary hearing. Now I'm going to warn you, Harry, the prelim may last some time: the judge has to read all those books, and that's a thousand a day."

"No problem."

"Every day I'm in court for you."

"No problem."

Chuck didn't want to tell him exactly *how* long this humungous trial would last. "When can we see this place on Queen Street?"

"This afternoon, if you care to run the blockade."

Chuck was another hour with Squire – the usual rundown of the facts and the law with a new client – and after seeing him to the door, he rejoined his partners in Leon's office and told them about the storefront for rent and the cash-in-hand money.

"We should pay taxes on what we earn like every other citizen," Leon said.

"Aw, man, cut with the communist propaganda. We don't have to receipt it all."

"It's dirty money," said Carrie. "Let's not get dirty with it. What did you get as a retainer?"

"Yeah, well, I figured instead of a big retainer, I'd ask him for a deal on the rent."

Carrie looked at him suspiciously.

"Queen West," said Chuck. "You're only a walk away from home."

"It's funny. I was thinking about having a practice down there. I worried it was a little too . . . Soho."

"She loves that street," Leon said. "I do, too."

"You would," said Chuck. "The beatnik barrio."

"It'll be trendy one of these days," Carrie said.

"Oh, yeah, and so will Cabbagetown," said Chuck. "But let's look at it."

"I like the idea, storefront lawyers," Leon said. "Right on the street. Part of the scene."

"We'll buy you a beret," said Chuck.

Chuck assumed the Queen Street branch of Squire International had been forced to close early that afternoon – the picketers, satisfied with their work, had departed by the time Carrie and Leon and he arrived. Down the street were a funky diner called Barney's, a jazz joint called Bourbon Street, and the Horseshoe Tavern – popular with local artists. There were buskers and handicraft stalls near the corner.

Squire's bookstore was on the lower floor of a two-storey building which was well recessed from the street. A separate entrance leading upstairs bore a sign that said HOGTOWN ACTORS' WORKSHOP.

The branch manager, a timid-looking fellow with hornrims, unlocked the door for them. "Mr. Squire is waiting for you." They saw him at the cash register.

"Have a gander around," Squire said. He scooped a few bills from the till and without counting them put them in his pants pocket.

The partners took a stroll.

The space was narrow and long and high, could easily accommodate about eight lawyers and secretaries. They tried to imagine it without the books and shelves, with typewriters clicking and phones ringing. A lot of work would have to be done.

"It's going to cost," said Chuck.

"Three months' worth of rent at the old place will pay for redoing it," Carrie said.

"The floor looks good," said Leon. "Nice, high ceilings. Put in partitions, do a little painting and sanding, move in the furniture, and we're in business."

"You want this, Carrie?" Chuck said.

"I kind of like it."

"Then you shall have it."

Squire advanced on them. "There's a little place in the back you can use as a lounge. It leads out to a patio, and I even have a couple of trees out there."

They looked at the back room and the patio. Possibilities.

"I'm prepared to pay half the cost of all improvements," Squire said.

"We may have a deal," said Chuck.

13

Speeder Cacciati didn't like all the veiled hints he had just got from Big Leonard Woznick on the phone. He didn't like the idea of discussing them with Billy Sweet, neither, who he wished would take a few tranks from time to time. But he went right into Billy's game room – though a little too quickly, forgetting to knock.

Billy was staring out the window, and he must have caught Speeder from the corner of his eye because he made a surprised, jerky motion.

"I told you not to *do* that," he yelled. "If I was carrying, I'd of blown your head off."

"Hey, Billy, cool, cool." Speeder whipped a comb through his hair. He wondered if it was the tension around here that was causing all this dandruff. Or something in the wake-ups he'd been taking. "I just got a call from Big Leonard. He asked me how we're doing on this Cristal thing."

"We are not doing nothing . . . anything on this Cristal thing. Big Leonard hired him, and Big Leonard can furnish the bail." Billy motioned Speeder over to the shuffleboard, dusted some sand on it. "You take first shot."

Speeder figured that whenever Billy was in a bad mood he had to humiliate someone at one of his games, that someone usually being himself. His first rock was lucky, a leaner to the left.

"Billy, what Leonard was sayin', I think, is Cristal's gonna sing if he don't get out."

"He said this on the phone? The *telephone*?"

"He spoke careful, Billy, very careful."

"Jesus Christ." Billy swept the counter off, and his rock stuck. "Mr. Normie the Nose – where is he? Why does it take so long for you to locate him?"

"Disappeared offa the face of the map. Maybe the bulls got him. Billy, things may be gettin' kinda dicey here."

Billy was quiet for a while, until they changed ends. Then he nodded and went, "Okay. Yes, that's what we'll do. We shall spring this canary. There's only one sure way how one can cure canary fever – I am going to tell Big Leonard to silence Mr. Cristal. Leonard hired a man who isn't very businesslike, he doesn't quite fit into the system. Big Leonard hired him, let him terminate him."

"Big Leonard ain't gonna want to grease this guy. Big Leonard –"

"Stuff Big Leonard! Flood the market with some of that high-grade Turkey, get the money to the lawyer and get this possible future singing star onto the street, and just tell Big Leonard to stiff him, understand?"

"Yeah, Billy." Speeder stuck one in a corner behind a guard.

"And if he don't . . . if he doesn't wish to do it, we stiff Big Leonard." Billy blasted the guard off and the counter went with it. "This lady lawyer, what does she know?"

"Sounds like too much."

"Lawyers have the biggest mouths of all. Lawyers, informers, thieves, and government regulators. You can't get ahead."

✢ ✢ ✢

There was no holiday for the lawyers on this holiday Monday. Carrie, Leon, and Chuck were sitting around in Leon's office, doing the paper on reforming their partnership. They had decided to move down to Queen Street at month's end. A lease had to be drawn up, decorators and carpenters hired.

The phone rang and Leon answered it.

"You got a Caroline Barr?"

"Carrington Barr. Can I say who's calling?"

"A friend of a friend of a friend."

Leon passed her the phone. "Sounds like it might be your underworld gentleman."

Carrie cleared her throat. "Yes, I'm Carrington Barr."

"Yeah, can we get together? It's about Cristal."

"What about him?"

"Not something I enjoy to talk on the phone about. Bar named Digger's Dell on Eastern Avenue. Nine o'clock."

"Just one minute – you can come up to the office –"

"Tonight. I'd appreciate it."

And click, that was it. Carrie was annoyed at the abruptness of this command. Obviously Big Leonard had done his job. She would meet one of Sweet's henchmen tonight. On his turf, but at least it was a public bar.

"Where?" said Leon, looking very worried.

"Oh, a crowded tavern, perfectly safe."

"Someone should go with you," Leon said.

"I don't want the contact spooked. This is *my* case. *I*'ll do it."

Leon shook his head. "Carrie, I'm not going to say this is not a woman's task because I would sound patronizing and sexist, but I suspect that bar is in some seamy neighbourhood with some kind of illegal back-room operation –"

Carrie cut him off. "Leon, you *are* being patronizing." Now she felt bad. "I'm sorry. Thank you for caring. I know you're just trying to be a friend, Leon, and you are. A *good* friend."

Leon looked so hangdog that she relented. "Okay, Leon, you drive me down there."

Carrie wasn't sure whom Billy Sweet would be sending to this Digger's Dell place tonight, a top lieutenant perhaps, maybe even Speeder Cacciati. She was a lot less bold than she pretended to be about this underground meet, but she'd braved Montreal and Big Leonard, and that wasn't so bad.

Still, Leon's company for the trip down there was welcomed – Eastern Avenue wasn't the most sophisticated part of town. Railway yards and warehouses mostly, so Digger's was probably a hard-hat bar. Leon's car – an old Chev rattletrap he used when he wasn't bicycling – blended well into the neighbourhood. Carrie was dressed down for the occasion, jeans and a light denim jacket, just a working gal meeting a guy on a date.

Digger's Dell was at a corner, a boxy-looking bar that didn't seem too well lit. Carrie told Leon to wait outside with the engine running – just in case.

"You're okay about this?" Leon said.

"We keep hoods out of jail. They like us." She hoped.

Alighting from the car, Carrie could hear the deep thrum of bass, heavy rock music from within the bar, and its volume increased as she opened the door. She should have expected this: strutting on a platform near the back was a so-called exotic dancer, and she was surrounded by a crowd of seated, drinking men.

Several turned to stare at her as she entered, salacious looks that gave her the willies. Were she and the stripper the *only* women in here? There, talking to the bartender, was one other, but she obviously worked here, a dancer or a prostitute. Then Carrie recognized her: Trixi Trimble had been a brunette when she last saw her, now she was blonde, and she wasn't wearing a cowboy hat. Barely covered, in fact, in something obscenely short and frilly.

"That was some of the weirdest dancin' I ever seen," the bartender was saying to Trixi as Carrie walked up behind her.

"I was grooving." Trixi spun that last word out, *groo*-ving.

"Yeah, you're groovin', all right. You better lay off that stuff." He lowered his voice. "I think we got heat." He was looking at Carrie – he must have thought she was a cop.

When Trixi turned, Carrie could see her pinned eyes, and she looked down at her arms and saw a spot of blood inside the elbow. Trixi erupted in a crazy, stoned smile and threw her arms around Carrie.

"Hey, Carrie, my main gal!"

Carrie thought: everybody is staring, trying to figure this out, thinking low thoughts, two hustlers embracing. The bartender retreated, satisfied she wasn't the heat.

"What're you doing in *this* awful joint?" Trixi said.

"I'm working."

"Not in *my* terr'tory." She giggled. "I just did my gig up there. Buncha staring morons. But it pays okay, and I'm broke, gotta do this." She was slurring her words.

"You're using again, Trixi."

"Can't help it. S'all over the street, twenty bucks a cap, can't turn it down at that rate."

"Trixi, you can't afford *not* to turn it down."

"Hey, Carrie, what're you *doin'* here?"

"Meeting someone. Never mind. Heroin – it's selling that cheap? That's unheard-of."

"Whole ship must've come in."

"Well, you look like you met it. You'd better get a taxi home, you're a mess. How could you dance in your condition?"

"Easy, 'cause you're not aware of the morons." She got off her stool. "But I'm goin', hon, I'm goin' home. I don't want to inn'erupt your scene here."

"Get some sleep. You come to see me tomorrow, okay? I want a serious talk with you."

"Yeah, I know, I gotta stop beltin'. Hey, you know that big old cute guy I kind of met in your office?"

"Mr. Moodie."

"He followed me all the way home that day. Weird. Is he okay?"

Carrie didn't like the sound of that at all. But no, Mr. Moodie was probably just lonely.

"I'll look at that secretary course. Love ya, doll."

Carrie watched her walk toward the door, sort of float to it, actually. She took Trixi's stool, checked her watch, and wondered where the messenger from Billy Sweet was, but she didn't look around, didn't try to catch anyone's eye – that could provoke unwanted interest. Billy's man would find her.

But unwanted interest came, in the form of the local charmer, Sly Stallone in a muscle shirt, who swung onto the stool next to her and asked her what she was having.

"That's very kind of you. A glass of water."

He frowned at this. "You one of the dancers?"

"I'm afraid not. I'm waiting for a friend."

"Maybe you've found one. Come on, how about a drink?"

"Do you know what I would like?"

"What?"

"Some solitude."

The charmer started to lean toward her, perhaps thinking she was playing hard-to-get, but a thin brown arm came between his nose and her shoulder, and its fingers grasped the edge of the counter.

Carrie swivelled around: a skinny young man, chinless and unshaven, an attempt at a Vandyke beard.

"Hey, asshole, I'm having a conversation," the charmer said.

The skinny man glanced down at him, apparently without much interest, then called out to the bartender: "Cholly, open me a Blue."

"I'll open your brain, smart-ass, you don't butt out."

Again, the skinny man looked down at him, this time with an annoyed expression. Carrie was guessing it was time to slide out of here, and she was about to do so when her way was blocked by yet another man, this one a barrel, short and powerful-looking, a long, diagonal scar running from a corner of his upper lip and across the bridge of his nose.

His voice was a bass rasp. "My friend wants to have your seat," he told the charmer. "I want you should tender it to him."

Carrie's seat-mate stared for a few moments at the long scar on the man's face, then decided to bail out.

"I take it you is the lady lawyer," said the barrel.

Carrie stuck out her hand. "Carrington Barr."

"I am pleased to make your confidence." His grip was not very firm; he seemed uncomfortable, his eyes cast down.

"And what is your . . . handle?"

141

"Hank Humphries is the name. And this here is Deeley."

The skinny guy smiled nervously. Carrie guessed their previous experience with women – especially professional women – had been rudimentary. What now?

The bartender brought Deeley's beer. He drank half of it in one long guzzle, and wiped his lips.

"We would like you to do the pleasure of joining with us to meet a friend," said Humphries.

"What friend?"

"He prefers to remain unknown."

"Where?"

"In the privacy of our moving vehicle."

"I'll meet him in public."

"He's got t'ree hunnert thousand other friends with him, lady. They want to meet you. Your honour and safety is guaranteed."

Carrie didn't like this at all – she was being treated by Billy Sweet like some chore girl or gopher. She wanted to insist that any transaction be done on her terms, at a place of her choosing. On the other hand, this didn't seem out of some old gangster movie where the bad guy tells the victim he's taking him for a ride.

And she wanted to meet those three hundred thousand friends. She looked over at the dancer, who was twirling a bikini top. And then she saw, seated at ringside, Staff-Sergeant Kronos, the man called Horse, gatekeeper to the cells at Provincial Court. He wore a big, goofy grin as he watched the dancer bobble her breasts. A kind of dirty-minded fellow – she hadn't known that of Horse. But she remembered she'd seen him reading a copy of *Hustler*.

"You comin', lady?"

She looked at herself in the bar mirror, between displays for Labatt's and Molson's. Those startled, innocent eyes. Maybe she was in the mood to take chances, maybe marital crisis had deranged her.

Her father would have done it.

"Okay, let's go," she said.

Deeley finished his beer.

A few minutes later Carrie found herself in the back seat of a yacht, an old gas-guzzling Chrysler, Deeley at the wheel,

Humphries up beside him. Deeley kept looking at his rearview mirror as he weaved – a little haphazardly – in and out of the traffic on Eastern Avenue, then Front Street.

They drove in silence. Carrie wanted to engage them, but they seemed shy.

Humphries leaned around and offered her a cigarette, which she unthinkingly took. Or instinctively. She held it between her fingers, caressing it, loving it, wanting it. A remembrance of good manners must have rung a distant bell in Humphries' mind, and he went through his pockets, finding some wooden matches. Fumbling, he dropped a couple of them, looking about despairingly for a place to strike one of them, finally ripping it across the brace between the windows. But he was too late – Deeley was passing her the dashboard lighter.

She declined it. "I just remembered, I don't smoke. But thank you, anyway, you're both gentlemen." Carrie preferred they see themselves that way, and perhaps they did. She put the cigarette in her handbag.

Deeley stopped the car on the quay near Harbourfront. A man appeared from the shadows and got in beside Carrie. Speeder Cacciati – she remembered him from the criminal courts. He was wearing dark glasses and carrying a cheap zip-around briefcase and was chewing gum like crazy, hyperactive. He ignored her for the moment and spoke to Deeley, who was back in traffic again, still glancing at the rearview mirror.

"Let me out toward Jarvis and Dundas, gotta run a chore."

Carrie watched him pick at a sore on his elbow. The man smelled of yesterday's sweat, and she shifted farther to her side of the seat.

"You're driving like a old lady, Deeley, stay in your lane."

A back-seat driver, to boot.

"Why do you let this heat-bag drive, Humph? He's gonna get us bulled over."

Deeley slowed down, and Cacciati finally turned and looked at Carrie, lowering the dark glasses. His gaze moved down her body, stopped at her crotch, and came back up. He smiled. She was revolted.

"You don't know who I am, Miss Barr," he said.

She didn't feel like enlightening him. "Okay, I don't know who you are. This is a bit silly, isn't it? You could have met me at my office. I very much resent being on orders, meeting your flunkies in that abysmal tavern."

"Hey, I'm doin' you a service. I just happen to know some people that know André, and these people took up a collection."

He unzipped one side of the briefcase. Carrie caught a glimpse: wads of rubber-banded bills. He closed it again, and passed it to her.

"I have to make out a receipt to someone for this."

"Give it to André. And maybe when he gets out, he should talk things over with Big Leonard, who is like . . . his counsellor."

"Mr. Cristal has a counsellor."

"Yeah, and a real good one – I heard about you. But André, he'll still wanna see Big Leonard. When Leonard talks to him, André should listen." He shouted to Deeley: "Stay in the same fucking lane, okay? The guy thinks he's an Indy race-car driver. I wanna ask about a guy named Normie the Nose, Miss Barr, he been in to see you? You gotta worry what a guy like that could say in court."

"I don't know what he's going to say."

"Well, I guess your job is to make sure he says the right things."

"I don't need advice about my job. I'll do whatever is in the best interest of my client. I also don't like all these games, Mr. Cacciati."

He stopped scratching and his concave face turned sour. "You know me?"

"About as well as I want to. You can tell Billy Sweet that I'm not a bag woman or a bonded carrier." Something, maybe the encounter with Trixi, was setting Carrie off, and she was no longer able to hold her tongue. "I have a good idea how this money was raised so quickly. Heroin is everywhere right now, and it's cheap, isn't it?"

"Where you gettin' your information? Your client been talking to you maybe too much? Frankly, I worry about that

Frenchman. I worry he don't seem to keep too many secrets. Billy, he especially don't like talkers, he likes the strong, silent type. Goddamn – Deeley, take a driving lesson!"

"I'm doing a evasive tactic, that's the t'ird time I seen that car. I think I got someone on my tail."

"I'm outa here," said Cacciati. "Pull over by that cab stand."

He got out, and strode to the first taxi in the rank. Carrie took the opportunity to make her getaway there, too, out the other side of the car with her briefcase of money.

"Hey," said Humphries, "we wish to do the compliment of taking you home."

"Thanks, anyway."

"There's that same car again," said Deeley.

Leon's old Chev pulled up beside them, and Carrie quickly got in.

The money locked in the office safe, Carrie invited Leon to her house to relieve the evening's tension with a wind-down drink. When she clicked on the lights in the living room, she saw that a whole rack of tapes and records were gone from beside the stereo, and her first thought was that thieves had daringly entered during the day. Then she checked the music library more closely – only Ted's rock and jazz were missing.

"Wait a sec," she told Leon, and went upstairs and found Ted's closets and drawers cleaned out. He'd made a quick raid.

He was worse than a thief. Did he try to clear this with her? No. Was there a note? Nothing.

She went downstairs, and forced Leon to listen to her excoriations of Ted over a couple of snifters of the five-star Rémy he'd foolishly left behind.

Leon just smiled. "You wanted to keep his underwear and socks?"

"It's the principle," Carrie said stubbornly. But she soon relaxed again – after all, it had been the best day she'd endured of late: new offices, three hundred thousand new friends.

"Carrie, do you really think Cristal wasn't involved in these murders?"

"I . . . I'd like to think he wasn't. Maybe he was framed." That was a growing possibility, his arrest seemed too convenient.

"I think you often blind yourself, Carrie. You *want* people to be innocent."

"Why shouldn't I?" Carrie didn't try to explain how she hungered for innocence, how she was emotionally trapped within the walls of this concept. But anything she'd say would sound banal and, worse, somehow defensive of her father, of her belief in him, his innocence.

She felt the old pain return. What a kangaroo court he'd faced, what a corrupt vendetta that tax-fraud case was, that *alleged* tax fraud. Charlie was innocent. Innocent. Charlie was *framed* . . .

Then the penitentiary term. And after his release . . . the family Pontiac sedan in the garage, locked, windows closed, engine running, carbon monoxide. His sad, limp body.

After Leon left, Carrie went to bed but was unable to sleep. She was startled by the sound of garbage cans clanking in the back yard. Raccoons, for sure, she told herself. Other sounds came. A soft, distant skritchy sound, as if from fingernails on a window pane. Don't be ridiculous. It's the night breeze hissing through the trees.

Spectres haunted her sleep again that night. Again the Midnight Strangler in his many guises roamed the dark paths and alleys of her subconscious. A masked ball of monstrous men, leering, demanding that she dance, and she is the only woman here, naked, ashamed. Who is this one now advancing? Inspector Harold Mitchell, hatless, his bald phallic head. A bigger man shoulders him aside, a man in the mask of a horse but wearing a sergeant's uniform: Horse Kronos, jailer to the halls of justice, and the ballroom becomes a courtroom, and she is pointing to Jock Strachan in his little bow tie. "That's the man, that's the man." But they don't believe her, and they take her away.

14

Harold Mitchell had assembled his team – the three male officers who made up Operation Sweet – in the drug-squad communications room, where under dimmed lights they viewed the latest videos. Mitchell had hand-picked these men, surveillance experts, masters of disguise.

The screen first showed a wobbly picture of a stripper peeling her clothes to loud rock music.

"Hey, hold on that," Hollis Lamont said, but too late: the picture changed to a scene at the bar, Carrie Barr on a stool in the company of three men.

"Twenty-one thirteen hours," Mitchell said. "On her left that's Humphries, and behind her, guy name of Deeley, a couple of Billy's foot soldiers."

"And here's me," said an officer named Chester. He was the charmer who'd sat on the stool next to Carrie.

From the video: *"Hey, asshole, I'm having a conversation."*

"It's the man of steel," Lamont said.

Chester's recorded voice: *"I'll open your brain, smart-ass, you don't butt out."*

"Oh, boy," said Lamont, "there's gonna be a fight. Watch Chester clean up on these guys."

Chester just grinned as he watched himself exit the scene.

"What were you trying to do, Chester, win an Oscar?" Mitchell said.

"I just wanted Hollis to get some sound levels, Inspector."

"Well, from now on just butt out of the scene, Steve McQueen. From now on everyone stays away from this lady. She's not dumb: she could pick up on the surveillance. She should spring Cristal today. We put eyes on him, instead, okay?"

"Roger," said Chester.

"All right, you guys, don't forget what you're doing out there. Don't forget what this is all about. Sweet fucking revenge. And goddamnit, someone bring in Normie Shandler."

Normie the Nose woke up that Tuesday morning to a powerful need, and his hands groped around for his jacket with his outfit and the last of his stash. He had no idea where he was, but it seemed like the outdoors: there were weeds growing everywhere around him. In agony, unable to find either his works or his smack, he rolled over onto his side, and saw he was beside some kind of culvert, and cars were passing over it. He couldn't remember how he got here last night. For some reason he must have decided to sleep outside.

Yeah, his landlord had kicked him out, it all came back. Some of it, anyway.

Shouldn't have pissed out the window. Should've tried to make it to the bathroom in the hallway.

Pissed right on the asshole's car.

The Nose thought that scene was funny enough to laugh at now, except he wasn't feeling well enough to laugh. Where was his jacket, where were his goods? He was feeling some morning chucks, he needed a straightener. He wondered when was the last time he ate. Did he eat yesterday? He wondered if he was hungry.

There, hanging from a low branch of a scraggly tree, was his jacket. He crawled to it on his hands and knees, unable to stand, not ready for heights. He reached up and pulled it down, and found his 'fit, the whole factory was in his pocket, the spoon, his tourniquet, a lighter, and the condom with . . . God protect him, his dope was almost gone, there was just a taste left. There had been a whole ounce here once, the condom had been fat and was now limp.

Could he have shot up a whole ounce in a week? He had shared some, yeah, he remembered passing the needle around with some friends a couple of nights ago. But a whole ounce?

The Nose felt the first prickles of panic. Carefully, though his hands were shaking, he swept the last of the dust into his spoon, turned the condom inside out, brushed it, and managed to get enough for a hit. He added some water from a sour-smelling puddle near the culvert outlet, heated up, tied off, and shot it in the line.

He felt the cooling rush, the glow. He could stand up now, he could be normal for a while. For long enough to call that lady lawyer, for long enough to score.

✤ ✤ ✤

Carrie had laid the money out on her desk for Leon and Chuck to admire, three hundred thousand dollars in rubber-banded wads.

"This pays off the loan, guys," said Chuck. "So we all understand, he is willing to sign this over as your fee?"

"Unless he changes his mind," said Carrie.

"But if he disappears?" Leon said.

Carrie recalled, then, Cristal's spooky words: *If I disappear, then you keep it all. If I die . . . then it will be a good year for your office.* What had caused him to pull that terrible thought from the recesses of his mind? Was it his so-called clairvoyance, a prophecy?

"Well, obviously, if he skips bail it's forfeit to the Crown," she said. "It's a chance we take."

Chuck fondled a stack of bills. "So what you have to do, Carrie, is make sure he stays around for the trial. What you have to do is convince him beyond a shadow of a doubt that he will be found not guilty."

"It's a *very* weak circumstantial case. I don't think he'll run."

149

Carrie repacked the money into the zip-around briefcase. It would go into their trust account. General and Commercial Trust would issue a certified cheque which would be deposited at the bail office.

Leon's secretary came to the door. "Cool Aid is here."

"Ah, yes, they want to start a counselling service for kids on drugs."

Chuck groaned. "More charity, eh? I know Cool Aid is a good cause and all, but we can't keep giving those guys complimentary passes."

"They do more for the street kids than the entire Department of Welfare."

Chuck stood. "I've got a sentence appeal this morning."

Carrie followed him out but stopped in the waiting room to greet the three fuzzy freaks who were the executive officers of Cool Aid: Roy, Elmo, and Parjanya.

"We've got a real problem with junk on the street," Roy told her. "Lot of sick people out there."

"I heard, twenty bucks a cap."

"Does the Lion sleep tonight?"

"He's just coming from his den."

Leon emerged, gave them hugs and pats and led them back to his office.

Carrie checked the mail. A note from G & C Trust complaining that her law firm had overlooked the last payment due on the loan – well, she would stop down there and speak to Mr. Barnsworth. Tickets for that bar do tonight for Mr. Justice Clearihue; how could they send *that* tyrant up to appeals? But she and her partners would have to go – they did a fair bit of work in the appeal court, and Clearihue, a stuffed shirt, would remember who didn't show up to honour him.

And here a couriered letter marked PERSONAL, from Prud'homme, Graves and Company, advising that Mr. Graves had been retained to represent Mr. Theodore Barr in "matters pertaining to the sad difficulties of your marriage," and could she give him a call at her earliest convenience. Carrie tore the letter up, disgusted – the coward was already hiding behind another lawyer's robes. Oh, yes, he was terrified that Melissa Cartwright would be named as corespondent, the client upon whose body he had committed numerous breaches of ethics.

She had never really intended to name Melissa, just to hang that grim possibility over Ted's head. But damn it, now she might. Get this B-and-E artist disbarred for life.

She wondered if she should hire her own lawyer, maybe Melvin Belli, or just do her own cross-examination of the adulterer. *Mr. Barr, please tell the jury about the night you discussed the evidence with Mrs. Cartwright until three a.m.*

She suddenly realized that today was the day the Cartwright divorce opened. She assumed Ted had had the good sense to retain someone to substitute for him. That someone would be unprepared. The case could be a schemozzle.

"For you, Carrie." Pauline handed her the phone again.

"This is Normie," came a low, lazy voice. "Remember me?"

Carrie was still silently fuming, and it took her a few moments to move from Ted mode to Normie mode. "Yes, of course, thank you for calling."

"I want, like, an appointment, only not in your office."

He was drawling, stoned – but he didn't sound as groggy as the time he'd encountered her on the street.

"Where and when would you like to meet?" She made her voice sound conspiratorial.

"I ain't ate nothin', I figure, for two or three days, so I'm gonna be over at a place I know in Chinatown, Sunrise Bar and Grill, just off Dundas and something. Bring ten grand in cash."

Carrie couldn't bribe a murder witness, that would create serious implications for her career, but she wasn't going to let this mercenary little junkie escape her hook. "I'll meet you there in an hour, and we'll discuss it."

"Ten grand down, and I want another fifty in a week."

"Order a big breakfast, Normie, it's on me."

"I need some cash, lady."

"I'll see if I can help you out."

He rang off after her vaguely worded assurance, and Carrie, clutching the zip-around briefcase, finally made her exit from

151

the office. In the elevator, silently sinking toward the ground floor of the G & C Building, she reorganized the morning's agenda. First the bank to deposit the money – no time to stop and chat with Barnsworth now – then breakfast with Normie, and then get André out on bail. Her client would understand why she was late.

In the spacious, antiseptic offices of this venerable trust company – founded in 1857, boasted the sign above the door – Carrie presented herself to one of the accountants. She saw that Robert Barnsworth's office door was open, and he was peering out at her.

How overdue was that loan payment? Almost a week – eight thousand dollars, mostly interest – and now the rent for August was also due, another ten thousand.

The accountant opened his eyes wide at the sight of the money, and he quickly filled out the slips. Carrie felt a presence behind her, and when she turned, she saw it was Barnsworth. He glanced from the money to her, his pink face a mask portraying false good will.

"Ah, Mrs. Barr, I'd rather been hoping to have a little chat."

"I'd enjoy that, Mr. Barnsworth, and I'd like to set a time."

Barnsworth lowered his voice while his clerk counted the money. "I shouldn't suppose you'd care to, ah, put things straight with us right now, Mrs. Barr?"

"I actually intended to speak to you about an extension on the loan, Mr. Barnsworth."

"I'm sorry – an *extension*?"

"Frankly, we don't have the money right now."

He looked from her to the stacks of bills, then back to her, his face animated with suspicion. She didn't attempt to explain where the money came from – let him think she was washing it.

"Really, Mr. Barnsworth, we've been quite reliable to this point, but since you cut off your referrals we've been *very* pinched."

"I also gather your firm is currently undergoing some, shall we say, disorganization."

"What do you mean?"

"You are divesting yourself of a partner?"

Carrie was suddenly at the end of her tether with this man. "Do you spy on all your customers?"

He was taken aback, and he sputtered a little. "We are a major financial institution, Mrs. Barr: it is our business to know these things. I rather think I must be blunt. Your husband developed several corporate clients for your firm – is he taking them?"

"Why you snotty little prig. Your nose is stuck in our business. Pull it out." She whirled, the certified cheque in her hand, and strode angrily out to the street. She wondered what was happening to her, what were these changes being wrought in her, anger so easily rising to boil. Uncool, uncollected Carrie.

She must pull herself together for this Normie character, be suave and smart. She took a taxi to Dundas West, the ever-lengthening spine of Chinatown, and found squeezed amidst the clutter of Cantonese restaurants an ordinary greasy spoon, the Sunrise Bar and Grill, where ham and eggs were a dollar-fifty.

Normie was in a booth at the back, and he'd already eaten. "Good morning," she said. He nodded.

As she sat across from him, he wiped his mouth with a napkin, and she saw his hand was shaking. Furtive, watery eyes. He looked as if he was coming down.

"Did you bring the money?"

"What are you selling?"

"I don't wanna horse around."

"Why should I trust you? How about a sample of what you know?"

"I'm tellin' you, I was there, I seen the whole thing."

"Did you see André Cristal there?"

"For the right kind of money, I didn't."

This was ridiculous, Carrie thought. "I'm not going to pay you any money, Mr. . . ."

"Shandler. They call me Normie the Nose 'cause I got this gift, I can smell almost as good as a dog."

He actually smelled as bad as a dog. His clothes were rumpled and grass-stained.

"That's why they hire me sometimes as a tester. I'm a expert.

153

I want ten grand to start with." He paused. "You got problems raising it that quick, I'll take half now."

He was licking his lips, twitchy, trembling. Carrie knew what he needed. "I'll lend you something to tide you over." She pulled fifty dollars from her purse and put it on the table.

Normie looked at it with dismay. "I guess you ain't been hearing me."

"Then let's hear you. Prove to me you know something."

"Okay, I was up there with Hiltz and Perez. I'm a friend of Hiltz, a kind of half-brother, and I was there to test the product. I can describe the place – you been there? – fulla movie shit. I remember the name, *Last Exit from Istanbul*, something like that. There was a crate with some veils – you know, the stuff belly dancers wear? That's where I hid. That a good enough sample for you?"

She said nothing. But it *was* a good sample.

"A couple of G's, lady, I'll trust you for the rest."

Carrie opened her purse again. "Look, I'm going to lend you another fifty dollars. Do you have a place to stay? Maybe I can help you find one."

Normie was looking agitated. He stared at the two orange-coloured bills on the table but didn't pick them up.

"I'm gonna give another free sample. I was there when Jerszy Schlizik came in unannounced with a heater."

"And what about my client?"

Normie's voice broke in exasperation. "I *told* you, I'm willin' to say I didn't see him in there." Now he leaned toward her with a smile that showed his crooked teeth. "You want me to say I saw him in that loft? That's what you want to tell the cops? You want me to say he came in just behind Schlizik and he blew the fucker away? 'Cause that's what I'm gonna say in court, I don't get compensated for my trouble. Two grand, lady, that's the bottom line."

Carrie didn't at all like the latter version of his evidence.

"I don't have two thousand dollars on me, Mr. Shandler."

"So sell your car. I'm wastin' my time here." He made motions as if to stand, but still had his eyes on that hundred dollars.

"I haven't been paid any fees for this yet."

"Then you better go see Billy Sweet right away. Billy don't want the Frenchman convicted – least I don't *think* he does."

"I'm not working for Billy Sweet."

She saw some tiny bubbles of perspiration on his forehead now, and he was fidgeting – he seemed to be slowly disassembling in front of her. He had a hell of a monkey, and it was becoming obvious he was out of heroin.

He snatched the two fifties from the table and got up. "Back here, same place, three o'clock this afternoon. A thousand bucks, I ain't takin' less, and it's just for starters."

"Just a sec, Normie . . ."

But he was walking rapidly out, on his way to get fixed. She wanted to chase after him, and had to keep herself from doing so. She worried she'd blown this one good chance. She'd given him too much money – with heroin going at twenty a cap he'd be higher than a kite when he showed up this afternoon. If he remembered to show up.

Carrie paid his bill and walked back downtown to the Queen Street courts, still pondering the alternative twists that Normie the Nose might give to his evidence. He could say he never saw Cristal. Or he could say Cristal murdered Jerszy Schlizik. She hoped he was making the second version up – if so, it was the most reprehensible form of blackmail, threatening to lie to convict a man of murder.

A loose cannon on the deck. She was resolved that for their next meeting she would conceal a tape-recorder.

At the bail office, she deposited her big cheque, the pledge for André Cristal's freedom. Cristal was brought out wearing a suit Carrie had picked up for him in a men's store, one she saw now was a little tight around the chest and hips. He was smiling.

"The first t'ing, I am going for a run, and then a long, hot bath."

"That suit looks awful. You couldn't have given me the right measurements."

"I t'ink I put on weight in here. From 'aving no exercise."

The trousers were so tight she could see – a quick glance, how embarrassing – the slight prominence of his sex.

155

The clerk passed him his belt, a set of keys, and his wallet. "Sign here, here, here, and here."

Cristal did so, his signature the letter *C* and a squiggly flourish.

"And here," said Carrie, who had scribbled upon the back of the bail receipt a direction transferring the money to her firm.

Cristal looked over it quickly, and signed it with the same flourish.

"Your fee, Carrington. As I 'ave promised."

He looked in his wallet. Carrie saw several dun-coloured hundred-dollar bills in it. He checked his credit cards – at least six of them. "It is fantastic," he said. "In Toronto you have honest police."

"Toronto the Good, we call it."

He stared at her for a moment, a careful appraisal. "Thank you, Carrington. For my freedom."

Something in those penetrating eyes gave her goose bumps. "Let's go have a nice healthy fruit juice or something. We have to talk before you go jogging off."

Outside, on the steps of the courthouse, he paused and looked about: the grass, the trees, beyond that the busy corner of Queen and Bay.

"The street," Cristal said. "In prison they call it freeside. It is good to be in freeside."

"I don't have my car."

"It is better to walk, yes? I t'ink you like to walk, I can see it in your legs, if you will forgive me for saying."

He was looking directly at her, the sun flashing off his teeth. Carrie decided to forgive him. Hard not for him to see her legs, since she was brazenly showing them under a short skirt.

"I like to walk," she said. "Come on, Toronto the Good by foot with Carrington Barr."

He took off his suit jacket and flung it over his shoulder, inhaled deeply of the freeside air and followed her across Nathan Phillips Square, past the two great curved arms of the City Hall.

Oddly nervous in his company, she talked non-stop, told him about her meetings with Humphries and Deeley and Speeder

156

Cacciati. Cristal asked few questions and listened mostly in silence, following her toward Dundas, into Chinatown – his tour guide would take him to Kensington Market, that little concentration of busy ethnicity in the heart of the city.

He drew her into a sporting-goods store on the way, and bought a pair of Adidas and shorts. He paid with American Express.

On Dundas, they passed by the Sunrise Bar and Grill. "That's where I met Normie the Nose this morning, and that's where he's supposed to be at three this afternoon."

"The tester?"

"Yes, he *was* in that loft, André. For a price he'll say he didn't see you there."

This caused Cristal literally to stop in his tracks. He turned to her, his eyes glinting fiercely. "And if his price is not met?"

"He may say something else."

"*Maudit*," he said softly.

"He may say he saw you shoot Schlizik."

She had never seen him display anger before, but now his facial muscles were taut and his voice was hard and tight. "Bastard! He is a liar!"

"Let me worry about him, André."

They continued to walk, and Carrie replayed for him her conversation with Normie.

"Will you pay him?"

"Not what he wants."

"Inspector Mitchell will pay him more."

"Oh, I'll *dare* the Crown to call him as a witness. I intend to record everything this time."

At Kensington Market, people were milling about, lots of activity in front of all the little shops and restaurants. Cristal picked out two rosy apples, and gave the vendor five dollars and told him to keep the change.

He extended an apple to Carrie, and as they walked, they munched. North through the suburban forest, the elms and maples that guarded Toronto's old imposing homes, past lawns yellowing in the heat. On Bloor, she turned east.

"My office is just down the street. I'd like you to come up after you've had a chance to get your bearings. Maybe tomorrow?"

Cristal didn't respond. He seemed lost in melancholic thought.

"André, I can't understand. You're an educated man, an architect, you had a future. How did you ever get into this? Dope. Gangsters."

He didn't reply for a while. She became uncomfortable with his silence.

Finally: "Okay. There was a . . . car accident. I was behind the wheel. A lady . . . well, my friend, my very good friend – she was killed."

"You haven't told me this."

"No, I . . . It's difficult."

"Okay, but I'd like to know."

"I went kind of crazy for a few years. She . . . she was . . ." He shrugged. "Never mind. Special. I got tied up with drugs, different t'ings, uppers, downers, coke, and at the end, the hard stuff. Heroin – it is an escape, but you cannot always escape from it. I lost my job. Borrowed to keep t'ings going. Street lenders, 10-per-cent-a-month men. Finally, I got clean, but I had to work my way out, selling their dope. That is the story, not a nice one."

"Okay." Carrie was the one now who was lost in her silence. This was a man who had loved too hard, and grieved with too much pain. She was moved by this brief history, so difficult in the telling, and she touched his arm, a gentle message.

"Yes," he said, "it is good to talk to someone. Maybe we can talk more soon, yes? But not now. Now I have the urge to run."

"Don't run too far. The bail restriction says you have to stay in Toronto."

"Don't worry, they won't let me out of their sight."

"Who?"

"*Les boeufs*. The cops. 'Ow are your eyes?"

"What do you mean?"

"The car that just went past. The man who 'as been a hundred metre behind us all the time." He shrugged. "It is their game. I am 'appy if they want to play it."

158

Carrie didn't look around. She assumed he was right. Mitchell would want to know if Cristal tried to make contact with former associates. They were going to a lot of trouble.

"Well, what are we going to do with you in the meantime?"

He grinned. "Whatever you like to do with me, I am 'appy to do."

Was he flirting? Or was she reading things?

"Where are you going to stay?"

They were in front of the Park Plaza Hotel, one of the city's older, larger hostelries. Cristal stopped at the entrance, and looked into the roomy lobby.

"Here, close to your office."

"You can afford it?"

"I t'ink so."

"Okay, André. Go for your run. Cacciati wants you to meet with Big Leonard. I guess the police are waiting for something like that, so don't do it. Don't talk to anyone, okay? Call me tomorrow at the office."

He smiled and bowed slightly. He raised her hand and kissed it – gentle, dry, no sparks, just an odd tickling sensation running up her arm. Then he turned and walked into the hotel.

15

The three Cool Aiders painted a mean picture for Leon – too many inner-city youngsters fouled up on drugs. Leon explained grants were getting hard to come by in these pinchy times, but he would get on the phone and lobby Metro Council members – a hearing was scheduled that night for Cool Aid's grant application for their counselling service.

After they left, Leon moaned to himself – he was a donor bank. He just couldn't say no. Maybe he should have gone into social work.

A call from Robert Barnsworth interrupted these sad ruminations. Leon listened to him grumble about the rude treatment he'd received from Carrie. Barnsworth wanted to talk with someone of calmer temper about the overdue loan and rent – would accounts be settled quickly or not?

"I'm afraid the answer is not," Leon said. "We're seeking to extend the loan, Mr. Barnsworth –"

"There will be no extension of the loan. I shall be serving you with formal demand, sir, and if payment is not received within two days – two days, Mr. Robinovitch – we intend to seize your chattels and commence a suit in damages. I take it that is clearly understood."

"Well, give us a break here. We've decided to look for cheaper rent somewhere, and we'll have some start-up costs."

"You are on a five-year lease, sir. Your former partner, I gather, has taken all the files of value?"

Leon made a face, didn't answer.

"Frankly, he was the only true businessman in your firm, and I suspect without him you are in shambles. You have all given guarantees, Mr. Robinovitch. We will not hesitate to execute on your personal holdings. Two days."

And he rang off. Leon groaned – Carrie, it would seem, had not performed the public-relations coup of the century in her handling of Barnsworth.

They had something like five thousand dollars in their general account. Leon felt trapped. He half-expected to find Robert Barnsworth standing petulantly by the door tomorrow, surrounded by bailiffs and sheriffs. What was to be done with this oppressive landlord? Was there no way to break the lease? Only fools would sublet from them at those usurious rates.

One new client today. Leon had demeaned himself, begged legal aid to send some business – and what had they sent him? A rape.

Conscience had always made Leon shun rape trials. If the defence was consent – well, it was always too easy to say the woman agreed. The whole process made Leon a little queasy.

But legal aid would pay five hundred dollars a day, and maybe one has to bend a few principles to get the banker off one's back.

The legal-aid form gave the client's name as "Blaine Johnson." He was without bail, in custody somewhere. And the trial was set for the Metro North Court . . . in just a couple of days – how could that be possible?

He phoned the legal-aid offices to find out why this application had been gathering dust, but was told the request had just come in.

He phoned the prosecutor's office. Yes, Mr. Johnson was coming before a jury Thursday morning. All the witnesses had been subpoenaed. No, the Crown would not agree to an adjournment – the accused had had plenty of time to get a lawyer. If Leon had problems he should tell them to the judge. This was a very

161

serious rape, the complainant had been beaten. The accused admitted the sexual act but insisted she'd consented.

Leon slumped in his chair. Woe. He tried some deep breathing, centring himself. As he was groping for a state of transcendental emptiness, his mother phoned.

"I don't like to call you in the office like this, Leon, but I assumed you must have been kidnapped by a flying saucer when you didn't make it up to the cottage on the weekend."

"Mom, the office is in crisis."

"Let me tell you about crisis. We're supposed to be seeing slides at the Walisches' tonight. I suppose you know they went to Russia again – Sid Walisch is still a communist even after Afghanistan, though I think Lenin would turn over in his mausoleum if he knew – but anyway, yesterday your father fell asleep on the grass at the lake and has third-degree burns, and he is going to be tonight's entertainment, the laughing stock. And everyone thinks *I'm* the family pinko."

His mother paused to chuckle at her joke, and Leon found an opening. "Mom, things *really* are in a mess here. Ted has left the firm and he and Carrie are getting divorced."

Leon heard just the phone static for a moment.

"Oh, my God. Not Ted and Carrington. Why, they were such a perfect couple . . . Forgive me, Leon, but who, may I ask, is the transgressor?"

"Carrie is the victim."

"Oh, how terrible. What happened?"

"Mom, not right now."

"You bring that poor woman over for dinner. This weekend. She must be desolate. Men can be such . . . well, not you, Leon, you'll never be unfaithful because you never seem to find anyone to be unfaithful *to*. What is this, a midlife crisis for all eternity?"

"I've got work, Mom. I'll call you from home."

He hung up, and thought: an evening with Carrie and Mom and Dad, it didn't seem overly romantic. But maybe it was the way to start – it could be followed by a concert, the theatre, a real date. He wondered if Carrie had the slightest inkling . . . But no, she saw him as a kind of avuncular figure, friendly old

162

preachy Leon, the cowardly lion of Oz: he'll never find the Emerald City.

Well, Mr. Johnson had to be attended to – Leon must see him quickly, and marshal his argument to adjourn this imminent trial.

But he was delayed in his flight – Pauline called, announcing the unscheduled arrival of Herbert Orff. Leon hoped he might speedily deal with this militant victim of the media barons and send him on his way.

Roly-poly Herbert Orff came in puffing under the load of several thick expandable files. "I've got three cabinets full of ammunition like this. Absolute proof. I phoned Dr. Yorvil in Alberta and he's sending more. He says this is our big chance to right the wrongs of history."

"I don't even want to look at this trash. I told you I'm arguing the Bill of Rights."

Orff whined: "But that sounds like a technicality."

"The judge is a tough sentencer, Mr. Orff. I'd hate to see you put away."

Orff's pudgy little eyes went into a squint, and his voice faltered. "But I'm only guilty of telling the truth."

Leon asked him for a retainer of five thousand dollars. It was a lot, but times were hard, and *this* gentlemen wasn't getting a free ride.

As Orff dumbly wrote out a cheque, Leon asked him: "Aren't you supposed to be at work?"

"Mr. Blumberg thinks I'm at the dump. He's not as smart as he thinks he is, I hardly ever go to the dump on Tuesdays."

Herbert Orff, garbage inspector. Leon led him out.

"Mr. Blumberg isn't the smartest member of your . . . racial persuasion, Mr. Robinovitch." Orff hesitated as if expecting a response to this; then, his big rear wobbling, he rolled out of the office. Leon was in a hurry, but he didn't want to share the same elevator.

Pauline Chong gave Leon a disgusted look. "Boy, that's the bottom of the barrel."

Then they heard what sounded like an argument in front of the elevator.

A loud, cranky voice: "You're a dirty, cocksucking racist, you want my opinion."

Leon couldn't identify the voice – another tenant of this floor? Had Orff muttered something offensive?

He poked his head around the door and saw that Orff was alone, staring at the closed elevator door. He was loudly debating with no one but himself.

"You're a fucking bigot," he said. "Fucking anti-Semite." Yes, it was Orff who was speaking, but as if from a different larynx, the voice street-tough and resonant.

"I should've told that lawyer I'll defend myself." This was his normal voice.

Orff then snarled, "You couldn't defend your dick, Hitler."

Now, yet a *third* voice issuing from the same throat: "Tell der stupid kike lawyer to stuff it, all he vants is your dough." A distinct German accent. Astounded, Leon realized he'd heard this voice before, as he and Orff had left court: *That asshole lawyer.*

Just then the elevator door opened – and there was Robert Barnsworth, his features set in grim determination. He had a folded paper in his hand: some kind of formal notice, Leon guessed. He was about to storm from the elevator, but then seemed unsure how to get around the hulk blocking the way.

"You can stick it up your fucking cunt, you Nazi swine!" Orff screamed at him.

Terrified, Barnsworth took a few steps back into the cage. Leon bolted toward the elevator as Orff, moving with zombie-like slowness, stepped inside.

"Stick it up *yours*, Jew-boy," Orff growled, still facing Barnsworth.

Leon got a hand in just before the elevator door closed, and it slid quickly open again.

"Herbert!" Leon shouted, and the man seemed to snap to. He turned and faced Leon, blinking – the guy had been in some incredible kind of trance. Leon could see Barnsworth in the corner, his hands covering his groin area; he'd assumed the attack would be sexual.

"I have to go to work. I'm on late shift on the twenty-four-hour emergency line."

"For what?"

"Solid wastes removal and blocked drains."

"Are you okay?"

"I have a headache."

"I want you to come back tomorrow, Herbert. I'm going to ask a friend to see you. He's of, ah, German extraction. I think you'll like him." Dr. Hal Kiehlmann, to be exact, doctor of the mind. Some kind of split-personality illness here.

"Okay, Mr. Robinovitch."

Trapped in the corner and cowering, Barnsworth spoke faintly: "Could you, um, ask this gentleman –" He didn't finish, sucked in his breath as Orff took a step back.

"Now, you mustn't bother Herbert, Mr. Barnsworth."

Leon let the elevator door slide shut.

✢ ✢ ✢

Chuck had drawn badly in the lottery of the appeal court: three law-and-order freaks, they made Torquemada look like a Sunday-school teacher. Mr. Justice Clearihue, the new guy, had to prove he was just as mean and fucked-up as the other two more seasoned sociopaths up there, and said Chuck's client – a forger of welfare cheques – deserved what he'd got.

"A particularly sordid endeavour. I cannot see that the trial judge erred. Appeal is dismissed."

Clearihue had been a corporate lawyer, a mouthpiece for the multinationals, what did he know about real law? Tonight he gets honoured, cash bar and speeches at the Four Seasons. Chuck didn't really want to go, but there would be a chance to schmooze and make some deals.

Now he had to get down to the Old City Hall for the appearance with Harry Squire. But he had some spare time, so he walked down the corridor to the main courthouse where a trial was under way that he was too snoopy to miss. The Cartwright divorce. He couldn't believe it was going ahead. Had Ted snapped?

Ted had called Chuck last night, his voice formal, tight and tired. He understood why Chuck had sided with Carrie. One has to do what one has to do.

"And I have to do Melissa's divorce tomorrow."

"You're out of your mind."

"Wouldn't it look odd if I suddenly backed out? Wouldn't that seem suspicious?"

"Just say you got sick, for Christ's sake. My God, man, Carrie could just walk into the witness box and blow your career to smithereens."

"Carrie wouldn't do that."

What was with this guy, representing his secret lover in her divorce suit? Suicidal.

Dr. Cartwright's lawyer, Ely Church, was a very skilled tactician. If he ever discovered this incredible liaison between the plaintiff and her lawyer – well, Ted wouldn't be able to get a job selling second-hand cars.

Chuck took a seat near the back; he didn't particularly want Ted to notice him there. But Ted had all his concentration zeroed in on Melissa's husband, Dr. Yale Cartwright, the heart specialist. He was in his sixties, at least thirty years older than his wife, and though a big man and somewhat stout, he seemed frail on the stand, his face sad and contemplative. Ted was badgering him.

"That was the night you blackened her eye."

"I'm afraid it was. I'd prefer to consider it an act of self-defence."

"Oh, I see, you were afraid of Melissa Cartwright."

"She has a temper."

Melissa was sitting beside Ted, making notes, not looking up. Chuck couldn't see her expression.

"And you called her a fucking, self-seeking bitch, if you'll pardon my language. But it was your language, wasn't it? Those were your words."

"I said that. I apologize."

166

"And I believe you smashed a fine antique crystal vase during this . . . this tirade of yours."

"I regret to say, yes."

"Threw it at the wall, narrowly missing her."

"No. She was some distance away. It was childish of me, though, Mr. Barr."

Dr. Cartwright was a good witness, Chuck saw, forthright, a gentleman. He had a sense things weren't going Ted's way. Case of cruelty, open and shut, Ted had announced. Practically a case of desertion, too: her old man was never at home. The divorce grounds would be quickly proved. The real meat of the action had to do not with carving up the witness but the roast, five million dollars' worth of land, chattels, and stocks.

"And you struck her with your closed fist."

"She came at me, she . . . It was the only time I ever hit her. Things had reached a head, I suppose. And I was tense – I'd been in the operating room all night, an emergency."

"Not just that night. Five other nights that week you'd been either at the hospital or in your office working. What kind of marriage was this, Dr. Cartwright?"

"A difficult one."

Chuck saw Madam Justice Swayzee smile a little at this. She was known to be a tireless worker herself, a fair and sympathetic judge. Chuck thought Ted was on the wrong tack, being so snide with the witness, especially about his workaholism.

"I can't blame her for finally blowing up at me."

"The next day, when she announced she was seeking a divorce, you told her to just go right ahead."

"Words to that effect."

"You said you didn't love her anyway."

"That was not true."

His voice broke a little. Alarms were going off for Chuck, but apparently Ted wasn't hearing them. "Are you *denying* you said that?"

"It's not true that I don't love her."

And he broke down. The tears were terribly real, Chuck saw, the man was no actor. And he could see Ted was shaken.

Now Ely Church was speaking with just the right gentle touch. "Perhaps we should take a break, your ladyship, while the witness recovers."

"Yes, of course."

Church then pulled the plug on Ted – his timing was immaculate. "I can save my learned friend any further agony by advising him we do not dispute the specific allegations of cruelty. But we say they are insufficient. My client seeks his wife's forgiveness and their reconciliation."

"Thank you, Mr. Church," said the judge, and court was recessed.

While his lawyer tended to Dr. Cartwright, Melissa sat still at the table, a motionless beautiful mannequin. Ted turned a dismayed face to the back of the courtroom where Chuck was seated. Chuck wanted to turn invisible. But he got up and met Ted halfway up the aisle.

"It . . . isn't going too well," Ted said.

"What in hell's name do you think you're doing, Ted?"

"Can't you see?"

"See what? I see you've gone wiggy."

"Maybe I have," said Ted. "Maybe I have."

There was a kind of madness in his eyes.

Tyrone Slocum, the prosecutor on the Squire case, was tied up in another court, so Chuck had to wait around with his client. Judge Revere's court, One-Eleven, was crowded, and several members of W.A.P. were in attendance. No clothespegs this time, but they were keeping the pressure up.

The Reverend would be moving on cycle at the end of the month to 124 Court to hear the non-custody trials he'd been setting down for his own docket. The list would include Harry Squire. Chuck smiled to himself: the Reverend was going to *hate* that case.

Squire mumbled in Chuck's ear. "You sure nothing is going to happen today? God, look at all the bloody suffragettes in here. Probably the usual quota of lesbians."

Judge Revere was frowning at a woman nursing a baby in the back row.

"Madam, this is a courtroom, not a nursery."

The woman made a face and left.

Squire seemed pleased. "He's obviously anti-feminist – looks like he could be on our side. Chuck, he's going to read those things and wonder why everyone's wasting their time with this case. Most of it's just good clean fun. You swindle banks, you're a hero. You sell books, you're a leper."

When Tyrone Slocum finally arrived, Chuck beckoned Squire to follow him to the front of the court. Several women glared at them.

Judge Revere looked balefully at Squire, then riffled through the many pages of the information, the list of nine hundred and fourteen titles. Chuck had read about thirty of them. All but a few were unsalvageable, penny-dreadful pulp.

"You're late, Mr. Slocum. I don't like late." Revere waved the information, flapped its pages. "This isn't an information, it's a catalogue. How long are we setting this down for?"

"Well, now, unfortunately all these books have to be read," said Slocum. He'd already told Chuck he didn't care if Squire were convicted or not.

"They have to be *read*?"

"Can't convict a book by its cover," Chuck said brightly.

Revere's eye tic became more pronounced.

"Crown estimates seven months," said Slocum.

"We're talking *months*?" The full horror of this case seemed to dawn on the judge now.

Revere began studying the information furiously. Then he leafed through his copy of the *Criminal Code*, pausing, reading, his lips pursed.

Finally, he looked down at the lawyers, and – incredibly – a nasty little smile began working its way onto his face. Chuck didn't like this smile.

"Gentlemen," said the judge, "I think the charge just *might* be deficient. In fact, it may be a nullity."

A nullity? thought Chuck. An information that weighs about a pound and a half is a nullity? He had to admit he hadn't studied it that carefully, if the truth be known.

"It would appear that in the drafting of it, an essential word went missing," Revere said. "The charge should read the accused was *knowingly* in possession of obscene books. Section 150A."

Slocum looked uncertain. "Well, this isn't the proper time and place for us to be debating an issue of law."

But the judge wasn't going to be denied his escape route from a seven-month trial from hell. "Isn't that your argument, Mr. Tchobanian? That the charge is void?"

Here was a dilemma. Chuck could just stand there looking stupid or accept the box of chocolates the judge was extending.

"Well, I must admit I was holding that one in reserve, your honour."

"Ah, yes," said Revere, "very wily of you, counsel. *Very* clever. Your argument, I take it, is that *mens rea* is an essential averment of the charge?"

"Exactly, your honour." Chuck felt himself choking on his words. "So I'm moving for a dismissal."

"Well, Mr. Slocum, what do you have to say to *that*?"

Slocum leaned to Chuck. "Well, there goes your golden goose, pal."

Chuck looked at Squire, who seemed confused: he didn't seem to have a handle on what was going on.

Slocum told the judge, "Guess there's not much I *can* say."

"Charge is dismissed," said Revere. "Next case, please. Let's get on with the day."

16

Wearing an artificial smile but feeling trapped in a thick wet fog, Chuck escorted Harry Squire into his office. Two hundred thousand bucks, he figured, that was what the case had been worth.

Squire was talking non-stop: "Here's to Canadian justice, it's the best damned system in the world. That's the green light I wanted. I'm planning to bring in some slightly more . . . shall we say, *exotic* material from L.A. I'd like you to look at some of it, really isn't for the ladies' bridge club. Between you and me, Chuck, I think we're going to break down some barriers."

"Yeah. By the way, Harry, we kind of slapped together that lease on the Queen Street place." Chuck pulled a file from a cabinet, handed him the lease papers. "You'll want to read it over."

Squire quickly glanced at the numbers, and signed it with a flourish. "I assume this case is a precedent affirming our basic democratic rights. Would I be correct in saying it repeals a bad law?"

"Not really, Harry. Afraid it's more of a technicality."

Squire appeared dissatisfied with that. He frowned. "But I'm not guilty."

"Correct."

"Okay, so I haven't done anything wrong, and I can keep doing it."

"Yeah, but we have to hope they won't relay the charge, Harry. They could change the wording on the information."

"How can they do that? Isn't there a principle of double jeopardy? A man can't be tried twice, right?"

"I'd say just lay low for a while, don't bring in the L.A. stuff just yet."

"Well, Christ, doesn't that cheapen the victory?" He was grumpy now. "Do I get my stock back?"

"I'll see what I can do."

Chuck picked up the phone and got Tyrone Slocum on the line.

The prosecutor was almost too obliging. "Yeah, he can come and pick them up."

"Great. So you're okay about doing that?" We're going to relay the charge, that was what Chuck wanted to hear.

"Sure, never had my heart in the case, anyway. Just tell your client to keep a low profile for a while."

Chuck hid his dismay. Hanging up, he told Squire, "You've got the books back."

Beneath the beetle brows, the frown was replaced by a beaming smile. "Excellent, excellent. A deal's a deal, Chuck, and the deal was a thousand dollars a day every day you were in court for me, so I gather I owe you exactly a thousand." Squire laughed to let Chuck know he was joking. "But there'll be a little bonus."

Squire pulled a roll from his pocket and Chuck began filling with hope.

"Three thousand. I don't want to hear anyone ever say Harry Squire doesn't reward his friends."

Chuck looked at the money, smothering his rage. The skinflint, he could stuff his bonus – Chuck had pride. "Naw, Harry, I'm not going to take this. It's on the house." He stuffed the bills backs into Squire's suit pocket.

Chuck was even more depressed because Squire didn't protest, didn't offer the money back. It could've paid for a valve job on his Oldsmobile or a couple of mortgage payments on his house.

They were back to square one. Broke.

When he phoned his wife to tell her he'd be late, he discovered she'd already heard about the Squire decision from her sisters who were in court.

"Congratulations," she said coolly.

"I have a bar reception, honey. I'll be late for dinner."

"Well, you'll just have to rummage in the fridge. Emergency meeting of W.A.P. tonight."

Yeah, Chuck thought, wap Harry Squire. "Complain to the attorney general, don't complain to me. Crown screwed it up."

"Well, we *are* going to complain to the attorney general, though I don't suppose it'll do a hill of beans of good."

Chuck had evil thoughts. "Oh, it might. Put enough pressure on them, hell, they might just relay the charges."

"That's possible?"

"Not that I'm advising it, of course. Wouldn't be in the best interests of my client."

✤ ✤ ✤

Normie the Nose wasn't in the Sunrise Bar and Grill when Carrie showed up at three o'clock, a tape-recorder in her handbag. She waited for an hour and a half, sipping what seemed like a gallon of tea, and finally gave up. He'd connected, spent the hundred dollars on habit feed, and was somewhere in dreamland.

He'd make contact again when the drugs ran out. But, deciding she'd been stingy, maybe he'd do so with Mitchell instead. Hell, she thought, worse comes to worst and Mitchell gets his hands on him, no jury in the world would believe the little weasel's lies anyway.

Three-thirty. She had clients coming to the office but she was bowed with a great weight of guilt over that lost soul Blaine (or was it Blair?) Johnstone, so she took a cab to the federal prosecutors' office where her friend Marcie Diagnello handled minor Narcotics Act cases.

Diagnello was in her office, just back from court, in a good mood after a conviction. Carrie explained about her rooster-tailed client's disappearing act and got a sympathetic ear. If he was still

173

in the system, Marcie would track him down. And she would drop the marijuana charge against him – the guy had suffered enough.

"But he was probably let go, Carrie, that's why you can't find him."

Carrie left there feeling much better. Obviously, that's what had happened. The error had been discovered, some judge had atoned by sentencing him to time spent in custody, and why would he bother to call Carrie to tell her? He didn't have her name or number.

✤ ✤ ✤

Lung Chan had seen the bum earlier, lurking around the garbage cans behind his restaurant. But he'd assumed the man had gone away, no sign of him all afternoon, thank heaven.

While the kitchen was getting ready for the early dinner crowd, Lung left the restaurant for the back yard – a truck had arrived with some fish, a late delivery. As he supervised the unloading he could sense a distasteful odour, and it wasn't coming from the fish truck. Seeking its source, he ventured toward a wooden fence and stepped onto something soft.

When he looked down, he could see he was standing on someone's fingers. He gave a yelp and jumped away.

Looking apprehensively over the fence, which enclosed a few plastic garbage containers, he and the delivery men saw a body sprawled there, a scrawny man lying in what was presumably his own vomit.

It was obvious he was quite dead. No one wanted to try mouth-to-mouth resuscitation.

Members of the first unit to arrive had gone through Normie Shandler's pockets, found his ID and his works. Some detectives came by, then the medical team, and then ident officers, and finally Detective-Sergeant Jock Strachan.

"Heavy habit," said a man from the coroner's office, showing him Normie's arms. "He's in rigor, early stages. I'd say four or five hours ago."

Strachan had already checked out Normie the Nose Shandler's record, damned pathetic. And he'd run a cross-reference through the computer system – Normie had been tagged some years ago jointly with a guy named Hiltz, a drugstore heist when they were both teenagers. And Hiltz had been gunned down in that back-end operation above the Roll-a-Bowl-a-Ball.

Strachan didn't think Normie the Nose OD'd on heroin. He would have developed a strong immunity. The vomit said he'd shot up with a hot needle. Or he'd *been* shot up.

That was soon revealed to be the case. In the lab, a tech showed him some blue-tinted fluid in a test tube. "Calcium arsenate. Rat poison."

Strachan smelled a rat all right.

✢ ✢ ✢

At the end of his working day, McAnthony decided to freshen up in his private washroom before Judge Clearihue's reception – while he waited for Harold Mitchell in a surly temper.

A hesitant knock on the bathroom door. McAnthony called out: "Come in."

Mitchell walked in and stood in silence for a while as McAnthony pulled a razor through the thick shaving cream on his face.

"Guess you heard about Mr. Shandler," Mitchell said.

"Jock Strachan phoned me."

"As far as the press is concerned it's just a dirty little junkie in an alley, Oliver. We haven't released the name. We're not issuing any press bulletins about how he died. We can tell Cristal's lawyer we've got him in a safe house, he's talking –"

"Have you no ethical sense whatsoever?" McAnthony barked, and in his anger, his hand shaking, he nicked himself.

"Okay, sorry. It was a thought. We still need some time on this."

McAnthony contained himself, dabbed at the blood. "We can assume this wasn't suicide."

"Billy Sweeticide."

"He knew of this man's existence?"

"Carrington Barr's card was found crumpled in his pocket litter. Figure it out."

"So he'd seen her."

"We assume."

"She's very much on the ball. Jock Strachan told me she has a theory you were attempting to set up her client for these murders."

"Where does she get that?"

"Oh, she thinks it was all too coincidental that your Constable Lamont was in the Roll-a-Ball that night. By the way, I told Detective Strachan about the bug in the film loft. He was, to put the matter mildly, in an absolute fury that the RCMP has been working at cross-purposes with the Metro homicide division."

"It's a sting, Oliver," Mitchell said quietly.

"What kind of sting?" McAnthony rinsed his razor, then towelled his face.

"Operation Sweet. Operation Sweet Revenge is the long form. The superintendent gave me a blank cheque to take him down. How I did it was up to me."

"I gave you the time you wanted, a few days to catch up with this Norman Shandler. I did that because you said his life was at risk. Now he is dead. And now I intend to tell opposing counsel that you had surveillance outside the film loft and an illegal wiretap within it. I am going to tell her you deceived me."

Mitchell moaned in dismay. "Christ. Where will that leave us?"

"The wiretap is inadmissible. I will have to argue that doesn't taint the surveillance evidence. You will testify you saw Schlizik and Cristal exit from the same vehicle outside the bowling alley. And then you will pray for a conviction, because if we don't get one your career as a police officer is over. I'd say your chances are substantially less than even."

There was silence as McAnthony buttoned his shirt and straightened his tie. Finally, he turned from the mirror and looked at Mitchell for a response.

Mitchell was leaning against the wall, studying the ceiling. He emitted a deep sigh. "Okay, you're right, I've been an asshole. I've been playing it too cagey. So what if we cut a deal with Carrington Barr? We drop against Cristal if he rolls over for us."

McAnthony had already considered this possibility. "Yes, I suppose it's a way to save your hide, though I somewhat doubt Carrington would go along with it. She may want to take her chances on a trial – she has all the chips."

Mitchell came closer, lowered his voice. "You can tell her we have someone inside Billy's organization who can finger Cristal."

McAnthony reacted with surprise. "You have a spy?"

Mitchell took a while, as if working on his phrasing. "You can tell her those are your instructions."

"Do I hear you correctly, Inspector? You want me to *divulge* this fact?"

"Actually, yeah."

"Word will get to Billy Sweet."

Mitchell shrugged. "Maybe it will smoke the prick out."

"This sounds like a very dangerous game."

"It's a sting, Oliver. Stings aren't played by Queensberry rules."

McAnthony understood then, from the nuances, that Mitchell was playing another of his games. There was no spy, of course; Mitchell was simply giving him the means to twist Carrington Barr's arm. He was filled anew with distrust for Mitchell. But there was not much point in trying to second-guess this hard-nosed cop with his single-minded devotion to ending the career of Billy Sweet. It was a cause McAnthony shared.

"I'll talk to Carrington," he said.

✦ ✦ ✦

Leon looked up from his desk as Carrie loomed in his doorway, fixing him with those big, maddening, green eyes.

"Come on, Leon," said Carrie, "we're going to that reception."

"I can't do it."

"Don't be a poop. It's five o'clock, we'll be late."

Leon stayed glued to his chair. "I can't handle the hypocrisy, not to mention the pomposity." He struggled with what he was about to say. "I have a better idea."

"Shoot."

"Why don't we have dinner instead?"

"You and me?"

Did she find that preposterous? Friends have dinner together. It happens all the time.

"I can stay here and do some work, and . . . you know, meet you after the reception?" How like a schoolboy he felt, stammering, his Adam's apple bobbing.

"Oh, Leon, I'd love to. Not tonight, I'm really bushed. Can we do a rain check on it? Maybe this weekend?"

Leon forced a smile. "Well, um, Mom was interested in having you over for dinner."

"Maybe she's going to try to line us up, Leon." Then she smiled, as if assuming Leon shared the humour, the manifest absurdity of it all.

Yes, it could be a disaster; his militant mother would embarrass him with a non-stop harangue. She'd left a message on his machine: she'd heard he was acting for some kind of Nazi.

"Listen, I'm going to beg off from that. How about just the two of us? You could come over Saturday – I'll do something special."

"I love your cooking, Leon. Sure, that'd be great."

The Bar Association had rented a salon in the Four Seasons to pay homage to Mr. Justice Clearihue – a cocktail-hour reception – and Carrie showed up late. The firewater had been flowing freely – the two hundred or so barristers here were becoming quite loud, a roar of loosened lawyers' tongues.

She saw Chuck gulping a drink at one end of the cash bar. Then she spotted Ted. Oh, God – she hadn't even guessed he'd come to this thing. There he was with a couple of divorce-court comrades. Not doing much talking, though, just listening, sort of sad-looking. Why was he not with Melissa, emboldening her for another hard day in court? How had the divorce gone today?

She wanted to turn on her heels, to flee, but something momentarily held her.

Suddenly it seemed as if everyone's eyes were on her as she stood hesitantly near the entrance. Gossip races like wildfire˙ through the legal community, and no doubt they all knew about her and Ted. To add fuel, they had seen him come in alone, and now her, and she couldn't retreat with dignity intact.

Chuck spotted her and waved her over. She'd have one quick drink and go. Maybe she should have taken Leon up on his dinner invitation for tonight – she felt bad about her refusal, he'd seemed lonely, in need of company.

From the corner of her eye, she saw Ted looking at her now, too. She put on a face that said, hey, I'm tough, independent, cheating husbands don't faze me, and she moved to the bar to join the lineup for drinks. There she was intercepted by Oliver McAnthony, who was looking very serious.

"Carrington, I have something to discuss if you can afford me a moment."

"Absolutely."

"Let me batter my way through this defensive line and buy you a drink."

"White wine, that's very kind, Oliver."

A spoon clinked against a glass, and the room hushed a little, and behind a backdrop of sodden, murmuring voices came the words of the president of the Toronto Bar Association, a ladder-climber whose name Carrie couldn't recall.

"The honour has fallen to me, ladies and gentlemen, to speak of greatness. To speak of honour and honesty. To speak of humour and humility. To speak of Thomas Gerard Clearihue."

Carrie joined Chuck, who was in an unhappy mood.

"Guess you heard about Harry Squire getting off. The milch cow has dried up. The tightwad offered me peanuts. I threw it back in his face. We're going to be on our uppers again if you don't bring in that three hundred grand."

"To no other practising lawyer could I say with such confidence, Thomas Clearihue, you've paid your dues."

"Now we've got to start paying ours," Chuck said, a little too audibly.

"Past treasurer of the Law Society and of the Canadian Bar Association –"

"Two-faced power-hungry opportunist. This guy's never been outside a boardroom in his life. He's a hammer in court, you should've seen him in action today."

"Will you all raise your glasses in honour of a new and vigorous presence in the highest court of this province: Mr. Justice Thomas Clearihue."

Chuck pantomimed being sick all over his shoes. His voice went lower: "Ted's here."

"I know. I'm going to hang around for a few minutes and smile a lot and then make a run for it."

"He's acting very odd. I watched him in court, he's blowing it."

"He, what . . . he's handling it *himself*? His girlfriend's divorce?"

"I'm kind of worried about him."

"Yes, we must weep tears for Ted."

This was interrupted as McAnthony finally escaped from the bar with her wine and his Scotch. He motioned her to follow him to a quiet corner.

"I'm afraid you've been done a small wrong, Carrie."

"I'm getting used to it." She smiled. "Not from you."

McAnthony didn't respond to that. She assumed he either didn't know about her breakup with Ted or was too courteous to acknowledge it.

"Perhaps we might want to sit down." But there wasn't a chair nearby.

"What is it?" she said. "I can take it."

"I haven't given you full disclosure. Facts have been withheld from me. You may assume that someone was playing childish games with us."

Ring around the rosy, she thought. With Harold the Bullet

Mitchell, no doubt. She had been right to be suspicious of him. How bad was this going to be?

McAnthony told her about the listening device in the prop loft and the surveillance unit outside. He told her that Hollis Lamont, the supposedly off-duty bowler, was actually working that night. "And Cristal was seen arriving in the car with Schlizik."

Oddly, what bothered her most about this sudden deluge of bad news was that André Cristal had lied to her – he *had* been partnered with Billy Sweet's number-one gunman on the night of these murders. Her faith in his innocence, half-hearted at best, was now shattered, and she was both saddened and angry at Cristal – and at herself for having been too easily misled.

"Mitchell . . . he had court authorization for this wiretap?"

"No."

"Well, he should be bloody charged." Stay calm, she told herself. She was trying to weigh all this, wondering how much the Crown's case had hardened.

"There's more, Carrie. There was a witness."

Of course, thought Carrie, the undercover unit would have spotted Normie. "Did you say 'was'?"

"He now exists in the past tense. One Norman Shandler, an addict."

She felt numb as he told her of Normie's death today. As she had waited for him in the Sunrise Bar and Grill, he had been lying dead in an alleyway behind it. Billy Sweet had done it – how had he found out he was there?

Then she thought: she had pointed out that restaurant to André Cristal, had told him Normie would be meeting her there. Now Carrie was feeling woozy.

"Your card was found in his pocket."

"He was trying to sell evidence, Oliver. He'd have been a terrible witness for either side."

"All that having been said, Carrington, I want to offer a proposition. Do you think your client will turn Crown's evidence?"

"For a dismissal?" She hadn't even contemplated that possibility.

"New name, new town, new job – I suspect I can give him money. But he has to give us Billy Sweet in return."

Cristal couldn't, she knew that. And she was sure he would not inform on Leonard Woznick. Or would he? Maybe he was capable of that, of anything. Surely he hadn't murdered Normie. No. Impossible.

"I'll have to seek instructions, Oliver. I'm not sure if he'll do that."

"I'm authorized to tell you another witness may be available who can point a more definite finger at your client, Carrie."

"Who, for instance?"

"Someone they have inside. I leave this information to your utter discretion."

Carrie tried to compose herself. She wanted to continue this intriguing discussion, but McAnthony raised his glass in a salute to her and discreetly turned to go. He'd seen Ted Barr bearing down on them.

There was no escape, and Carrie just sipped her wine and waited for him. He looked wan, distant, as if only a part of him was here. André Cristal and Normie's murder and deals with the Crown were suddenly shunted to the back of the brain. Her heart began to race. What causes this? The man is a jerk.

"I'm not interrupting?"

"No. How are you, Ted?"

"Do you care?"

"Frankly, no."

"I don't blame you. I know how much I hurt you."

"No you don't."

"Well, since you asked, I feel awful. I must have lost my touch in court today. It didn't go well."

"Oh, dear, you won't get all that money." She was sounding too caustic, she couldn't help it.

"Money?" He looked directly at her, pain radiating from him. "Who gives a shit about money?"

"What do you give a shit about, Ted?"

"I give a shit about . . ." And he stopped. "They're having dinner together. Melissa and her husband. The judge practically ordered them to, she . . . What a royal bitch the judge is. Anyway, I told Melissa to go through the motions, hear the poor slob out, she knows it's over, absolutely nothing between them . . ."

He may have realized he was muttering almost incoherently, and his voice trailed off.

"What in heaven's name is wrong with you, Ted?"

"Don't you see?"

"No, I don't see."

"That's funny. I thought it was obvious."

Then, before Ted spoke his next words, she saw. And she felt a stirring of nausea within her, had to fight it. Her fingers trembled as she tilted the rest of the wine down her throat.

"Melissa and I are on some kind of . . . cosmic wavelength. I don't know what it is – we laugh at the same jokes, we just kill ourselves sometimes, the same kind of books, the same kind of movies, whatever, tennis, the outdoors. The sex, it's incredible. It's like the gods matched us."

In a fury, Carrie slapped his face.

17

As Carrie walked quickly up Bloor Street, the ugly scene in the Four Seasons Hotel salon returned in waves and echoes, the stares, the gasps, the shame, the terrible expression on Ted's face. Unbelieving, beyond shock.

Had she slapped him awake, or merely addled his brains all the more?

Who gives a shit about money?

So it wasn't Melissa's millions, it was the knife of love, a horrid obsession that had blinded him, had cauterized all his senses. *We laugh at the same jokes, we just kill ourselves sometimes.*

In turmoil, she'd decided to walk to the Park Plaza – she needed the fresh air, needed to clear her head. She likes to walk, André Cristal said he had seen it in her legs. Yes, she must sit down with him, discuss this offer of clemency, do the things that lawyers do. Ask him about Normie Shandler, ask him bluntly if he killed him.

She rang his room from a lobby phone and was about to give up when he finally answered.

"*Allô?*"

"It's Carrie. I'm downstairs."

"I am t'rough in the shower. Come up."

Carrie waited for a discreet few minutes to let him dress.

When he answered her knock, he had slacks on but was bare-chested. His shoulders and chest seemed made of rock.

"How was your day?"

"I run maybe fifteen miles. Then some shopping for clothes. Then I run again, maybe twelve miles this time." He put on a loose-fitting shirt, silk, expensive.

"Are you going out?" she asked.

"Maybe. For dinner."

With whom? That young want-to-be law student from Montreal, Ms. Woznick?

"I won't keep you then," she said.

"Be comfortable, please. I 'ave wine, a fine estate Lafitte – can I offer you?"

"No, but thank you." She wanted a drink, though, something to help drown the memory of Ted's last ugly speech. Business, she told herself. Concentrate on business.

She sat in an armchair and watched him carefully, curious – would he lie about being in that car with Schlizik?

"The police were outside the bowling alley that night. They saw you and Schlizik pull up in a car."

"That is what they say?"

Just a smile. He didn't bat an eye.

"They are anxious to convict me. I am sure you will prove in court that they lie about this, Carrington."

His casual self-assurance suddenly had her in doubt again – she wouldn't put it past the Bullet to create evidence. And that other little piece of intelligence that McAnthony had passed on – the mole inside Billy Sweet's network – could that also be a smoke screen? Indeed, was André Cristal, as he had intimated, being set up for a fall?

"They also say there is a spy in Billy's organization, and that he can tie you into these murders. I'm not sure if that's true, though."

"Why do you t'ink they suddenly tell you all this business?"

"I think . . ." Well, yes, it was becoming apparent. "I think they want to put pressure on you to make a deal." *I leave this information to your utter discretion.* That's what McAnthony had said, the fox. He and Mitchell had conspired.

When she described the terms that McAnthony had offered, he did react, a surprised face, a low whistle.

"That is a very *good* deal."

"They want Billy Sweet, though."

Cristal sat on the bed, pulled out his makings and began to roll a cigarette, looking up only when Carrie told him about the death of Normie the Nose.

"Behind the Sunrise Bar and Grill, André, you remember I pointed it out to you."

"I remember."

"Well?"

"Well what?"

"I don't think anyone else knew he would be showing up there."

He continued making his cigarette. "Carrington, you disappoint me." Now he turned angry. "*Merde!* I am on bail for one murder, do you t'ink I would do another? I am innocent! Innocent of everyt'ing!"

"I know you say that, but –"

"Why don't you ask the cops? Everywhere I go they follow me. I run all along the Don River, there is a car behind me. *Les boeufs.* Ask your Inspector Mitchell where I was today."

"Okay. I have your point."

"This Normie, he was on Billy Sweet's list. Maybe I am, too. Maybe that is why he 'as put up bail, so he could kill me. A new identity is a good way to keep my 'ealth."

"It could mean implicating Leonard Woznick."

"I would never t'ink of doing that. But . . . maybe I can get something on Billy so they can drop my charge." He seemed to be concentrating hard. Then he blew out a stream of smoke, and looked at her with a strange glint in his eye. "If that is the police offer, I wonder how much Billy will bid?"

"I'm not interested in that kind of game, André."

"No game, an auction."

186

"I really don't like your laissez-faire attitude about this, André."

"Pardon me. Maybe I am talking crazy." He got up from the bed and put on a tie, carefully knotted it. "Let me t'ink about their offer, Carrington."

"Well, I should go, you have a date." Carrie couldn't help herself: "Anyone I know?"

"Waitress in the bar downstairs."

Fast worker, here's another two-timer – wasn't he practically engaged to Lenore Woznick?

The phone rang. "*Allô?* Yes, I will meet you in, say ten minute? If you do not mind to wait?"

Carrie propelled herself to her feet. "I'm off."

Cristal saw her to the door. "That is a . . . you say, exquisite? Exquisite dress. I t'ink you have very much taste. A lady."

"Thank you."

"But – can I say? – sometime I t'ink not a 'appy lady. Maybe there are other things in your 'ead that worry you more than a little murder trial."

"Maybe there are." She had tried to block Ted from her mind, but couldn't now. *The sex, it's incredible. It's like the gods matched us.*

Somehow she summoned a bright smile. "Well. Please come by my office. Ten o'clock."

He opened the door for her, but held her there for a moment. "What is it you like about this work, this criminal law, Carrington? Is it because it is work that is close to the edge, where you like to be?"

"I'm not sure if I do." Her life recently had been *much* too close to the edge.

"You go to dangerous places to meet criminals, you ride with gangsters in cars, you talk to a man who is murder the same day. It is how I see you, close to the edge. I t'ink about you sometime, my lady lawyer. But maybe you are not such a lady in court, eh?"

"I don't suppose I am, really."

"But always a lady with me."

187

She saw something in his eyes that was knowing and wry, something that seemed to penetrate her mask of calm professionalism, that made her feel slightly . . . unclothed.

She fled before he could offer his electric hand.

In the lobby, she still felt buzzed with his emanations, which were all mixed up with those very different ones from Ted and his incredible cosmic wavelength. Love. Melissa.

How transported Ted had seemed. And representing his mistress in her divorce . . . My God, she thought, it is *he* who is having the nervous breakdown.

She didn't leave the lobby right away, but looked around to see if she could spot the surveillance, one of Mitchell's cops. No likely candidates. Nor was any young, pretty waitress hanging about the lobby. Cristal was entirely too attractive, an unrepentant flirt – it was not surprising he could make opposite-sex friends so quickly. Sexy hit man. For a hit man is what he surely was. Removed from his magnetic presence, Carrie's doubts in him were restored. He'd seemed a little too keen on that deal to be innocent.

No alluring waitress showed up, but after a few minutes someone Carrie recognized did. Big Leonard Woznick. Heading for the elevator. She doubted he was here looking for a game of bridge. The wiry little man looked distinctly unhappy.

Carrie was confused. Was he an unexpected visitor, or was this Cristal's date? A liaison between Cristal and Woznick was one she had distinctly advised against. Obviously, Cristal had told him where to find him.

She assumed Cristal's friend and patron was here to convey a message of concern from the paranoid Billy Sweet. Should she walk in, catch them at this secret meeting? No, tomorrow she would talk to Cristal, and if he lied to her, she'd be comfortable in her doubts about the man.

She left the hotel, not looking forward to returning to her sad, lonely house.

In Cristal's room, Leonard Woznick's fingers were clasping a bottle of Löwenbräu that Cristal had fetched him from the bar fridge. Cristal noticed the knuckles of his friend's hand were showing white and that Woznick was grinning in a strained way. He was finishing a joke.

"He says, 'No, Doc, the liniment's for my arms. The girls never showed up.'"

He laughed harder than he had to at his own story. "The girls never showed up!"

Cristal chuckled. "Lennie, you kill me." He turned a corkscrew into his Château Lafitte.

"So how's everything, how's it all goin', they treatin' you all right in this town? You gettin' any action here?"

"I 'ave enough action. How's Lenore?"

"The same, you know. Great. She misses you." Woznick stretched out his arms – he seemed uncomfortable. He walked to the window. "Hey, that's somethin', that view."

"Take your jacket off," Cristal said. It was too warm for such a bulky jacket. Leonard wasn't very good at this.

But Woznick kept the jacket on. "I gotta take a leak. Beer, it just goes through me. I had two in the bar downstairs." He went into the washroom.

Cristal carefully poured himself a glass of wine, held it to the light, admired the ruby colour. He heard Woznick's loud peeing into the toilet bowl, heard his loud, tight voice, another joke, a two-liner.

When Woznick came from the bathroom his two shaking hands were directing a .32 revolver and a silencer toward Cristal. Gun still extended, he moved cautiously toward the bed and perched on it.

Cristal sipped his wine. "This is anod'er joke?"

"It ain't a funny one."

Cristal wondered: was this, then, what had been predicted? For he'd had a premonition of betrayal. No, he couldn't see it coming from Leonard. It wouldn't happen here and now. He suddenly knew that clearly, and this helped him to relax.

"This is not the work you do, Lennie. This is work for a professional." Casually, he drew on his cigarette.

"If you're gonna name names, you're gonna name mine."

189

Woznick took one hand from his gun, wiped his sweaty palm on his jacket.

"You took me in when I was broke. Do you t'ink I would rat on you?"

Woznick breathed heavily, his face lined with despair.

"Do you t'ink you can look Lenore in the face? You old *caba-chon*, I love your daughter, I want to marry her. This is crazy, it is ridiculous, a very bad joke." He blew two perfect smoke rings. "Lennie, *sacrifice*, you can't do it. You know that."

Woznick, shattered, lowered the gun and his whole body began shaking. "It means they'll kill me."

"They'll thank you."

"Why?"

"I can save Billy's skin. And yours. Everyone's."

Woznick looked up at him through bleak, raw eyes.

"There's an informer. Someone inside. I found out who he is."

Cristal saw the hope in his face. "You sure?"

"Absolutely."

"Who is it?"

Cristal shook his head. "I can tell you he is very close to the top. Explain to Billy I want to talk to his face. I will tell Billy, no one else. Tell him I need to be looked after, I'll need money, 'eavy money. I will 'ave a few expense. I may 'ave to disappear for a while after this t'ing is over."

Cristal gently removed the gun from Woznick's grip, and knelt and took the older man's hands in his own. "I am very angry that they try to make you do this."

"I'm ashamed."

"Be ashame for them. Billy will pay for this. *Beaucoup d'ar-gent.*"

Now he broke the revolver and emptied the shells from it, then returned the gun to Woznick. "There. It is safer. You won't shoot yourself in the foot, Lennie."

Woznick handed it back. "No, I want you should keep it. Maybe you gotta look after yourself."

Cristal shrugged, set it on a table.

190

"Who told you about this informer?" Woznick said.

Cristal hesitated. "My lawyer. She is a very good friend with the prosecutor."

Carrie sat in her living room seeking solace from Mozart, the clarinet quintet, music she thought might lift her mood. But her brain was still filled with Cristal, with Normie Shandler, with deals. With Ted. With the enormity of his having given his heart to another.

A noise outside, a dog barking, a distant male shout: "Get away! Get away!"

The Llewellyns' terrier, always yapping at someone. Carrie went to the window, but it was dark outside, almost midnight. She thought she could make out a man lumbering down the street, the dog at his heels, and she heard Mrs. Llewellyn calling from the front stoop: "Bingo! Bad dog! Bingo, come here!"

Suddenly Carrie felt exhausted. Another major day tomorrow.

That night Carrie had dreams of André Cristal. She was dancing with him in a nineteenth-century ballroom, and he wore a dress uniform. Now Ted was on the dance floor, too, his eyes wide and frightened. I have to speak to you, he kept saying. But she and Cristal danced on and on, his electricity flowing into her.

18

Leon was staring out his office window – not meditating: day-dreaming, mostly about Carrie – when Chuck wandered in with his morning coffee, and said, "You should've been there."

He then began describing in excruciating detail the drama of the slap heard around the world. How ghastly, Leon thought. Poor Carrie. Poor Ted. Leon was thankful he hadn't been at that function, the pain could not have been borne.

"She stalked out. Everyone stopped talking. You could've heard a pin drop. Ted stood around with a kind of puzzled look on his face for a few minutes before he left."

Leon wondered: What could he have said to her? What insult, what words could have been so cruel to cause Carrington to react that way in public?

The phone rang, and Leon answered.

"Uh, oh, Leon, it's me." Ted's voice, distant and hesitant. "I've got a . . . a problem, I . . . is Chuck there?"

Leon passed the phone over, and Chuck listened for a minute without expression. Finally he spoke: "I'll come right over." And he hung up.

"What?"

"I don't know, the worst, maybe. He sounded pretty garbled."
Chuck rushed away.

Leon envisaged Ted sorrowfully studying a vial of poison – he sounded as if he was in a total funk – Leon thought again of Carrie – he yearned to help her through this, but didn't know how.

Chuck found Ted where he had been told to expect him, in an office on the fourteenth floor of Royce Boggs's office complex on Richmond Street. Ted's door was closed, and no receptionist was outside it, so Chuck just knocked and walked in.

Ted, with tennis racket in hand, wearing a business suit, was listlessly bouncing a ball off the far wall of this massive, sterile office, stroking it softly on the rebound, never missing. His back was to Chuck.

"So what happened?" Chuck said.

Ted didn't turn around. *Clop, bounce, clop.* "The divorce action will be dismissed by consent, parties to bear their own costs. We worked it out this morning."

"She's gone back to Dr. Cartwright, eh?"

"She told me she was breaking his heart. She couldn't stand his pain."

"Yeah. She started worrying about that broken heart when she saw she was going to lose everything. Best thing that could have happened. She was a fucking mistake, Ted."

This time, Ted caught the ball in his hand. He turned around. He'd been crying: his eyes were red. Chuck didn't know whether to feel sad or disgusted.

"Carrie will have a good laugh," Ted said. His face suddenly twisted into a kind of sick grin.

"Yeah, she might find the irony amusing."

Ted hurled the ball at the thick pane window, and it caromed off his desk and against a wall, bringing down Ted's law degree with a tinkle of broken glass.

"I hate this office," he said. "I hate Royce Boggs, and I hate his work. I screwed up a contract for him. He's stopped inviting me up to the executive lounge."

"You're falling apart." To Chuck, this seemed obvious: the different parts of Ted were scattering to the winds.

"I've been an utter prick."

"Couldn't agree more."

193

"A ridiculous fool."

"Right on."

"Melissa, she . . . she ruined me. I can't believe . . . She . . . she said she loved me! I've been a blind, stupid, total fucking dunce!" He swung his racket at his desk lamp and sent it crashing to the floor.

Chuck grabbed him by both shoulders.

"You'd better wire yourself back together, buddy, you're losing it."

Ted's taut body seemed to slowly relax. "Please help me, Chuck."

"I'll clear my day. Let's meet at noon at the Kew Gardens courts."

Ted nodded. "Yeah. You'll probably beat me. Make the day a total losing experience."

Ted seemed to pull himself together, and Chuck felt it was safe to leave. At the door, Ted said, "Tell Carrie how lucky she is to be rid of me."

Exhausted by her day, Carrie had slept in until late that Wednesday morning, but decided to walk to the office anyway. When she arrived she found André Cristal already in the waiting room.

"You're on time. I thought your plans for last night might have kept you up late. The waitress in the bar downstairs." Carrie tried to smile disarmingly, but couldn't keep a nagging tone from her voice.

"I 'ave to talk to you about that."

"If you want to confess, I'm not a priest."

He laughed. "Carrington, I fibbed about the waitress."

She led him to her office. "Explain."

"The date was with Leonard Woznick," Cristal said.

Carrie was pleased at this frankness, but spoke sternly. "I dislike being lied to, André. And I thought I told you to stay away from him."

194

"I know. But I want to meet Billy Sweet. I want to give him to the police. To perform my end of the bargain."

"You're putting your life in danger."

"It already is. Leonard had a revolver. He had orders to execute me."

Carrie was shocked. "What happened?"

"Big Leonard, he could never do that. He is an old marshmallow. Maybe he just tried to scare me. Anyway, I told him I 'ave to meet Billy."

"André, I think things are getting out of hand here."

"I know what I am doing, Carrington."

"I don't like losing clients."

"I t'ink you don't like to lose, period. But you will win. I will give them Billy, and you will win our case." He puffed contentedly on a cigarette. "How much, do you t'ink, they will pay me, the police?"

"I can't believe how much gall you have. Are you trying to get it from both ends?"

"Maybe more fee for you, Carrington. We split it, everything the police pay."

"I am absolutely amazed at you."

He flashed his big smile. "They are all bastards, this horseman Mitchell, Billy Sweet, I want to bleed them. The bail moneys you 'ave, that is petty cash."

A bit of the con artist in this man, she decided. Real rogue. But a brave one, if not foolhardy.

"We can win a verdict, André. You don't have to take the deal."

"Now what I need is a small tape-recorder."

"I'm sure the police –"

"No police. I do this on my own. When I 'ave the evidence, you can ask them how much it is worth. Lump sum, never mind the safe 'ouse and the change of name. A million dollars, that is a good starting point?"

"And you want to scam Billy Sweet for a few million more. For agreeing *not* to turn him in."

"Let him sue me."

"This is preposterous."

"But maybe . . . fun, too?" His eyes were bright and hard upon her, mischief in them . . . something else, almost a little crazy. "I, also, I like it close to the edge. I do not get bored there."

The man was showing Carrie new dimensions, and they frightened her a little, but she also felt oddly attracted to the scoundrel in him – like a rascal thief played by David Niven or Cary Grant. She remembered last night's dream, dancing with him, the electricity that flowed from his hands.

"I'm not sure, André."

"Do you tell me not to? Is it your advice?"

She thought a long while about that. She couldn't tell him what to do with his life. The cause of closing the books on Billy Sweet was not an ignoble one. She thought of Trixi Trimble, wired, wasting her life.

"If you give me those instructions . . . okay. But I don't want to hear anything more about extorting money from Sweet."

"Then you 'ave 'eard nothing."

"I think it's a very, *very* dangerous kind of business."

"Those who don't risk don't live. But I will be careful. I am moving 'otels."

"How will Sweet's people contact you?"

"I don't want to involve you, Carrington, but . . . they will probably phone you."

"Well, that does involve me, doesn't it?"

"I t'ink they will understand you are just doing your job . . . Okay, it is a bad idea, I will not put my lady lawyer in danger." But he was looking intently at her, challenging.

"Oh, heck, do it . . . Keep in touch with me. We'll see how it's going. We can always call a halt."

Cristal stood, paused, looked at the wall: her degrees, her father's large mounted photograph, a wedding photo of her and Ted that she had not got around to throwing in the garbage.

She scribbled a note. "Here's my home phone number, don't give it out. Oh, and don't forget, you're in court tomorrow to set a date for your preliminary."

She walked him to her door, and there he put his hand lightly on her arm. She saw that Leon was standing just outside his office door, watching them. Cristal wheeled and walked away briskly.

"That's André Cristal?" Leon said. He came into her office.

"Yep."

"Not what I imagined. Clean-cut."

"He's . . . different. Guess you heard I slugged Ted last night."

"He's a wreck. Chuck has gone off to see him."

"The heart bleeds."

"Carrie, the dinner at my place Saturday, if you really feel you're going to be crowded . . ."

"No, that's on, definitely, I need to get away from all this craziness. What are your working on?"

"I have this nasty legal-aid case tomorrow, a rape, some schlemiel who attacked a girl in his truck."

"Poor Leon."

✢ ✢ ✢

Speeder Cacciati pulled up to Billy Sweet's guardhouse, flicked the gatekeeper a wave, then drove into the yard. He could smell Big Leonard Woznick beside him, the little jerk was reeking with fuckin' fear, he deserved to. Speeder was just glad he was not in his shoes. Billy was waiting. Wednesday brunch with Billy.

Last night Big Leonard was supposed to have hit Cristal, but the hit never happened, and Big Leonard had prepared a goulash of a story that Billy wasn't going to like. Bring him in, Billy had said on the phone this morning.

"You sure he ain't mad at me?" said Leonard.

"Billy? Naw, he's a real understanding guy. He'll have a chuckle over how the Frenchman shmooched the heater offa you." He rammed a big slab of Dubble Bubble into his mouth, and braked in front of Billy's brick fortress. Humphries and Deeley were across on the lawn, just lounging there, watching. So were Elvis and Izzie, the two boys who did such a good job on Normie the Nose with the rat poison.

Anonymous tip came in on that one, on the pager service, about where to find Normie. Speeder had kind of put out word on

197

the street they were looking, and he guessed some good Samaritan called in, maybe some guy who had a beef with the Nose.

One of the manservants opened the door and ushered them into the presence of Billy, in his big front parlour with all the books he never reads. Speeder saw he was smiling, but he didn't think it went very deep.

"Big Leonard," Billy said in a big, welcoming voice.

"Hey, Billy, you're lookin' great."

"The sun room, gentlemen," Billy said, waving them to the door. "How do you like your eggs? I'll tell the cook."

The sun room was a kind of greenhouse with tinted glass. Billy had fixed it up to look like something out of Hawaii: palm trees in pots and a fountain with a volcano and lava and a waterfall and a little beach scene.

A white garden-type table had place mats and cutlery on it for three, and after Billy put their orders in he motioned Big Leonard to a chair, and sat across from him. Speeder didn't sit, he felt a little jumpy, what with the pills he'd been doing and all, and he was worried that he was going to have to do something here for Billy, something not nice. Billy, who don't like to talk on the phone, didn't make his plans none too clear this morning.

He picked at his elbow – psoriasis, the doctor said, the skin was coming off like corn flakes. He made gum bubbles and listened to the friendly conversation that was going on, Big Leonard answering Billy's inquiries as to his health and everything.

The eggs came, and after the servant left, Billy asked Big Leonard how it went with the Frenchman last night.

"First of all, he don't want to squeal on no one," Woznick said.

Billy, with his big smile, said: "That's nice. That's nice that you tell us that. But it's not the news we wish to hear, Big Leonard." He stuck a fork into his fried egg, and mixed the orange goop up with the white.

"I coulda greased him, no problem, but I decided, you know, to squeeze some information from him, and it's lucky I did, Billy. Real lucky."

"Lucky for whom? Are *you* feeling lucky, Big Leonard?"

Woznick flinched a little. "He told me he knows something. I figgered it was worth saving his life. He's on your side, Billy, 900 per cent. Loyal like a brother. He helped knock off those guys for you, Billy, Perez and Hiltz, he told me about it, how Schlizik got hit and he had to finish the job alone. Yeah, he made some threatening noises, but only 'cause he had to get out on bail. He's got some information he wants to tell you."

Big Leonard was talking too quick, getting it out too disorganized. Speeder wasn't interested in breakfast right now. He was just watching Billy, waiting for the reaction.

"What does he know that could possibly be worth saving his life?" Billy asked, still nice as apple pie.

Woznick gulped down some scrambled eggs, chewed and swallowed and cleared his throat. "He says there's a narc inside. He knows who it is."

Speeder saw Billy blink a couple of times, that was all. Then his face started going a couple of shades lighter and his upper lip started quivering.

"It's a lie," he said in a tight voice, "and you bought it."

"Yeah, Big Leonard," said Speeder, "you bought it."

Woznick whirled in his chair to face him, but Speeder just grinned back. He had a piece in his pants pocket, loaded, he was ready whenever Billy said.

"Billy, I swear, I think it's the right goods —"

Billy cut him off, yelling: "Shut up! You're a stupid idiot! He scammed you!"

Woznick began talking, if possible, even more rapidly, sort of like he was pleading for his life. "Billy, we could end up kicking ourselves you don't ask André no questions. What's the harm? He wants to meet you, he doesn't want to tell no one else, the stoolie is high up, Billy, I think he's someone who got tight with you."

"There is no stoolie!"

"Turns out he's lying, Billy, I'll take him out, I promise. But if he's telling the truth, we're all going down the tube we don't do nothin'."

The servant put this conversation into stall by coming in and picking up some empty dishes and pouring more coffee. By the time he left Billy had calmed himself, had got some of his colour back.

"How does Mr. Cristal claim to know this information?"

"He found out through his lawyer."

Speeder saw that Billy was now a little hooked on this idea. He still remained behind Woznick, waiting for the word.

"How would she know?"

"Lawyers, they're in the loop, Billy, they hear this stuff. She's tight with the prosecutor. André, he kinda like promised her not to tell no one."

"Did he say he was a cop, Big Leonard? Or just an ordinary, garden-variety rat?"

"I got the impression a cop . . . Maybe I'm wrong."

"How high up?"

"So high up André only wants to talk to you about it, Billy." Big Leonard took a big gulp of coffee. He was bolder now, more confident, he had Billy mulling things over. "After he skips bail, he's gonna be on the run, and I told him you'd wanna look after him, Billy, maybe a few shekels to tide him over. He says leave a message with Carrington Barr, he'll meet anywhere, we'll make sure he's clean, no artillery on him or nothin'."

Billy looked up at Speeder. "Speed?"

Speeder slipped his hand into his pocket, around the gun butt. Woznick, turning again quickly, looked at the hand there, gripping something hard, and Big Leonard started stammering. "Speeder . . . listen, please, Billy –"

"Speed, are you still hawking those tickets to your Italian street carnival?"

Speeder was puzzled. "Yeah, well, for the charity night there at St. Francis of Assisi hall. Why?"

"I want you to drop one off to this Frenchman's lawyer with a note for him."

Speeder eased his fingers from his pocket, and used them to scratch his elbow. He had to hand it to Big Leonard, he got to Billy real good, just in time.

"Yeah, that's the idea," said Woznick, "fix up a meet, talk to André in a crowd, it's the best cover. Hey, Billy, he's okay. He's solid. Right in there. Jeez, well, I should get going." He eased his chair back. "I'll just call a taxi, have it meet me by the gate."

He didn't seem to know whether to shake Billy's hand or not, just had it sort of hanging out there. Speeder watched Billy slowly wipe a napkin over his lips, then rise. He finally extended his hand. "Have a nice day, Big Leonard."

After Woznick left there was silence. Speeder dabbed at his breakfast: the thrusters he'd been taking had ruined his appetite. He was waiting for Billy to start reacting, a little morning stroll down Paranoid Lane.

"This Cristal," Billy said, "does he think he's playing with children? A narc on the inside. What a joke." He rose, smiling, shaking his head, and left the sun room. Speeder could see him heading for the stairs to the games room.

Speeder grabbed his coffee and followed him. He didn't like the way Billy had become over the years this bundle of nerves. He had started off as a gutsy guy when Speeder first knew him. A gunner, he started off as, he had blasted the old Fischetti crowd right out of town and then went right to the top of the pyramid. But what is it with success? It changes you, and Billy wasn't his old self, like he was suffering some kind of creeping disease.

Speeder found him at the poker game, seven-card stud, betting a thousand, showing a high pair.

"Whom do you think it is, Speed?" he said. Lights blinked, cards appeared on the screen. One of the enemy players was showing four clubs.

"I think it's bullshit."

"You don't work for the horsemen, do you, Speed?" A small, unnatural laugh.

"Yeah, I'm head of narcotics."

"I worry about Artie, he does the books. I think there's something funny about him. That new guy, Robertson, the driver, you sure about him?"

"Yeah, Billy."

"Do you trust Big Leonard?"

"As far as I can throw him. It's a con, Billy. Shekels, he says. He and André think they got a play happening."

The flush didn't take, and Billy's three queens beat the table.

"Make the meet with André Cristal. Take him somewhere. Squeeze some truth out of him. Cut him if you have to. I want to know. What about the lawyer – can we find out what she knows?"

"She's a smart-ass broad, she ain't gonna tell us nothin'."

"Go down to the studios, see Nagler, he'll fix you up with a long-distance hearing aid. Stick it under her desk or someplace. Tell Nagler I want a relay from her office to the van."

19

Mr. Blaine Johnson was facing a jury trial tomorrow, Thursday, August 7, in the North York courthouse. A charge of rape for which Johnson could get put away for a dozen years or more. But Leon couldn't track him down.

He wasn't at the North York lockup. He wasn't at the Don. He wasn't in any of the regional jails. And he definitely wasn't out on bail.

The Crown had sent a courier over with some particulars about the case, along with Johnson's record. Two previous sexual assaults and half a dozen common ones. Leon Robinovitch would be defending some violent misanthrope tomorrow.

Johnson, a truck driver, had apparently picked up a young hitch-hiker and raped her in his rig, at his company's parking lot. In her complaint to police she said Johnson threatened to kill her if she told anyone. *His* statement was – predictably – different. He claimed she was all over him, and afterwards she wanted money or she'd go to the cops, and that's when he hit her. The material sent over by the prosecutor included a photograph: a girl of fifteen with a fat lip and swollen eye.

Ah, how noble Leon would feel going into the fray for this princely fellow.

But not tomorrow. Though the prosecutor, Ms. Genevieve

Flagg, would be showing up with her loins girded for battle, her witnesses prepped and ready, surely the judge would agree to traverse the case to the next sittings. Leon had not been able to reach the judge, who happened to be old Elliot Packer, the ancient, ulcer-ridden terror of the Ontario High Court. He was at home writing judgments all day, his clerk advised, and she was not prepared to interrupt him with anything short of a threatened terrorist attack on his house.

Well, Leon would show up in court tomorrow and simply demand an adjournment.

His phone rang. "That awful person is here again," said Pauline Chong on the intercom.

Leon put away the rape file. Yes, today he also had to deal with another of his favourite clients, the many-faceted Herbert Orff, and Dr. Kiehlmann was due any moment.

Orff ballooned in through the doorway and sat, squeezing between the arms of a chair. He'd brought his lunch, a bag of pork rinds.

"How goes everything, Herbert?"

"I have a headache."

"Well, Dr. Kiehlmann is on his way and we'll see what he can do for that."

"I know what he's coming for, and there's nothing wrong with me. He's a psychiatrist, and you think I'm crazy just because I believe in different things than you."

"No, Herbert, I want to prove you are absolutely sane."

"You do?"

"You see, there's a danger the prosecution will raise the issue of your competence to stand trial. We have to be ready for that. We'll need a psychiatrist to testify that you're just a normal human being."

Orff looked sceptical. "Is this usually done?"

"In your type of case, yes."

Leon answered the intercom, and then got up. "You sit tight, and I'll be back in a moment."

He found Dr. Hal Kiehlmann waiting by Pauline's desk. He

was a long-time friend of Leon's, about fifty, with short-cropped grey hair – he'd worked in a military hospital before going into forensic practice.

"I can hardly wait to see this interesting subject."

"Three different voices. The three faces of Eve, so to speak. What is that, it's not schizophrenic – schizoid?"

"Dissociative personality, possibly. The divided self."

Leon led him back to his office. "How does he manage? He has this long-time work record. A mainstay of the Waste Management Branch in Scarborough. One has to assume it's not taxing work."

In the office, they found Orff trying to squeeze out of his chair, lifting it as he rose. He'd polished off his pork rinds.

"Sit down, Herbert," Leon said.

"Up yours, shyster, you give us Jews a bad name," he snarled, sitting back down, glaring at them.

"Us *Jews*?" said Leon.

"I don't want no goddamn head doctor poking into my brain, okay? Kiehlmann, that's a German name, ain't it? No way."

Orff the Jewish other. Leon had heard this voice in front of the elevator, cocky, profane. He looked at Kiehlmann, who nodded, then took a chair near Orff.

"I'm Hal Kiehlmann." He offered his hand.

Orff – or whoever he was right now – hesitated, then took it. "No offence. I just don't like krauts. After what we went through . . . You guys'll never understand."

"And what is your name?"

"Hymie."

"You're proud to be a Jew?"

"Damn right."

"And what do you do for a living?"

"I help Orff. He's a fucking anti-Semite but I'm kind of stuck with him."

"I hope you don't mind talking about it."

Hymie pondered. "Yeah, well, I'm sort of puzzled by it all, so, yeah, shoot."

Leon was curious but he didn't want to get in the way, so he left the two of them alone.

When Dr. Kiehlmann finally led Orff back to the waiting room, Leon saw the psychiatrist was holding a copy of the book Orff had been peddling, *A Thousand Lies Exposed*. He also observed that his client was back to his old self, as it were, but looking more confused than usual.

"I don't want to do any tests, doctor."

"Tomorrow, please, just come to the clinic."

"Are you sure this is going to help my headaches?"

"Maybe. If you co-operate. Please sit down for a minute, Herbert."

"Yes, sir."

They returned to Leon's office.

"What we have here is a barely functioning, grossly neurotic, fucked-up individual," Kiehlmann said.

"Can you expand?"

"Multiple-personality disorder – infrequent but well-recorded. Form of psychoneurosis. *Grande hystérie* is the rather elegant name for it. In his case, it's complicated by an extreme paranoia about everything that talks, walks, or breathes."

"Well, how many people are walking around inside his skin?"

"Three, at least."

Okay, Leon had a plan. He would convince the Crown that Orff was unfit to stand trial, and persuade them to drop the charge.

"It's a rarity in the trade," Kiehlmann said. "I've always wanted one of them. I'd *really* like it if you picked him up tomorrow. Just bring him to my office on the campus. I don't trust him to come on his own."

After Kiehlmann left, Leon went downstairs to see the banker. It was nearly time for Robert Barnsworth to meet the new tenants.

At his desk, Barnsworth looked up suspiciously.

"Good news, we have the August rent. We'll still be a little behind on the loan, but that's coming." Leon handed him a cheque.

Barnsworth casually looked at it, and gave Leon a legal document.

"Notice of eviction."

"Too late. We found some subtenants."

"Subtenants? Dare I ask what kind of tenants?"

"Very solid people. They're dropping by, I'd like you to meet them."

"Professional people."

"Of course."

"You still have the loan to pay, Mr. Robinovitch. We've called it, as you know. One hundred and fifty thousand Canadian dollars."

Several minutes later Leon met Robert Barnsworth at the reception desk with a smile that promised not only a truce but hopes for a permanent peace. He led the landlord to his office with his arm in friendly embrace over his shoulder.

"I have the three signing officers in here now, Robert," Leon said. "I've made you an extra copy of the lease assignment. They're taking the place over for the balance, three and a half years, and for the whole renewal period."

"What kind of profession do these new tenants represent, Mr. Robinovitch?" Barnsworth was still holding himself in stiff reserve, hadn't returned to a first-name basis.

"The caring profession."

Barnsworth might have been hoping they'd be medical people, but in the doorway to Leon's office he stopped short: sprawled comfortably within various chairs were the three leading officers of the Cool Aid Society: lanky, long-haired Roy; fat, hairy Elmo, and mop-topped Parjanya.

Roy, wearing a FUCK THE CONTRAS T-shirt, had his long legs up on a corner of Leon's desk. Elmo kept sneezing and wiping his nose, looking vaguely like a man with a bad cocaine habit. He was also scratching his crotch, as if he had crabs. Parjanya was wearing an extremely transparent top, her breasts and nipples showing in prominent outline.

He had told them to be as bad as they could be, but they were overdoing it. "The new tenants," said Leon, introducing Barnsworth.

207

Barnsworth didn't move, just his eyes, flicking, jumping from Parjanya's bosom to the Friar Tuckish hippie with his incessant scratching.

"The Metro Toronto Cool Aid Society," Leon said. "They help kids with drug problems."

He urged Barnsworth in, led him to the little sofa, to the space beside Parjanya, who was reeking of various Indian essences. When she gave Barnsworth a little palms-pressed Hindu bow, he crossed his legs and sat like a man coiled.

"We're thinking of a kind of drop-in centre," Roy said.

"Yes," said Barnsworth, finally able to speak, "but the lease wouldn't permit any, ah, clinic or a . . . treatment facility."

"Nothin' like that. Some counselling, drug therapy. A lot of these kids are on the needle, they're pretty fucked up."

"Hey, man," said Elmo, "some times the courts refer them to us, like when they're really at the end of the road, and the straight social workers can't handle 'em. They're robots, most of them social workers, bureaucrats with initials behind their names, most of 'em couldn't organize a piss-up in a brewery." Elmo picked up what might have been a tiny flea between his fingernails and squeezed it. "Gotcha." A belch.

Leon was becoming annoyed, they were being *too* obnoxious. But Barnsworth was a person lacking as much in subtlety as in sense of humour, and maybe he didn't get it.

Roy said, "Elmo, he does stress therapy. Massage."

"Ever need any help with your body," Elmo said, "I know where some good spots are."

"I see," said Barnsworth, and he turned back to Parjanya. "And what do you do?"

"Oh, this and that. Kind of, you know, keep everyone happy." Her voice went husky. "And I do the books, so I'll be down in the bank a lot."

"Yes, well . . . I'm sure you all do important work, but I suspect there are better areas in the city –"

"Nope," said Roy, "this is perfect. Building with a little class, it'll help raise the kids' self-esteem. Besides, where we are now, we're always getting raided by narcs."

Leon handed Barnsworth the lease-assignment form, duly executed by himself for the firm and by Roy, Elmo, and Parjanya. "They'll be taking over end of the month when we have our new place ready."

Barnsworth leafed through it. "Isn't there a clause . . . I take it the landlord does not have to consent?"

"Nope. Of course I realize we have to make up any deficit if they fail to pay the rent, but we'll take that chance."

"Well, frankly, I doubt if they can afford —"

"No problem," said Roy, "we have some grant money coming from the boys downtown." He unfolded a couple of newspaper clippings. "Here, from this morning's rag. 'Metro Grants Cool Aid $12,000 for Centre.' That picture's from when we got an award from the provincial government." He showed Barnsworth the society's incorporation papers. "We're for real," he said with a menacing grin.

"Of course you are." Barnsworth's small pink smile, which had long ago deserted him, now clicked back into place. He gave Leon a look that said he knew his game. "Perhaps we could have a session in private."

Parjanya's hand reached for his before he could rise. "You seem a little uptight," she said. "You should open yourself up. The Lord Siddhartha says one must be constantly loving."

Barnsworth freed himself from her, stood.

"And we love you, Mr. Barnsworth," she said. "We really love you."

"Er, thank you. I, ah, well, Leon, just a few technical matters to iron out."

Leon took him to the library, and sat him before the table on which the obscene books were haphazardly piled.

"I take it you'd simply be prepared to cancel the lease."

"Oh, no, it's too late. We've signed that subtenancy agreement."

"General and Commercial Trust will not be held to ransom."

"Well, Robert, we borrowed a hundred and fifty thousand dollars from you to refurbish the space, and if we cancel the lease a lot of that goes down the drain. Of course, if you wanted to *buy* all the creature comforts we put in . . ."

Barnsworth paled. "How much?"

"Well, at least half of what we spent we'll never recover, it's gone into fixtures. We have a coffee room set up in there, carpets, partitions . . . So, half. Seventy-five thousand."

Barnsworth stared bleakly at a whips-and-chains book titled *Pain Through the Ages.* "That's far too much."

The negotiations continued until mid-afternoon, interrupted only once, when Roy wandered in with a tape measure and had to be shooed out. Afterwards, the Cool Aid officers stood outside the open library door, looking betrayed and grim.

Just after lunch hour, Barnsworth brought in a lawyer, and Leon reinforced himself with Carrie. The lawyer looked at everything, looked over Roy, Elmo, and Parjanya, and with his help ultimately a deal memo was signed: the lease cancelled, the fixtures sold to G & C Trust for sixty-five thousand dollars, the interest rate on the loan lowered by three points.

After the Cool Aid people left, Barnsworth mustered his remaining dignity and shook hands with the three lawyers, and said without cracking a smile: "We'll miss you."

Leon had to like him for that. Definitely sounded like a sense of humour.

Leon and Carrie celebrated in the lounge with a bottle of champagne they'd been saving should an occasion arise.

"Good on you, Leon," Carrie said. "You deserved a big win like this."

She gave him a hug and a big smack on the cheek. It sent Leon reeling. He had to struggle to keep from telling her he was hopelessly in love with her, but might have done so had Chuck not popped in.

Chuck was sweaty, in shorts and tennis shoes. "I, uh, I've been with Ted. I have a message from him for you, Carrie."

"Ted who?"

"He's coming over for dinner with Lisa and me. I'm going to spend some more time with him tomorrow. But . . . well, he wants to talk to you. Everything exploded in his face, Carrie. Melissa's gone back to Dr. Cartwright. They've reconciled."

"Yes." She gave him an impassive, wide-eyed stare and got up to go. "Well, I've been neglecting some files."

"Carrie, for God's sake, he's in pain."

She sighed. "What does he want?"

"To talk. To apologize. All he asks is a chance to give confession. Give him that much, for Christ's sake. The guy's been in fantasy land, it's like somebody drugged him. Now he's coming to. Carrie, you may hate his guts but he's a human being in agony. Worse now, I beat him two out of three sets, he kept smashing balls into the net."

"Is he suicidal?"

"I wouldn't say exactly."

"Call me when he jumps. I'll come running."

Carrie strode quickly through the midtown streets, thirty-seven minutes from office to home, that was her record. The forecast again called for rain tonight. The hot rain of summer that never really cools things off, rain by night and sweat by day.

She hoped Ted had enjoyed his tennis game with Chuck. Wham, ace, forty-love. In tennis love means zero. We both scored zero, didn't we, Ted? How deeply love wounds, my darling. How callously it betrays. How like fools we become in its grip.

How satisfying to see this happen to you.

Walking through Queen's Park, alone, finally able to escape from the hurly-burly of this day, she could luxuriate now in pleasant contemplation of the ironic vengeance that God had judged her husband must suffer. Do you and Melissa still laugh at the same jokes? It must have been such a jolly lot of fun enjoying those same movies and everything.

Don't you remember, Ted? *We* used to enjoy the same movies. *We* used to laugh at the same jokes.

You blew it, buddy. Don't come crying.

At home she found a message from Ted on the machine. "I'm at my hotel now, Carrie, in case you intend to call. Room 401, the York." The voice monotonic, stripped of emotion.

She made an omelette. André Cristal in court tomorrow at

211

ten – she must meet with McAnthony beforehand and agree on a prelim date. And keep that deal alive. Sweeten it with vague assurances about what André might know, a counter-offer for his services. How generous might the state be in bartering for the evil prince of heroin?

After eating and showering she went to her bedroom where she played her cello for an hour, a sonata for her father. She remembered him in his big stuffed chair, a whisky at hand, his eyes closed, his innocent, red-haired, spindly-legged daughter so anxious to entertain him.

Why, Charlie? You who fought so hard for others, why didn't you fight for yourself, for your innocence, for your life?

André Cristal phoned just as she was pulling on her pyjamas. "It's not too late?"

"No, you caught me just before going to bed."

"Good. I 'ave a new place. Furnish apartment, near downtown, off Davenport Road." He gave her the address and phone number.

"Comfortable?"

"Penthouse suite. They didn't seem to know who I was, but they liked the money."

"Where do you get all this money, André?"

"I 'ave savings. It is not good to spend money, Carrington? What is it for?"

"I'll see you in court tomorrow. Ten-thirty or so, okay?"

"*A bientôt*, Carrington. Sweet dreams."

That night she dreamed of him again. She was unbuttoning some sort of tunic that he wore and they were on her bed. His voice in her ear: "But I am innocent." And then she was suddenly running from him, running, running, and he was a large man now with a little moustache and little blue eyes. Mr. Moodie, don't you understand? You, too, are innocent . . .

The midnight show, and from the dancing stage Trixi watched the waiters hustle the google-eyed morons. Last call, a final beer for the road, then they go home and rape their wives. She had just shot up before going on: it was the only way she could stomach showing her crotch to the morons.

Led Zeppelin, heavy metal, how was she supposed to dance to this? She wanted this over, wanted to get out of here, wanted to go home, to bed, alone, and she was shedding her clothes as fast as good manners would allow. Here comes the bra, guys, it's the moment you weened-too-early teat freaks have been waiting for. But for a while she couldn't get the clasp undone, her fingers were all rubbery.

"Come on, show them," a moron shouted.

Her back to them, she peeked over her shoulder and stuck her tongue out. She wiggled her bottom and tugged at her panties and gave them all a moon. This has all got to end, she thought, it's fucking demeaning. Tomorrow, yes, tomorrow, she would call on Carrie Barr. Tomorrow begins the process of drying out. Look for a straight job, maybe apply to that computer school.

Now she was down to a G-string. Maybe she should give it to that big ugly bastard just beneath her – he'd probably like to eat it.

"Let's see it, honey." A voice from the back.

Up yours with a paddle, moron.

"You can't dance worth shit, do something useful." He wouldn't let up. "Let's see the old fruit cup, babe. Gimme the beaver."

Trixi stopped dancing and glared in his direction. "Take a douche, pal." And she gave him the finger and walked off the stage, grabbing her clothes, the guitars still screeching.

That really did it for her, the asshole in the back, she wasn't going to put up with any of this crap any more. She slipped her clothes on, not bothering with the underwear, and went straight to her boss at the bar and demanded her pay for the night.

"You're through," said the boss. "That was your last act."

"Pay me off."

"You get paid piss-all for sassing the customers."

"You shit, I'll get my lawyer."

She stormed out into the sticky night, her rage having eaten away the effect of the last hit. She had a little more scag in her purse, and for a second or two she thought about doing it, then decided, no, that's it. Clean life. Yeah, she'd get her lawyer on the case tomorrow, sue the guy's face off. Not enough bread on her for a cab ride, she'd spent everything on two caps of junk, the price was going up again.

She walked down Eastern Avenue – it wasn't a safe place to hitch-hike so maybe she should get over to a better-lit street.

A car pulled up at the curb alongside her and the driver leaned out the window.

"You like a lift?"

She recognized him. He was that big, bald moron who'd been in the front row, a regular customer, the possible G-string eater.

"No, thank you." She walked on.

He curb-crawled alongside her in his car, an old Mercury. "You sure? I'll take you anywhere."

She didn't like his tone or his leer. "I have a ride coming."

"Suit yourself." The car drove away, and slowed as it went around a corner. Trixi had a sense it might have stopped there, just out of her view. But the corner was well-lit, and she wasn't going to change direction just because this buffoon was trying to stalk her.

She had enough change for a bus, and a bus stop was at the corner.

Before she reached it, just as she passed an almost-empty lot where a building was in the early stages of construction, she heard what she thought were footsteps behind her, and suddenly she went prickly all over.

And then she felt hot breath on the back of her neck, and a hand went over her mouth and, flailing, she felt herself being lifted, carried to the construction site, a huge man, obese, she tried to twist, to turn, to see his face, she could hear his grunts, and she was in a state of terror.

She bit his hand and it was abruptly pulled away from her mouth, and one of her hands came free and she took a swing at him, but before she could take a breath to scream, his hand took her by the throat, then both hands, tight as a vise.

After the Midnight Strangler choked her to death he made love to her.

20

When Carrie showed up at the office Thursday morning, Pauline had an urgent message for her from Jock Strachan. She called him from the reception desk.

"I'll make this blunt and short, Carrie." Strachan's burr was prominent – that usually meant trouble. "A woman's body was found at seven-thirty hours at a construction site on Eastern Avenue. Behind a pile of concrete blocks. Naked, neck broken, dress torn from her. There's semen. The pathologist estimates time of death about midnight. All the trademarks."

Carrie sucked in her breath. "How terrible . . . Jock, why are you calling me about this?"

"Where's Edwin Moodie?"

She was confused, annoyed. Edwin Moodie? So typical of a policeman, the one-track mind . . . Mr. Moodie would probably be on the job at Kelver Cartage, where he toiled a few days a week.

"I think I can track him down."

"I doubt it. He has not been called in for work."

"How do you know where he works?"

"Och, lassie, give us a little more credit than that."

"I suppose you know where he lives then."

"All we know is he paid his bill last night at the Eagle Hotel and checked out."

She felt a distinct unease. "Dear God, Jock, I . . . Eastern Avenue? Has she been identified?"

"Young woman of ill repute. Patricia Trimble, she called herself Trixi."

Carrie felt faint; she clutched the edge of the reception desk for support. Pauline was watching her with concern.

Strachan's voice softened. "I believe you knew her."

"I was her lawyer."

"Aye. Did they ever meet – Moodie and the Trimble woman?"

Then she remembered Moodie – in this very waiting room – bashfully trying to respond to a flirting Trixi. What had Trixi told her later? *He followed me all the way home that day.*

"Jock, I'll have to talk to you later. Thank you for telling me." She hung up.

She turned her ashen face to Pauline. "Trixi . . . she's dead. She . . . worked near there." For a moment she thought she was going to be sick, and she had to fight it. "Pauline, they think it's the Midnight Strangler. Oh, God, I have to find Mr. Moodie before the police do. He's not very bright, the police could get him to say anything."

She leaned dumbly against the desk, breathing slowly in and out, full of Trixi's pain – and something else: for the first time a niggling note of uncertainty about her Mr. Moodie.

Speeder impatiently cracked gum as he watched the slaves entering the G & C Trust building. He was in a van with the motor running. In the back were Deeley and Humphries and Nagler, the tech from Heliotrope, the movie studio Billy sort of owned, a silent partner.

Nagler was twisting wires, clamping them, futzing around, he was an electronics wiz. Deeley and Humphries were just killing time, yapping when they should've been quiet.

Nagler slid up to the front and handed Speeder a thimble-sized transmitter with a suction cup on it.

"There's a stick-on chemical in the cup. Don't touch it. It'll hold for weeks."

Speeder put it in his pocket. They'd got here an hour and a half ago, before the morning rush, and had watched the suits pouring into the building, pod people heading for their desks and their filing cabinets. Speeder had watched the lady lawyer Carrington Barr almost running in, all anxious to go to work. Man, that redhead with her big green eyes, a little tall for him, but okay in every other way if she wasn't such a cold fish.

"Deeley, take the wheel. We're in a no-parking, but don't go nowhere unless you have to."

He brushed off his sports jacket, which was flecked with dead skin and dandruff, straightened his tie, and said, "Here goes," and stepped out of the van and joined the slaves marching into the building.

Accountants and secretaries, routine freaks, grind artists, what did they know of the rich funny fuck-up that was the real world outside their tinted windows? He made ten times as much as them guys for doing shit, just sucking around Billy all day, and he didn't want no one messing with his good life, not this lady lawyer and not André Cristal.

He went to the washroom down the hall first, and drew some water into a plastic cup and knocked back two caps full of tiny bombs that would go off when the gelatin melted. He took a piss – it was fucking orange, maybe he was cleaning out his system.

How was he gonna be able to get under her desk? Hey, lady, mind if I crawl down there and look around?

He got into the elevator and went up to the tenth floor, staring at the back of a bunch of silent suits with briefcases, they didn't know Speeder Cacciati was here, the right-hand man to one of the biggest business barons in the country, their lives were piddling in comparison. He could feel the cartwheels going off now, tiny surges of energy and good feeling.

Nice offices. Fancy furniture. Chinese chick at the front desk. Asked for his name and all, and if he had an appointment, and

217

when he said he didn't, she told him to be comfortable for a few minutes.

A beard with a long nose came hustling out of the offices, doing up a tie, one of the partners, Speeder guessed. "I'm off to North York," the guy said to the Chinese dame. "Johnson, a rape. I'll be back to help Carrie out with this Moodie thing. If I'm longer than a couple of hours, I'll call. If the old bugger won't adjourn me, I'm withdrawing from the record."

When Speeder got sent into Carrington Barr's office, there was a secretary in there, too, and they were talking about what sounded like a murder last night, a prostitute or something.

Speeder got sort of ignored for a while, just a "Please sit down, Mr. Cacciati," so he took a chair and pulled it up in front of the big desk.

He saw his chance immediately, when the two women went to the door and their backs were turned, and he stuck the transmitter under the lip of the desk, a couple of feet in, nice and close to her chair. When Carrington Barr came back to sit down he was calmly scratching his elbow as if nothing happened.

"I'm in a hurry, what do you want?"

Hey, you could be more polite, lady, Speeder thought. But he was glowing now, her cold-ass shit didn't bother him. He took an envelope from his breast pocket. "We took up another collection. A little advance on your fees and maybe something to tide him over."

She gave him this kind of big wide-eyed look, and went and slit open the envelope with a letter opener. She brought out the money, fanned it, twenty grand and a ticket to the St. Francis of Assisi Charity Night, which she frowned at.

"What's this all about?"

"Italian street carnival. André can win some prizes in the St. Francis of Assisi church hall."

She just looked at him.

"Tomorrow night, Friday."

"Why should he want to meet you?"

"He should make contact. We bailed him out, he owes us."

"Maybe he thinks you owe him more."

That stopped Speeder for a second. That's what he and Billy had figured. Whom do you think he is fooling, Billy had said, with this narc-on-the-inside stuff? He's on the con, him and Big Leonard. And maybe this Mrs. Barr, too.

Speeder turned on the charm. "Listen, lady, I got too much respect to bullshit you. Sure, we're worried. Look, we're gonna pay all his legal bills, whatever, you name it in reason. We just wanna make sure, you know, like our investment is gonna be protected. Wanna ensure him we're backing him all the way. Just a friendly meeting, me and André. A thousand people there. There ain't gonna be no damage to nobody."

She didn't say anything, but Speeder could tell she was thinking clearer. Twenty grand and she could just shove it in her poke and no one's gonna know, and that's just a dribble to what's coming. She's figuring: if I play my cards I could be Billy's full-time throat.

"I'll tell him. But I'll advise against it."

"That's a fair attitude," Speeder said as he got to his feet. "Glad you could see me on short notice."

"Next time, please phone."

Speeder shuffled quickly out of there. What a bitch, all the time wrinkling her snobby nose at him, did he forget to wash his armpits this morning or something? Screw her, he felt powerful, these pills were really doing it, he felt taped, zappy, in control.

Mission successful, the boss won't ask for his head. You got to worry about Billy, thinks everybody and his dog is out there to nail his ass. Uneasy wears the crown that fits the head. Or something. Sometimes he worried that Billy didn't even trust him. *Can I trust you, Speed?* Speeder had done time for Billy, had shoved guys off for him. He wanted to tell the suit with him in the elevator he had greased three guys in his lifetime – what would he think about that?

Outside, he put sunglasses on, he figured he looked pretty dapper. The van was still in the no-parking, and he jumped into the back.

"Getting anything?" he asked Nagler.

"Yeah, we got quite a reach if I use the aerial."

219

Speeder could hear two women's voices from the receiver's small speaker, he figured she had her secretary in the office with her again.

"*So who was* that *guy?*"

"*Speeder Cacciati. Reminds me of a slug. Leaves a trail of slime wherever he walks.*"

"*He's Billy Sweet's head honcho? Yech!*"

Speeder felt the cartwheels he'd done rushing to his lower gut, a kind of pain that settled in his bowels, magnified by the dope. He was looking at Humphries and Nagler, who were acting like he wasn't there, pretending they hadn't paid attention to the words.

"Yeah, that comes in real excellently," said Humphries, "like they're right in the room."

Speeder wanted to go back up to that office, just wipe the fucking cunts out. This was all being recorded, Billy will laugh his head off. A slimy slug. The bitch.

They listened to Carrington Barr connect with a guy named Oliver McAnthony at the prosecutors' office.

"*Oliver, can we meet before court?*"

They couldn't hear his answer but it was some kind of long speech.

"*Oliver, I know about it. Jock Strachan phoned me. Let's not jump to any guilty conclusions yet, okay? Maybe Mr. Moodie moved out of that room because he was feeling crowded.*"

More conversation from the other end.

"*Yes. I'm thinking about it, but I want chapter and verse on what you've got on André this time. No cagey little secrets, Oliver.*"

Silence for a couple of seconds.

"*No, I don't* quite *have everything.*"

Again, some kind of response.

"*Do I have to spell it out? Our friend that you have on the, ah, inside. The mole.*"

Speeder sat frozen, listening, wanting to hear more about this friend, the mole, the spy. There was one! But the conversation ended, with Carrington Barr simply saying, "*Okay, see you in court.*" Then nothing, maybe the sound of a chair being rolled back.

Cristal hadn't been bluffing. According to Big Leonard the Frenchman had found out about the narc through his lawyer. This lady was obviously in the know, chummy with cops and with the prosecutor guy, Oliver. Yeah, she was in on the Frenchman's scam, all right.

Billy was going to shit green. Billy, he won't have no time to laugh at Speeder Cacciati's expense, he was gonna go berserk.

✢ ✢ ✢

Carrie was in grief for the entire walk from Bloor Street to the Provincial Courts – like too many of her clients, Trixi Trimble had been a friend. And a sick feeling that she may have grossly misjudged Edwin Moodie had settled on her and stayed with her.

Could Moodie in following Trixi have found out she worked in that strip joint? Her body had been found only a block and a half from there. Had Carrie been taken in all along, blinded by her refusal to accept the ugly truth of guilt?

If she had won freedom for a serial killer, did she share blame for the death of Trixi Trimble?

Reporters outside the Old City Hall harassed her with questions about the Midnight Strangler, about Moodie – where was he?

She politely shrugged everyone off and escaped into One-Eleven Court, where the impatient Judge Revere was presiding. She saw André Cristal in the back row. He winked at her, and she waved back.

She seated herself on defence-counsel row. The judge was listening – barely – to a long-winded submission on behalf of a B-and-E expert. The tic in Revere's eye kept beat with the tapping of his finger.

McAnthony strolled in and took an empty seat beside Carrie.

"Your Mr. Moodie is behaving very unlike an innocent man. Disappearing as he did."

"It's just not like him."

"He's a drifter, though, isn't he? Though as your gentle bleeding heart would probably prefer it, a socially displaced person."

"Don't be sarcastic, Oliver. What do you think, three weeks be enough for the prelim?"

"M. Cristal is not enthusiastic about our offer?"

"He thinks you should sweeten it."

"Carrington, we are prepared to go to trial on this one."

"Prove to me you can win it. What does your so-called spy say about my client?"

McAnthony sighed. "I have to talk to Harold Mitchell about that."

"I think it's all a fairy tale, frankly. Oliver, what's the cost of keeping a thirty-three-year-old man in protective custody for the rest of his life?"

"Around a million dollars, I would suspect."

"More like a million and a half. What if we take it in cash?"

"And you will give us Billy Sweet?"

Carrie thought: what am I getting my client into? But these were his firm instructions. Still, she hedged: "We would try."

"I'll discuss it with the inspector."

Judge Revere sentenced the miscreant who was before him, intoning: "Though the mills of justice grind slowly, they grind exceeding fine. Thirty months."

McAnthony stood up, and spoke to the regular prosecutor: "May I play through?"

Cristal was called, and he came forward beside Carrie. He was dressed like a man on the way to a board meeting: a grey, expensively tailored suit, a conservative silk tie with just a dash of colour.

The judge granted a one-week remand. Carrie waved a goodbye to McAnthony and led Cristal from the Old City Hall courts. Outside, they talked in the shade of a tree.

"I think they'll go for it," she said.

"Then it is up to me. Has any of Billy's friends called you?"

"Speeder Cacciati." She handed him the ticket to the St. Francis of Assisi Charity Night. "The Italian community holds a street carnival every year out there and a fund-raiser in the hall."

"Tomorrow night I will turn up the 'eat for them." He smiled.

"You're not at all afraid?"

"Of course. But it is 'ard for me to explain – I enjoy the fear."

Was he suicidal? Again, she remembered those intimations of his own death as they talked about his bail money: *If I die, you can keep it all.*

"Cacciati also gave me twenty thousand dollars."

"Good. You can buy lunch."

It was nearly noon. She didn't have to scurry back to the office. Yes, a pleasant Thursday lunch with M. Cristal.

They went to the Courtyard Café at the Windsor Arms, a favourite haunt of glitterati wishing to be seen in public. She saw other lunchers glancing at them – at Cristal, mostly, perhaps mistaking him for some mid-level movie star, the kind of person you're not sure about, but think you *should* recognize. The food was good, especially the Caesar salad. The forty-five-dollar bottle of Beaune that Cristal ordered wasn't bad, either. She normally didn't drink wine at lunch, she explained a little stiffly. Miss Priss.

But, still in turmoil over Trixi's death, she ended up drinking more of it than he, and she felt, if not giddy, certainly slack-tongued by the end of the meal.

Oddly, their conversation didn't touch on the case, or on anything to do with the law, but was mostly . . . well, about her *life*. She found herself telling him about her early years, the loneliness of an only child. She told him about her parents, about Charlie Connors, his brilliance, his alcoholism, his final trial in defence of himself, and the terrible wrong that was done to him.

"It was eight years ago, I was twenty, studying law, here in Toronto. It was a terrible time, I kept flying back and forth to help Mother – she was sick, an awful cancer. I almost had to repeat the year. And then Mom died. He'd got compassionate leave from jail to be with her, but it was too late, she'd gone, and he . . ." She took a breath. "After the funeral he stuck a hose in his car."

Here she was, wet-eyed, babbling to a near total stranger, an alleged contract killer, a heroin trafficker.

"If it hadn't been for . . . Well, I had friends."

223

His silence forced her to continue. "Chuck Tchobanian – he's my partner now – he mostly got me through it. Worst time of my life, worse than what I'm going through now."

Whoops, her tongue had fashioned words without the benefit of thought.

"Worse than now?"

His intense eyes looked beyond her blushing face, through her sockets, into her soul.

"I've had a little marriage crisis."

"I 'ave notice the missing ring."

"I threw it out the window." Oh, just say it. "We're estranged." That was a namby-pamby way of putting it. "I'm seeking a divorce."

"I am very un'appy for you. It is sad when love is lost."

She remained silent for a while, then finished her wine and became brave and stubborn, and said, "He actually fell in love with someone else."

"*Calice*! He should see a psychiatrist."

"You're absolutely right." She felt better now, had got through it, she wasn't going to blubber.

"Can we offer a dessert?" said the waiter.

"Coffee," she said. The hard edge of caffeine to set her back on an even keel. Cristal must think she lives a life of misery. Not so, she wanted to tell him. I'm basically happy, happy, happy.

She became Carrington Barr, barrister. "Call me at the office tomorrow, will you, in case there are any developments? If Billy does make contact tomorrow night – please phone me afterwards."

And take care, she wanted to add.

Outside the restaurant he bussed her on each cheek.

"The French way," he said.

At a news kiosk she saw Edwin Moodie's picture beneath its Strangler-Strikes-Again headline. "WANTED! CHIEF SUSPECT, ONCE ACQUITTED, DISAPPEARS."

21

Leon assumed he was going to take a beating today from Judge Elliot Packer over his bid for an adjournment of his rape trial. The judge, in his mid-seventies, only a year from retirement, had all his wits but suffered a severe case of choler. Thankfully, the irascible old fellow was just as hard on the Crown as the defence.

Leon had to wait a couple of hours for his case to be called at the North York courthouse because a commercial fraud case was still being heard, a non-jury trial. Judge Packer spent most of the morning berating a police witness.

"'Attended at'? 'Had occasion to make examination'? Talk English. You went to McLean Motors and looked at their records. When I went to school they taught English. Have they stopped doing that?"

While the police witness tried to reorganize his thoughts, Judge Packer turned on the prosecutor, who looked liked a man on the rack. "Perhaps some time before this case concludes you will be good enough to tell me what it is about. I've never seen a more haphazard prosecution."

Leon's client, Johnson, the alleged rapist truck driver, had not yet been delivered to the building. A lot of people around here were nervous that his continuing absence, as Leon had begun to suspect, might result in a major cock-up. If Leon had not been able to locate Blaine Johnson, maybe the police couldn't either. Packer would go on a rampage.

The plan was that after this witness was finished on the stand, the fraud trial would be adjourned for several days. The rape, a jury case, would be late in getting under way if it got under way at all, and Leon had a feeling that Judge Packer, in an especially acerbic mood, might refuse to adjourn it – a panel of jurors was waiting outside.

But Leon hoped he might not have to ask for his continuance. He looked over to where his prosecutor, Genevieve Flagg, was fiddling nervously with her sleeve buttons. The arresting officers were on the phones, trying to make contact with the police van that was supposed to be bringing Johnson in for trial. Flagg's witnesses were all prepped and ready. It was nearing half past eleven. And no accused.

It was she, now, who was seeking his consent to an adjournment. Maybe, Leon told her. But let's wait and see.

The judge, tiring of his sport with the fraud-case prosecutor, ordered a break. "When we return we will empanel the jury. Mr. Robinovitch, you are counsel on the next case?"

He rose. "I am, my lord."

"And you are ready to proceed?"

Leon hesitated for only a moment, then took the leap. "Yes, sir."

Flagg looked at him with her mouth open, and jumped up. "My lord, I . . ."

"Yes, Miss Flagg?"

"Well, there may be some problem locating the accused."

"I thought he was in custody."

"He is. He doesn't seem to be at the Toronto Jail."

"Then it's your problem, isn't it? It's not Mr. Robinovitch's. It's not mine. It's your problem. And if you knew there was going to be a problem you should have told me. We have citizens waiting. Adjourn until eleven-forty."

They all filed from the courtroom. Leon tried to avoid Flagg, but she came flying at him. "You told me you hadn't even *seen* this client."

"Have you seen him?"

"No."

"Maybe he doesn't exist."

"Judge won't dismiss the case, if that's what you're hoping."

"You don't know Elliot Packer."

At eleven-forty, still no accused. Judge Packer glared at the empty dock, then barked to his clerk: "Call the case."

"Her Majesty the Queen against Blaine Johnson."

"Miss Flagg, you are appearing for the Crown?"

"I am, but —"

"And Mr. Robinovitch, you are here for the non-existent accused."

"My lord," said Flagg, "I am seeking an adjournment until this afternoon."

"Perhaps you might advise your employer that these courts are in crisis, Miss Flagg. I have a schedule that would tax the patience of the saints. Now you want me to waste a whole day because of some administrative blunder —"

Just then there was a rattle behind the door leading to the dock, and it was flung open by two florid, puffing court officers, who dragged in a reluctant young man in handcuffs, pale and shaking. A punk, sporting what they call a rooster-tail, but he had no stiffener in it, and the red hair was losing its dye, flopping onto his scrubby scalp.

"The Crown is ready to proceed," said Flagg, giving Leon a secret, triumphant look. Leon guessed she hadn't looked very hard at those mug shots of the accused. Fifteen years older than this fellow.

"You are Johnson?" said the judge.

"Hey, man, is this all part of the nightmare? 'Cause if it is, don't wake me up, I wanna see how it ends, man."

"Mr. Johnson!" the judge roared.

"I'm gonna *talk*, 'cause it's my own nightmare and I get to do what I want in it. Bring on the jury, man, let's get going. Sentence first, verdict after, like in *Alice in Wonderland*."

"Mr. Robinovitch, will you get your client under control?"

"You mean I got a *lawyer*? Hey, man, am I glad to see *you*."

Leon, not sure what was really going on here, decided to play this one by ear.

Johnson, if that's who he was, kept ranting. "They shipped me up to some godforsaken hole way up north, found out I was the wrong guy, and now they say I got a jury trial today on a rape. The only thing I ever raped was my own dink, man, gently by hand. Like this is total bizarro."

Packer had gone apoplectic. "That man is in contempt!"

Leon was beside the accused now. "Shut up," he ordered.

Blair Johnstone lowered his voice. "Where'd you come from, man?"

"Where'd *you* come from?"

"I got popped with some joints in my pocket. What I want to know, is this some kind of drug-deterrence program? 'Cause if it is, I wanna meet the guy who devised it, he's a genius."

"Mr. Robinovitch, I don't permit chats with clients in my court. Just get him under control."

By now, the two Metro officers running this case had come into the courtroom and were talking urgently with Genevieve Flagg. Her expression turned suddenly into one of dismay.

"My lord, I think we have the wrong man."

Judge Packer turned so still that Leon wondered if he'd died on the spot. Then he seemed to sag, as if a burden had descended upon him, the heavy weight of his long years on the bench.

"And what is this gentleman charged with?" he asked in a voice so faint Leon had to strain for it.

"I don't know."

"Half a gram of smoke, man. I'm guilty. Shoot me."

"Shut up," Leon warned him again.

But he didn't relent, pleaded loudly: "Hey, judge, man, you can't do nothin' worse to me than I been through. I been in the joint for two *weeks*. I share a cell with a guy called Bung-Hole Bertrand."

"Get your client under *control*," Packer hissed.

"He's not exactly my client," said Leon.

"My lord, can we, ah, regroup?" Flagg said tentatively.

"This is an abomination. An utter muddle! Both counsel, I

want you in my chambers. Now!" Packer had risen, and was shouting. "This court is adjourned!"

"Hey, man, what about me?"

Packer was leaving but stopped in mid-stride.

"You're going back where you came from." And he walked out.

The court officers grabbed the man in the dock and started hauling him away.

"You, the lawyer," he hollered to Leon, "you gotta help me!"

"Okay, don't worry. I'll be down to see you."

But during the half-hour it took for Judge Packer's vitriol to exhaust itself in his chambers, the young man had been spirited away. The Don Jail, the court officers said. Leon would just have to track him down there tomorrow. This afternoon he was dealing with Herbert Orff and Dr. Kiehlmann.

Herbert Orff lived in a lonely little house in East Scarborough surrounded by weedy, overgrown lots – probably, thought Leon, a subdivision that had never got off the ground. He assumed there were not many people wanting to live with the constant roar of the 401 Expressway in their ears.

Leon got out of his car and tramped along a beaten path to the side of the house, a ragged, patched 1950s bungalow – bare plywood and laths where patches of stucco facing had broken off. Urea formaldehyde insulation showing, deadly stuff – probably affected Orff's brain.

Other poisons, too. Leon saw two large spray canisters with DDT. Then he saw the swampy area out back: it seemed an ongoing struggle against mosquitoes had been fought here. The yard was strewn with junk-food wrappers.

Aside from incessant consumption of Fritos and Cheesies, how did the man pass his leisure time? No automobile – Orff was a user of public transit. He obviously had some money salted away – ten years holding down a union job, and he seemed to live on the cheap.

Orff came out before Leon could knock. He didn't seem to want to invite his lawyer in, though Leon was curious. Whatever was inside was obscured by frilly curtains on the windows. Dainty muslin trim, odd for a bachelor. Or in his case, several of them.

"Mr. Blumberg wouldn't let me have another day off. I had to change shifts and go on early sewer backups. He called me a *schtoonk*. I don't know what that means. He also called me a tutti-frutti, and I can guess at that. Ever since he heard about my case in court he's really been giving it to me."

"I'm going to see if I can't do something about that, Herbert." He escorted him to his heap, his '71 Chevie. "I'll have a talk with your union."

"They don't like me either."

"They don't have to like you, Herbert." Leon, seeking co-operation, was determined to be pleasant. "How did you get along with Dr. Kiehlmann yesterday?"

"Okay, I guess. I still can't understand why this is important. I hope I don't have to take any written tests. I'm not very good at them."

As Leon held the car door for him, he noticed a bandage on the fleshy part of his hand, between thumb and forefinger.

"Did you get in a fight with somebody?"

"I think I cut myself."

"You don't remember?"

"Maybe I was sleepwalking. It's something I do. It's my typing hand, it's really hard to work."

Easy access to the 401 meant they made it in jig time to inner Toronto, into the sprawl of the U. of T. campus, where Kiehlmann taught and worked. All the way, while working through a bag of corn chips, Orff read snippets aloud from his latest copy of *The Simple Truth*, the newsletter he subscribed to.

"This one's about the foreign immigrants, how they're imposing their customs on us." Then later, "Here's an article on how they use subminimal messages on TV."

Leon recalled: this character believes television is part of the international plot – but didn't he see a TV aerial on top of that little house? But maybe Hymie watches the tube.

They met Hal Kiehlmann in his office. The psychiatrist led

them to a small observation clinic in the health centre, where he gave Orff some of the dreaded tests to fill out – the Standard Weschler and a personality quiz.

In a room adjoining, they drank coffee and watched through a heavy-pane window as Orff struggled with his answers at a small desk.

"Any ideas on how Mr. Orff took on these extra personalities?" Leon asked.

"It's often a strategy for coping with childhood abuse. A person sets up a defence mechanism, using techniques of what we call dissociation and conversion. Bluntly, the guy probably couldn't deal with his past, never mind his present, so he sought escape into a personality with better coping skills. Basically, he despises himself."

Orff seemed hung up on an answer, started sucking the end of his pencil, and Leon could see the psychiatrist was becoming impatient. Finally, Kiehlmann returned to him. Leon could hear the conversation through an open intercom system.

"Why don't you relax over there?" Kiehlmann pointed to a couch. "More comfortable."

Orff rested his big bottom tentatively on the couch and Kiehlmann took a chair beside him. "How have you been?"

"I've had headaches. Ever since the last time."

"I'll see if I can't get you something for them."

"Mr. Blumberg doesn't like it when I change shifts. It's going to affect my next job performance review. Did you read *A Thousand Lies Exposed?*"

"Ah, yes, very interesting."

"Then you understand what I am up against. They're trying to silence me. That is what this court charge is all about."

"Who is *they*, exactly?"

He said peevishly: "It's all in the book if you'd read it. The power elite. The Jews. The lawyers."

"But *you* have a lawyer."

"We need some on our side. After we win, there will be no lawyers. They will be given useful work to do."

"That injury to your hand – how did you get it?"

231

"I don't know, I think I went out . . ." Words faded. He scratched his head.

"Do you mean you left your house?"

"I don't remember."

"Tell me, Herbert, do you ever hear voices?"

"I'm not deaf. I hear *your* voice."

"Do you sometimes hear voices when no one is around?"

Orff seemed to reflect. "I . . . think so. People. Talking about me."

"And who are they?"

He didn't respond.

"Okay, Herbert, I want you to relax."

Orff hesitated. "There won't be any tricks?"

"Lie down, and close your eyes."

This was said firmly. Leon observed Orff squinting at Dr. Kiehlmann, whose bearing and military haircut seemed to suggest high rank. After a few more moments of hesitation he stretched out on the couch and shut his eyes.

"I know what you're trying to do. You want to hypnotize me. It doesn't work on me."

"Just relax."

"I am not going to fall asleep."

"Herbert, I want you to help me. I want you to count backwards from five to zero."

"I am going to stay awake."

"As you start counting, your eyelids are going to get heavy. Very heavy. When you reach zero you will be very relaxed."

Orff began. "Five. Four. Three." He was slowing; the "three" was followed by a yawn.

"Two. Um, one. Ze–" His head went to one side and his mouth went slack, and Leon heard the soft rasp of a snore.

"Hymie," said Kiehlmann, "are you here?"

No response.

"Hymie?" Kiehlmann repeated.

Hymie's eyes popped open. "Okay, okay, don't get your shirt in a knot. I'm here." The tone was insolent, the voice rasping and snide. He sat up and looked around. "I wish that son of a bitch hadn't brought me here."

"What son of a bitch?" said Kiehlmann.

"Orff. He gives me the creeps."

"How does he bring you here, Hymie?"

"Can't leave home without him." He smiled. "That's a line from a TV commercial."

"You watch television?"

"Oh, yeah, at home. Orff won't watch TV, though. Thinks it's destroying his mind." He chuckled.

Leon watched all this with amazement.

"I come out after supper and turn it on, and Orff can't do dick about it. I come out sometimes at the Waste Management Branch, too, but Mr. Blumberg never notices. I come out when Mr. Blumberg teases Orff. He can't stand it, but that's what he gets for being a Nazi scum. I got Jewish blood myself, and I'm with Mr. Blumberg."

"Jewish blood?"

"Can I tell you something in secret?"

"Secret from whom?"

"From Orff."

"You don't think I should tell him?"

"He'd freak out. You see, Doctor, he's part Jewish, too. His dad was a Hebe. Like me. He went a little bonkers when poor little Herbie was seven and he had to go to this mental home, and his mother was like this fat, scolding German lady – I don't think she started hating Jews until she married Orff's dad, but she despised him so much I figure she drove the old guy insane. Anyway, she put Orff in a foster home. None of the relatives wanted him, because he was so screwed up."

Hymie leaned closer to the psychiatrist. "But he doesn't remember this. He doesn't remember his father was Jewish. And why we can't tell him is he'd probably kill himself. Good riddance maybe, but what happens to me?"

"You don't think highly of Mr. Orff."

"He uses me for his own ends. I don't trust him."

"How did Mr. Orff get along with his foster parents?"

"They were *weird*, Doc. Like, who else would have this fat nutty kid except the bottom-of-the-barrel foster home. Doesn't nobody check on them places? Made him dress up like a little girl sometimes. You see Orff, he has this problem with women, can't stand to be around them. I'd say from what I seen at the office the feeling is mutual."

"Or he's afraid of them?"

"I don't know. I like 'em."

"You do?"

"Yeah, there's one special girl. Dottie."

"Tell me about her."

"She's kinda skinny. I keep telling her she should put some meat on. Dottie tells me her problems. I tell her mine. There's nothin', you know, real sexual."

"Where do you see Dottie?"

"Oh, she lives with Mrs. Pinkerton. Nice lady. I go visit, oh, maybe five, six times a month."

"Where is that?"

"I don't wish to involve her."

"I see. When were you last with Dottie?"

"Last night."

"Was that when you got that injury to your hand?" Kiehlmann asked.

"I don't know. You'll have to ask Franz."

"Franz?"

"Yeah, he goes out with Dottie, too. But Franz, he's a shit."

"I'd like to meet him."

"Yah. Dis is Franz."

Before anyone had a chance to blink, Orff had assumed his third personality, complete with what seemed a ridiculously put-on German accent.

"Franz . . . ah, yes, do you know where you are?"

"In der crazy hospital, mit der lunatics. I hear *everything*."

Kiehlmann cast a somewhat nervous eye towards Leon, and cleared his throat.

"Well, you're in a clinic. You know why you're here?"

234

"Yah, Orff, the stupid guy, he bring me here. Mit der son-of-a-bitching Jew lawyer." His face became daubed with the colours of rage. "I hear you talk to Hymie. You vant to hear about Hymie? He is filth! Scum of the earth!" He raised his little fists in the air and brought them down. "Rotten filth! Ve vill destroy!"

His eyes rolled up to show only the whites.

"Franz?"

A high, almost girlish response: "He doesn't want to talk to you any more. He has a headache."

"Who . . . are you?"

"I'm Susie."

Susie. Kiehlmann drifted another look towards Leon. The guy was swarming with people, a little village. The doctor had hinted he might find other life forms in this weakly integrated personality.

"Do you know Herbert?"

"Unfortunately, yes."

"Unfortunately?"

"He's a nothing, a no one, a useless little wart."

"I gather you don't like him."

"Nobody does."

Poor Orff, Leon thought. Even his other personalities despise him.

"Why don't you like him?"

"He . . . he makes me do the dishes, and all the boring routine work at the office. He won't let me meet anybody nice. Just Franz, who is awful, and Hymie, who I don't like even more."

"Why?"

"Hymie's pushy. You know."

"I'm not sure."

"A Jew."

"I see."

"You're not Jewish, are you? Most doctors are Jewish."

"And what about Franz? Why is he so awful?"

"I know he likes to . . ." The voice descended to a whisper. "He does terrible things."

"Such as?"

235

"I won't tell you. It's too awful, it's sick. He . . . he . . . I can't . . ."

The struggle suddenly ended and Susie disappeared.

"Franz?"

No response.

"Hymie?"

No response.

"Ah, Herbert, can you awake now?"

"Yes."

"Well, please do so."

The eyes opened, blinked, then focused on Kiehlmann.

"I told you, whatever you're trying to do doesn't work on me. I have a headache." He whined: "You said you'd help my headaches and you didn't."

And that brought the session to a premature close. Orff stubbornly refused his further co-operation. "I want to go home."

"I'll get you some pills. Come with me."

Whatever was in the medicine worked, and Orff agreed – though reluctantly – to complete his tests. While a doctoral student helped Orff with these down the hall, Leon and Kiehlmann met in his office.

"*The Journal of Abnormal Psychology* will be begging for my paper." Kiehlmann rubbed his hands with glee. "The man is a veritable fruit salad of personalities in conflict."

"Orff doesn't know about these other sides of himself?"

"No, completely blank. He's obviously amnesic during episodes when the others come out. That's diagnostic of *grande hystérie*, bouts of amnesia. No record of being hospitalized that I can discover. He has just – somehow – slid through life like this. Some early emotional damage, that's obvious, and also typical. Amazing. Might be the only such case in history where the therapy is to *not* integrate the personalities. Could be dangerous."

Later, driving Orff home, Leon asked him how the pills were working.

"I feel okay now. That was a waste of time just to prove I'm not crazy."

"Dr. Kiehlmann thinks he can find a way to permanently cure your headaches. He wants to see you again this weekend."

"I don't want to go back."

"Well, you'll damn well go back." Leon spoke forcefully – he'd learned this could work.

But he just snivelled. "I don't *want* to."

Orff still didn't invite him into his house, and since it was late afternoon and the day had been taxing, Leon decided to go home and recuperate.

On the ferry to Ward's Island, he tried to blot Herbert Orff from his mind, and he sucked in the breeze from Lake Ontario: fresh, an intimation of cooler weather.

His mother phoned as he was making his salad. She went on and on about the Nazi.

"Leon, I have a theory. Not mine, actually, it's Maggie Dennis's, she's a school counsellor as you know, and they have to take psychology. This is the theory: you are defending this . . . *character* out of some need to rebel against who you think are your stodgy parents."

"That makes real sense, Mom."

"We're squaresville, right? Boring old farts with their lost causes, especially your mother who dedicated an entire lifetime to the struggle against fascism. *So* out of fashion these days. We're not *in*. We don't meditate, smoke pot, or listen to Fink Floyd."

Leon sighed. What was the point of protesting? So he just listened and continued to make his salad.

He wanted to tell his mother about the odder aspects of Herbert Orff, but knew that any secrets he shared with her would be all over Forest Hill by the weekend. So he just listened and continued to make his salad.

That night he dreamed of Carrie. He was walking with her in the woods, unable to talk, words wouldn't come. Someone else, formless, vague, seemed to be hovering in the background. It might have been his mother.

22

Carrie didn't sleep well that night. The Llewellyns' terrier, Bingo, was at it again, *yap-yap*, all night – she felt like phoning to tell them to put the dog inside. Midnight, that's what her digital clock told her before she was finally conquered by sleep.

In the morning, as she was dressing, the chimes rang, and she hurried downstairs, buttoning her blouse. Standing outside the front door was an ex-resident of these premises, a morose-looking Ted Barr.

"Just a token visit," he said.

She didn't know whether to say "how are you?" or "goodbye," but decided to put on a pleasant face, tough it out, to prove to him – and perhaps to herself – she could handle this. "Come in for coffee."

In the kitchen, she put the coffee on, and Ted picked out his special cup, with an engraving on it, some minor athletic award.

"I sort of miss this. Do you mind if I take it?"

"Of course not."

She added just a little milk to his, automatic, three years of marriage. They sat across from each other in the kitchen nook. She could think of nothing to say and waited for . . . what? The Apology, she supposed.

"I had a couple of good days with Chuck. We're still friends.

That hasn't changed. He helped me. Kind of the way he helped you once, I guess. Underneath all those porcupine quills there's actually a very tender guy hiding out."

"I know. Look, Ted, I'm sorry things went badly for you. I felt stupidly triumphant when I heard, but it's past, it's over." She said that with emphasis. She was determined not to show tears.

"I made two mistakes," Ted said.

"What was the other one?"

"Boggs. I can't stand him. He treats me like a paper-clip dispenser. I'm opening an office up on Avenue Road, Carrie, I'll stick to family law."

"I think that's a good idea."

"As long as I keep my hands off the customers, right?"

Carrie said nothing.

"Funny, I woke up this morning, and it was all gone."

"What do you mean?"

"Her."

"Mrs. Cartwright?"

"I'm over her, Carrie."

"So quick."

"Her returning to her husband, it was the best thing that could have happened. Saved my career. I was bewitched and made a fool of. It wasn't love. Infatuation."

What was infatuation but that special, undreamed-of love that people suffered? How could he make light of it that way?

"Carrie, I know it's not easy to forgive. I know I just reek of the egg that's on my face. I . . . well, I don't want you hating me for the rest of your life. I thought maybe we could talk, have dinner, see a show . . . I fell upon a couple of tickets for the Cohen concert at Massey Hall Saturday night . . ."

"No, Ted. I'm having dinner with Leon."

"With Leon."

"At his house."

"Sounds serious." Ted smiled.

"Do you need anything? Linen? Dishes?"

"Hey, no, I told you – it's all yours."

"Your coffee cup, your trophies, a bunch of books of yours are here. Maybe you should collect a few things – honestly, I don't need a lot of the stuff. Stick around and pick out what you need . . . I have to get to the office."

"Sure. Well, uh . . . Let's do lunch some time."

"Let's do lunch."

Carrie stopped at reception to pick up her calls and sort through her mail. Second notice on her overdue car loan, that had to be looked after. Invitation to speak to the Status of Women group, maybe she should do that, get more involved, help woman the barricades. Brochures from a travel agency. Jamaica. God, that would be nice.

Concert tickets. Appeals from worthy organizations. And here, a small plain envelope with her name in handwritten block print and no return address. This is the kind of envelope that the weird ones mail, she thought. On the lined sheet within were some words of poetry, carefully printed in pencil.

"In the star speckled night,
the moon darts among the darkling clouds,
flows gold, alone,
and in the remoteness of my heart
becomes a dream of you,
a dream of
inescapable
impossibility."

Rather nice. No signature. Mailed in Toronto. Who the heck? . . . Well, he didn't seem dangerous.

Chuck was strolling through the new office space on Queen West with his interior decorator, Charlene of Charlene's Interiors. She had good ideas but they didn't always coincide with his.

"Naw, I like the big high ceiling," he said. "I don't want it to be lowered."

"You'll get some noise from above," Charlene said.

Upstairs was the Hogtown Actors' Workshop, that's what the sign said out by their stairway door. Well, he'd seen some people go up there, and he couldn't hear a peep from them, so actors couldn't be *that* noisy. Didn't sound like a long-term tenancy, anyway.

Chuck looked around at the gutted interior, all the bookshelves gone now, rubbish piled in a corner. Didn't exactly look like a thriving law office yet, but wait.

Just then Harry Squire came through the front door, upset, waving a piece of paper.

"What the hell is this? I been looking for you all over. I went to pick up the stock they seized and they gave me this."

As Charlene wandered away with a tape measure, Chuck examined the document. Correctly worded this time, did *knowingly* sell obscene books. "Appears to be a summons."

"It's the same charge I was acquitted of. I thought they couldn't try a man twice for the same crime."

Yes, faithful Lisa and her friends from W.A.P. had done their job.

"Well, back to plan A, Harry, we're just going to have to wear them down. I'm afraid it's going to cost."

"Money isn't the point. I have money. How much?"

"Prelim and jury trial, two hundred days, so about two hundred grand."

Squire paled. "Two hundred . . . *thousand*? I expected maybe fifteen, twenty."

The cheap screw, Chuck thought.

"Tell you what, Harry. I'll do it for half that, flat fee in advance."

Squire's face went blank, unreadable. Chuck bought him a coffee at Barney's and spent half an hour trying to pump him up, promising him everything but the moon. The trial would be a great civil-rights case, witnesses would come from afar, democracy was at stake, he would beat up the Crown witnesses, the fascist feminists who laid this charge.

"The issue really isn't that important," said Squire. "I think I may enter a guilty plea."

Chuck grumbled to himself as he drove back to the office: he hadn't been able to dissuade Squire. W.A.P. had won. Freedom of the written word had lost. Criminal law, it's full of cheapniks. Maybe he'd get out of it, do the civil side. Personal injuries, that's where the bucks were, whiplashes and leg-off cases.

Another tennis date with Ted tomorrow. Chuck got his clock cleaned last match, so the therapy was working, Ted was feeling more like himself. All his fantasies about patching up with Carrie – dream on, Bjorn Borg. Ted, despite the three years of marriage, seemed not to know Carrie as well as Chuck did. He wanted to tell him: don't waste the effort, buddy.

As for Carrie, all Chuck hoped was she wouldn't go caroming off Ted into some disaster-on-the-rebound. He and Lisa would have to drop by this weekend with a bottle of wine and a pizza.

Still depressed, he walked into the office, where Pauline Chong said, "There's a Mr. Klovis here for you."

Chuck looked over at the young man sitting there, a long-hair with dazed eyes, staring into space. "Come on in, Mr. Klovis."

Chuck assumed he was right behind him, but about a minute passed before Klovis made it into his office.

"I got lost a little, man."

Chuck could smell a familiar aroma from his clothes, essences of marijuana. This doubtless accounted for Klovis appearing so zoned out.

"What's your problem?"

"Like, this guy, Blair, I was s'posed to put up a hundred dollars' bail for him? Like, he's my ace buddy, man, and I can't find him, like he's disappeared into the blue."

It took several minutes of halting explanation before Chuck could pick up the major threads of this apparent fiasco. Some character by the name of Blair Johnstone had disappeared into the maw of the system over a minor pot charge. That fact was confirmed for him when he phoned the Don Jail and found out the poor stiff indeed had been waiting in custody for two weeks.

He called the federal prosecutors' office and arranged to add Johnstone to this afternoon's docket at the Old City Hall.

"You got any money for fees?" he asked Klovis.

"I spent the hundred bucks. I got fifteen."

"Give it to me."

At the Old City Hall, Chuck found Leon having a coffee at the main-floor concession.

"What's up?" Chuck said.

"Waiting for Orff. He's late. Just a fix-date."

"Yeah, I got a quickie here, too, if they bring him in. Hey, what happened to your rape trial?"

"Complete schemozzle, I'll tell you over a beer tonight."

When Chuck went down to the cells to seek out Blair Johnstone, he found Horse Kronos at his desk, flipping through one of the beaver magazines the guy was addicted to. Maybe he'd like to pick up some of those porno books in the library.

Kronos looked like a uniformed pirate today, a black patch over his left eye.

"I told you, Horse, too much whacking off, it makes you go blind."

"It's healthy, smart-ass. I do it regularly three times a day, after meals."

"What happened, you stick a thumb in your eye?"

"Ah, a fuckin' infection."

"Wash your hands after, Horse, and don't rub them in your eyes. Blair Johnstone, narcotics in possession, they brought him in yet?"

"Think he's in the bullpen. Johnson!"

A man came to the wire mesh, stocky, in his forties. He didn't seem like the guy Chuck was looking for – a hippie, he'd figured, someone younger – but he answered to the name.

"I'm going to get you out of here," Chuck said.

In One-Eleven Court, Judge Revere was nearing the end of his list, cranky, hustling things along – like most of his brethren he liked to get away early on Fridays.

When the case of Blair Johnstone was called, Chuck kept it

short and succinct: the man was without a record, he had already served two weeks when normally you get a slap on the wrist for this, the court might see its way to letting him go with time spent in custody. He knew his judge: Revere, a time-and-motion freak, doesn't like it when the system snafus.

The drug prosecutor said he had just been given the file and wanted more time to look at it.

"This is Friday," said Chuck. "We want to get away. My friend isn't suggesting, I hope, that my client stay in jail all through Saturday and the Holy Day."

A man has a right to go to church on Sunday, Chuck might have added. Fifteen-dollar fee for this brilliant submission for a big ugly twerp who's probably not even going to thank him.

"Read the charge," Judge Revere said.

Chuck's client pleaded guilty to possession of cannabis and the judge gave him an absolute discharge.

The guy almost bolted from the courtroom, not looking at anyone. Chuck quickly followed.

In the corridor, he shouted to a fast-retreating backside, "Hey, pal, I'm sending you a bill."

Chuck had his address; he'd sock it to the asshole.

✢ ✢ ✢

Orff arrived late at Judge Singh's court, looking unusually foggy.

"What took you?" Leon asked.

"Those pills made me feel good, so I ate a couple of them. I think they slowed me down."

The bandage on his hand was gone now – the cut was healing. It looked like more of a bite than a cut. Maybe, Leon thought, Hymie or Franz bit him out of spite.

"You weren't off seeing your girlfriend last night?"

"What girlfriend? I don't have a girlfriend and I don't want a girlfriend."

That's right, Leon thought, he'd gotten confused: Dottie, the skinny girl staying at Mrs. Pinkerton's house, was *Hymie's* friend. Presumably Orff had never met her.

Leon led him into court. "When your name is called, come forward and say nothing." Leon planned to apply to put Orff over for another month, time enough to allow Dr. Kiehlmann to get a better fix on him.

Judge Singh was rendering one of his meticulous oral decisions on the law, and Leon waited at the counsel bench for the half-hour it took the judge to complete it. He turned around once, and saw Orff, seated directly behind him, grinning oddly at the court reporter.

"I have a doubt to be resolved in favour of the accused," Singh concluded. "Charge dismissed. Will you call Mr. Robinovitch's case, please."

"Regina versus Herbert Orff," the clerk announced.

Leon turned. Orff didn't move from his seat, was looking around, as if studying the courtroom.

"Herbert, get up here," Leon said in a low voice.

"Herbert's not here."

"Well, good Christ, who is?"

"Hymie. I'm Hymie."

Leon didn't know quite what to say. "What are you doing here?"

"Thought I'd check the scene out."

"Oh, for heaven's sake, come here."

Judge Singh said, "Mr. Robinovitch, I sense some difficulty."

"No problem, your honour." He tugged Hymie by his collar, brought him to his feet, and urged him toward the aisle. "I'm asking that this go over another month."

Orff – or Hymie – continued to ogle the court reporter. Her eyes widened with something akin to alarm. Leon feared he'd overdosed on those drugs Kiehlmann had given him.

Singh granted the month remand. Outside court, Leon checked to see whom he was speaking to. "Hymie?"

"I really like that chick in there."

Leon remembered: Hymie was the one who was fond of women. Bit of a lady-killer.

Leon didn't know what to do – should he drive him home? But Hymie didn't seem to need his help.

245

"Herbert's got the day off. I think I'll go visit Mrs. Pinkerton's house. See if Dottie's in."

"Your girlfriend."

"Sort of. Well, more Franz's. I have to take him there, you know, every once in a while, so he can do his thing. Anyway, it's embarrassing, not something I wanna discuss."

Leon wasn't quite following this. "I'll drive you to Mrs. Pinkerton's."

"No way, three's a crowd. Hey, I think Herbert would like some more of those pills, he's only got about ten left. Do you think you can get that shrink to give him more?"

"If he'll come to see Dr. Kiehlmann tomorrow."

Hymie lowered his voice. "Herbert, he doesn't want to come. He's afraid he'll learn stuff he doesn't want to know."

"Then why don't *you* bring him? And Franz, and everybody else." What was that line from *Casablanca*? Round up the usual suspects.

"I'll talk it over," he said.

✠ ✠ ✠

Oliver McAnthony, overcome with curiosity, seated the young police scientist in a stuffed chair. He wondered what was in the big leather case he'd brought with him.

"You're Sergeant Theophile . . . is that how you pronounce it?"

"Theo. Theo O'Doull, sir." A Maritime accent, a lilt. He had intelligent, confident eyes.

"And what brings about your presence here? You said you wanted to meet *in camera* – had you meant secretly?"

"I think *in camera* is appropriate." O'Doull unsnapped his case. Some kind of miniature projector. A video camera, too. O'Doull headed up the RCMP electronics lab; McAnthony had heard he had his Ph.D. "If you'll take that painting off the wall, I can shoot it up there at eye level."

"Movies?"

"I think you'll get a bang out of this."

246

O'Doull helped him remove the painting. They set it in a corner, and O'Doull plugged in his equipment.

"I knew Harold Mitchell from Newfoundland, worked on a major file with him there." O'Doull switched on a Newfoundland south-shore accent. "We were out bustin' a bunch of the b'ys."

So this was about McAnthony's dubious friend, Inspector Mitchell. McAnthony was prepared for anything.

"Bunch of happy-go-lucky Newfie sailors. Pot smugglers, for sure. Mitchell wanted them busted. He supplied fifty tons of hemp, a ship to carry it in, and even hired a crew. All he forgot were the rolling papers. Straight blatant entrapment."

"I recall reading about it. Things rather blew up in his face, didn't they?"

"They are about to again."

McAnthony surmised O'Doull had no love for the inspector.

"He has a bunch of hard-nosed sons of bitches in his special unit," O'Doull said. "Operation Sweet Revenge. They're like a bloody secret society."

"I, too, have that impression."

"But sometimes they have to reach out for a helping hand. That's where I come in. As head of the lab I get to see things."

"Sergeant, if this is about the listening device in the prop loft –"

"Listening device? We lent them a goddamn remote camera."

He lowered the room lights. On the wall, an image appeared with a clutter of movie props in the background.

"Special wide lens I developed, so it's a little distorted around the edges, but it covers a lot."

Bowling sounds. Anne Murray on a radio. In the foreground, a table. Two men packaging heroin in condoms: Hiltz and Perez. A voice: *That first hit was kinda chippy. Too much buff.* Normie the Nose Shandler.

McAnthony hadn't realized he was bending a pencil between his hands until it snapped.

"How did you get this?"

"I made a night raid, found the tape, made a copy."

McAnthony assumed the camera had been hidden in a wall.

The Nose strolled in front of it, a syringe in his hand. *"Reason you guys might wanna unload quick is ' cause Billy Sweet might think you're cuttin' him* out."

McAnthony watched Normie disappear into a washroom, re-emerge, step toward the door, and then go sprawling as the door was kicked open into his face.

McAnthony, horrified by the following images, knew he mustn't avert his eyes, and he saw Hiltz and Perez being expertly executed by Jerszy Schlizik.

"I'm just the tester!" Normie screamed from somewhere.

Schlizik was searching for him among the crates and wardrobes as André Cristal calmly entered, gun held loose at his side.

Schlizik wheeled, and pointed his gun.

"Vouz avez du visou."

"Talk my language."

Cristal did so, firing casually from the hip, and Schlizik staggered back toward the camera and collapsed.

McAnthony then watched Cristal adjust the position of Schlizik's body and place his own gun into Perez's dead hand. He watched Normie the Nose slither towards the back door. He watched Cristal calmly walk out the other way.

Then O'Doull turned off the machine. McAnthony was utterly confounded.

"I can't believe Mitchell would withhold this."

"He had a receiver unit outside. He just sat there and smiled and watched these characters shoot each other."

"I'd like to know what the hell he thinks he's doing." McAnthony picked up the phone. "Get me RCMP narcotics."

♯ ♯ ♯

In the smoke-filled back room of Lavanderie Woznick, with all the action finished for today's card at Blue Bonnets, Big Leonard was able to concentrate on this final critical rubber of bridge. He began chortling with glee as his nervous partner laid down the dummy.

248

"You're gonna kill me, I only got three points."

"But you got the king of clubs, you sweet baby."

Woznick stood up, leaned across the card table, and planted a kiss on his partner's forehead. Then he spread out his cards in triumph.

"Laydown! Eight diamonds, three aces, and a void! Doubled and redoubled! God finally smiles on Leonard Woznick."

As he raised his arms in ecstasy, the door swung suddenly open, and a man in a ski mask disembowelled Woznick with two blasts from a sawed-off shotgun.

23

Carrie was about to leave the office for the day when André Cristal phoned, in unusual distress. She couldn't make out what he said at first.

"Repeat?"

"They 'ave kill Big Leonard."

"Big Leonard? Oh, God, André . . ."

"The filt'y bastards."

"I'm coming right over."

RCMP Superintendent Kenneth Smith, realizing Operation Sweet held serious potential for scandal, had hurriedly conferred with Ottawa before inviting McAnthony and Mitchell to join him on an RCMP launch moored at the Toronto Island Airport. They made themselves comfortable on the aft deck as the launch purred along the inner rim of the islands.

Smith observed that Mitchell was very red of face, breathing hard. McAnthony had obviously taken the whip to him.

"We're off duty, gentlemen," Smith said. It was a way of announcing that what was about to be discussed was classified. No one would be taking minutes.

He pulled a bottle of single-malt from his valise, and passed shot glasses around. "This is the real thing. Can't get it at the LCBO. Have it flown in. Just a small still, really, in the hills of Kincardine. Doesn't sell anything under twelve years."

"Superintendent, there's just been another murder," McAnthony said.

"Oh?" said Smith. "Anyone important?"

"Fellow named Leonard Woznick, Billy Sweet's man in Montreal. It has implications. He was close to André Cristal."

"A thug, then? Terrible just the same. Too many guns, that's the problem. Like America."

"Thanks to Mitchell here, they're on a killing spree."

This thing was not going to be swept under any rug, Smith realized. McAnthony was a real problem, a proud man who played by the book. Dangerous because he was honest.

"I'm almost as much in the dark as you, counsel. When Harold came to me with his Operation Sweet, I'm afraid I told him to spare me the details. His show. My mistake. I should have sat on him. No idea shit would happen." He spread his arms in a helpless gesture. "Shit is what happened. Worse if it hits the fan."

"No one knew anyone was going to be shot in that loft," Mitchell said.

"I find that astounding," said McAnthony. "You must have known the heroin had been stolen from Billy Sweet. Why did you think Schlizik was on his way up there? To pin medals on those fellows?" His voice was raised, resonant. "You had a camera in there, you mindless bugger, and you didn't make a move until it was all over, and then you continued the game! For the last two weeks! And I was its dupe! I! The prosecuting attorney!"

"Easy on, old fellow," said Smith. "Things went awry. Didn't exactly have a SWAT team in attendance. Nobody hurt but some gangsters. Human garbage. Traffickers. Hit men."

"I may sound pious," said McAnthony, more softly, "but it is the system that got hurt. Our much-maligned system of justice." Then he asked Smith: "How do you propose to handle this?"

"Normally in these situations we look for someone to blame."

✜ ✜ ✜

When Speeder Cacciati walked out of Terminal One at the Toronto International Airport, the limousine was at the curb and, lo and behold, Billy Sweet himself was sitting there in the back seat, Billy who almost never dared poke his head out of his own house. At first, Speeder figured he was here to thank him for a job well done, because Billy likes a guy who is enterprising.

But the boss, holding a little tape-machine in his lap, looked kind of grumpy. What did he do wrong?

Speeder started in fast. "Had to do it myself, Billy, no one else I could trust on this job, took the little runt down with a shotgun, easy as pie."

Billy's tight, hard voice: "I didn't tell you to eliminate Big Leonard Woznick!"

Speeder began chewing his gum faster, talking at the same time. "Billy, I know I work for you, but I got a little leeway in using my initiative. That was the general plan, right? Off Big Leonard."

"And did you think the Frenchman wouldn't find out?"

"Not yet, word don't get out that quick."

Billy played a tape from the bug in the lawyer's office. Speeder could just barely make out Cristal's telephone voice, shouting, angry.

"They 'ave kill Big Leonard."

"Big Leonard? Oh, God, André . . ."

"The filt'y bastards."

"He was screwing Leonard's daughter! You brainless bedpan! He's got information for sale! You're going to meet him tonight, you think he's going to be in a nice mood to co-operate?"

"Sure, Billy, we let him know we mean business, scare him into talking." Speeder knew this sounded lame. Here he tries to do the right thing, surprise Billy, make him happy, and he gets this shit dumped.

Billy leaned towards Speeder, and hissed. "We have got a spy. You heard that lawyer dame on the phone. A narc, a copper, a finger. A fish that is swimming in our pond. This is who we want to know about. First find out from the Frenchman whom he is. *Then* you waste the Frenchman. Got it? You got the right order?"

"Yeah, I got it."

"You blow this, and I'll feed your testicles to the Dobermans."

"Well, they ain't gonna enjoy that meal, 'cause I got Deeley, Humphries, Elvis, and Izzie watchin' my back, and we're gonna pick up Cristal and we're gonna take him to a quiet place we know and we're gonna use some exotic forms of interrogation."

"Deeley, Humphries, Elvis – how reliable are they, Speed?"

"Deeley, I don't know, he's brainless, but I don't think he's a snitch. Elvis has only been around a year. Humphries, he's dumb, too, but okay."

"I need loyal men around me, Speed."

"Like who?"

"Vinnie's flying up from Medellin. Tommy Bogue from Amsterdam."

Good choices, Speeder figured. Vinnie Eng, half Chinese or Korean or something, he'd been around with Billy from the start, years ago, and now was heading up the South America end. Tommy Bogue did the overseas stuff, used to be Billy's main man in the old days.

"What about Shadow?"

"He's coming out of retirement for me. I trust Shadow."

He's been Billy's bodyguard from the start, a guy who thought the sun shone from Billy's asshole. The boss was getting serious.

Speeder looked at his watch. "I'm gonna be late." He popped a bubble, pulled the gum from his lips.

"And what if he doesn't show up, Speed?"

"Then we chain him to his fuckin' bed and cut him 'til he talks." They had the address, from the bug in the lawyer's office.

"There's a fish in the pond, just deliver me his name. I don't care how." Billy went kind of zombie-eyed, the neurotic thing that kept happening to him these days. He kept repeating, "Hook the fish, Speed. Hook the fish."

"You're goddamn rights I will. I ain't ascared of this clown, Billy. He's an amateur."

✢ ✢ ✢

Carrie and Cristal were standing outside on his penthouse deck, staring across the golden city, bathed in a sun two hours from falling. She had accepted his offer of wine this time, Chablis in a chilled glass.

Cristal was stiff, holding the railing with clenched hands, his face set, his eyes motionless. Carrie didn't know what to say, but she kept glancing at him. She had seen him angry before – but this was different, a silent rage.

Carrie looked out toward the islands, where Leon lived. The tree-shaded walkways, the busy little airport, the boats in the bay.

Beyond the islands was the unbroken horizon of Lake Ontario, and, directly in front of her, the vertical slash of the CN Tower, the so-called tallest self-supporting structure on earth: it reminded Carrie of a huge hypodermic syringe. She thought of Trixi. She thought of other ruined lives. Leonard Woznick. Poor Lenore, his daughter.

"How did you hear about it?" she said finally.

"I just 'appen to make a call to Montreal. To a friend."

"To Lenore."

"And it . . . she . . . well, she was hysteric, a man in a ski mask, she kept saying that. A shotgun."

Lenore . . . From her bag Carrie pulled out the photograph of Woznick's daughter, the snapshot he'd given to her. The sunny, smiling young woman in her graduation gown.

She offered it to Cristal. "He gave me this. He was proud of her, wanted her to be a lawyer."

But Cristal just glanced at it, looked away again to the horizon.

"I don't think you should go to that street carnival tonight, André."

He swung around, an odd, bright, biting light in his eyes.

"*Merde*. I'll go." Then, softly: "No one will stop me now."

"From what? What are you talking about?"

"They are garbage. Garbage that 'as to be taken out."

"Taken out? You mean *killed*? You'll do no such thing!"

He remained silent for a while, then turned and walked back into the apartment without a word to her. She followed, watched him reach into a bag in the closet and pull out a revolver and a shoulder harness.

"Where did you get that?"

"The gun is a gift from Big Leonard."

"The harness?"

He didn't answer. He placed the gun on a bureau and strapped on the holster.

"You *are* a professional killer, aren't you?"

Cristal shrugged.

She thought: this man is dangerous. Also, he isn't thinking straight.

As he reached for his jacket, she hesitated, then quickly grabbed the revolver and ran out to the patio with it. By the time Cristal reached her, she was holding the gun over the railing.

"Please give it to me, Carrington."

"I'll throw it on that rooftop, no one will get hurt."

Cristal checked his watch. "It's seven o'clock, I want to be there by eight. Before it is dark, Carrington, for another reconnaissance."

"You were there already?"

"This morning. I went into the hall, checked the exits. Nothing will happen to me, Carrington. I am very capable for what I do."

"They want to kill you, André. Think about what you've done, for God's sake, you've created a paranoid monster. Billy is sick with it. You went around spreading that story about a spy – that's why he killed Big Leonard, he probably thinks the spy is you, he . . ."

She went into verbal stall, rendered mute by the thought that had struck her and by the truth that was in Cristal's stone-cold eyes.

After a long silence, she said, "What is your real name?"

✣ ✣ ✣

The RCMP launch had left the inner harbour, and was skirting the rim of the outer island beaches. The lowering sun was flashing off the glass of the downtown skyscrapers. Superintendent Smith thought: Toronto the Good, but there was much evil behind the placid veneer of this city.

Smith was interrogating Mitchell now. McAnthony was just listening, sipping a second Scotch. Smith hoped it was mellowing him.

"What's his name?"

"Captain Michel Lachance," Mitchell said. "He's in the 2 Commando, Canadian Airborne Regiment."

"Why did you go outside the RCMP?"

"We'd been narked before, sir. We wanted an outsider. A volunteer. We thought of the Airborne. You know their reputation."

Smith nodded. "Yes, those fellows make the Green Berets pale."

"We did some interviews, looked at a few other people. But he was the cream. He was single, no family, adopted, a career soldier who didn't need training. He was a natural, an actor. He jumped at it. He wanted it."

"It sounds as if he was somewhat too eager," said Smith.

"Yeah. Maybe. He kind of turned out that way. We did some psych tests on him, and he was okay, a little headstrong, that's all. Anyway, we set him up with Leonard Woznick, gave him some pretty good cover – he was to say he was out of the Dubois gang. Billy is always looking for guys handy with guns."

"Did he know about the camera in the loft?"

"No, he didn't. He said he shot in self-defence when Schlizik turned his gun on him."

"But that's not true."

"No, he just greased the son of a bitch. I don't feel particularly bad about it, if you want the truth. Schlizik had just shot two guys, Captain Lachance probably thought his own life was in danger."

"That's not what we see on the film," said McAnthony.

Smith silenced him with a flick of his hand. "When did he tell you this, that he had shot in self-defence?"

"We had a couple of meets. There's a place we go."

"Headstrong, you say." Smith was still contemplating a way out of this. A police agent had committed murder on the job. If only there hadn't been that video tape. Or if it hadn't been discovered by that scientist, O'Doull, who apparently had it in for Mitchell.

"Okay, he went off on his own on the Schlizik thing," said Mitchell, "it wasn't in the script."

"What did the script say?" McAnthony asked. "Did the script say Schlizik and your agent were to murder a couple of heroin thieves?"

"We knew there was going to be some action. We didn't know what. We didn't expect to see Lachance there."

"I don't suppose you gave this James Bond a licence to kill," McAnthony said.

Mitchell looked at his tormentor with sullen hostility.

"We told him to look after himself."

"Okay," said Smith, "so what then?"

"So we decided, what the hell, alter the game plan a little bit. Make an arrest, get him bailed out, then put him right in tight with Billy Sweet as the guy who can save his skin."

"And hope no one would see the video," said McAnthony. "The arrest was a sham. You used the court system, Mitchell. You used me. You used . . . And how did you settle on Carrington Barr to defend him?"

"She was in the papers. Just won a big murder. Seemed logical."

"Or is it you thought she was a little raw? And tends to buy her clients' stories too readily?"

"Never really knew that . . . Goddamnit, Oliver, Billy Sweet runs millions of bucks worth of smack into this country and he's

257

crawled to the top of the garbage heap he helped to create. Your holy institution of the courts, they've done a damn great job of bringing Sweet to justice, haven't they?"

"Gentlemen," said Smith, "this becomes self-defeating. If you will permit me, let me pursue a line of thought. I hear they train these commandos until killing becomes an instinct, Inspector. Do you think he could have gone bad? An actor, you say – are you sure he just couldn't escape his role?"

"What do you mean?"

"This Big Leonard character. And Mr. Norman Shandler. Who's to say he didn't, ah, do away with them?"

"Well, that doesn't make sense."

"Headstrong, you say. Out there doing his own thing, as it were."

"Deserves a goddamn medal."

Smith said nothing. He knocked back his single malt. "My, that's tasty."

"What do you want me to do, sir?"

"I want you to pull him, Harold. Immediately."

Silence, just the purr of the motor, the wash at the bow. Finally, Mitchell said, "I'll be seeing him tomorrow. I'll pull him."

"He should be charged with murder," said McAnthony.

"He already is," said Smith.

"An . . . army officer." Carrie was dazed, her mind whirring. What were the implications here? She'd been made a fool of, to start with. "You're Operation Sweet."

"Basically, yes."

She had returned the gun to him. He was zipping a suede jacket over the holster.

"Everything has been a lie, then."

"Not everything."

"Your story about being an architect, becoming an addict after your lover who was killed – you really sucked me in, Captain . . ."

"Lachance. Michel Lachance. Part of it was true. The woman I loved, she died . . . Only she was my wife."

Carrie faltered a little. "Big Leonard's daughter. Lenore. You used her to get in with that gang. That's bloody awful. That's sick."

"I'm sorry for Lenore. It seemed the best way. You do what you have to do . . . She will have her revenge. *Merde*, Carrington, it's *they* who are sick. Sweet, Cacciati, those guys. They are the scum of this earth. I 'ave to go. We can talk later."

"Just a second here." She ran to the front door and, her arms outstretched, barred it.

He smiled and looked at her critically. "The image is of a woman on the cross."

"What are you then, a hired assassin?"

"Not quite, Carrington."

"I intend to end this whole operation."

"But you can't. Everyt'ing I 'ave tell you, it is privilege, yes? You are still my lawyer."

"I am *not* your lawyer."

"I will come back. Please, just stay here." He took a step, his hand moved toward the doorknob. She blocked it with her buttocks.

"Not until I have some answers."

His hand went to her waist, and she jumped – not from his touch, but from the sparks it caused. Lachance withdrew his hand and looked at it with mock horror.

"You are trying to electrocute me."

"I'm sure it's coming from you."

"*A bientôt*, Carrington."

Almost before she could blink, she was literally swept off her feet, and he was carrying her in his arms, both of hers pinned. He deposited her gently on a couch and was out the door before she could clamber up again.

24

Speeder Cacciati showed up at the street carnival just before sunset and mingled for a while. Big crowd, nice weather, sort of cooler now. Coloured lights strung from the trees of the park behind the church. Booths with pepperoni and pasta and plastic icons and pictures of Joe DiMaggio and Sophia Loren and the Polish pope. The sponsors, the Knights of St. Francis of Assisi, wore costumes of Roman centurions.

Speeder, though a Knight of St. Francis of Assisi himself, was in the same old clothes he had on when he took Woznick down, except now he had on a sports jacket. He was supposed to work one of the wheels in the hall, but had to beg off. He figured he'd spend some money, though, because it was all for a good cause.

A stage was set up in the centre of the park where a Centurion with a microphone was introducing some girls, the carnival-queen contest. Speeder moseyed over there to check them out. A dozen cute chicklets with corsages, all dressed up like Cinderellas, and Speeder figured all the Luigis standing around here with their wives, clapping, they were thinking about all that teenage pie, how sweet it would be to lay some pipe.

Not Speeder. He liked someone more mature. More, kind of, aristocrat, where you can have an intelligent conversation after. Like that fancy frosty Carrington Barr, maybe she wasn't so frigid in bed, he knew the type. If he couldn't squeeze it out of Cristal who the narc was, he might persuade her to kind of open up. Speeder thought he might not mind doing that at all.

No sign of Cristal outside the hall. But the idea was to meet him inside, that's why he gave him the free tickets. Humphries and Elvis and those guys would be covering the exits; Deeley was supposed to bring a car around.

He was speeding pretty good now, had done a couple just before getting here. He felt really fine, full of go and kind of lucky, like he could win some money tonight. It'd be a nice change to win, a guy gets tired of losing all the time with Billy.

The big persuader in his pocket, a .38, made him feel good, too. Just kind of lightly poke it in the Frenchman's ribs, and say, Hey, André, this ain't my love muscle, how'd you like to take a little stroll?

Those girls up there with their big boobs and nervous smiles, you think they wouldn't freak if they knew who he was? Speed Cacciati, gunslinger, cowboy, you look at me the wrong way, *blam.*

"Theresa," said the M.C., "what is your hope for the future of the world?"

"I think everybody has to get together and *really* work to love each other."

"Isn't that wonderful, folks," said the centurion. Speeder clapped along with the others. When the next girl was introduced, he gave a wolf whistle, then wandered off, stopping at a booth to buy some gum. They only had those candy-coated gum balls in a machine, three for a dime, not the kind he liked, the Dubble Bubble wrapped in a little comic strip.

In the hall he slipped around to the back of the stage. From there, hidden in the shadows of the curtain, he could pretty well see everything, three walls lined with concessions, but mostly games like roulette and crown and anchor, and a few other deals in which you're supposed to toss hoops or throw balls.

He couldn't see the Frenchman anywhere, and he worried maybe Billy was right, that he might be pissed off about Big Leonard. Blame it on a gang war, or something.

He sat on a bench at a crown and anchor where he could watch the entrance and invested a little money. *Plock, plock, plock* went the little rubber pointer, right on the lucky number. Twenty bucks, just like that, he does pretty good when Billy isn't around spreading his bad karma.

His streak continued. He got kind of excited and wasn't watching when he should've, and before he knew it André Cristal was right there beside him, on the bench. Where had the guy come from? He was here suddenly, quiet like a cat, right beside his gun pocket.

"I 'ope I don't bring you bad luck." Speeder saw the smile, but didn't like the look in his eyes. He'd met the Frenchman a few times, hired him on for Billy to work with Schlizik. Every time he saw him, he had this kind of look like he hated you.

"Hey, André, how are ya? Good you could come."

"Where's Billy? I said I wanted to meet with him."

"The plan is I'm gonna take you to him."

He watched Cristal put ten dollars on one of the squares.

"No, the plan is you're going to bring him to me."

Speeder decided the guy had a bad case of attitude. "No chance. You gotta know Billy, he don't like to go out much."

Plock, plock, plock. Cristal got paid off three to one. Speeder donated twenty dollars to the Knights of St. Francis of Assisi.

Calm, and kind of out of the blue, Cristal asked, "Did you kill Big Leonard today?"

"Who, me?" Speeder was confused by the bluntness of the question. Should he pretend it was all news to him? He really hadn't figured this part out. "Yeah, I heard. Naw, that was an outside job. Some money hassle is the word on that – he was runnin' a stacked game on the book."

From the look on the Frenchman he was obviously not satisfied. The guy had these cold killer eyes that went right through you and out the back. Speeder felt uncomfortable now, the speed was losing its zing.

"Honest, André. Outsiders, he kinda welshed on them. Juice dealers. Heavy people. And you got my commiserations. We all liked Big Leonard. His daughter, Lenore, listen, we got plans to see her through college."

The Frenchman was right up close to him where he could talk low, but it meant Speeder couldn't easy just reach into his sports jacket and grab his piece. He began to notice his pile of bills was shrinking and Cristal's was growing. He didn't see this as a good sign.

"When did you make these plans for Lenore? Before you killed him?"

Speeder thought: plans, that didn't sound too good, the hit was just a few hours ago . . . "We're *gonna* make plans, André. Hey, you're way out in left field on this play –"

"I t'ink I will break your goddamn neck."

Speeder shook his head with pretend disbelief and grinned nervously. He couldn't help looking around to see if any of the guys was in the hall. There was Elvis, just inside the exit through the kitchen, but standing there a little too obvious.

"You 'ave others outside, eh? At the doors? The ones standing around smoking and looking stupid? André, he is not stupid. Because André knows somet'ing that makes him smart. It is somet'ing Billy will kill to know. I am not going to give it to him so cheap as he 'oped."

"Like, who is he, André? This canary. He work for the government?"

"No. The cops bought him, paid him off big."

"How do we know you're not lying?"

"Take the chance."

But Speeder knew Cristal had the goods, the tapped phone call had confirmed that. This guy was a smart operator, smarter than anyone thought. He was confident, kind of scary-acting. Stay cool, Speeder, don't just grab for the piece.

Plock, *plock*, *plock*, the Frenchman doubles his money again, Speeder donates more to the Knights.

"So what're you thinkin' in terms of, André?"

"You tell Billy I want to meet with him on my ground. Tell him I don't do deals with some stinking flunky."

"Hey, frog, you don't start giving fuckin' orders to Speeder Cacciati. I speak for Billy. I run his show."

"You wipe his nose and wash his underwear. You are not'ing, a two-bit punk. I make my deal with Billy."

Speeder began to pat his pockets, as if looking for something, the breast pockets first, and he pulled out some empty bubble-gum comic wrappers he'd been saving to read. "What kinda deal are you talkin'?"

"The deal is I will snuff the stoolie."

"Good plan. Billy will pay you off real big for that."

"You're damn right. Because I want in."

"What's that mean?" Now Speeder casually slipped his hand into the gun pocket.

"Equal partners."

"The fuck you'll —"

Speeder felt fingers on his wrist, like steel clamps.

"I 'ave a big gun, too, Speeder."

"You're fuckin' crazy, you know that?"

"Tell him half of everyt'ing. His corporations, his import business. He signs over half the shares. Got it?"

Speeder's hand was in pain, and he started to get scared because he was losing feeling in it.

"I'll tell him."

"I will call your pager number tomorrow, eh? It's still the same?"

He grunted, "Yeah. Yeah, call me."

"Now go to the front door and tell your goons the action is off. I am going to walk out that door and into the crowd."

He withdrew his hand.

Speeder slid off the bench, got a few feet away from him. Now he had his hand in his pocket, on the gun. "I could just blast you off the face of the earth, asshole."

The Frenchman shrugged. "You wouldn't stand a chance. Anyway, where would it get you?"

Carrie, her mind in turbulence, watched the sun die in orange tatters behind the western smog, a false sunset, factory-made. Phony like everything else in her current world.

She thought she could make out the area around St. Francis of Assisi's, a distant twinkling of coloured lights. Cristal . . . Michel Lachance, whoever he was, was making contact there. Brave soldier. Maybe foolish. What drove him?

She was having a tough time reassembling the man. Captain in the somewhat notorious Airborne Regiment. Paratroopers. Commandos. Taught karate, he'd told her.

And here was Carrington Barr, barrister and solicitor, a pawn in someone else's game. It was unheard of. How, out of hundreds of criminal lawyers, had her name been chosen? It was bloody demeaning.

At least she was defending an innocent man. He hadn't killed anyone up in that prop loft: the murder charge was obviously just a ruse to gain Sweet's confidence.

Who knew about this? Oliver McAnthony? Surely not, it could mean his career . . . Still, she couldn't see the Bullet flying off on a fancy all his own. She should call McAnthony. She should also phone one of her partners, someone. But Captain Lachance had trusted her not to.

Here she was still playing their game. But just until he returns. If he returned. She would tell him thanks, but no thanks, and she'll be sending her bill to the attorney general along with a complaint to the Law Society. She'd take it to the media.

She poured the last of the Chablis into her glass, and spilled some: she realized she was just a little swizzled. A typical escape into alcohol, she had her father's booze genes.

She had a memory of him then, his gravel voice, his boozy kiss. Why did you do it, Charlie? You went to jail for a few years, Mom died, what's left of the world carried on. So why did you leave us?

Did you lie to me, too, Charlie? Were you actually guilty? I would have forgiven. I would have forgiven.

Or were you guilty?

You *were*, goddamnit.

265

And as she realized she could no longer lie to herself, as the truth about Charlie came to her with its full terrible force, she felt shattered. And the sun died while behind her banks of cloud rolled in and bathed her in reflected rose-pink light.

I forgive you, Charlie . . .

Suddenly she felt tears welling, and for a while couldn't staunch the flow, and she was swimming in memories of her father, of Ted. She should go, she thought. Return home. To that empty house . . . No, she would wait for Captain Lachance, reassemble herself, and be dry of eye when he returned.

Stupid to break down. It was the wine. Michel Lachance will return to find her staggering drunk. Give her that big neon smile as he gently escorts her to a taxi.

Chilly, she left the patio railing to seek something warm to cover her. For the first time, she looked around: a well-furnished, expensive place. Jacuzzi in the washroom, fitness room and pool downstairs. But Her Majesty was paying for it, wasn't she?

In the bedroom were some barbells and weights. Fitness freak with a nicotine habit. In a closet she found his gear all stowed neatly. Here was his bed, made up, crisp and flat. She should have known. A soldier. Bore himself like a bloody soldier. Forward march, one, two, pick up your shoe.

She put on one of his sweaters, large and woolly. It smelled slightly of him, a smoky fragrance she found horribly attractive. In a pocket, a packet of Drum tobacco and some papers.

She went back outside to finish her wine, sat at the patio table and tried her hand at rolling cigarettes. Not to smoke, thank you. Only as art forms. Her fingers were like rubber. The first cigarette bulged at each end, was soft in the middle.

She could have one little puff.

No.

She would tell him he could stuff his three hundred thousand dollars.

The callous heel, he had seduced a young woman with improper intentions. He had lied with blithe insouciance to his lawyer. Had he lost his wife, as he claimed? What were the circumstances of *that*? Where did the lies end?

She decided to resolve her bewilderment about him by hating him. The man was contemptible. Repellant. She despised him.

She bent furiously to her task of rolling cigarettes, trying to perfect her art.

The bastard.

Her heart seemed to skip a beat as she heard him enter.

"Carrington?"

She didn't look up, but he was beside her now. His hand appeared, retrieved one of her early, flabby efforts. She heard a match strike.

When she did look up, he seemed comical, the cigarette limp and crooked between his lips, a little grin.

"Perfect. Thank you. More wine?"

"I've obviously had enough."

"But I need a drink."

He returned a minute later with a freshly opened bottle and two glasses. "In case you change your mind. An Australian Chablis, more smooth, the other had sharpness."

"Did you develop your taste for wine out on bivouac some-place?"

"My father was a diplomat. Served in the embassy in Paris, mostly."

"Poor bugger. He sent you through architectural school and you went out and joined the army."

"I did actually study for a while at the Ecole Polythèque in Paris. I was too restless. Felt inactive. I switched to the military academy in Kingston."

"And have you been in lots of wars?"

He laughed. "This is the most action I've seen since I joined. Hostile enemies all around me."

"You find this funny."

"You. The look on your face."

"You're a bastard."

"I'm just 'appy to be alive. They had six or seven goons covering that place tonight. I t'ink they wanted to take me for a ride, like in the movies. And I was suppose to 'ave backup. Which never showed."

Carrie studiously ignored that bottle of Australian wine. She told herself she wasn't interested in his close call.

"What backup?"

"Operation Sweet. They were supposed to 'ave someone there. Those guys could have taken me out right at the door. But Cacciati acted scared. He really believes there is someone inside."

"How did you convince him?"

"I guess by daring him to kill me. Being cocky just enough."

"I see. An informer wouldn't be so brazen. How suited to your role you are, Captain."

"I enjoy a little t'eatre."

"The audience laps it up. And innocent Lenore, do you think she'll applaud after the final act?"

Lachance stopped smiling. "Carrington, I 'ave been a gentleman with her. I made her no promises of love or of marriage. She will survive my loss and the loss of her father. I will pay them both back for that loss."

"Do you expect me to sit idly by while this continues?"

"For twenty-four hours, Carrington. For the weekend. Please."

"I have to go. I'd like to see you in the morning when my head is clear." She stood, grasped the railing for support, and Lachance quickly took her elbow.

"Don't fall over."

"I'm fine, thank you."

"You're angry."

"Very."

Their eyes locked. His were sad, burning no longer.

"Can I see you to a taxi?"

"Yes."

But they just stood, immobile as statues. She felt rooted, paralyzed, held there by the force of him.

Suddenly he moved towards her, kissed her on the mouth, and she found herself opening to his tongue, and their bodies came together in a deep, crushing embrace, and they were still kissing, still clinging to each other with the glue of passion as a large moon clambered from the clouds, and for some reason all she could think of was a line from that mysterious poem. *A dream of inescapable impossibility.*

25

She couldn't be sure if she had slept. All she knew was that the room had been in blackness and now the grim light of dawn's beginning was seeping through uncurtained windows.

So there had been a blank, an hour or two perhaps, after he had kissed her lips one final time and closed his eyes and vanished into the void of sleep. Yet she couldn't remember even napping, just a long time of turmoil as she lay naked on the bed and listened to the sounds of night, the soft clamour of the city, the distant wailing of sirens, the nasal beeps of swooping nighthawks.

Her throat and tongue were dry, her head was throbbing dully. How much wine had she drunk? There'd been another bottle . . .

He was lying on his side, towards her, his eyes closed but moving. Do you dream of fields of battle, Captain Lachance, more strenuous conquests than this? Then she remembered her own dream. He had shed his uniform, she'd been in his arms – or was that not a dream but a memory of the night?

She felt sticky, embarrassed. The sex, she remembered vaguely, had been spectacular but the details of it were gone. She frankly couldn't remember how her clothes came off. Somehow he must have undressed her, but had done so while they were still standing, still kissing, and suddenly his hands were touching every part of her and every living cell of her body was screaming for him.

Lord almighty, what had happened to her? Cautious calm collected Carrington Barr, so proper, so reserved. In lust's mindless, savage thrall. *It is how I see you, close to the edge. But maybe you are not such a lady in court, eh?*

Or in bed . . . She remembered: oh, God, how *awful*: they had coupled standing up – was that possible? – then on the floor . . . It was terrible, that wild, jungle-animal scream of orgasm.

Her scream.

And later, in bed, he had brought her to another climax, with his mouth – her back arching, her hands clapped over her mouth.

God, twice. Not even with Ted . . . How simply incredible.

Three years of marriage. Of faithfulness to Ted. She doesn't do these things.

She remembered her ringing denunciations of Ted. "A client! He should be disbarred!"

No. Not the same at all. Her client was André Cristal. This was a fellow by the name of Michel Lachance. A knave. He had duped her into thinking he was a client, causing her mysteriously to go to bed with him. To spend the night with. Say it. To ball. To screw.

Why? . . .

Okay, he was ridiculously attractive, had been recently close to danger. Aphrodisiac element there. And then all the wine and all the loneliness and add to that all the anger at Ted. Mix in a dash of pure insanity. Recipe for complete lapse of control and judgment.

Now how was she going to approach Oliver McAnthony with her grievance about being used as a tool of the state? During the subsequent inquiry, would she be asked how she enjoyed the oral sex?

She thought she heard the city slowly awaken. She could smell their sweat, could smell the funky odours of spent sexuality. And she was . . . off the pill. No protection, my God, she'd been utterly *mad*.

Her unaccountable lust for him now satiated – at least she hoped it was – she lay there in the sobering light of dawn and wondered if she should dress and flee.

He could make an appointment to see her during usual office hours. She could pretend it never happened.

She urged Lachance to continue dreaming, slipped her legs off the bed, and looked around for her clothing. Not here.

She softly padded out to the living room and saw their sprawl of clothes, her blouse, her skirt, his pants and shirt. Bra and panties where they fell. She tiptoed to the kitchen and drank glass after glass of water. The drums in her head were easing now. She was exhausted – two hours' sleep, if that, but she'd get through the day.

She knelt to gather up her things and heard his voice.

"Carrington."

"I have to go." She stood, holding her clothes, not turning to look at him, sensing him close now, behind her.

"It is five-t'irty."

"It was a bad idea. It's my fault. I never do this."

His hands circled her waist and slid gently up to her breasts.

"Michel, please."

"Stay."

His body against her, his hardness. His hand now between her legs, finding her again so quickly in ripeness.

She turned, joined her nakedness to his, and kissed him deeply, with a hunger for him that she couldn't conquer.

Speeder saw that Billy had somehow got himself together this morning. Yesterday it was: "Half my *business*?" Screaming, totally demented, kind of foul-mouthed, which wasn't normal. "He can eat fuckin' *shit*! Bump him off!"

Then when he couldn't argue with the facts, that crazed, scary look came on. "Did they buy you, Speed? Did they buy you? Whom did they buy then? Give me a name. Deeley, Nagler, one of the accountants – whom did they buy?"

But Billy was almost like his old self at this morning's brunch, all business, no emotion: somehow he fought back from the brink. Courteous, even. He welcomed everybody, told them to jump in and have a swim if they wanted after.

Brunch was a kind of council of war out by the pool, with the core of loyalists Billy had brought in: Vinnie Eng out of Bogota, a skinny little guy, a cutthroat, and Tommy Bogue from Amsterdam, the big ex-enforcer with his beat-up face and crooked nose. They'd both flown in last night. And also Shadow was brought out of retirement from Florida, Billy's old bodyguard who was getting a pension. Shadow was about sixty-five, the only human being Billy *really* trusted, and he was a real pigsticker, mean as a knife.

So including Speeder, there was five of them, and he was happy to see he was still on the inner circle after Billy's paranoid rantings yesterday: "How do I know you aren't lying? How do I know you weren't plotting with him?"

He got into this real fixation for a while about Speeder, who got kind of shook up and decided to wean himself off a little from the speed, did some downers instead, Nembutal, Billy always complaining he had a garbage habit.

But being cool as a pool shark now, Billy was laying out the whole thing over coffee. He played for them that tape of Carrington Barr talking to the prosecutor: "*Do I have to spell it out? Our friend that you have on the, ah, inside. The mole.*"

"One," Billy said. "it is no longer safe to assume Mr. Cristal is lying or bluffing. Two, he is looking for a big payday – I don't know how much he'd settle for, some number in the millions. Three, his lawyer also knows who the fish is. These are the factors we work with, gentlemen. Did he say when he'd call, Speeder?"

"Some time today."

"Stall him. Get a couple of days off of him. We still have that little ear in the lawyer's office, maybe it'll hear something."

"Why don't we just pick him up," said Tommy Bogue. "Make him talk."

"I think he's got that figured out. Because it's obvious the lawyer's in it with him. Squeeze him and she goes to the police, and they pull out their stoolie, and then it's too late."

"Go after the lawyer, then," said Elvis.

"Then Mr. Cristal tips the men at headquarters. No, the bug will tell us when the time is ripe, when we can jump them together. I would like them brought here, downstairs to the sound-proof rooms. You put people in separate rooms where they can hear each other screaming, that's when people talk."

Speeder was relieved to see Billy Sweet was back in harness. Billy wasn't no dummy, that's not how he lasted so long in this business. When the toughs get going, the going gets tough. Something like that.

"Do you think he's boffing her, Speed?" said Billy.

Speeder almost swallowed his gum. "Naw, she wouldn't . . . not with that guy." The thought repelled him.

"I think he's boffing her. That will make it easier."

"Why do you think they're . . . doin' that?" Speeder said.

"Because her car's been outside his building all night. Right, Shadow?"

"Still was at nine when I left to come here." When he talked, which was hardly never, Shadow kind of wheezed like an old man.

Speeder was suddenly in a bad temper, cheesed off. The cunt, he thought she had more quality. Balling Cristal. How long had *that* been going on? He felt the goofballs he'd been taking lumped up in his stomach, bringing him down, and his elbows were itching like crazy.

"Maybe it's her that's running the play, Billy," he said. "Not Cristal."

"That's a thought."

"She'd be more co-operative to talk to than him. I think we should just grab her, and I could have it out of her in ten, fifteen minutes. I think I can deal with her pretty good."

"I spoke of the dangers."

"Yeah, but I say we take Cristal down. I don't think we should fuck around with him. After he's out of the picture, we grab her real fast. She'll talk, Billy, I know it." He blew a confident bubble.

Billy puckered his forehead in thought. "Okay, if the chance comes, do it that way. Mr. Cristal first."

Speeder's pager beeped.

✚ ✚ ✚

This time, when she awoke, his side of the bed was empty, and sunlight was pouring through the windows. Her headache, miraculously, was gone. She listened to the city's buzz, listened to her heart, listened for the sounds of Michel Lachance somewhere in this apartment. Music somewhere, classical, the Bruch concerto.

His bedside clock said ten-fifteen. Late for work. No, it was Saturday.

But for a while she couldn't get out of bed. She felt so . . . what did she feel? Complete. Good. Why the hell should she be feeling good? If it's good it must be bad. She should be embarrassed. How awful. Bloody ridiculous.

She finally pulled herself from the bed, this time with a rumpled sheet around her. She felt a patch of dampness on it, her own or his she didn't know. In her mouth, a taste of saltiness.

In the en suite bathroom she studied the mirror, seeking the madwoman in it, but saw only a frowning bright-eyed face, and . . . was that a smile? It's not funny.

Oh, God, *how* she had wanted a cigarette afterwards. But she hadn't broken down. Carrington Barr was made of steel.

A gentleman, he kept a spare toothbrush. A quality brand of shampoo. Big soft towels.

After a hot shower, she wrapped towels around her hair and body, and made a grand entry into the main room. The music had been coming from the radio, the Radio-Canada FM station, voices now speaking a melodious French. No sign of her host. Or her clothes – no, here they were, neatly hanging in the front closet.

The other detritus of the night had been put away, too, the wine bottles and the glasses, ashtray emptied. Compulsively clean, this soldier.

No explanatory note. Well, he was out running, no doubt. She didn't intend to tarry here. She quickly dressed and left.

On her windshield was a big ugly ticket. Okay, first the office. Then try to track down Leon and Chuck. Seek the advice of friends. Decide whether to confront Oliver McAnthony. But she would not do anything for twenty-four hours to sabotage Operation Sweet – she had promised Lachance that.

Outside the G & C Trust Building was a vending stand with the Saturday *Star*. Carrie looked at the big front-page photo of Edwin Moodie. The headline said: "HAS ANYONE SEEN THIS MAN?"

She remembered, though it seemed from another life: Trixi. Mr. Moodie. The search for the Midnight Strangler.

Mr. Moodie on the run. He's so . . . obvious, she thought. How could he have disappeared? Fleeing from the law – it didn't fit any picture she had of him. But how easily and often she'd been blinded of late.

Leon was in the lounge making coffee for Jock Strachan. She greeted them with – she realized – too much cheer. Leon looked at her suspiciously. She had yesterday's clothes on, pretty unusual for her, and she wondered if Leon noticed.

"Where were you last night?" Leon said. "I kept calling you at home."

There was a feeling of censure here, she felt vaguely scolded. "I . . . stayed at a friend's."

Strachan was lounging by the window, his hands in his pockets. "I have something I want to tell you in confidence, Carrie," he said.

"Want me to leave?" Leon asked.

"Leon can stay," Strachan said. "Your partners should know. You've had no contact from Moodie?"

"None."

"Do you still believe he's innocent?"

Leon had poured her a coffee, which she sipped as she thought about her answer. "I really don't know. If he calls, Jock, I'll try to bring him in. I'll explain to him that's best."

"No, Carrie, you'll nae talk to him alone."

"You know I have to tell him his rights."

"I think it may be dangerous to see him. Carrie, we spoke to another tenant of the Eagle Hotel, who'd visited Moodie in his room. There were pictures of you all over the wall."

"Don't be ridiculous. I'm his hero, why is that surprising?" But it was, to her, a little.

"Stories about his trial. Newspaper photos of the girls who were killed."

"That trial was a big event in his life."

"Always defending, eh, Carrie?"

"What do you have on him – other than the fact he hasn't shown his face recently?"

"If we find him, we'll soon know whether he's guilty. I haven't made this generally known – and I will trust both of you not to divulge it – but Trixi Trimble bit him."

"Where did she bite him?" Carrie asked.

"Her teeth were clenching a shred of skin. Dense epidermal skin, forensics says. From his palm, we assume. Not enough for a print, sadly. But a wee bit of blood. Not hers. She's type A. It's B and Moodie is B."

"That's still half the population," said Carrie, still defending. But there wasn't much point in it now, was there? If Moodie were arrested with that bite on his hand, the medical scientists could probably make a skin impression match.

"You had better be damn careful, Carrie," Leon said. "He's seen all the newspaper headlines. If he's innocent, why hasn't he turned himself in?"

"My thinking entirely," said Strachan. "He's waiting for the wound to heal. But if you're as much a *hero* to him as you think you are, he may contact you before then."

"I'll . . . If he does, I'll call you, I promise."

Strachan finished his coffee and stood to go.

"I suppose you think I am to blame, Jock, for getting him off."

"You defended fairly. That girl couldn't identify him in court." He smiled ruefully. "I dinna know what to think when that young woman pointed to me."

Carrie had to laugh. "She was so sure you were the Midnight Strangler."

After he left, Leon said, "Maybe it *was* Jock – you notice how he kept his hands in his pockets?"

"He always does that . . . Leon, don't be ridiculous."

"Sorry, I have an incredible sense of humour. I have a better candidate for the Midnight Strangler anyway. Pour yourself another cup, sit down, relax."

Carrie listened raptly to Leon's account of the injury he'd seen on Orff's hand: a human bite, it had looked like.

"When did you first notice this bite?"

"Thursday afternoon. The day after Trixi was murdered."

And he told her about Susie, the female voice within Orff who had come out under hypnosis. He described her odd reaction to bellicose Franz. "'He likes to do terrible things,'" that's what Susie said, "'awful things,' she said, and then we lost her. Orff hates women, or has some kind of psychotic fear of them. Physically, he fits the bill, a big guy."

"Short, though . . . Where is he now? Somebody should check him out."

Leon looked at his watch. "He's supposed to come in to see Hal Kiehlmann in an hour. I'd better go over there *tout de suite*. And if you'll pardon my French, *comment ça va* your client, M. Cristal?"

"Um, okay, I guess. I saw him yesterday." All of him. She realized she didn't dare talk about Captain Lachance for fear she would blurt out something about last night. Leon might not understand – *she* didn't understand. "I'll wait for you here. I have some stuff to tell you." She would explain later, when more composed.

As Leon strolled across the campus to Hal Kiehlmann's building, he worried about ethics. He was going to ask the psychiatrist to look for a Midnight Strangler hidden within one of Orff's personae. But Orff was Leon's client, entitled to his protection. Anyway, the state couldn't convict Orff for what Franz had done – or could it?

The Midnight Strangler attacked only every six or seven months, so there was some down time to think about this. Find out who this Dottie is, who Mrs. Pinkerton is, persuade Orff to undergo a little more hypnotherapy, and if they couldn't get a confession from Franz, one of the others might be prepared to rat on him. No . . . that's wrong, Strachan had to be informed right away, before that wound to his hand could heal. A conundrum.

Kiehlmann was waiting for him. Leon had already recited his concerns to him by phone, breaking his promise of silence to Detective Strachan about the bite on the hand.

"The guy could not possibly be the Midnight Strangler, could he, Hal? In one form or the other?"

"It's possible. Orff suffers a deep-seated antipathy toward women. Fear, perhaps, or a form of neurotic misogyny. But I can't believe he would have the wherewithal to commit all these attacks and not get caught. He is a man of simple mental resources."

"Maybe Franz has more."

"I wouldn't want to make any, ah, over-hasty diagnoses."

"Maybe there are others we don't know about. He could be a walking whodunit, full of possible suspects. Maybe Hymie is a collaborator – he takes Franz off to see Dottie and that's when he goes dotty."

"When he comes in, I'll see if I can't get Hymie to talk about Franz. He doesn't seem to be withholding anything."

"Let's find out how he got that injury, Hal. And where he was Wednesday night."

Leon told him about Hymie's recent appearance in court, standing in for Orff. And later, Hymie's enigmatic reference to Franz and Dottie: *I have to share her with Franz . . . It's embarrassing, not something I wanna discuss.*

"I think he's using too many of those pills, Hal. What's in them?"

"Barbiturates with codeine. Hope he's not abusing them."

Leon looked at his watch. "He's late."

26

Running hard, feeling his lungs burn, Lachance saw the heavy clouds continue to roll in from the south, a coming clash of fronts. The air was oppressive today, fragile, buzzing with electricity. But above was still the scorching sun.

His route took him through the winding tree-lined streets of sedate Rosedale, district of the rich. Afterwards it took him north, through parkland on the banks of the Don. He would make one rest stop, a pay phone near a public convenience, the number of which he had already given Cacciati's pager service. And a time: eleven hours, fifteen minutes.

He pulled up there to a puffing halt. He was a few minutes early, so he opened his packet of tobacco. In it he found one of the cigarettes Carrington had rolled last night. A very limp one. He smiled as he remembered her, how astonished at her own inexhaustible desire. He could still smell her fragrances.

From the first time he'd met her, he had known they would make love.

Just as he'd known he'd be betrayed – though he didn't know by whom.

He had told Carrington he was psychic. Of course she didn't believe him. It was impossible to explain. It didn't please him to have a sense of the future. It was depressing, in fact.

His first premonition of betrayal had come to him many months ago, when Mitchell had brought him to Toronto for the interviews. But he had volunteered for this work, to live and maybe to die on the edge.

The pay telephone rang. Lachance simply said, "Yes, it's me."

Cacciati seemed uneasy. "He'll meet you Tuesday night, late. Has to be a private place, and we got some ideas –"

"I will tell you when and where. Tonight. Half past nine. In public. At the revolving bar up in the CN Tower." The safest place he could think of, three hundred metres above the surface of the earth. Not easy to take a shot at someone and get away – he'd been up there, and it was a long elevator ride back to the ground.

"Billy don't wanna –"

"*Sacré*, I don't give a damn! I have a quarter and I am at a pay telephone. It is easy, I just tell the police their paid informant is in danger."

A pause. "The CN Tower, I don't know, Billy's ascared of heights."

"Give him a sedative. Just Billy and me, eh? Nine-t'irty tonight will be a deadline."

He hung up. The scabrous Speeder Cacciati with his fat floating pupils. A garbage-head. Drugged and dangerous.

But Lachance would be armed. He would be wired. The inspector would hear everything. Again he wondered – why hadn't there been backup last night? Mitchell's expert, Lamont, in one of his many disguises. But maybe he'd been disguised too well.

He continued running, north again, up a little strip of park in a creek valley, to Mount Pleasant Cemetery.

The thunderheads billowed closer, yet the sun still shone upon the gravestones. Lachance checked his watch. Eleven forty-five hours, no Mitchell. Just Lachance and the silent remains of many dead.

Now he saw a hearse turn in through a distant gate, cars following in slow procession. How languorous the rites of death. He smoked and watched the people in black, sad men and women following a coffin up a pathway among the trees.

Around a bend in the path came Harold Mitchell, purposeful, wearing a floppy hat to cover his bald scalp. He waved but did not look Lachance in the eye.

"It's over, Michel," he said.

Lachance wasn't sure what he meant. "Where was my backup last night? It could have been very dangerous there."

"I pulled them. And I'm pulling you."

Lachance was incredulous. "You're serious?"

"Dead serious."

"I'm there! It's almost zero hour. Billy Sweet's hungry for the bait. *Maudit!*"

"You blew it. And now my feet are in the fire."

"Blew it . . ."

"It's all on video, Michel. We have you murdering Schlizik."

There was silence as the realization hit Lachance. Then he said, "You had video . . . you *showed* it?"

"Someone unauthorized saw it."

"What does that mean?"

"Means you're charged with Schlizik's murder for real. They want to proceed."

"Schlizik? Does someone care? Schlizik? He shot your two undercover men, you told me to –"

Mitchell cut him off quickly. "I didn't tell you anything. I told you to use your judgment."

"And if I had the chance, to take the bastard down! I had licence. I had *carte blanche!*"

Lachance felt his control go – he felt unhinged, he was almost shouting.

Mitchell looked about apprehensively. "Easy, Michel, there are people over there."

Lachance lowered his voice to a hiss. "I was asked to go inside and root the maggots out. I've risked my life to do so, and you're saying they want to prosecute me for murdering Schlizik? I will go to jail for my life?"

"It was blown wide open, Michel. I don't have options. Look, I can make a hell of a pitch –"

"I'm there! How can you . . ." So this was the betrayal that had been divined. And the thought that it had to come calmed him a little.

He flipped his cigarette away, looked around for Lamont, for the others. "Am I under arrest?"

Mitchell shifted uncomfortably. "Well, Michel, right now I'm alone."

Lachance smiled his coldest smile. "So this is my chance to disappear? I'm to be saddle with everyt'ing. I am to be sacrifice to the altar because I eliminated some stinking pustule. Ah, Mitchell, you're a Judas."

"Take your time. Pack your bags. We won't hit your apartment for six hours." Mitchell started backing away, again glancing nervously at the mourners near their burial plot. "I'll say you must have been tipped. You never showed up."

"You corrupt shit. I am not running."

"Suit yourself." Mitchell strode away.

✢ ✢ ✢

Alone in the deserted office, Carrie anxiously awaited Leon's return from Dr. Kiehlmann's office. Outside her window she saw a distant ribbon of lightning over the lake, and she thought of Lachance's electric touch.

How convincing he had been in his role of mobster, this glib commando. In just six months he had parlayed a friendship with Big Leonard Woznick into a role as enforcer for the underworld – sucking in crooks and lawyers. Brilliant. Yet there seemed something just slightly off-centre about the man, something askew she couldn't identify.

How was she going to deal with him when they next met? Awkwardly, no doubt. Hands-off relationship from now on. Pretend it never happened.

She found that didn't work. Her memory insisted on embarrassing her with instant replays of her long night of dissolution.

Impatient because of Leon's lateness – it was mid-afternoon –

Carrie was readying to leave when he finally came back. He looked a little exasperated.

"Well, is your Herbert Orff the Midnight Strangler?"

"He didn't show at Kiehlmann's. I drove all the way out to his house, but he wasn't there either. All locked up and windows closed."

"We have to tell Jock Strachan about that bite mark, Leon."

"Let me try to track Herbert down first. Maybe he's working weekend sewer backups. I'll try to reach that Mr. Blumberg. I could try calling all the Pinkertons in the phone book and ask if Dottie is home."

"Leon, I have to talk to you."

"Sure." But he seemed distracted. She followed him into his office, where he started leafing through the phone book.

"Leon, André Cristal isn't really André Cristal. He's a cop. Sort of. A rent-a-cop."

Leon reacted as if she had told him it was going to rain tonight. "Scarborough, Waste Management, probably closed today." He looked up from the phone book. "What did you say?"

His eyes kept widening as she repeated it for him in detail, the shenanigans of Inspector Mitchell, Lachance's role as a government mole.

"That's incredible!"

"I don't know whether to sue or scream or what."

"Do you want me to call Oliver McAnthony for you?"

"No, I . . . I promised Michel I wouldn't rock his boat for twenty-four hours."

Leon shook his head stubbornly. "I'll call McAnthony."

"There's something else, Leon. Something worse." Leon would understand – he would be her confessor. "I went a little nuts last night. I slept with him."

Carrie could scarcely believe the amount of pain that registered on Leon's face. He seemed slowly to withdraw into himself.

"You're shocked. So am I."

Leon had no response. He broke eye contact, went back to his phone book. With a mechanical slowness, he dialled a number.

His voice seemed to break as he talked to someone about an emergency, asked how to reach Mr. Blumberg. He wrote down a number.

Still not looking at her, he said, "Let me deal with this first. We'll talk later."

"Well, we do have a date this evening."

"Yes. Dinner." His words were faint. "Is that still on?"

"Of course. Can I bring anything?"

"I have everything. Thanks."

Carrie felt enormously guilty now about her night of sin, her lapse. It had been a scandalous thing to do – she could see that now from Leon's reaction.

He was looking past her, at his door. She turned and saw Captain Michel Lachance standing there.

"I took a chance of finding you here."

She was suddenly flustered, and felt a burn rise to her cheeks.

"Oh, hello. Have you met Leon, my partner?"

Lachance walked in and held out his hand. "André Cristal. A pleasure."

"*Mon plaisir*," said Leon, expressionless, half-rising to meet him.

Carrie, weak of knee, led Lachance out into the corridor.

"I need a drink," he said. "Do you have a whisky?"

"We have some Ballantine's."

She led him into the lounge, and sat him down. "Ice or anything?"

"No. Neat."

She poured just a little for herself – for her nervousness.

"Did something go wrong, Michel?"

"Now I really need a lawyer," Lachance said. "And it is time for the whole truth. What I tell you now is utter secret."

He looked at her with eyes that were spear points, black and sharp – something manic in them, she thought.

"Okay, you're my client. There is absolute privilege."

"I did shoot Schlizik. I murdered him in cold blood. They 'ave everyt'ing on film."

285

"Murdered . . . What film . . . ? The police had a camera? My God, Michel –"

He took a big swallow of whisky and made a face. "They didn't tell me about the camera. So I t'ought I could get away with it. I really t'ought I could."

"Michel, I'm not following this."

"I will slow down, and start again."

An edge of bitterness was in his voice as he told of the killing of Jerszy Schlizik and of his encounter today with Inspector Mitchell.

"They are washing their hands of me. He wants me to go on the run so there will be no embarrassment. Mitchell is a cocksucker. Garbage. Like all of them."

Carrie didn't know what to think – this seemed yet another version of her client: dour, spiteful . . . and guilty of murder? Was there a reason? Had he gone haywire?

"Michel, there could be a defence – did Schlizik threaten you?"

"As I told you, he had just lowered his gun. No, it was not in self-defence. I just shot him. All I could feel then was a blindness in my heart, a hatred I could no longer fight."

"Why this . . . blindness in your heart?"

"Because of Céleste."

"Céleste . . ."

"She died of a 'eroin overdose." He bit his lip, and swirled the liquid in his glass tumbler.

His wife . . . an addict.

"The truth, finally, as I 'ave promised. It is a . . . difficult story. She was well-off, from a good family. Spoiled, crazy, experimenting with everyt'ing, fast cars, drugs. I loved her as no one must ever love." He swallowed the last of his whisky.

Carrie was pulled to him in his sadness. Céleste's death had impelled him to undertake this dangerous undercover role. And perhaps it had derailed him slightly in that loft: the blindness in his heart.

"If I live past the night, I will tell you more about it."

"Live past the night – what's that, a joke?"

He shook his head. "It's not'ing."

286

Carrie frowned at him, wondering about this enigmatic man. Behind that charming front, a tortured soul?

"A blindness. Well, a lack of intent. Irresistible impulse, temporary insanity. God, Michel, I can come up with a dozen defences. Schlizik was a vicious murderer, a cop-killer. No jury would dream of convicting you."

"There was full intent. I tried to cover up. I moved the bodies. I put the gun in a dead man's hand. I t'ought I was being very clever."

He wasn't being co-operative. She couldn't understand this, it was if he *wanted* to be found guilty.

"The video tape – it's illegal without a court order, it's not admissible. No *chance* of a conviction – that's why Mitchell wants you to skip town."

But Lachance was coolly eyeing her. He seemed to want to tell her something else, but was unsure whether to do so.

"Okay. You will not like this. I did anod'er thing to cover up."

He was the first to break eye contact. He bent his head and studied his empty tumbler of Ballantine's.

"I made an anonymous call to Cacciati, to tell him where he could find Normie the Nose. He was a useless germ, a scheming junkie, I didn't care. But I am guilty of that, too, aiding in a murder of a witness against me."

Carrie was rendered mute by this. She was having trouble believing it. And she was feeling a discomfort with him now: there was a cold-bloodedness about all this – a man on some mission of his own, yes, but vaguely . . . what? Sociopathic?

They are garbage that 'as to be taken out.

She had been standing near his chair, but she now moved away a little and leaned against a table. "So what exactly are your plans now?"

"To finish my job."

"To kill Billy Sweet."

"Maybe. If I 'ave to."

"I'm starting to think you are a little sick."

He shrugged. "Now it doesn't matter what I will do. I knew I would be betrayed. I know there will be death around me."

"I don't want to be hearing this. It's absurd."

"I have an appointment to see Billy. Tonight. Soon it will be over."

"I won't allow it."

He suddenly switched on his five-alarm smile – it came from nowhere. "You look like her. Céleste. You remind me of her, too, sometime. She liked it too much on the edge . . . Anyway, 'ow are you after last night? I 'ave forgot to ask."

"I'm . . . fine." Her cheeks glowed but elsewhere she felt goose pimples. "I think it was a kind of madness."

"When it is good it feels like madness."

"It's not something I often allow myself to do." It sounded of simpering apology, cloying, defensive.

"I believe that. It was special for me, too." He reached his hand out to her knee and stroked it, and she felt a chill run through her. The muscles of that leg were clenched, giving him a message, she hoped.

She spoke softly. "Let's just call it a night we both enjoyed, Michel, and leave it at that."

"Don't try to deny what 'appened. Our energy was fantastic." He looked at her with strange intensity. "I t'ink you want to deny, Carrington, but you can't hide from your heart."

She picked up his empty glass and escaped from him, refilling it at the counter.

"Stay here. I'm going to call the prosecutor."

She left for the secretarial area, but he followed her.

"I ask you not to, Carrington."

"Trust me on this."

She picked up a receiver from a desk, but Lachance gripped her wrist, quite hard.

"And will you, too, betray me? My lady lawyer who felt madness in my bed?"

"Let go of me."

"We made love. We shared our bodies. Our souls. Please, Carrington, keep faith with me. I have only you. I have nowhere to turn."

His hand was hurting hers, and he was looking at her with an intensity that frightened her.

"Michel, I'm not going to say you're here. I just want to find out what's going on. Now let *go.*"

"I . . . Forgive me. I guess I am upset."

He released her hand and she dialled Oliver McAnthony at home. Annoyed, she saw Lachance pick up another phone and plug into the line, covering the speaker with his hand.

"I'm sorry to pull you away from your pool or whatever, Oliver . . ."

"My leisure hours are spent in menial mental labour, my dear. I am writing a report."

"About Michel Lachance?"

A pause. "Yes. I suppose you wouldn't be calling out of hours if you haven't just learned something distasteful. I take it you've talked recently to your client?"

"Yes . . . on the phone."

Lachance nodded to her, seemed to relax.

"I danced to the same tune you did, Carrington. My report details the whole indecent matter. Whether it will remain in my desk or be widely read will be up to you."

"It's too absurd. Mitchell?"

"Yes. The whole thing was his doing. His immediate superior didn't have him under control. Rather a serious case of negligence."

"Whose idea was it to have Captain Lachance face this murder charge?"

"I take it you know about the video footage?"

"It's *not* admissible."

"A judge less intelligent than you or I might not agree. May I be brutally frank with you, Carrie? They want his silence. They fear the reputation of the entire RCMP will be tarred. If he agrees to say nothing – to the press, to anyone – they will drop the charge. I will go along with it only if you do. I think we owe you at least that. You can either take a trial and blow the entire thing sky-high, or we all hold hands and duck."

"I take it no one is trying furiously to nab my client."

"You might advise him not to be too apparent. Call me when you've talked to him."

After hanging up, she turned to Lachance. "Well?"

"I am going to finish what I started."

✢ ✢ ✢

Leon could no longer feel the pain; a numbness had set in. His voice sounded hollow in his own ears.

"I'm sorry to call you on the weekend, Mr. Blumberg."

"It's about Orff, right? You're his lawyer."

"I'm trying to find him."

"Well, I don't babysit the fat little fart. He's supposed to come in on emergency septic backup tonight and I'll leave a message."

"Do you know anything about his friends? A Mrs. Pinkerton? Or Dottie?"

"Never knew he had friends."

Leon started calling Pinkertons. From the secretarial area he could hear Carrie's and Lachance's voices, raised sometimes, then softer. Obviously she was enchanted with that man. He had read it in her face, an open book.

He guessed they wanted him to leave. They wanted to be alone. He couldn't face them, yet couldn't avoid doing so unless he left via his tenth-storey window. He'd have to say something to them, *See you folks later*, or *Have a nice day*. Maybe comment on the weather: *Looks like we're in for it tonight*.

A rumble of thunder.

How could he bear to see her when she came for dinner?

He was at a dead end with his Pinkertons, and finally he willed his legs to move and stumbled his way out of his office, where Carrie was saying something to Lachance in severe tones, admonishing him. She cut her speech short when she saw Leon.

"I'm off." He managed to get two syllables out.

"About six?" said Carrie. "I'll help you in the kitchen and then we can relax over a drink."

"Sure. Great. See you." Sure, relax over a drink.

He offered a limp wave and fled.

In a fog of despair, he somehow found his way out of the G & C Trust Building, managed to unlock and mount his bicycle, to wobble into the traffic. Must stop at a liquor store. A light Chablis. That's what Carrie usually likes.

"You are having dinner at his 'ouse?"

"Yes."

"I want to see you tonight. Is it possible? After?"

Lachance had been wandering from desk to desk, looking at everything, letters, memos, unapologetic about it.

"After what? After Billy's body has been carted away, and you're in a cell?"

"Not'ing will happen tonight. The meeting is only for evidence."

As he moved towards her, he undid the buttons of his shirt. This unnerved Carrie, and she lowered herself onto a swivel chair and slid forward until she was tight against a desk.

Lachance revealed a body pack strapped to him, a miniature tape-recorder. "I am going to deliver Billy to the cops, just as I promised."

He came closer, and her hand jerked as he clasped it in his.

"Why are you acting so strange?" he said. "So distant. Last night we were as close as two humans can become."

Last night was a mistake, she wanted to tell him. A thoughtless act of lust. "I just feel . . . odd about it."

He bent to her, sought her mouth, but she twisted her head away.

"I 'ave never had a night like that with a woman," he said huskily into her ear as his lips grazed her cheek.

"Michel, no!" She tried to push him away, but he resisted. Dissuade him somehow, placate him, don't anger him. "Let's go have a coffee and talk. The building isn't locked – anyone could come in." Please do, someone. But it was a weekend – the other tenth-floor businesses were closed.

He moved his face next to hers. "It is like we are brought together by the gods."

291

The phrase was a horrible echo of Ted's words, *matched by the gods*. She pulled away from him, but his hands were upon her now, ungentle, demanding, and he was still trying to manoeuvre her mouth toward his lips.

"Give me breathing room."

She thought for a moment he was going to force her – she'd discovered a beast inside the gentleman. But he withdrew, and started to button his shirt.

"*Je m'excuse.* I t'ink I understand, an office is not for romance. But later, yes? Maybe I can come to your home tonight."

"I'd rather you phone me. I'll be at home about midnight." She stood, tugged at her blouse. "I'm going to wash up. Then I think we should go."

The truth was that Carrie's nervousness had suddenly filled her up – she needed to relieve an intense pressure in her bladder. She escaped into the washroom, then headed quickly for the toilet. She sat and thought about how to avoid further entanglement with this man.

She didn't feel safe with him at all. He wasn't exactly the gentle knight she had taken him for, this soldier who had executed a man and assisted in the death of another. Of perhaps more import and more menacing was the fact he had read too much into last night.

She'd been fascinated with Lachance, tantalized, and, yes, she probably *had* wanted to go to bed with him. Now she was paying the price.

His meeting tonight with Billy Sweet – could any evil result from that? By midnight, when he called her, he could have his evidence. Mitchell would be pleased, McAnthony would be forgiving, Operation Sweet Revenge would be complete, and Michel could win the Victoria Cross instead of a murder sentence. And nothing need be said about Lachance's misdeeds outside the line of duty – the RCMP need not be embarrassed.

Okay, a plan of action. But she must call McAnthony, speak to him in private before the night was over.

At the wall mirror, she repaired herself, washed her face, daubed away a smear of lipstick. She looked into her bright, scared eyes, took out her contacts, and put on her reading glasses. There. A proper lady, genteel. Unavailable.

She found Lachance wandering about and had the impression he'd been going through cabinets and drawers. Looking for what?

In the elevator, he was in a silent, childish sulk.

"Where are you going to stay?" she asked.

"I'll find a place."

Suddenly, just as the elevator door opened on the ground floor, Lachance took her by the shoulders and pulled her roughly to him until she could feel the heat of his breath.

"It was more than a madness. Do not reject me, Carrington."

"Let me go, Michel."

His eyes had gone crazed again. She was frightened, but couldn't break free: his hands were like clamps. Through plate windows in the lobby, she saw there were customers in the trust office – it was open Saturdays – and there was Robert Barnsworth, studying sheets with numbers. He looked up, saw them inside the elevator, Lachance clutching her, their faces inches apart.

"For God's sake, people are staring," she said.

Lachance let go, but followed her. Carrie waved a taxi to the curb and quickly got in. "The islands ferry, please," she said.

Speeder had a different van this time, a '77 Dodge with an interior-decorating business painted on the side. Tinted windows you couldn't see inside of. But Speeder could see out, and what he was watching was Carrie climb into a taxi, not looking as good as she usually did, and there was the Frenchman still standing on the sidewalk, rolling a cigarette, looking kind of sour. Dumb asshole had no idea he was being watched. Now he turned around, walked back into the building.

"What's he gone back in there for?"

Deeley and Izzie, who were in the van there with him, just had stupid looks on their faces.

Who else was up there? All sorts of coming and going, but nothing from the bug under the lawyer's desk.

"What you want we should do?" said Izzie.

"We play it by ear," said Speeder. He turned up the volume on the receiver but still all he was getting was a deathly quiet from up there. He chewed like crazy on his gum, nervous, no dope in him today: he had to score something to brighten it.

Lachance had only glanced at the van, but that one quick look told him all he needed to know: smoked-glass windows and an aerial that seemed too complex for ordinary ham equipment.

Back inside the G & C Trust Building, he returned to the elevator and ascended again to the tenth floor where, using keys he had taken from a secretary's desk, he quickly entered the offices of Robinovitch, Barr, and Tchobanian.

Carrington's office – that must be where they put the transmitter. He assumed Cacciati hid it when he visited a couple of days ago. He tried to remember if he and Carrington had been in that office today. No, he was lucky: they had been in the lounge and the secretaries' area.

It took him only seconds to find the bug. He didn't touch it, didn't want to make extraneous sounds.

He tried out Carrington's chair, a tall-backed swivel, put his feet upon her desk, rolled a cigarette, and looked at her wedding picture: her husband, a weakling who hadn't known how to satisfy her.

He picked up Carrie's phone and dialled a number at random. A recorded voice: "I'm sorry this number is not in service."

"*Allô*, Carrington?" He spoke loudly. "In case you gave me your only key, I left the office door unlocked for you. Meantime, I am going to take a nap on the couch in here, I am exhausted."

He was silent for a few moments, as if listening to her voice. Then: "Yeah, Billy Sweet, he will go crazy with shock when he finds out who the spy is. But what if he is such a fool to think we are bluffing? What should we do?"

294

Another pause. "I agree. We will not give him a second chance."

A shorter pause.

"Yes, I love you, too."

He hung up, and waited for them.

27

Barnsworth had been summoned from home that evening to the G & C Trust Building. Now he was suffering nauseous tremors as he viewed the two bodies on the tenth floor. Near the elevator, a skinny young man with acne and horrible staring eyes, and just down the hall, another man, stouter, only his legs showing outside the door to the stairs.

"Ever see them before?" asked a detective.

Barnsworth felt his throat constricting, and was barely able to get words out. "They *are not* tenants of these premises."

There were emergency vehicles outside, reporters and police all over: a nightmare beyond imagining.

He had been told that someone from the custodial staff had found one of the bodies lying across the elevator entrance, the door opening and closing on it in rhythmic intervals.

"How did they . . . er, meet their demise?"

"Both looped, Mr. Barnsworth."

"Do you mean intoxicated?"

"Wire loop. Professional job. Could be a robbery – their wallets are gone. More likely they were just rubbed out, though."

"I'm sorry –"

"Underworld hits, Mr. Barnsworth." The policeman turned to

one of his colleagues. "Okay, get some prints and let's find out what we got here."

✛ ✛ ✛

Leon had just shooed Carrie from the kitchen, insisting his own hands and his alone would create the special of the evening, poached Atlantic salmon *al estragon*. Exiled to the living room, she stared outside at the gloomy, tossing waters of the harbour.

She had arrived two hours earlier after a strenuous hike in a wind-whipped drizzle from the Ward's Island ferry dock. They had talked pleasantly enough – if one can talk pleasantly about murder – but Leon was by turns contemplative and filled with a manic cheer.

He'd been clumsy, had spilled wine on his apron. Things were getting to him, Carrie decided. That madman, Orff. Her embarrassing dalliance with Captain Lachance.

She felt so ashamed of herself. She had gone to bed with Dr. Jekyll and he turned out to be Mr. Hyde.

The episode hadn't been mentioned this evening. Having seen how Leon reacted earlier to her stupid blurt that she had slept with Lachance, she was now resolved not to speak of it again. He certainly wouldn't be interested in the details.

But even privileged communications may be shared with partners, and she had told Leon about Lachance's rash quest to right the wrongs that had been done to his wife, Céleste. Leon had insisted: get on the phone to McAnthony.

But say what? *What I tell you now is utter secret.*

She sipped her wine and stared outside into leaden skies that promised an early, black, wet night.

"Phone him, Carrie." Leon came into the living room with canapés, a yogurtish dip with multi-grain bread sticks. "You have to tell him this Lachance character is acting on his own and he's on some kind of vendetta."

This Lachance character. A stern note of disapproval.

"Okay, Leon."

297

He disappeared. So like a hurt puppy. She wondered: did he have feelings for her that were beyond the avuncular? He'd never given a hint, though she remembered, after the crisis with Ted, how he had stayed at her bedside for nine and a half hours. Maybe it was more than just the caring of a good friend.

She almost wished she could fall in love with Leon. He was such a nice man.

McAnthony answered after one ring. "Have you put our offer to him?"

"He's considering it. Oliver, I want to know about him. All about him – do you have his file?"

"No, but I insisted on seeing it. I shouldn't be telling you this; every page is stamped 'top secret' in capital letters. But I believe you should know. For starters, he's a career soldier, went through officer training."

"Before that?"

"Adopted son of a couple up Noranda way, mine foreman and his wife."

"His father wasn't a diplomat? Served in Paris?"

"What has he been feeding you?"

"Céleste – what about her?"

"Who is she?"

"His wife . . ." Her voice trailed off. "Did he have a wife?"

"No record of that. Number of female companions over the years, quite a number. His relationships seem to lack a . . . lasting quality. Apparently some history of abuse."

Carrie felt a shiver, then a weariness that permeated all her limbs.

"Were psychological tests done on him?"

"Yes. Mitchell should have seen right away he wasn't the man. Slightly sociopathic, Carrie. Not sick in any medical sense, but lacking a strong conscience. Little appreciation of workaday concepts like right and wrong. Gun collector, military-knife collector. Black belt in karate – he teaches it, of course. Subscribes to *Soldier of Fortune* – well, it's the whole package, isn't it? You know the type. And something odd: he claimed to have some sort of paranormal power. Disastrous choice of candidate for this work."

Carrie couldn't find words.

"Carrie?"

"Yes . . . I'm just thinking."

"If you're wondering why I'm so eagerly telling you this, it's perhaps to hint that you should be a little wary of him – especially if he has not been, as it appears, totally open with you."

Carrie was silent again for a long while, then she bit the bullet. "Oliver, he's going ahead with it. He has a body-pack recorder and he intends to meet Billy Sweet tonight."

"My God. Where?"

"I don't know. I don't think I want to know. He's going to phone me at midnight and I need you to be up and alert. And, Oliver?"

"Yes, Carrington."

"I didn't tell you what I just told you."

"Do you feel you need any protection?"

She thought about that. "Maybe you could have a car sit outside my house tonight. But I'm above the fray, I'm just the lawyer. They don't shoot the messenger."

"I'll send a car."

She hung up, fuming to herself. She'd been an unmitigated fool to have gone to bed with that man. And now he was hung up on her – or was he just using her? He seemed more possessive than caring. Frightening, in any event. Sociopathic, the tests said, so he was incapable of love of others. But convincing in his lies, that fit the profile.

Yes, an unmarked cruiser in front of her house seemed not a bad idea.

✢ ✢ ✢

It's not like Speeder screwed anything up. Deeley and Izzie maybe could of, though, and it sounded like they did.

Nervous about breaking the news to Billy, Speeder had

dropped by the chemists to get some of the new mix he'd ordered, then called in, hinting Billy should meet him at a convenient location. So here was the boss making another rare appearance outside the Kremlin walls, with Shadow and Vinnie Eng sheltering him, and Tommy Bogue at the controls of one of the luxomobiles – the little Rolls, not the Phantom.

Speeder got in the front and explained the problem, which was he sent Deeley and Izzie up there to the lawyers' offices to snuff the Frenchman in his sleep, and half an hour went by and no sign of them, so Speeder decided not to hang around in case there was heat, in case they'd got theirselves busted.

"I don't think I am hearing very coherently," Billy Sweet said. "You tell me you sent Deeley and Izzie into that building. Why didn't you go instead, Speeder? They're too brainless to go somewhere on their own."

"I didn't think it was necessary. You heard the tape, Billy, the Frenchman was gonna be asleep."

Billy wasn't giving clues about how he was feeling over the disappearance of the two guys. Speeder couldn't figure out if Billy was furious at him or what. It *seemed* like he was in control of himself, all coiffed and neat in a three-piece suit.

"They just never came back out," Speeder said.

"They just never came back out." Billy mimicked Speeder's voice, squeakier than it really sounded.

Speeder nervously slid a Dubble Bubble into his mouth. He should do one of them whizbangs now, get on top of things. "Maybe they turned chicken, and went out the back way or something."

"Or is Deeley our informer? Or Izzie. Have you ever thought of that, Speed?" His voice cracked, the old terrors finally showing through, and he started yelling. "When you want to do something right, you fucking do it yourself!"

He sat there red and glaring. Eng finally broke the silence. "Did this Cristal guy ever come out?"

"Not through the front door, anyways."

"What about the lawyer dame?" Eng asked.

"Got into a cab. Maybe went home, I don't know."

Billy got himself composed, like he was earlier, and Speeder could tell he was trying to get his head around the problem.

"We go for the lawyer. Right now."

✥ ✥ ✥

Leon had tried to create a cosy mood with candlelight and Bolivian flute music, but the flickering flames and the haunting, reedy melodies only made Carrie feel jumpy. Outside, across the harbour, the buildings of Toronto seemed ghostly pillars, white-lit behind a rain that had begun to pelt the roof.

Leon was looking solemnly at Carrie's plate now. He had finished his meal, but hers was only lightly picked over – she had had to force each forkful down her throat.

"I'm sorry, I . . . just don't have a great appetite."

"You can't do this to me. I have a fruit compote for dessert."

"Well, it's not the food." It was Lachance, his lies, her shame – a deceitful seduction it now seemed. Earlier, Leon had listened with sad-dog eyes as she recounted what McAnthony had told her about this undercover commando.

"Leon, thank you for this evening. It's been rough. I needed your company."

"It makes me happy to have you here." And he added: "Would you like to camp here tonight?"

She should. It was beginning to storm outside – she'd be like a wet rat by the time she made the ferry. But there would be a police car outside. And she had to be at the phone when Lachance called at midnight.

"Thanks, Leon, but I think I'll be safe."

"I'll put some coffee on."

As Leon disappeared into the kitchen, the phone rang, and Carrie picked it up.

A contralto whisky voice: "Mr. Robinovitch, is he there?"

"May I tell him who's calling?" Carrie would protect Leon; clients call at the damnedest hours.

"Pinkerton. Mabel Pinkerton. Hymie, he's one of my customers, a regular, and he's being kind of difficult. He insists on seeing his lawyer. Tell him he better get his ass down here right away. We don't want no trouble."

"Just hang on a sec."

Leon answered her shout and came back and grabbed the phone. Carrie watched his eyes widen as the woman repeated her concerns.

"Mrs. Pinkerton, ah, what do you mean, a customer?"

He slumped into a chair.

"I see."

He wrote down an address, and disconnected. "A brothel on Parliament Street. She says he's freaking out. She didn't explain how. I can imagine. No, I can't. I have to get down there. I'll call a water taxi."

"I'll phone you at home," Leon said, and as he was about to alight from the taxi cab, Carrie leaned over and kissed him on the lips. He climbed out and watched the car accelerate away.

Standing in a wash of rain, Leon could still taste those soft lips, a touch of velvet. He shuddered, overcome by the moment.

Then he turned and examined a dilapidated brick building. This was the address he'd been given. That was the number on the upstairs doorway: a big apartment above a used-clothing store.

Orff – Hymie, to be exact – had been making regular attendances upon a woman named Dottie at a house of pleasure. No wonder Mrs. Pinkerton wasn't in the phone book, at least by that name.

Leon rang the bell as he'd been told, three shorts and a long, and in half a minute a thick-waisted woman wearing a pair of ornately framed spectacles met him at the door.

"I'm Leon Robinovitch."

"Hymie's up in one of the rooms," said Mrs. Pinkerton. "Only he's not Hymie, he claims he's someone else. Anyway, he's under a bed and he won't come out. I mean, there he was oompa-pa'ing around the room, and suddenly the guy freaks out."

"Oompa-pa'ing?" Very little of this was making sense. He followed her up the stairs. "Does Hymie come here often?"

"Sometimes twice a week. Dottie's the one he drops by to see.

302

Has this thing about her. He's been coming for . . . oh, hell, I don't know, five years. He never *does* anything with her, just plays his funny games mostly, so we don't really charge him the full rate. He's one of the strange ones."

"Just how strange?"

"Well, sometimes he carries on, eh? Goose-steps around the place, comes on with this funny German accent, and he . . . well, we keep some extra clothes for him here."

"Extra *clothes*?"

Nothing about the many renditions of Herbert Orff was very surprising to Leon any more.

From an open doorway, he peered into a rather frilly room, curtained with lace. Stuck beneath the bed was Herbert Orff. He hadn't been able to squeeze all the way under, and his head and shoulders were poking out. Squatting on the floor, talking to him, was a thin young woman wearing just underclothes and an over-sized military cap.

"Come on, Hymie," she said. "It's *me*, Dottie."

"Go away. I want my lawyer. I am going to sue everybody here."

This was Orff's normal voice, Leon realized, thin and timid. He was staring at Dottie fearfully.

Leon studied his client a little more critically. He was . . . yes, Leon's eyes weren't deceiving him, Orff was wearing a dress, a frock with a flower pattern.

Leon drew Mrs. Pinkerton down the hallway a little.

"The dress. Explain that, please."

"Well, um, he likes to play, like I said. Sometimes he gets into this kind of other character with a German accent, marching around, giving orders. Only he likes to wear a dress when he does that. Sort of your tranny type."

Tranny. So this was Hymie's big embarrassing secret about Franz. A Nazi cross-dresser.

"Has he ever been violent?"

"Not Hymie. He's real charming. Funny little fat Jew, but I'm not prejudiced, you understand. My attitude is it takes all kinds."

"And when he's being this German character?"

"Oh, we have to tell him not to shout so much. He rants."

Leon peeked through the doorway again.

"Come on, *Hymie*," the skinny hooker pleaded.

"I told you, I'm not Hymie. This is a case of mistaken identity."

Leon cleared his throat. "Herbert, what seems to be the problem here?" That sounded pompous to his own ears: here he was in a brothel talking to a guy in a dress.

Orff looked up. "At last. I want you to see what they did to me. I want to sue them to the ground."

"Exactly what have they done to you?"

"They kidnapped me and made me dress up like this."

"But that's *your* dress," said Dottie.

"It's *not* my dress. They're holding me hostage, Mr. Robinovitch. They want two hundred dollars."

Leon wished he had more of a sense of humour and could properly enjoy this. "Why do you say you were kidnapped?"

"Well, how did I get here then? They *drugged* me."

"You've never been here before?"

"Never once in my life."

"Two hundred dollars is a little steep, Mrs. Pinkerton."

"He's been here two *hours*. Just get him out of here. It's free."

"Free?" said Orff. "This is going to *cost*. I want to know exactly who these people work for, Mr. Robinovitch. I want to know who runs this operation. And I want my clothes and I don't want anyone watching while I change."

While his clothing was being retrieved from a closet, Leon lifted the bed up, allowing Orff to crawl out. The floral frock came down to his knees.

"It's part of the effort to silence me, isn't it? They'll stop at nothing, Mr. Robinovitch."

While he dressed in private, Leon talked in the hallway to Dottie, who was confused and in some distress.

"He's just not himself."

"What happened?"

"Well, we were marching, like we usually do – I have to

salute him, too, and everything – anyways, he just stopped in his tracks and he started blinking and looking around, and then he screamed, and crawled under the bed."

"He's never done anything like that before?"

"No. I thought it was pretty odd behaviour."

"Was he taking any pills earlier?"

"A whole lot of them."

"Dottie, when was he here last?"

"Um . . . I remember, Wednesday night. It was funny, he sort of goose-stepped right into the closet where I was hiding – we have this game, okay? – and he collapsed all over me, and he's kind of heavy, you know, almost broke my leg, so I bit him on the hand to get him off of me."

"Wednesday night . . . you're sure?"

"Yeah, pretty close to midnight."

For some reason, Leon felt relieved. He guessed it was because he was hoping Orff was really not the Midnight Strangler. In an odd, unsettling way, he had grown fond of him.

Orff came from the room, still indignant. "Typical communist trick. Tell this girl if she thinks she can make of fool of Herbert Orff, she should think twice. This is obviously some kind of sin palace. Look at her, she's barely dressed."

"Hymie, how could you?"

"Don't call me *Hymie*."

"I'll take you home, Herbert."

"I want this whole thing exposed."

"Let's go."

"I'm hungry. Can we stop at a 7-Eleven?"

✣ ✣ ✣

Lachance twice walked around the inner perimeter of Horizons, a cocktail lounge revolving high above the city in the CN Tower. No sign of the enemy, but he didn't really expect them.

He wondered if he had sent too brutal a message in eliminating the men assigned to kill him. Two useless *morviats* with revolvers and silencers. Very quietly, he'd taken out the thin one as he poked his head inside an office door. The other man was exploring elsewhere when Lachance crept behind him. It was so easy.

Lachance had waited to see if they'd send a couple more victims his way, but it seemed the enemy had been scared off, so he just dragged the bodies out of the law office and sped down the stairs and out the back.

If they were in retreat, he would just have to pursue.

But first he ordered a glass of white Bordeaux, and as he relaxed he thought of Carrington. Finally he had found a woman worthy of him. The others had been bagatelles, bland, uninteresting. Carrington Barr was different, special. *Une bonne botte.*

The cocktail bar inched around its axis and all the lights of Toronto passed by him, shrouded by rain, and the blackness of the lake went by, and the sky devoured him, the tumultuous sky and its tentacles of lightning. He felt powerful here, perched on top of the world. He had a sense of impending victory against the enemy.

28

Speeder was soaked right through to his skin, uncomfortable as shit, dripping all over the seat. He couldn't see anyone's faces, because the interior lights were out and there was no streetlamp or anything in the alley.

Speeder could hear their steady breathing, Shadow with one half-stuffed nostril, sounding like a baby's rattle. Vinnie Eng back there beside him. And he could make out Billy in the back, too, where the cologne was coming from. Speeder couldn't believe it, Billy was here, armed – it was like the old days, he was back in action.

"You're getting me all wet," Tommy Bogue complained. He was the wheelman for tonight.

"Well, fuck you. I been on an intensive reconnoitre and I almost died of the elements –"

"Shut up," said Billy.

"Okay, I shut up."

Billy sighed impatiently. "Tell us what you observed."

"Her car's in the garage so it means she's gotta be home. There's no lights on anywhere except one upstairs, which I figure it's a bedroom, facing the front, and she's probably in it. Nobody can hear nothin' in this torrent, so I say we just go in through the back way where there's a couple of windows we can jimmy."

"And you don't think anyone else is in that house?'

"Who? The guy she's fucking? He's a mile up the CN Tower. This is the time we got to do it, Billy. I'd say we got half an hour leeway, maybe forty-five minutes. Grab her and hustle her outa there."

Speeder checked his jacket pocket to see if the crankers had got soggy, but they were protected by Zip-loc. Whizbangs, the chemist called them, with a little coke and a little junk added, a sort of medicine cabinet.

"I'll do the interrogation, Billy, I think I got her number – gotta pull her down first from her heights."

"Do you want to be alone with her?"

"That's the best way. Tie her up first."

"Do you like her, Speed?"

"Whatta you mean? She's a whore."

"I think you like her. I think you just want to make out with her, and that won't encourage any questions to be answered."

"Aw, Billy, come off of it."

"Or do you wish solitude with her for other reasons? You wouldn't help her escape, would you?"

"Billy, when I hear stuff like that from you, I get kinda pissed off, you wanna know the truth."

"Speed's okay, Billy," Vinnie Eng said, who'd been around from the start, before Speeder's time. Speed was happy for the recommendation: he couldn't figure out why Billy was always on his case.

"What do you think, boss?" said Bogue.

"Tommy remains at the wheel. The other four of us go in. We get her."

We? Speeder didn't see Billy exposing himself this way. But it was like he wasn't expecting much of nobody else any more. Billy and his *You wanna do something right, you fucking do it yourself.* The Crown Prince of Paranoia, but he could still get into that kind of control thing he was capable of. Speeder hoped it wasn't just a skin-deep thing but was the old Billy Sweet back in form.

"Flashlights and weapons, gentlemen," said Billy. "Everyone has gloves? Ensure your silencers are on. This is to be timed for a maximum of fifteen minutes."

And the car doors opened and the four of them got out into the rain, Speeder leading them single-file down the alley to where there was the lawyer's big semidetached house, with a garage behind it, a brick patio, a narrow walkway to the street out front.

The door to the back porch had a kind of flimsy lock, and Vinnie Eng, who brought a small pry-bar, just wrenched it until it gave. The French doors to get into the house proper were even easier. Maybe they were making a lot of noise, but the weather was co-operating to the point Speeder could barely hear the scritching of metal and the popping of wood.

The French doors led into a large kitchen which was in total darkness, no lights anywhere downstairs. Billy gave whispered orders to them to fan out with their flashlights, and they covered all the rooms on that floor, and met again in the living room.

Shadow had the rope with him and the tape for her mouth, and he was assigned along with Vinnie to go up to the bedrooms. A couple of minutes passed, and Speeder couldn't hear any noise from upstairs and he figured it was going okay and he did a couple of his whizbangs. Billy wasn't saying nothing, all that could be seen of him was his wrist, the illuminated dial of his watch – Billy checking the time.

When Vinnie came back with Shadow, he said: "She ain't here. One of the bedrooms has a light on but she ain't in it."

Without seeing him, Speeder could tell Billy was blaming him as if it was his fault. Now they had to probably split fast from here. Speeder didn't want the Frenchman walking in on them, he was kind of crazy and dangerous.

"Well, Billy?" said Vinnie. "You want we should check outa here, or what?"

The phone rang, and Speeder almost jumped out of his skin, the crank taking effect faster than he expected. It rang two more times, and then they could hear a voice with a French accent on the answering machine going, *"He didn't show up."*

"It's Cristal," said Speeder.

"Shut up," Billy whispered fiercely.

". . . no 'urry, so we can meet in the morning and decide the next move. I will come to your oYce at nine. Have nice dreams."

A click.

"We just bought some time, Billy," Speeder said.

"Yes. We will wait for her."

Speeder felt the cartwheels spinning wildly in his head.

✥ ✥ ✥

Constables Chip Fogerty and Ann Wilcox, fresh-faced recruits in the Metro Police, had been paired off for the last two weeks, mostly pressing the bricks, but tonight they'd got a forthwith from head office and with it an unmarked car and an easy job. Surveillance – for no specified reason – of the home of Carrington Barr, barrister and solicitor. All they had to do was run a make on anybody hanging around.

They'd had trouble finding a parking spot, and were three houses up from the Barr residence. It was pounding rain. Chip Fogerty was in the passenger seat, reading a sci-fi thriller under the dashboard light. Behind the wheel, Ann Wilcox was half-turned, squinting at the Barr house through the rear window.

"Looks pretty dead. Aren't we supposed to take a little stroll around the neighbourhood once in a while?"

"I'll take a rain check," said Fogerty, not raising his nose from his paperback. "You go ahead."

Later, Wilcox decided. She turned and slouched into her seat. There were no sounds but the rain pelting the car roof and the sonorous voice of the police dispatcher. All units to keep all eyes open for the Midnight Strangler. *That* would be a collar.

✥ ✥ ✥

With one of his gloved hands, Speeder silently scratched at his elbow, the cartwheels making him itchy all over, there was always some damn side effect. His bladder was burning, too, he had to take a major leak.

Billy and Vinnie and him were in the darkened kitchen, with Shadow waiting inside the front door. Billy was acting nutty again, but the wheels were making Speeder like a fucking giant, he wasn't ascared of him no more.

"She went to the cops, didn't she? That's why she's not here. You aren't leading us into a trap, are you, Speed?"

"Lay offa me, Billy."

"Gentlemen, you heard that tape. The Frenchman said I will be very shocked to find out whom exactly is our spy."

"Yeah, Billy," said Speeder, "except what he said was you'll go *crazy* when you find out. You're halfway there, you want my opinion."

"I oughta have you taken out right now."

Vinnie Eng to the rescue again: "Hey, Billy, get off his case. He's onside."

Billy didn't say anything for a bit, then went, "All right. It ain't . . . isn't getting us anywhere. Ten minutes more." Speeder could see the dial of Billy's watch again. "Speed, I want you to go out back and tell Tommy we'll be longer than expected."

Billy sounded like he was getting back on base, thank Christ. "Yeah, okay, Billy."

But in the darkness, Speeder couldn't find his way out to the kitchen, and he banged into a wall and knocked down a picture in a glass frame that broke into pieces.

Billy blew up again. "What kind of drug salad have you been doing, garbage-head? You wanna leave *evidence*? You want the neighbours to hear?"

Speeder turned on his flashlight to try to find his way out.

"Turn that light off!"

Speeder did, and felt his way to the kitchen and out through the splintered back doors to the bricked-over patio, into the sea of rain.

Tommy Bogue had snuggled the car right up to the garage so it looked like it was just parked there empty if anyone came. Speeder told him to just hang tight because the dame wasn't home yet.

Coming back across the patio, he stumbled into something metal, a barbecue stand, he realized. It fell with a clatter you could hear even with all the rain, and suddenly there was this dog making an uproar from over the fence and, just as Speeder was finding his way to the porch steps, it came out of nowhere, a little mutt but yapping like hell.

And then a light came on next door, and he almost pissed himself as he went down flat on the bricks.

A lady's loud voice: "Bingo! Bad dog! Bingo, come here!"

Shit, he thought. He was worried more about Billy than anything else – he was gonna have a total conniption.

"Bingo, goddamnit!" A man's voice now, and sounding as if he was in the back yard next door. Speeder scrambled up the porch steps as the dog kept barking and the voice came closer: "Bingo!"

The dog turned tail just as Speeder made it through the door. The faint light from the next house disappeared.

"You doorknob, I oughta kick your head in . . . Did they see you?"

"Naw, Billy."

"Did you want them to see you?"

"Jeez, Billy. Listen, I gotta take a leak."

"You'll stay here!"

"I gotta real bad."

"Vinnie, accompany him upstairs to the facilities."

"Aw, for Christ's sake, what's he gonna do, hold it for me?"

"Don't let him go near any windows."

As her taxi crept through the black streets of west Toronto, she saw there'd been power outages – whole districts were in darkness. Too spooky, she thought. But her own street was lit, thank God.

Where were her watchers, the surveillance team McAnthony had promised? There, up ahead. She told the cab driver to cruise past her house, and they drew abreast of their car: a man and a woman in uniform, short-haired rookies.

Carrie rolled down her window. The officer behind the steering wheel rolled down hers. Her companion quickly closed a book and slipped it into the glove compartment.

"Hi. I'm Carrington Barr."

"Oh, hello," the policewoman said. "Nothing to report. Don't even know what we're looking for. Is it something to do with the Midnight Strangler?"

"You watch for *any* unexpected visitors. Want to come in for a coffee?"

"Thanks, Mrs. Barr, but we have a thermos. I think our orders are to stay outside."

"You're here 'til . . . ?"

"Just to dawn, and then we get relieved."

"Well, thanks, I'll sleep better knowing you're here."

"We'll take a boo around your yard after a while. Have a good night, Mrs. Barr."

And Carrie braved the rain, dashing back down the street and up her steps. Home sweet home, and wait by the phone.

As she fumbled for the light-switch inside the door, she heard a raspy breathing sound.

A gloved hand grabbed her wrist.

She was caught in a bear hug from behind that took her breath away.

Before she could scream, a sticky, thick tape was rolled across her mouth, and she was dragged toward the living room.

She kicked backwards, and nicked her captor's shin with her heel, and he grunted in pain and threw her to the carpet.

In near-hysteria, she kept flailing, but her legs were pinned, and now her arms, a knee painfully thrust against her lower back. She heard a soft, clammy voice.

"Tie her up quickly, and let's go."

Her wrists were bound, then her ankles. Her brain was seething with fear, but somehow she summoned everything that was in her, and commanded herself to think clearly. They worked for Billy Sweet. She was being kidnapped. They would torture her and they would murder her. How could she alert those police outside? But they were too far from the house.

The same voice, now coming from the area of the staircase.

313

"Wait for them to come down. Why is a simple piss taking so long?"

The only sound was of falling rain. A faint radiance from a streetlamp outside gave only dim detail of the men inside the living room.

The phone began to ring.

Leon's voice on the answering machine. *"Carrie? If you're in bed, hey, get up . . . Carrie? You there? Listen, the Strangler isn't Herbert Orff. I have absolute proof. That leaves Moodie. I just talked to Jock and he has a line on him, someone recognized him from his picture. But something else, Carrie – look, I'm meeting Chuck and we're coming over there even if we have to drag you out of bed, because this is important – we had two men murdered outside our offices today, apparently a couple of thugs –"*

"Murdered?" someone said. "Shit!"

A flash of lightning painted the room in sickly white tones and Leon's voice suddenly died. The panel light on the answering machine died with it. The radiance from outside, too. Power outage.

Carrie had vaguely made them out: a middle-aged man standing rigid in a suit and raincoat; an older man, in his sixties, a brute. Two of them, and others upstairs.

Carrie tried to wiggle her hands, bound behind her back, but her bindings bruised and cut.

A flashlight coming down the stairs. This voice she recognized. A squeaky voice. Speeder Cacciati.

"Billy? You there?"

So the leader was Sweet himself.

"You imbecile, don't mention *names*! We have a *guest*."

The beam of Speeder's flashlight caught Carrie's supine body.

"Oh, yeah. Shit, sorry."

"Turn that off!"

Sweet, having been unmasked by Speeder and his flashlight, seemed to be losing control. His voice was under strain, cracking. "Where the fuck is Vinnie? Didn't he come down with you?"

"He was right behind me."

"Someone look for him."

Another flashlight blinked, and Carrie saw the older man climbing the stairs, and again there was absolute darkness. And an ominous silence. Where were those cops? Damn them!

Then Billy's voice again, brittle now, like breaking glass: "What did you do with Vinnie? Are you the rat? Those guys in the law office – did you tip off the bulls? Are you our scummy *rat*?"

Suddenly he seemed to be almost hysterical, and Carrie sensed that the danger to her life was the more immediate.

"That's bullshit," said Speeder, sounding rattled, too. "Let's get the fuck out of here."

"She's going to talk!" Billy barked. "Right here! Now!"

He was nearly on top of her now, and she felt something blunt and hard at her temples, the barrel of a revolver.

"You scream, you die," said Billy, pulling the tape from her mouth.

"I won't scream." Be in control, she told herself. Think. Be smarter than they.

"Who's the fish? Who's the squeal? *Spill it!*"

"I'd be suicidal to tell you."

"You have five seconds or your brains are all over your shag carpet." Sweet's voice rose: "Do you hear me? *Five seconds!*"

Carrie chose a new tack, and talked fast, but Sweet didn't seem to be listening.

"Don't you see what they're doing? They *want* you to kill me . . ."

"Four . . ."

". . . I know too much, they've set this whole thing up . . ."

"Three . . ."

"Damn it, listen to me . . ."

"Two . . ."

". . . They bought the only man who can make a perfect case against you."

The countdown stopped. Sweet repeated her words: "The only man who can . . ."

"If you kill me, he'll be the star witness."

315

A flashlight was now coming fast down the stairs. Carrie saw it was the old guy, and he was in a hurry. She decided, without knowing why, that this moment must be seized.

"Because he's right beside you, Mr. Sweet."

"Beside me?" Sweet's voice went faint. "Not . . . Speeder."

The other man was with them now, his voice hushed, scared. "Billy, we got a real problem . . ."

Speeder sounded hoarse. "*She's* got a problem, the crazy cunt!"

". . . Vinnie's dead. Found him with his skull caved in."

Sweet gasped and moved away from Carrie. An eerie silence claimed them.

Her voice was calm cool collected Carrie: "You know he murdered Vinnie, Mr. Sweet. He was up there alone with him."

"She's lying, I didn't do it," Speeder said, his words becoming strangled, losing force.

"Of course you didn't." From Sweet's throat issued an oddly gentle and comforting laugh. "Did you think I'd fall for her bullshit? Speeder, Speeder, when do you think I was born, yesterday? The lady made a nice try, I give her credit. Gag her again, Shadow."

Carrie tried to twist away. The tape again went over her mouth, stifling her scream.

"Okay, Speed, beam onto her head, so we can see exactly what we are doing."

Speeder's flashlight went on, blinding her momentarily.

The *whump, whump* of the silenced revolver in Billy Sweet's hand.

She could see blood spurting from two wounds to Cacciati's heart. He crashed against the wall and slipped down it into a heap, and the flashlight bounced and rolled, then held his face within its cold white beam, his gap-toothed ghostly grin, his pinned, staring eyes.

"What was your price, Speeder? I hope you didn't come cheap." Sweet knelt and clicked off the flashlight and they were in blackness again. "Shadow, dispose of the lawyer, and let's go."

But another light came on just then, a powerful beam from the direction of the entrance to the hall, and Carrie could suddenly see them in grim detail, Sweet and Shadow in synchronized movement, guns turned to that source of light. And just as suddenly that light went out.

The men backed toward safe positions against the walls, ignoring Carrie for the moment. Then she felt a familiar, smoky breath close to her nostrils, and quickly she was floating upwards, scooped from the floor by muscular arms, carried away.

Lachance whipped the tape from her mouth and stuffed her unceremoniously into the hall closet amid the coats and jackets. She fell with a rattle of clothes-hangers, and a beam of light pierced the darkness of the hall.

Without shutting the door, Lachance whirled around and dropped to the floor, and Carrie could hear a soft fusillade, bullets fired through silencers, and she saw Shadow stumbling, wounded, dropping his flashlight, retreating into the kitchen.

Lachance fired once again, his bullet sending the flashlight spinning, and darkness was upon her again.

"It's stopped raining," Constable Ann Wilcox said. "Let's do our walkabout."

"Soon as I finish this chapter," said Fogerty. He was still glued to his book.

Wilcox, again peering through the rear window, thought she saw a flicker of light from a downstairs window of the Barr house – but she realized it was probably a reflection from the streetlights, which were blinking into life. Power had just been restored, but the house they were watching remained dark and peaceful.

✣ ✣ ✣

Lachance had simply vanished, leaving her tied up in the closet. But not hidden, because the door was open at right angles from the wall. Now the house was drowned in silence – even the muffled patter of rain had ceased and the wind had died.

Lachance must have had been here for some time, had heard everything, had played a reckless game with her life.

A soft thud. Silence again.

She tried to wiggle farther back into the closet, felt precarious there, standing on tightly bound ankles. If she could just balance herself, reach down behind her, feel for the knots, free her legs . . . the front door was only five feet away.

A tinkle of breaking glass, a dish, maybe her crystal – someone was in the kitchen.

Then: *whump, whump.*

A clatter as if someone had fallen over a stool or chair.

Then not a whisper of sound for several minutes, maybe more. Slowly, Carrie lowered herself into a squat, balancing herself, and felt for the knots behind her ankles.

A soft squeak from the hallway floor. Carrie knew exactly where it came from, a loose floorboard only six feet from the closet. Then she heard a quick intake of breath – someone was heading quickly for the front entrance.

Wobbling, she tried to stand, but the man crashed into the closet door, and this brought Carrie falling forward, helplessly, onto his back. She knew it was Billy Sweet, knew it from the smell of him, fear and cologne.

He was furiously trying to wriggle out from under her as a ceiling light snapped on – the power was back. Sweet suddenly pulled Carrie closer to him and stuck the barrel of his revolver under her chin.

Then she saw Michel Lachance standing near the kitchen door, his gun in his hand. He was wearing a flak jacket, and over that a leather bandolier with ammunition pouches. Like Sweet, he was wearing gloves. Unlike Sweet, he was smiling.

Sweet's voice was raspy, raw. "I'll kill her."

Lachance strolled slowly forward. His laughter was guttural, demonic.

"Do it."

"I have nothing to lose! I will!"

"You're alone now. Your soldiers are dead. I sent your driver away, too. He won't be coming back. Ever."

"I said I'd kill her and I will!"

"*Merde*. Do it, Billy. I dare you to do it."

In speechless fear, she stared into Lachance's fiery black eyes, and she knew Sweet was seeing something lethal in them, too, inhuman and unhealthy. Perspiration dripped from Sweet, and slowly he withdrew the gun from her chin. He spoke rapidly.

"Listen, André, I'm beginning to understand things here. We were just looking for information, and I think you gained the wrong impression what we were doing. We can work things out. You have a grievance, I'm aware of it. Little misunderstanding, that's all."

"Put the gun on the floor."

"I've been thinking, we should come together. I have the assets, you have the skills. Hey, what a team! Here, my gun's going onto the floor. We'll work it out, whatever. You need me, I can use you. Fifty-fifty, or anything you think is honourable."

"Move away from him, Carrington."

She wriggled back toward the closet.

Sweet gulped. "And her, too, because I understand you're in it together. Half for you guys. We blast out of here right away, nobody will know we was here or what happened."

"How about a third for you and two for us?" Lachance said, still smiling that manic smile.

"A deal." Sweet started to get up and began brushing himself off. "Hey, we'll go to my place, I'll show you the files. We're big, André, twenty million turnover each of the last three years."

"So you trust me, Billy."

"You have to believe it, André. Okay, let's go."

"Okay, Billy, I'll follow you."

Sweet hesitated, then turned and started walking toward the kitchen door.

Lachance shot him in the back, a single bullet through the heart that sent him sprawling onto the kitchen tiles.

As Carrie looked on, horrified, Lachance glanced at the body with an almost supreme indifference, then pulled a gleaming six-inch blade from his boot. She flinched as he came toward her, but he merely began to slit her bindings.

"I came in the same way the enemy did. In the dark. It was almost too easy."

Now anger displaced the immense relief she felt.

"You son of a *bitch*, you set me up as a target."

"Now you *know*, Carrington, what it is like on the edge." His laughter seemed black, brutal. "Now that you know the taste, the t'rill of it, you can never go back."

"You . . . shot him in the back."

"In war, people die. I 'ave save some trouble for the state." He packed away his gun and the silencer. "I t'ink those lazy cops are still outside, so we'll go out the back way."

He took her hand and tugged with a force that propelled her past Sweet's prostrate body, pulling her into the kitchen, where he stopped and gripped her arms fiercely with both hands. "Don't let me down, Carrington. Because we are together. There is no choice."

She couldn't hold the gaze of his burning eyes, and looked away – and then saw an overturned chair, Shadow's body, two ragged bullet holes in his back. She gasped and turned away, fought the dizziness that was overwhelming her. She had to clear her head, to devise a way to appeal to what was left of this man's reason. Lie, stall, cajole, offer him some way out.

"Run, Michel, get out of here. Save yourself. Those police will be coming."

She tried to release her arms but he held them in an iron lock.

"I'll wait until you're gone before I call them."

"And what will you tell them, the police?"

"Michel, let *go*."

"That I 'ave murder some people?" A raised, demanding voice: "I saved your life. Now you owe it to me." Then softer: "Come with me."

This was not some fool of love – the man was obsessed,

unreasoning. Carrie summoned a calmness she didn't feel, and spoke with firmness. "I'm not going anywhere."

"You 'ave no *choice!*" He was practically shouting, surely someone could hear. How to appease him?

"I . . . I'll meet you after."

"Don't lie!" He slapped her hard with the flat of his gloved hand, and she almost fell onto the overturned chair.

"You *bastard!*"

But he only smiled, and twisted her arm and yanked her toward him in a two-armed grip that forced the air from her lungs. "You like a strong man, admit it."

He pulled her toward him and kissed her. She bit him on the lower lip, drawing blood.

Still holding her wrist, he drew back and slapped her again with even more force, snapping her head sideways.

"So you are like the others, just a slut."

And he began to laugh in a low, cruel voice that sent a shudder up her spine.

"You will not talk to any police, Carrington. But I will." He nodded, as if affirming something to himself. "When they ask what 'appen, I will explain I tried to save your life. But I was too late. You were already dead."

29

Traffic downtown was jammed up, just emergency lights on at intersections, stalled streetcars, confused drivers piling into each other. Chuck could have kicked himself for not taking the Gardiner Expressway out to Parkdale – he and Leon had been half an hour getting from Jarvis to Bathurst. But it looked as if they were finally tunnelling through, and here were the lights back on again, just in time to run a red.

"Jesus," said Leon. "Don't get us killed. You're sure Carrie's house is under guard?"

"McAnthony said not to worry, a car's sitting outside, and they've got orders to prowl around on foot."

"She *couldn't* have been asleep when I phoned. She was waiting for a call at midnight. From that guy Lachance. He's dangerous, Chuck."

"Stop fussing, Leon, Carrie's in her bed dreaming of tripping through fields of daisies."

Chuck finally slowed to a safe speed as he entered the maze of streets that was Carrie's neighbourhood: tall elms and neat lawns, a law-abiding street, Chuck had always thought, well-mannered and crimeless. The sky was suddenly clear and the night warm, mists dancing upon the grass.

They parked on the intersecting avenue, and as they rounded the corner on foot, Chuck's reaction was relief: no ambulances, no cruisers with flashing wig-wags. Where were Carrie's watchers? Then Chuck spotted them, two uniformed cops in a parked car, a light on inside. "Find a place to park and check on Carrie," he said. "I'll see what these harness bulls have been up to."

He alighted and approached the police cruiser. The woman at the wheel had been listening to the police radio, and jumped as he appeared at her window, her hand going to her holster.

"Easy," Chuck said, "I'm one of the good guys. Chuck Tchobanian, Carrie's partner." The male cop was closing a book. Chuck recognized him from court, a lip mover, dumb as cowflop. At least he could read. "What's happening?"

"Nothing," said the woman. "Peaceful as a country graveyard around here."

✣ ✣ ✣

Carrie tried to scream, and Lachance hit her not in the face but the throat, a jab of a middle finger, and she choked and gagged, felt herself passing out, wanting desperately not to, fighting against oblivion.

Lachance, still holding her wrist, knelt toward Shadow's body and reached for his revolver, which was still equipped with a silencer.

"It is this old man, Shadow, who murders you. It is perfect, yes, Carrington? No 'idden camera this time. They will believe a hero."

As he bent, he went slightly off balance. Flailing, she yanked his arm hard, and they fell to the floor, his limbs tangling among the legs of the fallen chair. Her arm now free, she scrambled to her feet, and propelled herself toward the kitchen door as Lachance rose.

Out past the French doors, hanging loose on their hinges, onto the porch. Three long strides to the back door.

Lachance was five strides behind her.

Outside. Down the steps to the grass. A bare yard, lawn and roses. Nowhere to hide.

She stopped, confused. She suddenly didn't understand why she'd been running or what she feared – the many terrors she had endured this night had abruptly ignited, consuming her, and she felt something snap, and she descended into a kind of giddy empty choking madness.

She turned and saw him ten feet behind her, standing at the bottom of the porch stairs, bracing the gun, aiming it at her head.

Yet she no longer felt fear, just a strange soothing calmness. She didn't want to move. She felt rooted here, finally at peace, the mindless bliss of madness – or was this death?

But the angel of death – if that was who was emerging from the shadows – was embracing not her but Lachance: a massive dark shape that seemed to surround him like a tent.

She watched as the dark form carried Lachance high into the air, then headlong onto the grass, covering him, swallowing him up.

"I got his gun, Mrs. Barr."

She couldn't make sense of this. It wasn't real. Nothing was.

"I didn't want to bother you. I only came to drop off some of my poems."

Leon rang the doorbell. No response. But there were lights on inside. Then he heard voices from the back, and he sprinted down the walk between the houses, and suddenly stopped. The scene seemed surreal to Leon: Carrie sitting on the back steps, her chin cupped in her hands; Edwin Moodie squatting on top of Michel Lachance in a pool of rain water. He was reciting poetry.

A reading. A literary event.

Moodie's voice was soft and thin.

"I think of that lonely rose
Scarlet in the silver starlit night,
A blink of gold.
And I see green eyes and crimson hair,
And her golden-ringèd finger bare."

He looked up at Carrie. "I'm not sure about that last line. It's kind of . . . ponderous – is that the right word?"

Leon saw Moodie was holding a sheaf of papers in his hands. No bandages, no bite marks on those hands.

"Continue, Mr. Moodie," Carrie said. "That's very *good*."

"I just don't know if this is the right time," Moodie said.

"It's the *right* time."

Lachance groaned and Moodie shifted a little. Now Chuck came trotting around from beside the house. He stopped, stared, mouth agape.

"Carrie . . . ," Leon began.

"Don't interrupt, Leon," Carrie said.

"Don't *interrupt*?" Leon said. "For God's sake, what's going on here?"

"Well, um, I came over to leave these poems in her mailbox," Moodie said, "because I just moved into the neighbourhood, a real nice basement room where it's quiet to write, and anyway I been meaning to ask Mrs. Barr to look at them, and maybe help my spelling . . . Well, it's a good thing I came, I guess, and found her in all this trouble."

"Let's hear more, Mr. Moodie," Carrie said with an eerie calmness.

Something was definitely wrong with the picture of Carrie: she was unnaturally serene.

Something was *very* wrong with her.

"Now, Mrs. Barr? It don't feel right, not now. Anyway, I'm not very good yet, I'm kind of learning. I get poetry books from the library, John Milton and, um, Byron, and a lot of poets you never heard of, too. I know lots of stuff by heart."

"Read the poem you mailed to me."

"I . . . can't. Not right now."

"I think I remember part of it," Carrie said. " 'A dream of you, a dream of inescapable impossibility.' Where did you come up with that?"

"Oh, I just liked those words together, Mrs. Barr. I get some of my words in a book called a thesaurus."

"Call me Carrie, please."

"I don't know if I can."

Leon looked at Chuck, who was blinking, reacting as if he'd just awakened from a strange dream.

"I'm going to get those cops," Chuck said. He raced off.

"Why have you been hiding, Edwin?" Leon asked.

Moodie frowned and his little moustache twitched. "I wasn't hiding. I moved, and then I got sick with a flu."

"And so you didn't report for work."

"I'm only part-time."

"No, Edwin," Leon said. "You should have phoned to tell them you were sick."

"Oh, I didn't know."

He went to his pocket and displayed a small gold ring on the palm of his huge paw. "I got your ring for you, which I kind of found, um, one day out under the window there." He began speaking quickly. "I never wanted to bother you, I just . . . I been embarrassed to let you see my poems, I been trying to get up the courage . . ." He was stammering now. "They're all dedicated to you, Mrs. Barr."

Chuck came back through the house, leading a man and a woman in uniform. Leon observed they seemed more than a little rattled.

The policewoman froze in her tracks when she recognized Edwin Moodie. Her gun was quickly on him.

"Honest, I didn't do it," Moodie said.

✛ ✛ ✛

Jock Strachan, deciding he had seen enough blood for the night, worked his way through the melee of investigators in the house, and went outside for a breath of the hot, clammy air that had descended on Toronto after the storm.

The back yard was only slightly less busy than the house – Strachan had brought in two entire crime-scene units. A crew from the morgue was standing by with stretchers, waiting for ident to finish with the corpses.

326

Four bodies in this house, two in the G & C Building. Strachan was a little in awe of the efficient killing machine that was Michel Lachance.

Harold Mitchell had played Dr. Frankenstein to the hilt, he had created a monster.

The inspector was standing over there leaning against a tree, his hands in his pockets, looking too smug for a man who had jeopardized his police career with all his hanky-panky. But though the best laid schemes o' mice and men gang aft a-gley, Operation Sweet Revenge had somehow succeeded. Strachan assumed there'd be a hush-up of some kind.

Lachance had long ago been taken away in a wagon, cuffed, shackled, silent, his face locked into an expressionless mask. But Strachan had seen the burning hatred in his eyes as they settled one last time on Carrington Barr.

And she had stared right back, with a puzzled look – as if she had not recognized him. Carrie had been taken beyond the gates of hell tonight. War trauma – Strachan had seen it before, in the faces of the men he had served with in the battle for Brittany. Some had never completely recovered.

A doctor had now joined the nurse attending Carrie, who sat swaddled in a blanket, shivering despite the heat of the night. She was studying some papers at the wooden patio table. Her two partners were standing by.

"Fogerty. Wilcox."

The two young officers jumped simultaneously. They'd been standing about uselessly, whispering nervously to each other, their debriefing finished. Strachan had left that task to his partner – he'd needed time to get his temper under control.

"Get your rear ends over here."

They came forward, neither able to make eye contact.

"Taking a coop in the car, were you? You dinna want to get wet? A wee too much effort to check on the house once in a while?" Strachan fished from his back pocket the paperback found on the front seat of their car. "But maybe you just couldn't tear yourself away from *Invasion of the Ant People*. In *my* book, there'll nae be a happy ending. Bugger off now, the both of you, and be in my office at eight o'clock sharp. Now get out of my sight!"

His bellow chased them away and for a few moments silenced the buzz of conversation in the yard. Strachan looked at his watch. Three o'clock. He would try to catch a couple of hours of coop himself. More important, it was time for Carrie to get some rest.

He walked over to Leon and Chuck. "How is she now?"

"I'm not quite sure," Leon said. "She keeps reading those poems Moodie gave her. Over and over. She doesn't seem to want to talk."

"I asked her if she wanted me to call Ted," Chuck said, "but it only seemed to make her more upset."

"The doctor's taking her to Women's College Hospital," Chuck said.

Strachan bent to her. "Carrie?"

She looked up, her eyes slightly glazed. "Yes, Jock?"

Good, she recognized him. "You're a brave bonnie girl, Carrington. I want you to go with the doctor. We'll nae need you for a day or so. Just rest."

"Where's Mr. Moodie?" Her words were barely a whisper.

"He's over there talking to some policemen."

"He's not the Midnight Strangler."

"No. He's a hero."

"I think I know who it is." She frowned, looked puzzled. "I thought I did. I forgot."

Strachan turned to the doctor, who nodded. "I'll be giving her something," she said.

Strachan patted Carrie's arm and walked down to the alley. Time to feed the ravenous press, a large number of whom were standing outside the ribbon barricade.

But he detoured to join Moodie and the officers attending him. "We're going to put you in a hotel for a few nights, Edwin. I don't want reporters bothering you, okay?"

"Thank you."

Strachan turned to go, then paused. He couldn't help smiling a little, remembering the time he'd been cuffed to Moodie in the courtroom – when the witness fingered Strachan as the Midnight Strangler.

"You ever read Robbie Burns, Edwin? He said an honest man's the noblest work of God."

Moodie smiled broadly. *"My love is like a red, red rose, That's newly sprung in June.* I know that one."

"Good lad."

Strachan adjusted his bow tie, then went off to deal with the press.

30

September 10, 1980. Temperature outside plus nineteen Celsius. A perfect day, though hinting at the bite of coming autumn. A day for walking. Carrington Barr had made it from her new apartment to the new Queen Street offices in seventeen minutes, twenty-five seconds. Not exactly a world record, but not bad for a smoker trying to quit. Again.

She had spotted Leon down the street at Barney's, enjoying breakfast with a few dignitaries from the Queen West Merchants' Association. Good old Leon – companion, care-giver, full-time mensch. Two tickets to the symphony tonight. Picnics, bike rides, dinners out, dinners in. A lovely Labour Day weekend with him and his feisty, gregarious mother at his parents' cottage. If only Leon had more of *her* genes, less of his solemn father's.

She saw the new awning had finally been put up. Sort of classy. BARR, ROBINOVITCH, TCHOBANIAN. Leon had insisted Carrie get first billing for the new offices.

Carrie gave a cheery wave to Pauline. The waiting room was full: a new whiplash, an impaired, and . . . Oh-oh, the computer traffickers had tracked them to their new lair, three suits, three sets of pleading eyes.

"Mrs. Barr, might we show you the new units today? Desktops and portables."

"We'll take a look. This afternoon at three? I have to rush off to court."

As the suits filed out, there came from upstairs, from the Hogtown Actors' Workshop, a shrill female voice: "*Henry, your behaviour is utterly vile.*" Then: "*Well, you can stuff it up your bleeding arse, Ingrid.*"

The interior designer had recommended sound-absorption tiles. No, Chuck said, we stick with the tall, high ceiling.

Pauline Chong said, "*What* are they rehearsing now?"

"I think it's a comedy of manners."

Carrie piled into the mail. A postcard from her dentist: her pain-free year was over, time for a checkup. Letter from her real-estate agent – the market was a little soft right now, and would she be interested in lowering her asking price? And here, rerouted from the old offices on Bloor, was a letter from some poor sod in the Don Jail. Mail-delayed a *month*. Some kind of embattled plea for mercy from "our system of injustice." Blair Johnstone. She knew she should remember that name, but for the moment nothing clicked for her. She would put him on her list of things to do.

Here, a scrawled note from Edwin Moodie. *I'm pleased to tell you I am now working full time at Kelver Cartage.* Clipped to the note: a newspaper photo, the mayor giving him a medal for bravery. *For your memorybilia,* he wrote. What a guy. Street poet laureate.

"*With vigour, Lawrence.*" A voice from above, the director's. "*You can stuff it up your* bleeding arse! *Sing it out.*"

Carrie marched into Chuck's office.

"Chuck, install some goddamn *sound*proofing."

"Okay, okay, I'll look after it. Carrie, you sure you want to go to court today?"

"I don't want to. I have to." She was not looking forward to seeing Lachance again, but she had to prove to herself she could. Her psychiatrist had said, "Do it if you feel strongly about it."

"So you're okay."

"I'm okay." She pulled out her pack of Player's Lights and broke a cigarette in half and lit the part with the filter.

"I thought you were quitting on Labour Day."

"Moved it back a weekend. How is everything on the home front?"

"Lisa's gone off the deep end, predictably. Gonna divorce me if I don't stop acting for Harry Squire. The Wappers claim they have proof positive now: over-consumption of beaver *does* lead to rape, murder, and pillage."

Carrie shrugged. "I gather the Midnight Strangler's room was piled to the ceiling with those magazines."

"Yeah. Turned out he was Squire's best customer. Harry says the publicity is killing what's left of his business."

"*Such* a shame."

"Saw Ted the other day. He's been concerned about you, ever since –"

"I know. We've talked on the phone. What's he up to?"

"Still picking up the pieces. He has an offer to join Justice, do some drug prosecuting."

"Oh, good. It'll be interesting going up against him."

"He thinks you've got something happening with Leon. What do I tell him, just old friends?"

"I don't know, Leon can't seem to make a proper pass at me." Chuck laughed.

Carrie returned to the waiting room to greet Leon, just back from Barney's.

"I'm ready," she said. "I'm tough. I can do it."

He smiled. "That's the old Carrie."

She bussed him on the cheek. So supportive. She wished she could light more of a fire for him.

As the morning sittings got under way, Old City Hall was full of bustle and clamour – witnesses rushing into courtrooms, lawyers haranguing each other in the corridors. Carrie had missed this, the nervous excitement, the pain and joy of working the courts.

Judge Vandover had the September shift in One-Eleven Court. A silent, staring mannequin: one hardly even knew he was there. What a relief after I-Don't-Like-Late. Lots of media here, two mass murderers appearing on the same docket.

Oliver McAnthony was at the counsel table, playing with his fob and chain, lounging, making a hard chair seem comfortable. All the other chairs were occupied, so Carrie crouched down on one knee beside him.

"Carrington," he said in a hearty, welcoming voice. "Excellent. Good to see you back in harness." He started to rise, offering her the chair, but she gently pulled him back into it.

"I can't sign that statement. Really, Oliver, it makes me sound as if I *frequent* that place. I can hardly say he was a habitué of Digger's Dell if I only saw him there once."

"I shall alter the wording to suit your regard for your reputation. I'm being facetious. We owe you a debt of gratitude. Several, I suppose. But your suggestion that we should check out a man called Horse – why, Carrington? Where did that brilliant deduction come from?"

"I don't know. I saw Kronos slavering at those strippers at Digger's Dell. Then Chuck told me he turned up at work with a black eye – just after Trixi was murdered. You don't get a black eye from reading girlie magazines at a desk in the city lockup. Do you have him, Oliver?"

"The teeth marks hadn't faded. Blood and serum matches. We have bruising on her knuckles. And the manager of the club saw him following Trixi outside just before her murder. No statements – but then Kronos is an officer of the law. He knows his rights."

"Well, I hope you collared the correct gentleman this time."

"I would hazard that we have. Practice makes perfect, Carrington."

"Good luck."

She found a seat close to the prisoners' dock, not far from the stairwell that led to the holding tanks. Where Staff-Sergeant Horse Kronos once held court.

"Call the case of Kronos."

He lumbered up the stairwell, eyes downcast. Carrie remembered the last time he was in court – sitting innocently in the gallery during Mr. Moodie's trial – and she remembered that spunky young witness studying him, studying him, then rejecting him.

Horse Kronos's appearance took twenty seconds. He was remanded for psychiatric observation.

"Would you call the case of Regina versus Michel Lachance?" McAnthony asked the clerk.

Carrie steeled herself.

Up he came, up the stairs. Dapper in his grey pinstripe. The smile.

He looked around as he reached the top step. His eyes met her eyes.

"You will recall, your honour, that the information charges a number of counts of murder," said McAnthony. "The accused is being remanded week to week until he obtains counsel."

"Are you still unrepresented, Mr. Lachance?" said the judge.

"I t'ink I am well represented. Better, if my lawyer would answer my calls. But I see she is here."

The court officers didn't restrain him, and he stepped closer to her. In a low voice, he said, "I guess I went temporary insane."

She just stared in astonishment at him. One of the charges was the attempted murder of herself.

"But I 'ave a better defence, Carrington. I was trying to save your life. Justifiable homicide. It's perfect."

She drew away from him, feeling all the horror upon her again.

"I believe my friend has an application," McAnthony said.

Carrie willed herself to stand, to break the black grip of Lachance's eyes. She made her way toward the judge.

"Apply to remove my name from the record, your honour."

"Granted. I regret we had to bring you here for this, Ms. Barr."

She nodded, then turned and walked toward the door. Past the dock, past Lachance, beyond the range of his angry electric charges. And as she went by him, he turned and shot knives at her. But he couldn't touch her anymore, she felt free of him, free of all her pain and terror.

She went out into the streets of Toronto and walked for miles.